HANKYPANKY

CLOVENHOOF

HEIDE GOODY

IAIN GRANT

1

Jeremy Clovenhoof loved Wednesday evenings. He had a whole Wednesday night routine which mostly involved him laying sprawled on his sofa with a glass of lukewarm Lambrini in his hand.

The sofa wasn't exactly a sofa, it was the leftover bits of his bed. It turned out that you could, in fact, cut a bed in half with a chainsaw. He'd not only won a drunken bet, he had also invented a new piece of furniture. The sawn-off end sat on top of the larger bit. Clovenhoof had named it a sleeping sofa and it was surprisingly comfy.

Wednesday night was also *Great British Bake Off* catch-up night. Clovenhoof had spent most of the past ten years mocking anyone who watched the competitive cooking show. The idea that you should watch other people making and eating food and not actually get to try any yourself was as nonsensical as watching porn without being allowed to vigorously pleasure yourself (a belief which had resulted in him being kicked out of every arthouse cinema within a twenty mile radius).

However, Clovenhoof had found fresh enjoyment in the cooking show when he started compiling a mental list of which baked goods he would most like to eat off which contestant's body. Was it macarons off Samayah? Was it a sloppy cream gateau off Ashley? The list had turned into a complex tally chart, then into a series of badly executed photoshop images, and then into a whole viral thread of online posts that had ended up with him blocked by the TV company and no less than six celebrity chefs.

Jeremy Clovenhoof also loved Wednesdays because for the last month or more, Wednesdays were the nights when he would have a visitor from the Old Place pay him a visit.

There was a knock at the door. Clovenhoof paused *Bake Off*.

"It's unlocked!" he shouted, which was technically true. Clovenhoof had lost his flat keys on Monday and had booted the door in with a well-placed hoof kick, ripping the lock from the door and taking a decent portion of the door frame with it.

Rutspud, a small sack over his shoulder, peered carefully round the door before entering the room. Rutspud was a demon of the Sixth Circle, and he was visiting the disgraced former Lord of Hell, so perhaps he was right to be cautious. The great and powerful, both above and below, might have opinions on demons wandering the mortal world and consorting with a dictator in exile. In particular, the great and powerful below might want to take action against such a demon and make an example of him (or perhaps a dart board or a string of sausages – Hell could be very inventive when it chose).

"Good evening, Lord Satan," said Rutspud.

Clovenhoof always thought Rutspud had watchful and expressive eyes. Expressive eyes which hinted there was a whole range of thoughts going on in Rutspud's brain at any one time; but since the little demon possessed the rare gift of intelligence, he mostly kept his mouth shut and those thoughts to himself.

"It's Jeremy, Rutspud," said Clovenhoof. "Big Jezza. Hoofmeister. King Dong. Any of those. I haven't Satanned in years. Get in here, get comfy with me and give me all the goss from the Old Place."

Rutspud plopped down onto the edge of the sleeping sofa. "Things are much the same as the last time we spoke. There is a good deal of interest in some of the apps we've developed in the lab. We won a special commendation for the parking app we created. It charges a booking fee for a parking session, even when parking is supposed to be free. It also contains a signal blocker, so that it always take a minimum of twenty minutes to pay for parking, no matter where you are."

"Incredible work." Clovenhoof wanted to applaud the evil, although he was glad he never paid for parking. It was one of the benefits of always getting other people to do the driving. Clovenhoof loved the concept of driving, but his hooves just weren't ideal for pedal pushing.

He waggled his half-empty bottle of Lambrini at Rutspud. "Libation?"

"Ah," said Rutspud and reached into his sack to pull out

an unremarkable wine bottle. There was a cork inexpertly shoved in the top of it.

"Is that what I think it is?" said Clovenhoof.

"Do you think it might be fermented fizzy monk's piss?" said Rutspud.

"I do," said Clovenhoof.

"Then you'd be right." Rutspud pulled out the cork with a satisfying plosive sound and topped up Clovenhoof's outheld glass.

"I normally drink the commercially produced stuff," said Clovenhoof, savouring the drink's rough bouquet. "But when in Rome..."

"You ever been to Rome, lord?"

Clovenhoof snorted. "Who'd you think gave Nero the idea to crucify Saint Peter upside down?"

As Rutspud poured himself a small cup of monk's piss, Twinkle crossed the room to have a sniff.

Rutspud drew back in surprise. "It is a miniature monster, but unpleasantly fluffy," he said.

Twinkle was a Yorkshire Terrier and the description of unpleasantly fluffy miniature monster was not far wrong.

"I'm looking after him while Nerys is away on this training course with her frenemy, Tina."

"Training course?"

"*Jungle Boss* or something. A load of bollocks that involves messing about in the woods and burying your own turds, I think."

Twinkle looked at Rutspud expectantly. Rutspud poured a splash of the monk's piss into a little bowl that had been put down for the dog. Twinkle inspected it and then gave a tentative lick.

"Wouldn't Nerys prefer the other one to look after her dog? You know the one. The weedy human who looks like he's just discovered life is a joke but he doesn't understand that punchline?"

"Ben?"

"Is that his name?" said Rutspud.

"He would do, except he's thrown himself back into getting his bookshop profitable again. Thinks there's going to be renaissance for small local high street shops."

"Renaissance? As in...?"

Clovenhoof shrugged. "Cheap labour, poor hygiene and deadly turf wars, I guess. Now, what do you need help with this week?"

Rutspud emptied the remains of his sack onto the low coffee table. He placed a bottle of liquid, a thing looking like the leg of a cheap pottery cat, and a scrappy fragment of a map onto the table. "Your help is requested. We have urgent questions, my lord."

"Ah, as always I am happy to help." Clovenhoof puffed up with self-importance. "Do we have the usual rounds on Geography, History and Science?"

"We do indeed," said Rutspud.

The reasons for Rutspud's visits were due to a complex series of events, involving a dangerous rise in the average temperature of Hell, an incursion by a band of Welsh monks, a magical wardrobe built by the author of the Narnia books, and a monstrous flood that had destroyed Satan's magnificent

Fortress of Nameless Dread. The simple, short-sighted version was that Hell's newest ruler, Lord Peter, was a fuck-up and Hell was in a mess. The simple long-sighted version (which Clovenhoof preferred) was that the Big Guy Upstairs was a fuck-up and subsequently Hell was just one of many places in a mess.

And it turned out that Clovenhoof was the only guy who could help fix it. The folks downstairs still needed him.

"Brilliant," he said. "What do you need?"

Rutspud smoothed the map flat onto the table. "This small fragment is the only remaining record showing the inner courtyard of the Fortress of Nameless Dread. Partial features only. You can see here that there is a *correctional fountain* – whatever that means."

Clovenhoof scratched his belly in reflection. "From what I recall, it flowed with fabric softener. A pungent scent of springtime flowers. Anyone who took a dunking would be soft and fluffy for weeks."

Rutspud quivered in horror and looked at the very fluffy dog which had made short work of his drink. "Good grief, that sounds awful. Right, thanks."

Clovenhoof thought there was something awfully familiar about the map, but he was already on his second bottle of Lambrini and starting to mix his drinks, so thoughts didn't necessarily come easy to him.

"Okay, next one." He grabbed the weird little cat leg from the table and heard it crack in his grip.

"Be careful with that!" said Rutspud. "It's St Zita's Pipe of Order!"

"Is it?" Clovenhoof looked at the two broken pieces in his hand. It was indeed a small clay whistle.

"That's what the box said."

"What box?"

"We just found it while digging out the foundations for the new Fortress of Dread. It was in a capsule with 'St Zita's Pipe of Order' written on it."

"But there were no instructions or anything to indicate where the 'order' part comes in?"

"No," said Rutspud.

"Right." Clovenhoof stood up. "Maybe you blow it and it gives you whatever you order. I need to go and get some superglue. Keep talking. Tell me about the bottle."

Rutspud was forced to shout as Clovenhoof wandered across the landing into Ben's flat in search of glue. "The liquid is called The Tears of Lilith."

"Are they like the actual tears of Lilith?" Clovenhoof shouted back. "Or is it just a poncy name? Like for a perfume or something?"

"I don't know."

Clovenhoof walked straight into Ben's flat.

The place was like a super-distilled answer to the question 'What does a single man's home look like?' The dining table was covered in wargaming figures and the paraphernalia needed to craft hundreds of over-priced wargaming miniatures. Underpants were drying on the radiator. Recently, Ben had decided to put some of his Heavy Metal LPs on the wall, like they were pieces of art. To Clovenhoof's eyes, it just looked like they were there because he'd run out of space to store them in the cupboard.

Ben was hunched over his laptop at the kitchen counter, a look of disgusted consternation on his face.

"Glue, Kitchen," said Clovenhoof, hoping Ben realised he was referring to the man's surname and not the room they were in.

Ben was so taken with whatever was on his screen, he didn't even bother to tell Clovenhoof off for not knocking. He just waved a hand at the wargaming table. "Somewhere on there," he said vaguely. The horror on his face seemed to be permanently fixed.

"You watching that *Two Girls, One Cup* video again?" said Clovenhoof.

"Huh?" said Ben, finally looking up, blankly.

"I said, you had a good day, mate?"

Ben blinked. "Busy. More than busy."

"Good," said Clovenhoof. He spotted a yellow tube of superglue among the snippers and abrasive tools on the table and snagged it up. "Heard from Nerys at all?"

"Huh?" the fazed Ben repeated before replying properly with: "She sent me some photos. I think they were doing folk dancing and singing business mantras this evening or something."

"Fascinating," said Clovenhoof who really didn't care, and left.

2

Ben's attention was pulled back to the screen, even though its contents were stomach-churning.

Saying he'd been busy at the bookshop was an understatement. He'd sold more books in a single transaction than he had in the previous three months. A woman had carried a series of huge piles to the counter and bought the lot. Ben had to hunt around for boxes and extra-strong carrier bags. Customers purchasing large quantities of books was not a problem he often had to deal with, but she had a car outside and filled up the back seat with piled-up volumes.

As Ben had helped her to carry her purchases out, he saw a large folder on the car's seat, with *Crystal's Crafts* emblazoned across the front. Now he was staring at the website for Crystal's Crafts, his stomach in knots.

"One of a kind gifts, hand-made with love," he read in an appalled whisper.

It sounded so very wholesome, but there was image after image of mutilated books, folded so that they formed a sort of sculpture in profile. The pages were folded with mathematical precision, so that the open book showed a 3D pattern on the edges of the pages. It was all very clever, but at its heart was still a mutilated book and Ben wasn't sure he could bear to look at the rest. Of course he did look. He scrolled through and saw books folded to resemble hearts, cats, and even a T. Rex.

He sighed heavily as he realised the one thing all of the books he'd sold had in common was that they were chunky hardbacks, priced cheaply.

"It's not right," he whispered to himself. "It's just not right."

Books were there to be read, or at the very least be kept in a state where some future person might pick one up and read it. Admittedly, one of the books he'd been very surprised to sell to Crystal was called *The Schoolboy's Book of Everyday Science* which dated from around nineteen fifty. It had a pompous tone, with out of date content that would be (rightly) rejected by any modern schoolboy, yet surely it still held some sort of historical interest?

Crystal's website also had a section dedicated to vintage books commanding a higher price, especially where the finished sculpture related to the book's title in some way. He expected the science book would end up there, after it was turned into a retro rocket sculpture.

He swigged from a can of cider and wondered what he'd do if Crystal returned to buy more books. In business terms, he should welcome her with open arms, knowing she was the best customer he'd ever had. But he couldn't get over the queasiness he felt at the fate of those poor books.

He briefly entertained a fantasy where he screamed "Book Murderer!" at her and chased her from the premises. It was a pleasing but impractical thought.

What he needed was some sort of checking system for customers, so that he could assess their suitability for book ownership. Like with guns. He searched the internet for the rules people had to satisfy in order to buy a gun. Predictably, it varied hugely across the world. It was straightforward in the United States and a handful of other places. The strictest countries insisted upon an interview with the police, background checks, a firing test and checks on storage facilities. It might be impractical to enforce such restrictions on his own customers, but he noticed many places required potential gun owners to present a written statement, declaring why they wanted a gun. Could he use that idea? Customers would resist writing large amounts of text at the till, but maybe he could design a questionnaire?

"That might work," he said and opened up a fresh document on his laptop.

3

Clovenhoof returned to his flat with a tube of glue. "If those are the real tears of Lilith," he said, "I remember her back in the day. Adam's first wife, you know. She and I, we had a thing going for a bit. Incredible bird, she was."

"I think women find the term 'bird' derogatory," said Rutspud.

"No, no. Actual bird. She had eagle's feet at the time I knew her. A bold look."

"Adam?" said Rutspud. "As in *the* Adam? The first man?"

"Yep. Eve wasn't his first wife. First there was Lilith, but it didn't work out. She was too – what was the word they used? – wilful. I think that basically meant she wanted to go on top."

Glue and broken pipe in one hand, Clovenhoof picked up the bottle. It was made of clay, had a rough, knobbly exterior not unlike a pineapple, and was indeed carved with ancient Akkadian script that said *The Tears of Lilith*.

"Huh," he said, thumbing off the top and dropping a splash into Twinkle's bowl.

"Hey!" said Rutspud.

"A bit of animal testing never hurt anyone," said Clovenhoof. "Except possibly animals."

Twinkle lapped it up. Clovenhoof shrugged and took a swig. He smacked his lips.

"And?" said Rutspud.

"It's salty," Clovenhoof concluded. "But lots of liquids are salty." He gave an experimental belch in case that yielded further results. "Nope. No idea."

He put down the pipe and glue, recorked the clay bottle and tossed it onto his sofa.

"Right, I need to concentrate while I glue the other thing back together." Clovenhoof held the two pieces in his hand, rolling them together so that he could align them correctly. "Watch and learn. Superglue isn't for everyone you know."

"I've used superglue before," Rutspud assured him.

"A lot of people are afraid of its awesome power. Ben has told me many times it's all about moderation. You just squeeze out one drop at a time."

"Watching and learning," said Rutspud, sipping his monk's piss.

Clovenhoof looked up, suspicious that Rutspud was somehow mocking him. He looked down again at the tube. "Ooh, it's a new tube so I get to break the seal. I screw down the nozzle like so." He screwed the plastic nozzle onto the neck of the metal tube. "Now just the tiniest squeeze to get out a single drop." He gave a squeeze which was actually a fairly large one because of his sausage-like fingers. No glue came out.

Rutspud coughed and looked as if he wanted to say something.

"It's fine, I will just give it another small squeeze." Clovenhoof half crushed the tube, figuring he might as well. No glue came out.

"I think it's possible that you didn't break the seal," said Rutspud.

"Rubbish! I put the top on, that's supposed to break the seal." Clovenhoof sighed and unscrewed the nozzle to see. Rutspud was right. "Fine. I will poke a hole through, get it started." He looked around for something sharp and thin. He didn't have to look far, because the sleeping sofa's broken spring kept poking holes in him. He angled the sharp, pokey end into the top of the tube.

"Wait a second," said Rutspud, "that might be quite—"

A geyser of superglue erupted from the nozzle. It went so high into the air that Clovenhoof couldn't help admiring the spectacle of it, before he remembered it was superglue. "Oh crap! Need to make sure it doesn't go all over the place!" he yelled.

"Maybe just—"

Clovenhoof reached out a hand to catch some, having the presence of mind to dab the broken end of the pipe into the pool now sitting in his palm. "Perfect! Now I'll just line it up with the other piece and squeeze it gently to set." He clamped his hand firmly around the pipe and gave a satisfied smile.

Rutspud stared at Clovenhoof's hand in horror.

"What? What's wrong—? Oh, oh shit!" Clovenhoof flexed his fingers to open them again but they were glued fast into a fist, with the pipe in the middle.

Rutspud sighed. "I am in awe of the glue's fearsome power. Have you, by any chance, glued the pipe to your hand?"

"Fuck. My hand!"

"The pipe!" Rutspud shot back. "I was only borrowing it. I need to take it back, you know."

"How do I get my hand open?" Clovenhoof yelled. "You work in Hell's lab! You're one of the smartest demons down there. You must have some idea!"

Clovenhoof saw the little demon turning it over in his mind. "You have options. You definitely have options."

"Excellent. What are they?"

"Option one, you can try and find someone with a solvent for this chemical, and hope that it doesn't melt your hand off."

"Keep going," said Clovenhoof with a frown. "More options."

"You could rip it open, then seek urgent medical attention for the skin you tear off in the process."

Clovenhoof shook his head.

"You could just leave it, and hope that it wears off, or that your skin sloughs off?"

The questioning inflection at the end of Rutspud's sentence told Clovenhoof he was now out of ideas.

"Slough? Slough?! Do I look like a fucking snake?" he

roared. "I mean, at one time I might have done, yeah, but not now. I cannot slough my skin!"

"Not all in one go maybe, but—"

Clovenhoof threw himself backwards onto his sleeping sofa, ignoring the noises from the springs. He held his right hand up to the light, hoping to see a point where it wasn't quite so stuck. He plucked at his pinkie finger with his left hand. It was stuck, but maybe not as thoroughly as some of the others. It was quite uncomfortable to move it too much, but he gave it a gentle waggle, and tried to find a way to ease it free.

"You're going to have to be my right hand man now, Rutspud," he said. "Quite literally. It takes two hands to control my todger when I piss. I use the word control loosely, by the way."

"I need to get back," said Rutspud. "I'll be missed if I'm not back for poker night."

Clovenhoof knew they played with real pokers and he was briefly nostalgic; then he remembered his predicament. "But what about my hand?"

"And I need a pipe! If Lord Belphegor finds out I took it from the infernal secret museum then there will literally be hell to pay—"

"Wait! What?" said Clovenhoof.

Rutspud paused. "Yeah. If I don't get that Pipe of Zita back, you'll have demons queuing up to cut off your hand."

"No. Wait." He fixed Rutspud with a steely glare. "You said you'd just found this while digging the new foundations."

"Er, ah. We did."

"And now you say you borrowed it from the infernal secret museum."

"Yes, well..." Rutspud nervously twisted his fingertips against each other. "We're *going* to put it in the museum when we've worked out what it is..."

With his one usable hand Clovenhoof grabbed at the map Rutspud had brought him. "I *knew* this looked familiar," he growled. "You've shown me this before. You've asked about the fountain before."

"No, I don't think so."

"You're recycling old questions!"

"I'm not!"

"You're bringing me things that you understand perfectly well then ask me to help identify them!"

"It's not what it seems, boss," said Rutspud, his face twisting wretchedly.

Clovenhoof gave a sudden gasp. "Shit! I know what you're doing!"

Rutspud's face fell. "I'm sorry..."

"You've been coming here, week in week out, with all these questions, these made up requests, designed to appeal to my vanity and – yes! – this has all been a huge distraction ploy! You're doing this so I don't see what's really going on in Hell!"

"Er..." said Rutspud.

"There's some plot afoot, isn't there? There's a vast conspiracy. Forces are moving, threatening to bring down the cosmos, and if you don't keep ol' Jeremy Clovenhoof distracted, he'll see what's what and he'll come marching into the pits of Hell and put the miscreants in their place. That's right, isn't it?"

"Honestly?" said Rutspud.

"Honestly! If I need to put on my big boy pants and go on a massive crusade across time and space to put things back the way they should be – even if the Almighty Bastard himself needs saving – don't you dare stand in my way! So – tell me!"

Rutspud was cowering beneath the pillar of Clovenhoof's fury. Twinkle, who had seen Clovenhoof flip out more times than he could count, sniffed at pieces of fluff along the skirting board.

"The truth is..." Rutspud began.

"Yes?!"

"The truth is that a few weeks back I did have some honest questions for you. That thing with the map and the fountain. That's real."

"Yes?"

"And there were some other things. Like which key was the right one to open the fuse box on sub-level K."

"Yes?"

"And it was helpful when you shared that handy mnemonic for remembering which demonic Titan was held in which pit."

"And?"

Rutspud shrugged. He was a little demon and didn't have much in the way of shoulders for shrugging, but somehow he did it with expressiveness and panache.

"And then there were no more questions," he said. "Literally. We had it all figured out. But I could see you really liked to share your wisdom and experience."

"Yes?"

"So I thought you might like it if I kept doing it. Make you feel, you know..."

Clovenhoof was stunned. "What? Useful? Relevant?"

Rutspud looked up at him. He didn't answer or even nod, which somehow made it worse.

"Fuck's sake, Rutspud," Clovenhoof whispered in horrified embarrassment. "You do know that you're a demon, don't you? You thought I'd *like* it? How is this demonic? You are the worst demon ever. You took ... *pity* on me?" He spat the word out like it was poison in his mouth. "I don't need your pity, you disgusting little scrote! I'm Jeremy Clovenhoof! I'm Satan! My face graces the covers of a thousand bad Heavy Metal albums. I'm a god! Or at least the next best thing!"

Clovenhoof banged his fist down hard on the settee. Something went *twoing* deep within the mattress and a piece of broken spring poked out. Even his furniture was attempting to stab him.

Rutspud waved a sad arm at the television. "You spend your nights watching cooking shows, boss."

"Ironically," said Clovenhoof in self defence.

"You sit on broken furniture and look after the neighbour's dog."

"Fuck you! I am a monstrous tyrant. The world trembles at my name!"

"It used to," said Rutspud. "Now, you're just ... a has been. A lonely old man. Sorry, boss."

Clovenhoof stared.

"Oh, fuck," he said. "You're not the worst demon at all.

You're the *worst* demon. You build someone up and then smash them down. Give them hope and then whip it away. Bollocks. You should get an award or something."

"I'm sorry."

"No. Fuck off."

"Please, if I could—"

"No. Fuck off!" Clovenhoof stood and all but chased Rutspud to the door. Rutspud managed to grab his sack and the scrap of map before Clovenhoof had him out of the room.

"The pipe—" he began.

"You can have it when you prise it out of my hot sticky hands!" Clovenhoof yelled.

He slammed the door after Rutspud, but because the lock was utterly gone it simply bounced against the frame and rebounded into his hand.

He whirled. He was furious. He was betrayed. But above all else he was humiliated.

Twinkle looked up from his skirting board explorations.

"You don't think I'm a pathetic has-been loser, do you?" he said.

Twinkle said nothing. He didn't have to.

4

When Ben opened up the *Books'n'Bobs* shop on Boldmere High Street the following day, he set about making a few changes.

He'd gone to bed listening to Clovenhoof yelling at whatever or whoever it was that had annoyed him – those cooking shows really seemed to rile him up – and Ben had woken the following morning full of plans on how to save his books from the hands of predatory crafters.

Spartacus Wilson came through the door. On paper, Spartacus was an employee of the bookshop. In reality, his wages were funded by a series of grants Spartacus had obtained – from the local chamber of commerce, apparently – and he was there to establish a more effective online presence for the bookshop.

Ben secretly thought maybe all of the local figureheads had combined their thinking in an effort to keep Spartacus from wreaking havoc in the community if he got bored. It seemed lanky Spartacus was everything that the older generations feared about youth. He was foul-mouthed, disrespectful, ignored the temptations of formal education yet possessed a wealth of modern skills, and looked set on a course to build a personal fortune before he hit thirty.

Last week, Spartacus had introduced a barcode scanner into the shop, and every day he sent off a bigger pile of books in the post. Whatever he was doing, it was starting to work.

"Morning, Spartacus!" said Ben. "Cup of tea?"

Spartacus waved his can of Monster energy drink at Ben as a polite refusal.

"I need to walk you through a few changes I'm making," said Ben.

"Yeah? I'll walk you through my changes if you want. I think I've nailed the SEO for anyone looking online for bookshops in the area."

Ben knew that SEO was Search Engine Optimisation. It was a nugget of knowledge at the very edge of his technological understanding and he clung onto it while the world still made sense.

"Who would do a search for local bookshops?" Ben asked. Then he realised Crystal from Crystal's bloody Crafts probably had.

"Passing trade's a thing of the past," said Spartacus with a shake of his head. "So what are these changes you've made?"

"Some of the newer customers we're getting," said Ben carefully. "They might not be suitable for book ownership."

"Not suitable for book ownership? Who's that? Isn't everyone suitable for book ownership?" Spartacus asked.

"No!" said Ben. "Read the questions on here and you will see what I mean." He handed over a sheet of paper.

"We're supposed to be going paperless," said Spartacus, waving the sheet. "Anyway ... so you want to know why I am buying books today, and I can select from this list?"

Ben nodded.

"Reading for enjoyment, reading for work, buying for a gift or planning to use as source material for crafting." Spartacus looked up. "Is this market research? Because if it is, there might be better—"

"—No, not really. It's to stop the destruction of books. See, if anyone ticks that final box about wanting books to use for crafts, then they are only allowed to buy books from this shelf here." Ben ushered Spartacus to a low shelf with a small selection of titles.

"It's all the out of date Guinness Books of Records, and those ones about how to get a job in computers from the eighties." Spartacus frowned. "In fact, it's that box of books I put in the back and said you should get recycled because nobody will buy them."

"Exactly! So this is like recycling, isn't it?"

"I've missed something haven't I? What happened?" asked Spartacus.

Ben told Spartacus about Crystal's Crafts and what he'd discovered.

"Wait? You sold thirty five books in one go? That's incredible! If you could find some more customers like that then—"

"No! That's the point. I don't want customers like that.

Customers who buy books to destroy them are not welcome here."

Spartacus gave Ben a long, hard look. "Right, Mr Kitchen. You know how I feel about reading. Reading books is something you do when you've run out of internet."

"Yes. You've said."

"But when I hear you talking about reading, which is *a lot*, I hear you say a particular phrase all the time to people."

"Yeah? Really?"

"That the reader *owns* the reading experience, that there is no right or wrong way to read a book."

Ben recognised his own words. "Well, yes. Yes, I do say that."

"So that means they can read it in a careless way and dog-ear all the pages if they want, yeah?"

Ben gritted his teeth against the trap that was approaching. "I suppose so, but it's a mark of someone who—"

Spartacus held up a hand to silence him. "So if they read the book and fold the pages as they go, that would be a similar thing?"

"I'm not playing this game!" said Ben. "I don't like it and I won't have them as customers. It might not be logical, but it's my shop and my rules."

Spartacus shrugged. "Yep. OK."

Ben was mildly put out that his minor tantrum was so easily shrugged off. He suspected Spartacus would just sell books to customers and lie about using the questionnaire. He resolved not to leave Spartacus alone with customers if he could possibly help it.

"Oh yeah," said Spartacus, sliding a box across the floor with his foot. "I brought this up from the basement."

"I thought you were frightened of the basement," said Ben.

"Yeah – back when I was kid and thought it was full of spiders and rats with rabies. It's old junky book stuff. Really old. And I thought you might want to look through. We can put it back out if it's no good."

"Thank you," said Ben, lifting the box onto the counter to take a look. "Oh, I know what this is. This is some of Desmond Rothermere's stuff."

"Desmond. As in Dirty Desmond?"

The myths surrounding the owner of the shop before Ben took it on nearly twenty years ago were as numerous as they were apocryphal. Ben had heard it said that Desmond Rothermere not only ran a 'respectable' bookshop but also provided literature of an entirely different sort for local gentlemen.

"I don't know about 'dirty'," said Ben primly.

"They said that the local Women's Institute threatened to burn down this place and hang him by his goolies if he didn't stop selling porn."

"Well, that shows that you know. It was the Mother's Union, actually."

Despite the shop being in Ben's hands for a considerable time, there were still some remnants of Desmond's time to be found: notably boxes of stock in the furthest and most cobwebbed corners of the basement, as well as the stout safe built into the shop counter that would have been very useful indeed if Ben had any means of opening it.

Ben perused the box before him. There were some older magazines in there, mostly *Woman's Own* and *People's Friend*. He riffled through the books, making sure they weren't mouldy . They were interesting enough to put out for sale. He smiled at the one promising Christmas recipes. There was interest in the weird celebration cookery of the seventies, where savoury jellies were considered *de rigueur*. He was delighted to see a gaudy centrepiece dish called a *festive vegetable mould*, which featured layers of overcooked vegetables and slices of boiled egg set into a clear jelly. It was spectacular, and not in a good way. He left the magazine open on the counter so that he could show Spartacus. He might even leave it there for customers to enjoy.

"Okay, what other delights do you have for me?" he asked the box.

He dug deep and pulled out a smaller set of thin books. They were older than the magazines. The style suggested the nineteen-fifties. Nestled between them was a battered pair of 3D glasses with one red lens and one blue one. Ben put them to his eyes, but the plastic was quite degraded and he couldn't see much. He opened one of the books and saw that the pictures inside were photographs in the blurry style which looked good through the 3D glasses.

"Oh my!"

As Ben flicked through the pictures he realised they were soft porn. Very much in keeping with Dirty Desmond Rothermere's reputation. The book was entitled *A Bosomy Beauty* and the woman in the images, whose name was apparently 'Lois', was featured in various poses, completely naked. 'Lois riding her bicycle', 'Lois playing tennis' and

'Lois drinking tea on the lawn' – all the while completely starkers. It was oddly charming, as though Lois simply lived that way and someone had captured a few casual snapshots.

"Nice!" said Spartacus, leaning over to look.

"No, you can't look at these!" said Ben.

"Why not?"

"Because it's ... well it's unsuitable," said Ben.

"You're looking at it," said Spartacus.

"Only in an appraising way," said Ben. "To see what we have here."

"Yeah. That's what I'm doing too. Why's she so blurry?"

"Well—" Ben couldn't stop himself. He was about to launch into the nerdy details and he knew it. He sighed. "It's a three dimensional photography technique called an anaglyph. The photo is taken in two different colours, and when you look at it through the 3D glasses, the coloured lenses give it depth. We have the glasses here, but they are a bit too worn."

He showed Spartacus the glasses.

Spartacus picked them up and turned them over. "These are coloured cellophane or something?"

"Yes, they just need to be the right colour."

"Maybe this is as good time to tell you that I ate all of the Quality Street," said Spartacus.

"What? There was over half a tin left! That should have lasted another six weeks. What on earth— Oh wait, I think I follow what you're saying."

Ben hurried over and fetched the tin from its hiding place, clearly now compromised. He took the lid off and found the tin was empty, apart from the wrappers swirling in the bottom. "Good grief, what kind of monster leaves the wrappers in the tin?"

"The kind of monster who is about to help you improvise some new 3D glasses," said Spartacus.

The shop door slammed open and Jeremy Clovenhoof stormed in, rattling the glass in its frame.

"If you break that door, you're paying for it," said Ben.

"Can it, Kitchen," snarled Clovenhoof. "I need to ask you a question."

"Oh?"

Clovenhoof put his hands on the counter in the manner of a man who meant business. "Am I an old, over-the-hill, pathetic, has-been loser? Or am I a man in his prime? A free-wheeling cool-as-fuck rebel, flipping the bird to 'the man' while he storms through life?"

Ben and Spartacus looked at him.

"Is that the question?" said Ben eventually. "*That's* the big question?"

"Is there a third option?" suggested Spartacus.

"What do you want as a third option?" said Clovenhoof.

"No, I was just asking. The answer's 'A'."

"'A'? Which one was 'A'?"

"Old and pathetic loser," said Spartacus. "That'd be the one. You can't even do up your buttons properly."

Clovenhoof recoiled from the counter as though he'd been punched. Ben saw he had indeed misaligned the buttons on the hideous Hawaiian shirt he was wearing that morning.

"I had to get dressed one-handed this morning," said Clovenhoof and shook a fist at the two of them.

"Did you ... did you superglue your hand together?" said Ben.

Clovenhoof's nose wrinkled grumpily. "You don't think I'm a pathetic has-been, do you, Kitchen?"

Ben wasn't ready to give Clovenhoof the un-sugar-coated truth. "I mean, none of us are as young as we used to be, are we? And you're—" Ben realised he had no clue how old Clovenhoof was and had fallen into a trap of having to guess "—around sixty? Fifty-five?"

"Add a few zeroes on the end, why don't you, you bastard," spat Clovenhoof. "I'm not some old codger. I'm always tearing it up, causing mayhem, a party animal."

"Yeah?" said Spartacus. "What are you up to tonight?"

"Well, it's Thursday so I might be saving myself for a big blow out weekend."

"Oh," said Spartacus, unimpressed.

"Why?" said Clovenhoof defensively. "What are you doing that's so much cooler?"

"Me, PJ and Kenzie are off to a pop-up nightclub in Birmingham."

"Pop-up what?"

"It's in a disused factory by the canal. It's invite only."

Clovenhoof sneered. "Just sounds like a tarted up version of kids drinking cider behind the bike sheds."

"We don't drink. Kenzie's scored some weed off Jefri's uncle's girlfriend. We're gonna get high, get off with whoever we fancy, then at dawn we're going to 'borrow' some kayaks and graffiti anti-capitalist slogans in the canal tunnels."

"At dawn?" said Ben. "You've got work tomorrow."

Spartacus grinned. "You never pulled an all-nighter and then gone into work before?"

Ben, who liked to be tucked up in bed with a hot chocolate and a graphic novel before ten each night, thought the notion was sickening.

"We ... we can pull an all-nighter," said Clovenhoof with unconvincing bravado.

"Sure you can," said Spartacus.

"We can. We're going out tonight, aren't we, Ben?"

"Are we?" said Ben.

"We're going to go and paint the town red. We're going to hit the clubs of Birmingham."

"We're leaving Sutton Coldfield? That sounds like effort."

"We're painting Boldmere red then," said Clovenhoof. "The Boldmere Oak have a music night on a Thursday, don't they?"

"Loud music makes my ears ring these days," said Ben.

"We're fucking doing it!"

"Oh. Okay."

Clovenhoof stepped away from the counter. "Yeah! Rock and Roll!" He backed away towards the door, giving the finger to them both with one hand and a fist with the other. "You have to imagine I'm giving you the finger with this one. It's stuck at the moment."

When he'd gone, Ben returned his attention to how they might make replacement 3D glasses to look at antique erotica. "We've got the coloured plastic, but we need to fix them together."

Spartacus slid a box for collecting old spectacles closer.

"What? No we can't use those." Ben put a hand on the

box. "They are to help people in Africa with eyesight problems."

"We're just borrowing them for a few minutes," said Spartacus.

Ben dipped into the box and picked out a low prescription pair. He pulled out a red wrapper and a blue wrapper from the Quality Street tin and sellotaped them to the spectacle frames. "One red lens and one blue. See if it works." He handed the glasses to Spartacus.

Spartacus put them on and looked around. "Freaky." He turned his attention to Lois on the page. "Oh wow. It's like a weirdly tinted hologram or something."

"Yes!" Ben was thrilled that the experiment had worked. Then he remembered he was encouraging a young person to look at a naked woman. "But that's probably enough for now."

"Enough?" said Spartacus. He waggled his phone at Ben. "You have heard of the internet, right? PornHub? RedTube?"

"I wouldn't know about that," said Ben, whose forays into racy internet images tended to be limited to looking at images of TV's *Xena Warrior Princess,* or Frazetta and Boris Vallejo cover art.

Ben closed the book and Spartacus removed the glasses. "What will you do with them?" the lad asked.

Ben was thoughtful. "I suspect these are reasonably valuable. A bit niche, but the right buyer will pay a good price for them. Let me think about how we go about selling them."

Spartacus looked at the pile of slim volumes. "There's four of them."

"All featuring Lois." Ben spread them across the counter. Lois was featured at the seaside, the circus, and the farm in subsequent books. Apart from location, Lois changed her hat between books but was otherwise to be found spending time sightseeing or sitting against a picturesque view. He smiled down at her rosy cheeks. There was something utterly charming and innocent about this vintage porn, and he couldn't help but feel a pang of adoration for wonderful, carefree, Lois.

He looked up to see that Spartacus was staring at him. He cleared his throat and he tidied the books into a neat pile. "Good find, Spartacus."

"Now, do you need a bit of a sit down?" suggested the youth. "Maybe a little nap?"

"Eh? What?"

"You and Mr C have a got a big night out ahead of you." Spartacus grinned. "Wouldn't want you getting over-tired."

"How old do you think I am?" Ben scowled. "No! Don't answer that!"

The truth was, Ben realised, he felt tired just thinking about the idea of going out on a work night. Maybe if he reminded Clovenhoof that he needed to stay home and looked after Twinkle, maybe even drop a sly text to Nerys that Clovenhoof was shirking in his duties, then the old devil might be coerced into dropping his midlife crisis plans for an unplanned night out...

5

"Ah-ha!" declared Tina with a victorious point of her finger.

Nerys Thomas whirled guiltily, phone in hand.

"I knew you were taking the digital cleanse too well!" said Tina.

Nery shoved her phone under her pillow, but it was too late. "I'm sure they didn't expect everyone to give up *every* device," she said. "Besides, I needed it for emergencies."

"Was that an emergency?" said Tina snidely.

"It concerned Twinkle, so yes," said Nerys. It had, in fact, been a weird message from Ben saying Clovenhoof was shirking his duties by intending to go to the pub that night and requesting Nerys step in and stop him. Nerys thought that was as unnecessary as it was futile and told Ben that as long as Twinkle was getting his walks and his meals, Jeremy Clovenhoof could do as he damned well pleased.

"What would Guru Gary think?" said Tina. "Hmmm?"

Nerys tried to shrug off the ridiculous question, but it was hard.

They had paid for a full week in a two-person rustic lodge at the '*Wild Boss*' training weekend ('*Because it's a Jungle Out There!*' the literature had declared) and Nerys had hoped it would be a fun but informative boost to their new designer handbag business. Going into business with Tina, who she'd known, worked with and frequently loathed for much of the last twenty years, was a difficult proposition and they needed all the help they could get.

However, after four and a half days of living in tiny cabins in the woods with no running water and no heating, Nerys had concluded the week's activities could be best described as a mixed bag.

The first night's 'Cosmic Networking Mixer' had simply been a chance to get to know the other attendees and swap business cards, all the while dancing under the night skies with glow-in-the dark patterns painted on their faces. It had actually reminded Nerys of a couple of raves she had attended in the nineties and she'd felt unexpectedly nostalgic.

Some of the activities, like the 'Animal Spirit Guide Hikes' (aka taking alpacas for a walk) had been fun, but nothing more. Others, like the 'Abundance Manifestation Meditation Workshops', had just been spiritual mindfulness claptrap that hadn't helped Nerys understand her business any better. And as for the incessant chanting of 'Profit Mantras': that had just been silly.

All of this was overseen by Guru Gary. Gary was a goat.

Not a man embodying the spirit of a goat, but an actual snowy white goat, no more than two feet tall, whose role appeared to be to wander from session to session, staring at participants with unnerving intensity. Bizarrely, the goat was really good at his job. To be stared at by Guru Gary was to have your soul seen and judged.

If anything, Guru Gary had facilitated the few valuable insights Nerys had taken away from the week. During days of pointless and tiring activities, Gary's laser-beam glares had forced her to face certain truths about herself and her shared business. And so, in those few snatched moments of respite between activities or at the end of the day, Nerys and Tina had felt compelled to have a series of frank discussions about what problems their business faced and how they were going to fix them. By the end of the week they had agreed one of them really needed to finish that sales analysis, one of them needed to source a fresh supplier of new materials, and neither of them needed to devote any more time to Instagram photo-shoots of their wares.

"Guru Gary would not like me to be on my phone," said Nerys.

"No, he would not," said Tina solemnly. "It's dinnertime soon, then we've got the Morris Dancing Executive Stress-Relief session to wrap up."

"Morris Dancing Executive Stress-Relief?" said Nerys.

"I've seen the Morris dancers they've hired. Wednesbury Wallopers, they're called. Bunch of weirdos with heavy sticks. I think we're going to whack each other with sticks and stomp our feet until we're too knackered to be stressed."

"Sounds like the perfect end to a weird week."

Nerys grabbed her coat – her now grubby and mud-streaked coat that was going straight to the dry-cleaners as soon as she got home – and followed Tina out of the door.

Nerys's tummy rumbled as they crunched over the woodland mat of soggy pine needles towards the meeting hut. "What's for dinner tonight?"

"It's celebration curry night," said Tina. "Because nothing says spiritual improvement like eating curry and then spending a night in a tiny airless shack with you. I think the options are chicken or chickpea."

"Yeah," said Nerys thoughtfully. "I'm definitely going for the veggie option."

"Really?" said Tina. "I think if I don't get a full portion of fat and protein I might just go light-headed and keel over from lack of energy."

"If you do, claim you're going on an entrepreneurial astral journey and you'll probably get an extra brownie point. I'm surprised goat curry isn't on the menu."

"Nerys!" Tina gasped and then, in a conspiratorial hiss, said, "What if Gary hears you?"

"I don't know what came over me," said Nerys. "Anyway, I'm steering well clear of the chicken. They're cooking everything on open fires. You seen a fridge or freezer for hygienic food storage anywhere?"

Tina wasn't listening. As they neared the central meeting area, where rough log seating had been arranged around a fire in front of the main meeting and teaching hut, Tina was looking over at the Morris dancers who were donning their gear by their van.

"Is it me, or is there something about a man with bells

strapped around his calves that's somehow intrinsically sexy?"

"Oh, God, you are light-headed," said Nerys.

They made to join the line of fellow spiritual businesspeople waiting for food. Guru Gary stood on a tiny hillock and surveyed the queue. Most of the people could not meet his eye.

Nerys let Tina get a little way ahead and then turned to Gary. She didn't exactly bow to him but she could not help but put a little servility into her posture.

"If I've done anything to offend you, Gary, I'm truly sorry."

Gary simply stared back at her. She retreated from his painful gaze and rejoined Tina in the line.

"I can't wait to get home tomorrow," said Nerys. "I wish I was there now."

Tina tutted. "And miss out on this fun? What would you be doing if you were back home, huh?"

Ben's message had suggested Clovenhoof was dragging him out for a boozy and raucous night on the town, and Nerys wanted to be able to say that she'd totally be joining them. In truth though, she couldn't imagine anything better than a long hot soak in a tub followed by a night sprawled on her sofa in her dressing gown, with Twinkle at her side and the trashiest celebrity reality TV on the telly.

That image would have provided her with a fuzzy comfort while she waited, bowl in hand, for her dollop of chickpea curry. However, for some reason, her daydream image of indulgent luxury had Guru Gary planted right in the middle of it. No matter how she tried, she couldn't shake the dinky goat from her mental image. He stood there resolutely, in the living room of her mind's eye, watching her; judging her.

Nerys shuddered. "I can't wait to get home," she muttered to herself.

6

C lovenhoof walked into the living room in his finest shirt, his funkiest cravat and his cleanest pair of Bermuda shorts. "What do you reckon, Twinky-boy?" he said, giving the dog a twirl of his outfit.

Twinkle sat on the sawn-up bed sofa, gnawing and licking at something. Clovenhoof realised it was the clay flask of 'Lilith's Tears'.

"Hey, don't mess with what you don't understand," said Clovenhoof, snatching the bottle away. He secured the loose stopper and stuffed it in his pocket. "Now, pay attention and tell me what you think of my outfit."

The little Yorkshire terrier looked at him with disinterest, then give a little doggy burp that to Clovenhoof's ears sounded like, "Great."

"Damn right, I do," said Clovenhoof. "Don't stay up late and don't answer the door to strangers."

He waltzed out of his flat and collided with Ben, who had

dressed up for their big, debauched night out in on his usual faded T-shirt and shapeless jeans.

"Fuck me," said Ben, recoiling from the sight of Clovenhoof's multi-coloured shirt, scarf and jacket. "Those patterns were never meant to go together. They literally hurt my brain."

"Evidence that their mesmerising power is working, causing you to subliminally desire me," said Clovenhoof.

"More like warning people off, like a brightly coloured poisonous frog."

"'Brightly coloured poisonous frog' is not the insult you think it is," said Clovenhoof.

They wandered down Chester Road to the Boldmere Oak. Over many years, their favourite boozer had remained a constant. Oh, things changed over time. Grab-a-granny nights and chicken-in-a-basket dinners had given way to pub quizzes and a range of sloppy TexMex menu items. Landlord Lennox had handed over more shifts to his fierce, no-nonsense niece Florence. And the place had had more fires, renovations, and inexplicable acts of God occur to its material structure than almost any other building in the world. But throughout all of that it had remained constant: constantly a bit more shit than it wished it was, constantly unable to draw a better class of patron, constantly willing to accept Jeremy Clovenhoof and his friends as customers.

As soon as they entered, Clovenhoof and Ben were forced to yell at each other over the sound of a band doing a sound check in the back room.

"I'll get the drinks in before they start," said Clovenhoof.

"Thanks!" said Ben, but his face fell as Clovenhoof held out a hand for his credit card.

Clovenhoof went to the bar. "This lot any good, Lennox?" he asked.

Lennox poured Lambrini into a glass, then pulled out an earplug. "Eh?"

"This lot." Clovenhoof tried to jerk a thumb at the music but used the hand that was still mostly glued together. "Any good?"

"They come highly recommended."

Clovenhoof rolled his eyes. "Obviously *someone* will highly recommend them. Probably their moms. What sort of stuff do they play?"

Lennox shrugged and automatically poured a cider and black for Ben. "Covers I think. Rock and heavy metal. They are from Denmark. They love a bit of rock over there."

Clovenhoof took the drinks back to Ben and nodded towards the band. "Rock covers coming up. Should be good."

"Brilliant!" said Ben. He hovered near the door to the back room. "I can't quite read their name on the drums."

Clovenhoof looked. The bass drum was painted with the name, but it looked very much as though some other name had been there previously and this new one had been added over the top.

"There's an old name there. It looks like it used to say Panda People."

"Yeah, and someone's gone over it with Djævlehund."

"Djævlehund it is then. What instrument would you play, if you were in a band?" Clovenhoof asked.

Ben eyed him shiftily. "I hope you're not thinking of

pinching their equipment for a cheap Christmas present, Jeremy!"

Clovenhoof pulled a face. "I wasn't thinking anything of the sort," he lied.

Ben sighed and thought for a moment. "There was a time when I seriously considered learning to play bagpipes so I could join in with some of the AC/DC songs that feature Bon Scott playing them."

"Rock bagpipes?" Clovenhoof said. "That's a thing?"

"It's a thing," said Ben. "And it's so very niche that a covers band would almost certainly let you join in if you wanted. I don't think any of them have their own bagpipe players."

"You've thought hard about this, haven't you?" said Clovenhoof. "Why haven't you ever done it?"

"I have. We did. That mad, crazy Devil Preacher band we briefly formed ten plus years ago."

"*I* formed," said Clovenhoof. "And you didn't get to play rock bagpipes then, either."

"No? I was doing a lot of drugs at the time. It's hard to remember."

Clovenhoof clapped his hands, stood up and looked all around, as if there might be bagpipes in the room if he looked hard enough. "Time to change all of that. You need someone to give you that prod to follow your dreams. Let's make it happen!"

"I'm not sure I'd describe it as a dream, exactly," said Ben. "And there are health issues associated with bagpipes. There's a thing called 'bagpiper's lung' where you get a sort of pneumonia from spores in the bag."

"You're backpedalling. Why are you so afraid of adventure?"

"I'm not afraid of adventure at all. Shush now, the band's starting."

Clovenhoof and Ben tapped their feet to some warm-up tracks, mainly middle-of-the-road rock anthems. They joined in with the shouty parts as they consumed more alcohol. Jeremy got a round of Jack Daniels shots on Ben's credit card and managed to hand them to each member of the band while Ben had his head down doing a complicated air guitar solo, mirroring the intense concentration of the lead guitarist.

"Here's one that you might know," said the lead singer. His accent was Danish (Clovenhoof had a great ear for languages) and his smile was broad and charismatic. He had chains hanging from his belt, looping down over his tight, leather trousers. "A cult classic, available only as a bootleg from their legendary appearance at Symphony Hall. It's a favourite of ours, so give it up for *Spineless Disciples!*"

Clovenhoof wasn't often lost for words, but he pointed at the band, and gaped at Ben as the opening chords sounded. Ben was lost in his drunken air guitar playing, so Clovenhoof had to prod him to make him pay attention. "Listen! Can you believe this?"

"Yeah, it's great!" slurred Ben.

"No, pay attention! It's one of my songs! It's *Devil Preacher!*""

"You mean one of *our* songs?"

"One of *my* songs. From when I was rock god!"

"You're not a rock god."

"Only a rock god would glue his fingers together like this!"

Clovenhoof held up his hand. He had managed to pry loose his index and pinkie fingers, but the others remained tightly glued to his palm. He was now, 24/7, making the sign of the horns. His hand was an unchangeable rock music tribute. He jabbed his fingers at the band as they started *his* song and several of them responded in kind.

Clovenhoof lost himself in the memory of his time in Devil Preacher. It was a high point of his early days on earth. He had played amazing music and been appreciated by adoring fans. He sang along with the song, bellowing the words with such vigour that the guitarist caught the eye of the lead singer and nodded at Clovenhoof.

The singer gestured for Clovenhoof to join them on the tiny makeshift stage. He didn't need asking twice. He took the microphone and howled the final verse of *Spineless Disciples*.

"THREE TIMES *the cock did crow!*
   Christ denier! Christ denier!
   A bunch of cocks all in a row!
   Cowards and liars! Pants on fire!"

WITH A FEW SHORT gestures they moved onto another of Devil Preacher's songs, *(Never Trust a) Man in a Dress*. It was a favourite of Clovenhoof's: a song where he'd been able to express some of his frustrations with the interfering Archangel Michael. He found himself wishing that Michael was here to witness him re-living his glory days, but Michael was in the Canary Isles or somewhere with his boyfriend Andy. Clovenhoof glanced around the room and saw that people were enjoying the song. It was exhilarating, and he knew he had to have more of this. The song was over much too soon. With a final shout of *"Run away from the man in a dress!"* the band moved on to play the opening chords of a Queen classic, and the singer took the microphone back. Clovenhoof sat back down, giddy with the experience.

"Did you get any photos?" he asked Ben.

"I was living in the moment," said Ben. "I was playing air bagpipes, did you see?"

Clovenhoof had not seen, and he wasn't even sure what air bagpipes looked like, but he couldn't crush the mood. It had grabbed them both. He hauled Ben to his feet and the two of them started headbanging in front of the band. Neither of them had long hair to swish, and so they had to make up for that with attitude and vigour. Clovenhoof thought he might have pulled something but he kept going. He adopted a lunge position and whacked his head up and down in time to *We Will Rock You*. He raised his hand again, showing the horns, mainly because it was no good for anything else. Clovenhoof and Ben kept headbanging through the rest of the band's set. Clovenhoof refused to stop until Ben did, and he began to wonder if Ben was thinking the same.

When the final encore was over, the two of them stood straight, and immediately clutched hands to their necks.

"Ooh!" said Ben. "I think I'm going to feel that in the morning."

Clovenhoof nodded, immediately regretting it.

"We will be back later!" the singer shouted to the small but enthusiastic crowd and jumped off the tiny stage onto the floor. He walked straight across to Clovenhoof. "You were so cool, man. Old school rock!"

"Old is right," muttered Ben.

"You have no idea," said Clovenhoof.

"You Brits love to rock. I am Aksel. Come join us!" he said.

"I think I need a lie down," said Ben.

"Fuck that noise," said Clovenhoof. "We're hanging out with the band."

The band were sitting at a corner table.

"You were very good up there," said Aksel to Clovenhoof. "You sound so much like the original."

"I *am* the original!" said Clovenhoof.

"Yeah, sure you are!" laughed Aksel.

"The original singer of Devil Preacher died, didn't he?" said the lead guitarist. "Burned down his own flat after consuming human blood."

"Well, that second part happened," said Clovenhoof.

"No," said Aksel. "I heard he pumped sewage into an evangelical church and drowned in the flood."

"Fifty percent true," said Ben.

"No," said the sharp-voiced drummer, an unlit cigarette between her lips. "He formed his own breakaway country, tried to buy the Church of England and died in a guerilla war."

"Again, so close," said Clovenhoof. "And yet I live."

The singer, Aksel, stared at him. "No! Can it be real?"

"Jeremy Clovenhoof, the one and only," Clovenhoof leered.

"Is your hand permanently stuck doing the horns?" asked the lead guitarist.

Clovenhoof nodded and held his hand aloft. He wasn't going to mention the glue. "You're Djævlehund then? Where are you from?"

"Three of us are from Copenhagen." The singer put a hand on his chest. "I'm Aksel Vaskebjorn. Valdemar Slange plays lead. That silent monster is our bassist, Rasmus Kakerlak." The big hairy man gave a grunt of greeting. Aksel pointed at the fourth member. "Camille, our drummer, we picked up in Paris."

"Ah, Paris," said Ben in a drunk and wistful voice.

"—Is a shithole full of dog turds and fascists," said Camille.

Clovenhoof shrugged. "I mean, yeah. I love the smell of dog turds in the morning."

"We are on a tour of the UK, living the rock'n'roll dream," said Aksel.

Ben leaned over. "What is it though? Really? What is the rock'n'roll dream?"

Clovenhoof knew that Ben was in an advanced state of intoxication, so his question was intended in the abstract, rambling sense, but Aksel took it literally.

"It is a well-trodden path!" said Aksel, clearly animated. "I have written down the ones that I want to achieve, especially while I am here in the UK, where so many famous bands were born."

"You have a rock star bucket list?" Clovenhoof perked up, suddenly interested. "This is great! What's on it?"

"All the usual things," said Aksel. "Crowd surfing is one. I want to learn some moves like David Lee Roth, the flying splits and so on. I might need a yoga instructor for that. Then there's the obvious ones like trashing hotel rooms and getting arrested for public indecency."

"No time like the present," said Clovenhoof. "I've got a full bladder and I'm always happy to help with a bit of public indecency. What shall we go and piss on?"

Camille spoke up. "If you get arrested then what happens to the Scarborough gig? It's all about timing, Aksel. We need to make sure someone's on hand to get photos as well."

Clovenhoof was impressed with the way that Camille managed to speak entire sentences while a cigarette was clamped in her mouth. She oozed a certain frosty charisma from her tiny, leather-clad frame.

"Camille's brand manager wants to manage some sort of Instagram campaign," said Aksel with a sigh.

"You need a bucket list," Clovenhoof said to Ben with a nudge. "It's liked we were saying earlier, you need adventure in your life."

"Sounds good!" said Ben, raising his glass to the idea.

"Come with us," said Aksel. "We could really use some roadies."

Clovenhoof grabbed Ben's elbow. "Yes! We get to go on the road with a rock band! This is exactly what you need, Kitchen, and you know it."

"I have got a lot of band t-shirts," said Ben with a nod.

"Yes! You can wear them all with pride while you do all of the fetching and carrying," said Clovenhoof.

"You'll do some as well," said Ben.

"Of course," said Clovenhoof, already lining up his own personal bucket list. It involved less of the fetching and carrying, and more regaining his former rock god prowess. Pathetic has-been loser indeed!

7

"**B**rilliant, lads," called Rutspud as the crane of scorched iron swung the next girder into place over a currently part-built Fortress of Nameless Dread. Scampering worker demons waited to receive. A couple of them waved at Rutspud.

It was hard to enjoy life when one was a demon.

For a start, demons weren't alive. They weren't born and they didn't grow up. They certainly didn't possess that vague and nebulous thing called a soul. They didn't have the spark of life with which the Almighty Above had imbued even the tiniest of creatures.

Secondly, it was kind of hard to enjoy life when your natural milieu was Hell itself. People often pictured Hell as dark and fiery, and for the most part it was, but it was also freezing cold and damp. It had fields (where the grass cut like razor blades) and forests (where the trees whispered hurtful things about your hairstyle). Hell was a vast and varied domain, but its overall theme, its quintessential raison d'être, was that it was horrible, just plain horrible. Hell was a terrible place to live in, regardless of whether you were a wretched human soul or the wretched demons sent to torture them. *you* ?

Thirdly, the demon society had evolved over time into such a form that it punished every demon who existed in it. Things sometimes went wrong in Hell, and long, long ago, someone had decided that mistakes should be rewarded with punishment. Let a damned human have a moment's relief? It was pitchfork up the fundament for you, old chap. Miscalculate how many souls you could roast in the Lake of Fire at any one time? Your skin would be used to make the towels draped over the sun loungers at the lake's edge. Owning up to your mistakes wouldn't help either. Honesty was an undemonlike quality and also needed to be punished. Therefore, if mistakes were brutally punished and honesty was quashed, then demon society naturally evolved into one where the individuals at the top excelled at hiding their incompetence and maintained their position by deflecting blame (and the attached punishments) to those directly beneath them. And if you pointed this out to the demons they would point right back at government bodies and corporations on Earth as evidence this was the natural way of things.

The girder slid into place and the demon Umgolgoth and her thousand spiderling offspring swarmed over it to cement the girder in place with their spider-silk. Rutspud preferred the more reliable application of rivets, nuts and bolts, but the spider demon seemed to enjoy being part of the building process. And who was Rutspud to stop her?

"Nice work!" he called out. "Bring in the next one!"

It was indeed hard to enjoy life when one was a demon, but Rutspud felt he gave it a jolly good go. He knew that his existence, long or short, was ultimately pointless. He knew that generally he lived in a vast cosmos which did not care for him, and locally in a small subset of that cosmos which gently despised him and wished him harm. No achievement he made would outlive him, and he would only be remembered by a handful of individuals as a series of increasingly sketchy and self-serving recollections.

And yet Rutspud did manage to enjoy himself. He had long ago decided to detach himself from worrying about his place in the big picture. If nothing he did mattered, and he had no control over the colossal machinations of the universe, then he couldn't hold himself accountable for anything that happened. He was a free-wheeling ball in the big pinball game of existence and he might as well enjoy the ride while it lasted.

Rutspud had met more than a few Buddhists in his time in Hell and felt his philosophy was not a million miles away from that of the Buddha himself. Buddha wasn't in Hell and he wasn't in Heaven (Rutspud had checked), and if he ever caught up with the slippery bugger, he'd love to share his own personal philosophy with the man.

A companion crane was already hoisting up the next girder.

Hodshift, an engineer demon, wandered over with a clipboard in his hand and pencils tucked behind each and every one of his many ears. "Right, guv," he said, "Couple of fings for yer."

"Yes?" said Rutspud.

"Three actually."

"Okay."

"First up, we need to make a decision about the sub-basements."

"Yes?"

"They're still flooded."

"I know."

"Well, we need to pump 'em out if we're gonna use them, don't we?"

Rutspud nodded dubiously. "But Yan Ryuleh Sloggoth, elder demon of the impenetrable depths, has taken up residence down there."

"Exackerly," said Hodshift. "We can pump 'em out but old Sloggy ain't gonna be happy. He's already eaten four of my best blokes."

"Do we have to pump them out?" said Rutspud.

"What – and just leave them as flooded?"

"How about, we lay a floor of thick glass over it and make it like an aquarium."

Hodshift gave this some thought. "And 'ow are we going to deliver Sloggy's victims to 'im, eh, chief? Those oil executives ain't gonna torment themselves, you know."

"Right, right," said Rutspud. "So hear me out." He spread his hands wide as though painting an imaginary canvas. "Water flumes."

"Water flumes?" said Hodshift.

"Water flumes. Put them up on the third floor. Big coils of

tubing. Nasty evil humans go in the top. Wheeee – plop! Chomp!"

"Wheeee plop chomp?" Hodshift mused on this and, with one of his many pencils, sketched out some ideas on his clipboard. He started to turn away.

"The other things?" Rutspud prompted him.

"Oh, yeah," said Hodshift. "First up, yer don't need to tell the boys what to do – with the iron girders and the cranes and wotnot. They've got their orders. I've got 'em well trained. You do the science-y stuff and share the infernal plans; my lads will make it as ordered wivvout your help."

"I know," said Rutspud, shrugging happily. "I just like being involved."

"All right, you weirdo. And secondly, there's an angel for you."

Rutspud coughed. "—What?"

"There's an angel for you, out by the gate. Says he needs to speak to you. Something about divine substances being taken up to Earth without permission."

Rutspud would have coughed again if he'd properly recovered from the first one.

"Divine substances?" he said, and tried not to think about the broken Pipe of St Zita he'd left in Clovenhoof's fist, in case somehow that guilty fact became instantly written on his face.

"I'm just the messenger, mate. Angel, gate, waiting fer yer."

"Right," said Rutspud and immediately scampered off towards the entrance to Hell.

It was hard to enjoy life when one was a demon, and

although Rutspud put the effort in to do so, the universe seemed hellbent on making it even harder.

The entrance to Hell was what Rutspud considered to be a class 'hell mouth'. It was high and wide like a monstrous maw. Its very architecture seemed to say 'Come on in! We've got room for all of you!' The high and well-lit nature of the space, coupled with the queues of the damned waiting to get in, also gave it the feel of a large airport terminal. Inspired by this, the R&D department had worked long and hard on developing an app so that the recently deceased could check into Hell in advance via their phones, and thereby skip the queues. Bizarrely, this app proved popular with those in the queue. Even though on-line check-in only hastened mortals towards the actual torture – the *eternal* torture – there was something in human nature which couldn't resist a funky little phone app and the chance to skip a queue.

Rutspud walked past the fast-track lane of the smug and soon-to-be-tortured and out towards the gate itself. Hell's watchdog Cerberus was laid out snoozing, or at least two of its heads were snoozing while the third kept a lazy watch over proceedings. Snoozing or not, Rutspud gave the huge dog a wide berth and went out into the grey nothingness of limbo where, indeed, an angel was waiting for him.

Rutspud swallowed his fear and stepped forward.

8

Ben woke up in his bed to find morning light streaming in through the half-drawn curtains, Clovenhoof standing over him.

"What are you doing up before me?" groaned Ben, feeling the appalling dryness in his mouth and the pounding onset of a major hangover headache. "This is against the natural order of things."

"We're off on the road!"

"What?"

"There's no time to be lost. We don't want the van to go without us."

"What van?"

"They're coming to fetch us in fifteen minutes. I'm wearing that leather jacket Nerys said made me look like I belong in the seventies. It works for the roadie look, don't you think?" He gave a twirl.

Ben remembered it all then. The Boldmere Oak, the

band, the talk of bucket list items and adventur
seemed such a good idea last night, but now he
the cheese in the fridge that was due to go out of date.

"Oh, I don't know Jeremy. It all seems a bit hasty."

"Of course it's a bit hasty. It's an adventure. Now get up!"

Ben levered himself up from his pillow. "Ow! My neck!"

Clovenhoof rolled his eyes. "I'll get you some paracetamol if you hurry up."

"What will I do about the shop?" Ben said.

"Surely Sparts can take care of it?" said Clovenhoof.

"What? No. Ridiculous." He sat on the edge of the bed, massaging his neck. "I am not going to start roadying for a band just became it seemed cool when we were pissed as newts last night."

"But you promised!"

"I don't think I did."

Clovenhoof tutted and Ben heard him go out of the flat and across the hall. Ben blinked at the weak sunlight and imagined what it would be like doing the lifting and carrying for a two-bit metal band. The negatives instantly outnumbered the positives. What did Ben want? What did he really want? He wanted to get to his shop. He wanted to sit behind the counter with a hot cup of tea and music playing faintly in the background while he thumbed through some much loved books in stock. His mind leapt to Lois – beautiful, untainted, spirited Lois in those vintage 3D nudey pictures. Ben wanted to sit and drink tea and sink in the happy, innocent world of Lois.

Clovenhoof barged back in. "Painkillers," he said and put two tablets in Ben's hand.

Ben tossed them in his mouth, then saw his bedside glass was empty.

"Need wa'er," he said around the tablets.

Clovenhoof patted at his clothes, then pulled a pottery flask from his jacket pocket.

Ben inspected its rough surface and the weird lettering on it. "What's this?"

"Water. Special water."

"If that's code for your piss..." Ben put his lips around the narrow neck and sucked in enough water to swallow the tablets.

"Now, let's get out there, hit the road and make this rock'n'roll dream come true!" said Clovenhoof.

It was a patently stupid idea, but as a sudden warmth flooded Ben's body, washing away the ache from his body and the pain from his head, he felt that it was, in fact, not such a stupid idea after all. Spartacus *could* look after the shop. Ben *could* spend a few days on the road with a cool band. He *could* spend a few days finding himself and living a little of that rock and toll lifestyle.

"Yeah." Ben jumped out of bed. "Let's do it!"

"Fuck yeah!" crowed Clovenhoof.

Ben pulled on trousers and slipped on his shoes. "Listen, there's something I need to fetch. Can you pack me a bag, please? I will be back in just a few minutes, then I'll be ready."

"Pack you a bag? Sure. Leave it to me," said Clovenhoof.

Ben trotted out of the house and, as swiftly as he could, went down to the shop. He unlocked the security shutter, ducking under it before it was half-raised, and went inside.

They were on the counter: the 3D adventures of lovely Lois. It was, he decided, the one thing he could not afford to leave behind. Spartacus had seemed confident he could find a specialist buyer for them, but Ben realised he wasn't ready to sell them.

It would have been brilliant if Ben could have stored them for safety in Desmond Rothermere's old safe in the counter, but since he'd never had the key for the thing, it just wasn't possible. Ben scribbled a note for Spartacus, put the vintage books into a black bag, zipped it up and carried it out.

He hurried back to the house and found there was a large, very shabby transit van waiting outside. It had a trailer hitched to the back, piled high with equipment, and a tarpaulin strapped down with elasticated bungee ropes. The name *DJÆVLEHUND* had been painted on the side in a naïve and amateurish font.

Clovenhoof stood on the pavement, looking very pleased with himself. "Chop chop! We're off to North Yorkshire. I assume that's in the north, is it?"

"We should tell Nerys where we're going," said Ben, hesitating.

"All dealt with," said Clovenhoof. "Twinkle's been out for a crap and I've given him his breakfast. Even said 'thank you' to me."

"The dog?"

"At least that's how I interpreted his noises. Nerys is back later on. It'll be fine. Come on, get in!"

"You packed me a bag?" Ben asked.

"Of course. It's in the van."

Ben climbed in. The van was quite a large one, but it seemed very full with six people sitting inside. He nodded in greeting to the members of the band and tried to put names to faces again. Aksel the singer, Valdemar the guitarist, Rasmus the bassist and Camille the drummer. The three men looked like they'd hit the booze hard last night: empty shells, like spent tubes of toothpaste. The drummer still wore that fierce bitch look on her face. Even the unlit cigarette was still jammed between her lips.

He looked at the empty seat. "Where's the seatbelt?" he asked.

"It's a vintage vehicle," said Aksel, "they are not fitted. Don't worry, we won't be going on the motorway."

"No? Why not?" asked Ben.

"The van cannot go quickly enough. It will be fine though, I am a very good driver."

Clovenhoof sat next to Ben, shoving him sideways to get comfy. "It's a proper tour bus. It even smells right."

Ben sniffed. There was definitely a hint of old takeaways, with a heavy dose of body odour and something that might have been shoe polish, but he wasn't sure.

The van sagged heavily on its suspension as it pulled away from the kerb. Ben really wanted to ask if it had a current MOT, but knew that it wasn't a very rock'n'roll question.

"Everybody!" said Aksel. "Our two new roadies are Ben and Jeremy. Jeremy joined us on stage last night and was in the original *Devil Preacher*.

Ben was about to point out that so was he, but

Clovenhoof chipped in. "I wasn't just *in Devil Preacher*, I *was Devil Preacher*."

"So, ah what are our duties going to be?" Ben asked.

"You're roadies," said Aksel. You will do all of the jobs that arise. Mostly that will mean you carry our equipment and set it up for each gig. It's pretty easy, and you will soon learn how it goes."

"In addition to our roadying duties, we will of course be here to help you carry out those important rockstar items on your bucket list," said Clovenhoof. "Happy to suggest more if you need a bad influence."

"Number one item is to get home unscathed," said Valdemar. "I need to get back to my little Frederik."

"Oh, has Valdemar got a little baby boy at home?" said Camille, from the front, in mock surprise. "Did anyone else know that?"

Hairy big guy Rasmus grunted.

"I am just saying," said Valdemar.

"You say repeatedly," said Camille. "We get it. Your balls work. You have a child."

Valdemar reached out with his phone.

"No. No photos," said Camille. "No one wants to see photos of your little shitting machine right now."

"Say shitting again!" said Clovenhoof. "It sounds much better with your accent. Sheeting. Sheeeeting. It doesn't work when I say it."

Camille ignored him.

"So how many gigs have you got planned?" asked Ben.

"Shows. We're calling them shows on this tour. We do gigs

back home, but this is a much bigger deal," said Aksel. "Anyway, who knows? Our promoter is working to add some extra places, but right now the next is at a theatre in Scarborough on Sunday."

Ben wondered what sort of a place Scarborough was. It was probably all part of the adventure, finding out.

"So, is flamethrower guitar on your bucket list?" asked Clovenhoof, tapping Aksel on the shoulder.

"Er, no? I have not heard of such a thing," said Aksel. "Do they exist?"

"If they don't, then they should," said Clovenhoof. "Take it from me, there are very few things that can't be improved with a flamethrower. Leave it with me."

"If you make such a thing, it will need a risk assessment," said Valdemar. "We can't afford to be reckless."

There was a long silence in the van. Ben thought it sounded sensible, but what did the others think?

"Sure Valdemar," said Camille. "Got to get home to that product of your balls, don't you?"

"I didn't say—"

"Can we not argue while I am driving?" said Aksel. "I need to concentrate on the road. I am perhaps still a little drunk from last night."

"Do you need someone to take over?" said Ben. While he had not thought it necessary to speak up in the matter of flamethrower risk assessments, he definitely felt like he didn't want to be killed by a drunk driver. If an initial crash didn't kill him, having an overladen trailer of band gear piling up and over him might just do the job. An image of him being decapitated by one of Camille's cymbals flashed through his mind.

"Is one of you okay to drive in a bit?" said Aksel.

"We're fresh as daisies," said Clovenhoof.

"Yeah, absolutely," said Ben. It was surprisingly true. "Those paracetamol you gave me, Jeremy. Were they super strength or something?"

"Er, yes," said Clovenhoof. "And guaranteed to keep you worm-free for up to six months."

"What?" Ben swallowed. "Did you give me some of Twinkle's dog-worming tablets? You didn't, did you?"

"Tablets are just tablets. They're all the same."

"Jeremy!"

"It's all a con, you know. Big Pharma tricking us into buying drugs."

Ben threw his hands in the air. "You gave me ... ugh! And Nerys actually trusted you to look after her dog. I can't fucking believe you sometimes."

"I know," said Clovenhoof. "I am amazing, aren't I?"

9

As he strode into Limbo, Rutspud recognised the multicoloured sparkling lights dancing over the slender angel and his glossy luminescent wings.

"Eltiel?"

The angel gave a little jump of surprise. "Ooh, you snuck up on me there."

"Literally just walking," said Rutspud, gesturing at his footprints in the snow-like non-stuff of Limbo.

Eltiel clutched the grey stone tablet he held against his chest a little tighter. "It's sort of spooky round here, isn't it?" he said, casting wary glances at the cave entrance.

"It *is* Hell," said Rutspud.

"I suppose it is," said Eltiel and attempted a nervous little smile.

Finding out that the angel seeking him was Eltiel gave Rutspud some relief. Angels, like demons, were big on hierarchy. Thrones, dominions, orders and choirs marked out the complicated map of angel power structures. In that great hierarchy, Eltiel was somewhere near the very bottom. He was a messenger angel, a gopher, a doing of deeds that greater angels couldn't be bothered doing. As much as he'd dislike to be compared to this naïve, weak-willed and frankly unintelligent angel, Eltiel was, rank-wise, one of Rutspud's opposite numbers in the Celestial City.

If one of the big guns of Heaven – a Gabriel, a Raphael or what have you – had come to speak to Rutspud about divine substances being taken up to Earth, he might have been quaking in his metaphorical boots. But this was just Eltiel.

"What can I do for you, disco-wings?" said Rutspud.

"Thank you for your time, Rutspud, craven worm of the sixth circle."

"Rutspud'll be fine," said the demon.

"A pressing matter has come to light," said the angel. "The Heavenly Moral Records Centre has detected several unusual readings."

Rutspud was familiar with the Heavenly Moral Records Centre or HMRC. It kept a tally of sins carried out by individuals and calculated the penance or punishment owed by each. Rutspud had even visited it a few years back when the Celestial City's sins readings had all gone screwy and all manner of hell-bound individuals were sent to Heaven by mistake.

"Yeah? You still got a drunk saint in charge of that place?" said Rutspud. "Have you lost control of the sin valves or whatever."

"St Hubertus enjoys a drink," admitted Eltiel. "It's part of his charming character. And, no, there is no problem with human sinning."

"Tell that to our processing team at the gates," said Rutspud, offering a cheesy grin to underscore the joke.

"Oh, would they like me to?" said Eltiel, giving Hell's entrance a nervous glance.

"No..." Rutspud both tutted and sighed. "What's the issue, Eltiel? I've got building works to oversee."

Eltiel flipped his stone tablet around. On it, in sparkly golden lines of light, was a graph. It showed a straight light which abruptly peaked.

"Spikey graph," said Rutspud. He tried to read the legend along the side. "Anima?"

"Anima, spirits, humanity, will," said Eltiel. "We're struggling to come up with a single theologically sound definition."

"Really?"

"Yeah. It's the thing that separates humans from animals."

Eltiel gestured across his rectangle of carved stone and the imagery changed. The angel waved the tablet over Rutspud, then held it up to show him. There was a hollow outline picture of Rutspud, and next to it a big zero percent.

"You have none. You are not alive," said Eltiel. "You are entirely a tool of evil."

"You're a tool," Rutspud shot back instantly.

"Of the Heavenly Father," Eltiel agreed readily. "We act as we are instructed. We, as individuals, cannot deviate from the Divine Plan. Humans, on the other hand can—"

"Fuck up," said Rutspud. "Do what they want. Act like

dicks. Become capable of acts of great self-sacrifice or waste their lives eating chips and watching reality TV. You're talking about free will, aren't you?"

"That's definitely part of it," said Eltiel. "It's not just the freedom to act but also the 'will' to change the Lord's creation, to pull history down this track or that."

"Or just sit on the sofa and watch crap telly."

Eltiel flicked back to the graph on his stone tablet. "This spike is most alarming."

Rutspud realised a couple of things. First of all, and most annoyingly, he realised that Eltiel's tablet was literally his *tablet*. One of the joys of Hell was its willingness to leap upon human technology and use it for its own perverse ends. The internet, YouTube, phone apps, self-driving cars— Hell had stolen Earth technology, perverted it for its own use and, in most cases, fed their infernal improvements back into the Earth original. Heaven either had no desire to use Earth technology in this way or was somehow incapable, and here was Eltiel holding the physical proof. Someone Up There had heard that humans were using 'tablets' to find and display information, so what did Heaven do with that knowledge? They made dancing magic lights appear on the surface of a slab of stone that belonged nowhere except tucked under Moses' arm. Heaven had made tablets and made them stupid.

The second thing that Rutspud realised was that Eltiel hadn't thrown any accusations at him at all.

"How can I help you with all this?" he said casually.

"I know you're a clever demon."

"Lies and slander, buddy."

"And I know you are often Hell's go-to guy when it comes to dealing with matters on Earth."

"Again, don't know what you're talking about."

Eltiel waggled his fingers over his tablet and several fresh images appeared, like medieval woodcut illustrations but executed in golden light: Rutspud playing frisbee with a monk on a green hillside; Rutspud scampering along a familiar residential street in Birmingham.

"You get around a lot," said Eltiel. He waved his hand. The next image showed Rutspud and a squad of demons running through the Celestial City itself towards a monstrous tunnelling machine.

"Shit," said Rutspud. "I didn't know you guys knew about that."

"Few of us do."

"We were on a mission from Hell itself. I didn't have a choice—"

"Because you are a tool."

"Er, yeah. Right."

"I want you to help me because I think you can."

"Ohh – this is like a general request?"

"It is," said the angel primly. "I am asking you."

"Truth is, I'm kinda busy. I mean, I'd love to help you lot do your job but, you know how it is? Anyway, it's just a bit of – what? – Free will? Spirit? Chutzpah? I'm sure it will all even out in the end."

Eltiel drew back, surprised. "I don't think you understand the gravity of the situation."

"Well, it can hardly be important if you lot can't agree on the name of it."

"It's of paramount importance," said Eltiel. He was probably trying to sound commanding and forceful, but from his lips it just sounded tetchy and borderline hysterical. "Have you any idea of the profound impact this could have? Unchecked, it could create mass Satanic sex rituals, cause the beasts of the field to turn on their masters, and set up a calamitous situation where the Djævlehund drags a thousand souls down to Hell."

"The what? Those are oddly specific situations," said Rutspud.

"I've run the equations!" said Eltiel and thrust his tablet in Rutspud's face. Those very items were indeed listed. "Actually, I don't know what an equation is, but it sounded like the right thing to say. I have sought predictions and it's not good, Rutspud. Trust me."

"Sound like a regular week on Earth if you ask me."

Eltiel let out a big dramatic sigh, trying to expel his anxious energy. "Listen, please. Let me put it into context. Long, long ago, the Almighty created the Heavens and the Earth."

"I might have heard this one."

"He created the seas and lands and the plants and the animals." As Eltiel spoke, golden lines of light sprang from his tablet to create an attractive 3D rendering of God's creation in the air between them. "And though this world was perfect, the Almighty was not yet done. He created man and woman, and to them alone he gave this anima, this soul, this free will." In the image between them a naked man and woman appeared among all the creatures in the crowded garden.

"Some of us downstairs consider that to have been a generally bad move," said Rutspud.

"The Almighty is perfect and never makes a mistake. Well—" In the image, the man and the woman visibly argued and the woman ran off. "The Almighty had made the woman too wilful."

Rutspud might have retorted that this sounded like a bedtime story written by and for the patriarchy, but any snide remarks were cut off by another realisation: he'd heard this story very, very recently.

"Balls," he whispered. "That's Lilith."

"Lilith indeed. So filled with wilfulness that she rejected Adam, rejected the Lord Above, and anything she willed to be true became true."

The crying woman in the image magically gained bird feet, sprouted wings and flew off.

"For some reason," said Eltiel, "a not insignificant quantity of that wilfulness is now loose in the world and I hoped I might enlist your help to find and contain it before any of these bad things occur."

Rutspud stroked his little chin in thought. He hoped, to Eltiel's eyes, it looked like he was contemplating whether he could be bothered to assist the minor angel. In truth, he was contemplating what the hell might happen if Jeremy Clovenhoof chugged down the rest of that bottle.

"Yeah, yeah, I might be able to help you..." he said.

10

They swapped over drivers somewhere just outside the Midlands before lunchtime.

Clovenhoof considered himself to be a well-travelled man. In fact, as the devil he would once proudly have said that he had been everywhere. Indeed, was to be found everywhere, lurking around every corner, waiting to ensnare weak souls with his wiles. Of course, that was really a load of bollocks. Running Hell had kept him busy enough, and he only popped out now and again when the whim took him. Humans didn't need the devil to tempt them. Humans had as much resistance to sin as a dog let loose in a sausage factory.

But Clovenhoof did pretty much know everywhere. Unfortunately, everywhere was mostly like everywhere else. One pointless dreary town with an amusingly named pub on the high street, a trio of supermarkets on the outskirts, and miles and miles of indistinguishably dull housing estates between them was very much like another.

They stopped in such a town to swap over.

Aksel gratefully got out of the driver's side, wide-eyed but barely conscious. Clovenhoof began to clamber over from the rear to get to the driver's seat.

"Er, you're driving?" said Ben.

"I am," said Clovenhoof. "Unless you'd like to sit on my lap and do the gears."

"You don't have a driving licence."

"I did my test back in June."

"Did you pass?"

"I've done my driving test twelve times, which by my calculations makes me twelve times better than the average person."

Ben looked pleadingly at Aksel, who shrugged. "I do not know how your driving laws work. I am not even sure if this vehicle is technically legal on your roads." He looked to Rasmus, who grunted. "No. Possibly not."

X that   "Well, in the case," said Ben, climbing into the front and displacing Valdemar, "I'm getting one of the seats with the seatbelts."

Clovenhoof looked at the dashboard and the pedals. He absolutely knew how to drive. The main issue had always been that his hoofs were too small for the pedals. But he knew he could do this. Only a pathetic old has-been of a devil would accept they couldn't drive.

Momentarily thirsty, he dipped into his pocket, found the Lilith's Tears and took a hearty swig. It was salty invigorating passed it to Ben.

"Come on, Kitchen. We can do this."

Ben, sighing sceptically, accepted the bottle, took a sip and passed it back. A warm smile appeared on his face. "I do believe in you, Jeremy. Together, we can do this."

"That's the spirit." Clovenhoof waggled the hot air events, twiddled the knob of the defunct radio and put the wipers on. "Final instruments check. Tower, we are ready for take-off."

Rasmus gave an almost wordless mumble.

"Yes," said Aksel. "It is very important that we do not go over sixty kilometres an hour."

"Why?" said Clovenhoof. "Do we travel back in time?"

"No. The van will overheat and die."

"But not travel back in time?"

"No."

"Shame."

Clovenhoof started her up. The van chugged into life. Clovenhoof found the clutch on his second stomp and shoved it into first.

"Oh no. The crazy old man is driving. We are all going die," said Camille, without a hint of emotion.

Clovenhoof accelerated away.

In the back, Valdemar plucked out a metal tune on his guitar.

"*Storm rages, thunder roars. Through chaos landscapes we endure. Side by side on life's battlefield we stand...*"

"That is good," said Aksel. "A new song?"

Valdemar nodded and slipped into a chorus. "*Frederik, oh, Frederik, your daddy misses you soooo. Fredrick, oh, Frederik, your little nose, your tiny toes.*"

"*Baise-moi!*" Camille swore emphatically and stuck her earphones in.

Clovenhoof grinned, sped over a roundabout and made for the A-road north.

NERYS PRESSED the button to wind down the passenger side window again. Tina stabbed at the controls on her side to put it back up.

"Leave it down," Nerys snapped.

"But it's cold."

"And I need to be able to breathe if we're not going to crash. You focus on keeping that bucket on your knee and your vomit off my upholstery."

Tina did not look well at all. Their stay at the 'Wild Boss' retreat had come to an explosive end when Tina had been spectacularly sick in the early hours. She'd barely got to the door of their grubby shack before expelling the contents of her stomach. The hurling had woken Nerys and she sat up to see Tina running across the clearing towards the communal toilet and shower facilities. Tina was to find no relief there as it appeared there was a crowd of people already gathered around the meagre facilities, clutching themselves to hold the sickness in.

A food poisoning outbreak seized the whole site and more than half the participants were afflicted. In the cold light of morning, there had been nothing for them to do except throw their belongings in the car and make the journey back to civilisation.

"I'm so cold," mumbled Tina over her bucket. "I think I'm going to die."

"You're not going to die," said Nerys. "You're going to puke and shit your guts out, spend a weekend on the sofa watching TikToks of fashion fails and discover you weigh five pounds less on Monday. Win-win."

"There's nothing left to puke," said Tina, gagging halfway through the sentence. "I think I'm about to throw up one of my kidneys."

"Well, you only need one," said Nerys. She tried to crank up the aircon to dispel some of the disgusting acidic stink filling the little car. All that seemed to do was recirculate the smell and spit it back in distilled form. The aircon could only offer hot vomit stench or cold vomit stench.

"I warned you about having the chicken option," said Nerys.

"I know, I know," said Tina, repentantly. "Everyone else seemed to be enjoying it. Those Morris men were wolfing it down."

"And I'm sure they're regretting it now," said Nerys. "They'll probably need to put their hankies on a hot wash when they get home."

Nerys couldn't wait to get home. Specifically, she couldn't wait to dump Tina at her flat, leave as soon as was decently possible, get back to her own flat, give her little dog a big fuss, slide into a soapy bath, and put all this horribleness out of her mind.

She put her foot down on the accelerator to try to get home that little bit sooner. And if the increased speed blasted more of Tina's stink out of the window, so much the better.

THE ROAD ahead was flat and straight. Clovenhoof coaxed a few more miles an hour out of the elderly van.

In the back, the band were quiet. Aksel had gone to sleep. Rasmus too. Possibly. Valdemar was still idly picking out Heavy Metal love songs to his infant son. And Camille appeared to be on a business video call to somewhere which slipped between French and German – which Clovenhoof understood perfectly well – and seemed to be about a 'social media portfolio' and 'curated presence' – which Clovenhoof didn't understand at all.

Next to him, Ben was looking through some yellowed and dog-eared picture books and staring meditatively at each page. He was also, oddly, wearing glasses with bits of coloured paper stuck over them.

"What's that then, Kitchen?" said Clovenhoof.

Ben automatically recoiled from him. "It's none of your business. You wouldn't understand."

"What wouldn't I understand?"

"These are vintage. Works of beauty."

Clovenhoof tried to peer over at the books, only wobbling slightly on the road as he did so. Ben held back for a moment before showing him.

"I know what you're going to say," he said.

Clovenhoof screwed his eyes up as he looked at them.

"It's blurry pictures of women in the nud. You looking at blurry porn?"

"See? I knew you were going to say that. The pictures are 3D. And it's not porn."

"It's naked women. It's porn. Say it loud, say it proud."

"And it's not wom*en*," said Ben. "It's *one* woman. Lois. They're all of her. It's like a little picture book of her adventures."

"Oh, right. A little bedtime picture book but with 3D tits."

"It's not about the tits," said Ben. "You're missing the point."

"What?"

"Forget it," Ben said with a harrumph.

Clovenhoof looked at him askance. "Do you fancy her or something?"

Ben drew himself up haughtily. "I think it's a fabulous window into a more innocent time and I think Lois is ... charming."

"Fuck. You do fancy her. Ben's got a boner for red and blue totty."

"I can be drawn by the beauty of it all. A woman who had curves in all the right places, who isn't trying to fit some supermodel template. A beautiful woman just going about her day."

"With her norks on show. How old is that thing? Your Lois must be in her eighties now."

"Stop trying to make fun of it."

Clovenhoof sighed. "I think it's lovely. You're taking your first steps into a bigger, seedier world. Go on. Let's have a look."

"No," said Ben, holding his book back protectively.

"I won't damage it."

"You will. Just by looking. Everything you look at turns ... grubby."

"That's a fine way to talk to your oldest friend."

"You're not my oldest friend."

"You don't know how old I am."

Ben sighed and relented, holding the book open to a page. "Your eyes are meant to be on the road."

Clovenhoof gestured to the road ahead. "Nothing coming." He looked at the pages. "*Lois at the Holiday Camp*, eh? I need the glasses to see it properly."

Ben tutted, reached over to steady the wheel, and passed Clovenhoof his glasses. Clovenhoof slipped them on and was in a world of reds and greenish-blue.

"Cool. It's like I'm on drugs," he said. "Crap and unexciting drugs, but drugs."

"Take a quick look and then take them off," said Ben.

Clovenhoof looked at the page. "Ooh, she's come right out at me. You humans are really inventive sometimes. It's like 'Pop!' Lois doing calisthenics by the poolside." He could see what Ben meant about her physical appearance. She was just an ordinary woman, not especially attractive or conforming to any expected body type. She just happened to have been caught on film doing jolly activities in the nip. Clovenhoof approved: male, female, young, old, he was an equal opportunities sex pest.

"You can almost reach out and touch her," he said, fingers hovering over the page.

Ben pulled Lois out of his reach and shut the book forcefully. "Don't you dare!"

Clovenhoof laughed. He held out his hand to inspect it at a distance through the 3D glasses. "It's like it's really there..." he said dreamily.

"Of course it's there— Car! *Car*!"

Ben was right. There was a car on the road coming towards them. And, yes, Clovenhoof had drifted over to the right while looking at the book. And for a moment, his 3D-focused brain thought '*Wow, it's like that car is REALLY coming straight at us*' before he realised that, of course, the car was doing exactly that.

He floored the accelerator and wrenched the wheel round.

11

Nerys didn't notice the transit van and trailer drifting into her lane until it was almost too late. The road was long, straight and boring, and she'd been distracted, both by the vomit stink coming off of Tina and also by the curiously high and secure fencing of the farm she was driving past. High fencing, like it was a prison for naughty vegetables and the farmer didn't want any of them escaping.

Nerys only realised they were on a direct collision course with the van when Tina gave a weak and sickly burble of alarm.

"Crap," Nerys breathed and, with the thought that 'crap' might be her last words on Earth, steered the car violently up onto the leaf mulch covered verge, feeling that awful weightless sliding sensation of the car losing control, bounced off a little mound, and spun back onto the road where – thank fuck! – the tyres reconnected with the road. She steered back into her lane, facing the right way.

She slammed on the brakes, turned off the ignition, and stormed out of the car to remonstrate with the idiot van driver, but he was almost out of sight, fishtailing across two lanes as he went, steam or smoke rising from his vehicle.

She could make out the word *DJÆVLEHUND* painted on the back of the trailer, but the vehicle was too far away for her to read the registration number.

"Get your eyes tested, you absolute bell-end!" she yelled. Then, because there was nothing else to be done, she got back in her car.

Tina was sitting perfectly still in the passenger seated, covered head to lap in her own vomit. The bucket, which she still held, was now mostly empty.

"I want to die," she whispered in a tiny and miserable voice. "I want to die now."

"Not until you've paid to have my car valeted," snapped Nerys and started the engine up.

THE MEMBERS of Djævlehund and their two new roadies stared at the van. It had come to a juddering halt in a dirt driveway, steam hissing noisily from its open bonnet.

"Heap of shit," growled Camille.

"It will be fine," said Aksel.

Rasmus grunted.

"Did you go over sixty kilometres an hour?" Aksel asked.

"I may have tapped the accelerator a little to swerve

around that crazy driver," said Clovenhoof. "But I treated this van with all the respect I would give an elderly lover."

Aksel's lips drew into a firm line. "We will need to let it cool down, and possibly top up the water. Stopping for an hour will not mess up our schedule."

Rasmus contributed some sort of wordless grunt and pointed ahead.

"I see it, my friend," said Aksel. "A business premises. We can ask them for some water. And perhaps they will give us coffee too, if we are lucky. I am very thirsty."

The premises, down the short drive and across a yard which served as a car park, was a set of squat buildings. Clovenhoof wondered what sort of business it was. The location suggested it should be a farm, but this place had high fences, and the signage discreetly called it RIBBLE-LORENZ HORTICULTURE, with no additional information.

"I'll go and ask for some water," Aksel said.

The group trailed after Aksel in an untidy straggle. Clovenhoof peered round the edge of the metal entrance building. Polytunnels stretched into the distance on the other side of the high security fence.

"I bet there's something amazing inside here," said Clovenhoof.

Aksel pressed the button on an intercom. "Hello? Hello? Is it possible that you can help?"

"Aye?" said a tinny voice from the speaker.

"We need some water for the radiator of our van."

There was a pause. *"There's a garage in Little Cheddington."*

"Is it far?"

"About twenty-minute drive?"

"But our van is going nowhere and I must apologise for it is blocking your driveway."

There was a long pause before the answer came. *"Hang on."*

There was silence thereafter.

"'I must apologise'," sneered Camille. "Hardly a Heavy Metal attitude."

"Actually I find that Metal fans are some of the sweetest and most polite people around," said Ben. "It's quite a nerdy little musical genre."

Clovenhoof made a half-laugh of a noise. The man was right. Metallers were the sort who'd be kind to their grans and tried really hard at school. If you wanted to get music-related violence, the best place to look for it was at kicking out time on the pavement outside the most popular and poppy nightclubs. Most Metal Heads would be tucked up in bed with cocoa and their headphones on at that hour.

Camille cast out the cigarette between her lips and pulled another from her crumpled pack. Clovenhoof hadn't actually seen her smoke one yet.

"You know you're all morons if you think that someone is coming," she declared, grinding out the discarded cigarette with the heel of her boot.

A door opened and a figure in a white coverall stepped out, complete with hood and a mask. Only their eyes could be seen. "I were in t'clean room," said a man with a broad Yorkshire accent and a Velcro fabric name badge that said *Bilal.* "Tha wants some water, yeah?"

"I would like to use the bathroom," said Camille.

"Oh, tha can't come in. This here's a secure facility."

"We have waited here for a long time," said Camille with a frosty glare. "What would you have me do? Piss in the car park?"

"I, er." The man, Bilal, cast his arms about as if he wanted to suggest an alternative, but could think of nothing he was prepared to offer. "Fine. Tha'll have to be in and out, sharpish."

"Very good." She strode past him into the building.

The others followed. Bilal made small noises of anguished surprise, but didn't stop them. They entered a space that Clovenhoof considered extremely dull. It was a grey room with other doors leading off it, and a single chair. There was no reception desk, no water cooler, no coffee machine, not even a low table with out of date magazines.

Bilal turned to address them all. "Right, now this is important. Tha needs ter stay in this room. The rooms beyond are carefully controlled and tha must not go in them."

They all nodded.

"What are you? A pub band?" he said.

"We are metal band," said Valdemar.

"Who play at pubs," said Aksel.

"Hmmm. Well, just stay here and..." Bilal led Camille through a doorway.

Clovenhoof nudged Ben as they all stared at the other doors. "What do you reckon's in there, then?"

"We will probably never know. We'll get the water and be on our way in a short while," said Ben.

"What? Let this slide without satisfying our curiosity?" said Clovenhoof in horror.

"Why so curious?"

"Because it's odd," said Clovenhoof. "It's a farm back there but he's all done up like one of them end-of-the-world pandemic scientists, and there's big scary fences everywhere. They've got something odd back there."

"They're growing genetically modified crops?" suggested Valdemar.

"Rabid monkeys," said Aksel.

"Growing rabid monkeys?" said Clovenhoof.

"Containing them or something," said Aksel. "Like it's a research centre for rabid monkeys."

"What would we learn from studying rabid monkeys?" asked Ben.

Aksel shrugged. "Why it's a bad idea to give rabies to monkeys?"

"So it would be cool to go find out," said Clovenhoof. "All we need to do is look. Watch and learn." He went to one of the doors and nudged it open. "See how I am not entering the space at all? I am merely observing."

The space beyond looked like a locker room. There were outdoor boots on a rack with clothes hung up nearby. Small personal lockers faced them. There was another door on the far side, labelled CURING ROOM.

"Curing room," said Aksel. "For the rabid monkeys."

Clovenhoof tried the next door. It revealed an office space, with a desk and noticeboard.

"Not even a water cooler," said Aksel. "I am very thirsty."

"Here, mate," said Clovenhoof and passed him the still mostly full flask of Lilith's Tears. "Salty refreshment for you."

Aksel popped off the stopper.

"There are some leaflets on the desk," said Ben, peering into the room. "Can you see what they say?"

"Not from here," said Clovenhoof.

"I know what to do," said Aksel enthusiastically as he wiped the back of his hand and passed the bottle back to Clovenhoof. "This is like 'the floor's lava', right?"

Clovenhoof shrugged. "It definitely could be."

"Here we go." Aksel dragged the chair over to the doorway and pushed it inside the room. "If I stand on the chair then I haven't entered the room, have I?"

"Of course you have," said Valdemar. "Are you a *hjerneløs* idiot? Not entering the room is quite different to not touching the floor."

Clovenhoof gave Aksel an encouraging tap on the arm. "Go with your instincts."

Aksel took a huge step onto the chair and then grunted as he heaved himself up. "I can reach the leaflets!" he crowed. "There's a letter here too, something about testing samples being scheduled for pickup today."

"But what samples?" said Clovenhoof.

Aksel leaned over, sticking a leg back as a counterbalance, and picked a leaflet from the top of the pile. "Got it!"

At that moment, the chair slid out from underneath him and he landed heavily on the floor of the office. The chair clattered backwards across the reception floor.

"Lava! Lava!" hissed Ben.

Bilal and Camille chose that moment to return. Clovenhoof stepped over and smartly shut the door, holding it closed (with his usable hand) to stop Aksel blundering out.

"Ah, you're back. Sorry, I fell over your chair. Oh hey, did you say that you needed the toilet as well, Ben?"

Ben was startled, but caught on quick enough. "The toilet? Yes please, if it's at all possible. You know what it's like when you've been on the road for a few hours. Ha ha."

"Fine." Bilal shook his head and beckoned to Ben to follow him.

Clovenhoof could hear muffled groans from behind the closed door, so he groaned even louder himself. "What?" he said as everyone looked at him. "Anyone else got the tummy rumbles? If anyone hears any noises, it's definitely my stomach, not anything else. I once had voice recognition switched on when it was doing this and it wrote a brand new Devil Preacher song. True story."

12

Rutspud led the way deeper into Limbo, Eltiel scurrying to keep up. The pinks, greens and oranges of the angel's halo cast unusual and jaunty colours onto the otherwise colourless landscape.

"Where are we going?" said Eltiel.

"Earth," said Rutspud. "Specifically to Jeremy Clovenhoof."

"Satan?"

"That's the one. For, er, reasons, I suspect he's the one with the extra willpower free will juice in the form of Lilith's Tears."

"Oh, my," said Eltiel. "And how are we going to get to him in Limbo?"

Rutspud cast his gaze back in the direction of Hell. "We just need to get away from prying eyes."

"Oh?"

Rutspud did not elaborate further, but pressed on with:

"One thing I don't understand is, listen, you're telling me that whole business with wilfulness and Lilith really happened?"

"Well, it's not scriptural orthodoxy, but yes, it happened."

"So that literally means Adam and Eve and the garden of wossname really happened. I weren't around at the time to see, and yet...?"

"And yet?"

"This cosmos is billions of years old. Dinosaurs, woolly mammoths, the whole kit and kaboodle. Humans evolved from ape-like creatures."

Eltiel's expression was dark and puzzled. "I don't concern myself with such things, Mister Rutspud. I'm too busy for that. Messages, duties, being the best version of myself."

"Yeah, but you get my point."

"I remember Eden very well. Fabulous place. It was a garden, like totally wild, but in a cool and well-organised way. An angel could be happy there."

Rutspud considered they had walked far enough. He took out a device he had yet to give a proper name. He currently called it the InstaDoor and hated the name. It needed to have a cool name, like Dimensional Gateway Generator, or Riftmaker 1.0, but he'd not settled on one and his hind-brain kept calling it the InstaDoor and he worried the name would stick.

"Where'd you get that from?" said Eltiel.

Rutspud waggled the little handheld box. "Oh, it's something me and Hodshift knocked up together, based upon the impossible geometries of a stairway from Hell to Earth. It replicates the same dimensional folding techniques."

"I mean where did you get it from? You weren't carrying it a moment ago, and I can't help but notice—" the angel looked meaningfully at Rutspud's unclothed body, "—you don't have any pockets."

"Oh, I'm just very good at hiding things," said Rutspud with a grin. "Now, I need a while to calibrate this thing. It's not very accurate so we want to target Clovenhoof's residence as tightly as possible."

He fiddled with the controls of the InstaDoor. Eltiel kept a watchful eye on the swirling mists of Limbo, as though he feared some terrible Limbo-monster might come barrelling across the empty landscape and try to eat them.

"I never understood why the humans did anything to jeopardise their place in Eden," said Eltiel. "It was beautiful. They had every green plant on the Earth to use as they wished. Adam could have spent an eternity relaxing, giving names to the animals. His mates, first Lilith then Eve, were supposed to make him happy. I mean, I don't quite see it myself. That whole sex business. Ugh. Messy and squelchy."

"Tell me about it," said Rutspud as he played with the calibration settings. "That whole sex thing was an epic fail in the design department." He felt irritation at his choice of words. "But which is it? Design or evolution?"

"Hmm."

"If you were there, you know what I mean. Did the Big Guy make humans on day fifty-seven of creation or—"

"Day six, actually," said Eltiel.

"Really? Wow. He really cranks out his creations. Maybe if He slowed down He wouldn't give them stupid looking genitals and an unnecessarily complicated reproductive system. But did He do that, and literally give them free will and what-have-you, to separate them from the animals or did they evolve? Cos I've seen fossils. We've made our own copies of dinosaurs down in Hell. Let them run riot in the Pit of Embittered Creationists."

"The way I see it," said Eltiel, "it's like that box."

"What box?"

"Oh, this clever physicist, Mr Bohr, was telling me about it. Not sure I understood it fully. He did use some big words. But it's a box and you put a cat inside it."

Rutspud shuddered automatically. "I don't have dealing with cats. Horrible, fluffy things."

"And you put some poison in the box with the cat."

"Okay. I'm back on board. Poisoning cats. You've got my interest."

Eltiel looked up as he tried to remember. "And then there's something about some radiation or particles and the cat gets poisoned, or it doesn't."

"Oh, I'd go for poisoned. Every time."

"Ah, but this was the clever thing," said Eltiel. "You don't know if the cat is dead or not until you've opened the box."

"Throw extra poison in. That'd do it."

"No, you misunderstand me. It's science apparently. It's not that you don't know if the cat is dead or alive before you've opened the box. The cat is both dead *and* alive."

"Like a zombie?"

"What?"

"Like a zombie cat. Dead and alive."

"I fear you're truly missing the point. The cat, dead or alive—"

"Dead. Definitely dead. Locking it in. Final answer."

"—the cat is both those things at the same time, and I think the whole creation or evolution thing is like that."

"Like a zombie cat in a box?"

"I probably need to try again," said Eltiel.

"Hang on," said Rutspud. "I've got it." He stabbed the activation button and a vertical shaft of purple light rent the air directly in front of him. "Come on."

He reached into the light with both hands and forced it wider with his arms to allow him to slip through. Eltiel followed closely behind.

They came out in a small room with unpainted concrete walls. Shelves were filled with buckets and plastic bottles. A mop and broom stood in the corner.

"This is not Jeremy Clovenhoof's house," said Eltiel.

"It is not," agreed Rutspud. He hopped nimbly over a bucket, opened the cleaning cupboard door, and stepped out into a noisy concourse. "It's a train station. And in Britain," he added, noting the signage around them. "That's better than it could have been."

Eltiel stepped close to Rutspud and whispered. "Won't the humans be stunned by a visitation from a heavenly being."

Rutspud looked up at him. "You think they'd find *you* stunning? You're basically a human with bonus wings and glitter. You could just be someone going out to a nightclub. I'm the demon here."

"You're right!" Eltiel tried to enfold Rutspud and conceal him in his robes, but the demon batted him away.

"You may have noticed, mate, that no one has been

awestruck by our appearance yet. I don't know if it's divine intervention or human stupidity, but in my experience, which is broader than you'd think, humans ignore our kind."

"Oh." Eltiel sounded somewhat disappointed.

"But if you could lose the wings and maybe ditch the robe for something more modern, we might fit in better."

"Lose the wings?" said Eltiel, affronted.

"I saw Michael do it tons of times. Just sort of, you know, pull them in. Clench your bum cheeks or something. Just..."

Eltiel screwed up his face in concentration and, without a sound, the wings were gone.

"Good," said Rutspud. "Then clothes. Look at the people around you. Just normal people."

There was another soundless shift, and abruptly Eltiel was wearing boot-cut jeans and a simple but stylish checked shirt. And Rutspud abruptly realised he was dressed in baggy little trousers and a pink T-shirt.

Rutspud looked up at Eltiel. The angel pointed at a man and his young daughter not twenty feet away. Eltiel's angelic powers had copied their outfits precisely.

Rutspud pulled at his own T-shirt to read it. *"Daddy's Little Princess*? This ... this is creepy on so many levels."

"I think pink suits you," said Eltiel.

"Speaking of pink, you need to lose the halo, too."

Eltiel raised his hands to the sparkling nimbus of light around his head. "You go too far, sir! This is my signature look."

"It looks like someone put a rainbow into a blender."

"Oh, trying to be hurtful now, are we?" quailed the angel.

Rutspud was about to offer a comment which would

hopefully stop the angel moaning and convince him to hide his halo for now, while simultaneously making it very clear his multi-coloured lights looked like Care Bear vomit, when he spotted a sign.

"Ah! Coventry!"

"What-try?" said Eltiel.

"We're in Coventry. Not crazy far from Clovenhoof's place at all."

"Good. Which direction?"

Rutspud cast about. "Well, we could go back to Limbo and recalibrate. Or we could catch a train." He looked at the board of departure times. "Or we could just steal a car from the car park."

"Which would be quicker?" said Eltiel.

Rutspud scratched at the itchy Daddy's Little Princess T-shirt. "Stealing a car, I reckon," he said. "This way."

13

B en trotted after Bilal along a nondescript corridor. "What is it that you do here?" he asked.

"We are a horticultural centre," said Bilal. "A start-up tha'd probably call it."

"Yes, but what is it that you grow that needs so much securit— Oh." The pieces came together in Ben's mind. "You grow medical cannabis, don't you?"

Bilal swivelled on the spot. "How did tha know that?"

"Oh, just put two and two together and..."

"Tell me that you lot aren't planning to nick our stock."

"Um, no. I mean would people do that? I wouldn't. And if I was about to do so I probably wouldn't tell you."

"True, true. Paradox. I've put everything into this venture, mate, I tell thee."

"I can honestly say we had no idea where we were stopping. We're travelling up north and we got some problems with the van, that's all."

Ben shut himself in the toilet cubicle, while Bilal waited outside. He hoped Aksel would have sufficient time to get out of the office, and that they would all be grateful for the distraction he was helping to create.

Ben didn't need the toilet, so he gave himself a countdown with a whispered 'plop!' in the middle before emerging. When they got back to the entrance, Ben couldn't help gasping as he caught sight of Aksel, blood pouring from a wound on his head.

"Now don't get mad," said Clovenhoof, "because I was given bad advice. This lot here said that a curing room would have first aid supplies in it."

"No we didn't, we said that it sounded a *bit medical*," said Valdemar.

"You went in the curing room?" Bilal exclaimed. "No! Tell me you didn't!"

"Not all the way," said Clovenhoof. "Just far enough to see if there was a first aid box.

"Tha bloomin idiots!" Bilal fumed. "It's a clean environment in there, I need to invoke the decontamination protocol. It's going to cost a fortune. I need to speak with Hector and Robbie. The three of us have worked night and day on this latest batch. Yer'd better not have buggered it up."

"Would they be the guys with Dutch accents who said they were going to leave this shitshow for you to sort out and organise the testing bale?" Clovenhoof asked, smiling as if he expected praise for passing on the message.

Bilal sighed with frustration. "Right. I'm gonna get you some first aid things and water for your van, then you lot have to piss off."

"That would be lovely," said Aksel. The blood ran freely down his forehead, lending him a crazy Halloween look as he tried to smile at Bilal.

Bilal disappeared for a moment, then returned with a first aid box and a bottle of water. "Go now, bugger off the lot o' you."

He all but chased them from the building.

They all trouped out to the van. Rasmus put Aksel into the rear of the bus and topped up the water. The engine radiator hissed greedily as it took it in. When he'd finished he gave Clovenhoof the thumbs up to start the engine.

"Hey, wait for the rest of us!" said Camille who was photographing Aksel's head, insisting that Instagram was an essential first step when it came to triaging a wound.

Ben got the job of first aider as he was the one who'd picked up the supplies. "There's some of those fancy plasters that are like butterfly stitches. We should use these."

He tended to Aksel's injury as they bumped out of the car park and rejoined the road. They all toppled to the side as they swerved to avoid another van pulling into the car park. Ben used the tiny antiseptic wipes, wishing they came in sizes suitable for people who were so covered in blood you couldn't see where they were actually hurt. He finally found the cut high on Aksel's forehead and used the butterfly stitches to hold the sides closed, which seemed to slow the bleeding to a mere trickle.

"Feels bouncy on the suspension," murmured Aksel.

"You're just not used to sitting in the back," said Valdemar. "It's like this for us all of the time."

"You are breaking my heart, Valdemar," said Camille.

It occurred to Ben that Clovenhoof had been unusually quiet since they'd left. "You okay, Jeremy?"

Clovenhoof gave the widest smile in the rear view mirror. "You'll never guess what that place does."

"They grow medical cannabis," said Ben.

Clovenhoof scowled. "No. You're not meant to know. You're meant to guess. And then I tell you. They—"

"Grow medical cannabis. In the polytunnels out back. I worked it out."

"You're no fun."

Ben frowned. "How do you know anyway? Oh, wait, you went into the place where they process it." It was another few seconds before a terrible thought occurred to him. "You didn't steal any, did you?"

Clovenhoof unzipped the top part of his leather jacket and waved strands of purloined greenery at him. "I didn't just steal some. I stole every bit that I could find in the lab."

Ben was appalled. "But that's supposed to be for sick people!"

"Hey, I'm as sick as they come, Ben, you should know that."

"But the police?" Ben looked out of the rear window of the van, half expecting to see a police car already giving chase. "This is serious, Jeremy. We will get into so much trouble for this."

"The faster we smoke it the better then? Destroy the evidence. There's barely enough hear for a couple of spliffs anyway. Look, guys," said Clovenhoof, waving his herbs. "I've scored weed."

"Cool!" said Aksel.

As Ben turned away from the rear window, something caught his eye. There was a luggage compartment behind the back seat. Most of the band's gear was in the trailer behind them, but some of their bags were stashed in the back of the van. A large plastic-wrapped cube sat on top. Ben was fairly certain it hadn't been there before.

"Hey, what's that in the back?"

Aksel and Valdemar clawed their way over to look.

Valdemar reached over and tilted the package to look at it better. "There is a label. It says that it's for WonderLab Sciences testing facility,"

"Does it say what's in it?" Camille demanded.

"CBPM material, five kilos," said Valdemar.

Ben groaned. "No, no, no."

"What?" said Aksel. "What is it?"

"What's the betting that C stands for cannabis?"

"Cannabis-based products for medical use," said Camille.

"You looked it up?" said Ben.

"No. I am just clever," she said.

"That letter in the office. The testing sample. The guys tossed this in the back of our van, thinking we're the ones picking it up."

"Easiest drugs heist ever!" called Clovenhoof from the front. "Five kilos. That's like a least ten big spliffs."

"We passed another van back there," said Valdemar. "They will discover the mistake very soon."

"We could turn back and give it to them?" said Ben.

"We would not want to get into trouble," agreed Valdemar.

"Hey, hey, what about the rock and roll dream?" demanded Clovenhoof. "The bucket list."

"Theft was not on the list!" said Ben.

"But smoking a shit ton of drugs is, surely."

Aksel tilted his head. "Our Devil Preacher friend is right. This is a rock legend in the making. I have already sustained a serious head wound on a massive drugs heist. It's so damned sexy I want to kiss myself!"

"Fucks sake, he's delirious," said Camille.

"A little lightheaded maybe, but you know I'm right. We go on the run with a massive bale of cannabis. We smoke some, we share some, we give it away like Robin Hood, eh? We go down in flames!"

"We don't have to actually go down in flames," said Valdemar. "It would be quite nice to just make it home in one piece."

"Yeah yeah, baby-daddy," muttered Camille.

"Tell me you wouldn't like to enjoy a few last spiritual moments of hazy bliss with your bandmates before you settle into your domestic routine?" said Aksel.

"We need to find somewhere quiet," said Valdemar. "We only had a five minutes start, they might follow."

"As if lab scientists would engage in car chases," Camille said.

"It sounded as if their business is quite new and a little financially precarious," said Ben. "So maybe they will."

"Oh. I didn't realise you were there to audit their accounts," pouted Camille.

Clovenhoof banged the steering wheel with his hand.

"We need to get off the beaten track. Navigator! Find me an alternate route!"

It wasn't clear who Clovenhoof thought the navigator was, but a couple of them looked at their phones.

"There is a 'bridle' path up ahead on the right," said Valdemar.

"But it's bridle path," said Ben.

"This is for horses, yes?" said Aksel.

"Yes, it's for horses," said Clovenhoof, "but if a horse can get along it then so can this beast of a van." He leaned on the accelerator. "Let's take this party bus off-road!"

14

Nerys made sure Tina got safely to her doorstep before abandoning her there as quicky as possible. The vomit had mostly dried onto her in a lumpy, stomach-turning crust.

"I just want to curl up and die," said Tina.

She'd been repeating it like some sort of mantra for the last half hour, as though if she stopped she would be forced to either drop dead for real, or face up to the fact she was horribly sick and disgusting both inside and out.

"Go stand in a shower," said Nerys. "Fully clothed. Leave the clothes in there and go to bed."

Tina nodded miserably. "You are a true friend," she sniffled.

"I know."

Tina reached out to hug Nerys.

"Get away from me, you fucking mess," said Nerys, scooting out of reach.

She backed away, got into her foul-smelling car and raced home as quick as the roads would allow.

She was filled with a pent up list of things to do. It started with her getting out of the car and ended with her slobbing out in cosy comfort, but there were like twenty things between the first and the last.

She parked. She got her bags out of the boot. She'd already decided to leave the vomit-stained car for another day. She just had to drive it to one of those car wash valeting places and let them deal with it. She went up to the door of four-hundred-and-something Chester Road and put the key in the lock.

"Ben! Jeremy! I'm home!" she called, before remembering some unclear phone messages about them going off to a music concert or something. That was all well and good. A day or two without the boys would be very welcome. As long as they'd looked after Twinkle, and as long as Clovenhoof hadn't raided her flat for his own petty Satanic ends in her absence, all would be fine.

She lugged her bags upstairs to the top floor and let herself into her flat.

It looked fine. Her underpants weren't strewn everywhere (that had happened before) and her kitchen cupboards weren't all open and empty of food (that had also happened before). All seemed fine.

"Twinkle!" she called. "Mummy's home."

There was a scrabble of claws on floor and Twinkle came in from the hallway, a happy and expectant look on his cute hairy face.

She bent to fuss him. "Aw, I bet you missed me," she cooed.

"You have no idea, darlin'," said Twinkle.

She sprang back, propelled by horrid surprise. Twinkle wagged his tail.

Nerys shook herself. She hadn't heard him speak. That was impossible. It was a trick. It was a curious improbable effect of atmospheric conditions. It had been the sound of a distant TV or radio somehow carried into the apartment.

"You got any food in, luv?" said Twinkle. "I'm not sayin' I'm famished, but I could eat a bladdy 'orse right now."

"Oh, fuck. You spoke," she whimpered.

"Tell me about it," said Twinkle. The voice coming out of his throat was far deeper and gruffer than she'd expected from such a little dog.

What the fuck am I saying? she screamed in her own mind. She shouldn't be expecting *any* voice to come out of her little dog.

"One minute I'm mindin' me own business," the dog continued, "and the next it's words and thoughts and— Oh, listen to me rabbitin' on. You were gonna make me a nice bit o' lunch, right?"

"Why the fuck do you sound like Bob Hoskins?" she whimpered.

Twinkle sniffed and scratched himself. "Or does Bob 'Oskins sound like me, huh? Now that nosh you were gonna make me..."

Nerys had to cling onto a chair to keep herself upright. "What the fuck happened...?" she moaned.

"I reckon it was that spooky bottle of hoodoo juice old

Jezza left on the sofa," said Twinkle. "I got a nice slurp of that and – wallop! – it was like a switch bein' turned on."

The fear and horror inside Nerys turned almost instantly into a rising rage. It was a good rage. Nerys couldn't utilise fear, but she knew how to utilise rage.

"Jeremy? Jeremy Clovenhoof did this to you? That bastard. That utter fucking bastard!"

"Tell me about it," chortled Twinkle. "That man's a bladdy liability. You shouldn't've left him in charge if you want my opinion, sweetheart."

Nerys tried to slow her impassioned breathing. She held onto her rage – God! She was going to use it when she caught up with that man! – but she needed clarity for now.

"I'm going to kill him," she said simply. "I'm going to kill him and then I'm going to undo this horrible thing he's done to you."

"Fair enough," sniffed Twinkle. "Now, I don't wanna be that guy, but about that plate of grub you promised. Let's get to it, eh? Chop chop."

15

Clovenhoof kicked the van's tyre and stroked his chin. "Yeah, it's going nowhere."

It was his contribution to the diagnosis of their current predicament. He had driven into the ford with everyone (apart maybe from Rasmus) urging him on and insisting all would be fine, but it had definitely not been fine.

The van had made it most of the way out of the ford before the engine died, and now they all stood next to it arguing about what to do next.

Clovenhoof realised his phone was ringing. It was Nerys. He picked up. "Hi Nerys. You're back? Great. I'm in the middle of something—"

He was forced to stop by the tirade of incomprehensible, high-pitched questions and abuse that exploded from her. He held the phone at arm's length.

"I'll speak to you when you're a bit less hysterical!" he said loudly to the phone and killed the call.

"It's pretty simple," said Aksel, adopting a manly pose on the rocky track they had come to a halt on. "It got wet so it can dry out, yes? We push it up the road a little, onto higher ground, we camp out for the night and it will be fine in the morning."

"A great plan, except we have no food or water and we will undoubtedly wake in the morning to a van that still won't start," spat Camille.

"We could—"

"—If you're about to suggest that we trap a rabbit or forage for mushrooms, then seriously, don't."

"How far to an actual road?" Ben asked. "We could hitch, maybe?"

Valdemar pulled out his phone. Everyone looked at him to see what the answer might be, but instead of consulting a map he made a call. "Oh hey, baby. It's me. Just wanted to check in while we have stopped. Everything fine? How's the feeding?"

He wandered away from the group and Aksel checked the map. "It's not far. About a quarter of a mile through the trees, that way."

"Well then, you have your answer," said Camille. "There is no way we can drag all of the gear that far. Someone hitches to find food while the others make a campfire. I will have a pepperoni pizza."

Everyone stared at her.

"It makes sense," she said. "We make camp and send someone for supplies and help."

There was some embarrassed shuffling as they all accepted her plan was probably the best one.

"Well, these boots are for performing really. They pinch my feet at the best of times," said Aksel. "I would say that hiking is not for me. I will stay and make the fire."

Rasmus made an exasperated rumble, like a peeved volcano, and started to shamble off into the woods.

"Someone needs to go with Rasmus," said Camille. "You know, in case actual words are needed."

"Coming!" shouted Clovenhoof cheerfully. A jaunt through the woods to jump out on passing cars sounded just the thing.

He and Rasmus pushed through the undergrowth, the bickering from the rest of the group fading behind them.

Rasmus was powerfully built, so the branches and thorny brambles didn't impede his progress. Clovenhoof found it easier to walk in his wake, navigating the brush after he'd already trampled it.

"So, Rasmus," said Clovenhoof. "What are you getting out of this tour?"

The big man grunted, and Clovenhoof thought perhaps he was dismissing the question, but then he spoke for the first time. "All my life I wanted this."

"Huh. Wanted what exactly? Obviously not to be whacked in the face by a wet branch," said Clovenhoof, spitting out bits of leaf.

"It's easy enough to get a bass guitar, join a band, play some gigs," said Rasmus. "But then you must go to work the next day and answer calls from people who didn't get their deliveries. That is not the dream."

"I can't imagine that's anybody's dream," said Clovenhoof. "Me, I have the one about opening Boldmere's first drive-in hot tub experience. One day I'll make it happen, you see."

Rasmus turned to look. "How does a drive-in hot tub experience work?"

Clovenhoof wagged a finger. "Yes, there are teething problems and you just identified one of them. There's definitely work to be done on the design."

Rasmus shook his head and carried on walking. "My husband, he has different dreams. Kitchen extensions, sunshine holidays, early retirement..."

It was only then, listening to the gruff and weathered voice, that Clovenhoof realised Rasmus was significantly older than the other members of the band. Behind that untamed beard, beneath that soiled black T-shirt, was the body of a middle aged office drone.

"Is this your midlife crisis?" said Clovenhoof.

Rasmus barked with laughter. "Isn't this yours?"

"I'll let you know when I get to middle age."

Rasmus chuckled. He waved a big hand back the way they'd come. "I sunk half my redundancy money into that van and this tour. Every day, texts from my Henrik. Half worried, half demanding I go back. I shall enjoy this while I can."

There was a change in the quality of light filtering through the trees and Clovenhoof realised they were coming to the edge of the wooded area, and he thought he could hear the sound of a car. "Hey, we're nearly at the road! Let's see if we can get ourselves a lift."

They hurried through the last of the greenery. Rasmus burst out onto a single track road at the exact moment a van rounded a curve. It clipped Rasmus with its wing mirror and sent him spinning away and onto the verge.

Clovenhoof ran over to check on him.

"Fuck!" said Rasmus. "That was close." He rubbed a bruised upper arm and started to get up.

"No, stay down!" hissed Clovenhoof. "This could work for us. Follow my lead."

"Eh? Oh, okay."

The van had pulled over and its four occupants hurried over. There were three men and a woman.

"Oh my God, he just came out of nowhere," said the driver. "Is he okay?"

"I've got this," said Clovenhoof. "I think I can bring him back from the veil. Clear!"

They all stepped back instinctively, then looked at each other, confused.

Clovenhoof made a show of patting Rasmus all over, pausing only to use a hand to close Rasmus's eyes when they flickered open to see what was going on.

"Rasmus! Rasmus! I think your leg is going to be fine, once it's healed," shouted Clovenhoof. "You probably won't be able to drive though! Can you hear me? You can wake up now, or maybe I'll start chest compressions."

"I think I'm awake now," said Rasmus, clearly trying to withhold a grin. "Aargh, my leg," he added as an afterthought.

"I am so very sorry," said the driver. "Christ. Do you need to go to hospital. I can drive you where you need to go."

"Within reason, Jacob," said the woman at his side,

forcing a smile at Clovenhoof and Rasmus. "Obviously we're on a tight schedule."

"You might be able to help," said Clovenhoof looking thoughtful. "The thing is, we were just packing up our campsite and Rasmus was supposed to drive us all north. I don't know what we'll do now. The kiddies will be so disappointed."

"We're heading north," said Jacob. "Whereabouts are you going?"

"What do you mean by 'all'?" the woman asked Clovenhoof. "How many of you?"

"There are six of us," said Clovenhoof. "A band on tour."

"Marcee! Musicians!" said Jacob with a little clap. "This is fate!"

Marcee rolled her eyes. "There's musicians and musicians, Jacob." She pushed him aside to address Clovenhoof. "We're just dealing with a terrible loss."

"We did run them over, sweetness. We are duty-bound to help," said Jacob.

"Don't you bloomin' well 'sweetness' me when you want a favour!"

"But you are my sweetness."

"And you're a fool."

Clovenhoof decided to ignore their domestic squabbling. "We could help Rasmus into your van and show you where we're camped," he said.

Jacob got the other men to carry Rasmus carefully into the van where they put him into a seat.

There were little sleigh bells on leather straps, and

multicoloured tassels hanging above the chairs on one side of the van. The woman, Marcee, caught him looking.

"We are a Morris side," she said.

"That's where you go out and kill someone called Morry?" hazarded Clovenhoof.

"Morris dancers," said Marcee. "We're the Wednesbury Wallopers."

"Of course you are," said Clovenhoof. "I think it's fate that we met each other."

16

Nerys stopped outside Books'n'Bobs on the high street to address Twinkle.

They had walked down here without her putting Twinkle on his lead. He didn't ask her not to but... Well, it seemed odd, somehow: putting a lead and collar on an individual who could speak. Individuals who spoke were, in her mind, people. And people on leashes, well, that suggested certain kinds of passions and fetishes. Nerys didn't want to admit to herself that putting a lead on a talking Twinkle was somehow oddly sexual, but it did feel all kinds of wrong.

She crouched down. "We're going to go in to talk to Ben," she said.

The tiny terrier licked his own nose. "Righto, darlin'. You pin 'im down and I'll do the talkin', yeah?"

"No. Exactly not that. Exactly the *opposite* of that. You don't do any talking in there at all."

"I can be very persuasive when I put me mind to it," he said.

"You'll freak him out."

"Nah. Silver-tongued, me. I've known 'im nearly all me life. I know how that long streak of piss thinks."

So many questions filled her mind. She glanced at a passerby who was looking at them. She gave a polite smile and tickled Twinkles ears for show. When the passerby had gone, Nerys said, "Listen, you can talk now—"

"I can. And we need to have a word about a few things, sweetcheeks. Dinners, for one thing."

"No. I need to ask. You can talk now. Does that mean your brain is more ... is it smarter? Or is it just the talking?"

"What's it matter?"

"It matters because I've said all kinds of things in front of you before today. You've seen me in all kinds of situations."

"Love a duck! Tell me about it."

"Exactly!" she said shrilly. "There's been more than a couple of times when I've been in the bedroom having, um, some 'Nerys time' and you've just stood in the doorway, looking at me. Like a creepy weirdo."

"Says the woman who openly watches me when I'm tendin' to me intimate groomin' routine."

"Licking your arse for hours on end, you mean?"

"Entertainment can be thin on the ground in that flat," he said. "Which brings us back to dinners. Now, what I'm saying is that you sometimes have a nice lamb chop or two in the fridge, but when it comes to servin', you seem to forget you've got a hungry lad in the 'ouse—"

"I don't – I don't care about your dinner needs—"

"That's what I'm talkin' about!"

She gripped his little head, gently but firmly. "I'm asking you, Twinkle. Have you changed? Do I need to worry that I've been living with a ... a sentient being all this time?"

"Listen, darlin'. Apart from the lack of chops, and you could do to drop a few more biscuits on the floor, you've treated me all right. No need to worry about us. Now, are we goin' to go in there and talk to this muppet or not?"

She sighed. "I will do the talking," she said firmly and led the way in.

The shop was, as it usually was, empty. There were no customers, and behind the counter there wasn't even a Ben. Instead, there was Spartacus Wilson.

"Where's Ben?" she said.

Spartacus looked up from the box of books he was taping up. "Not here. You want him?"

"It's Jeremy I want," she said.

Spartacus instantly recognised the underlying tone in her voice. "What's he done now?"

Nerys glanced down at Twinkle and held back an honest answer. "I just need to find him. And then possibly kill him."

Spartacus nodded like this was the most normal and commonplace thing in the world. "He's not here either."

"I can see he's not here."

"No, I meant neither of them are." He pushed a sheet of paper over to Nerys. On it was a message in Ben's neat hand.

SPARTACUS,

.   .   .

Jeremy and I are going to be away for a couple of days. We're roadies for a band we saw at the Boldmere Oak last night. I've taken some vintage books with me for safekeeping. Do NOT sell any more books to that woman from Crystal's Crafts. Some things are sacred.

Ben

PS: Remember to lock the shutters at the end of the day.

Nerys saw that the box of books Spartacus was taping up had an address label that began with the words *Crystal@Crystal's Crafts.*

"She's paying full price," said the teenager. "I'll just tell Ben I sold them to one of them antiquarian book collectors. He'll never know."

"What band?" she said.

"*What* band?" he asked.

She crinkled the note. "The band they've decided to be roadies for. Christ, what a moronic thing to do. The band. What band? Where are they?"

Spartacus shrugged. "No idea. You could try calling Jeremy."

"Neither of them is picking up," Nerys fumed.

"You could ask the Boldmere Oak, if it's that important," said Spartacus.

"He's right," said Twinkle by her feet.

Spartacus leaned over the counter and looked down at the dog. "Did he...?"

Twinkle coughed and retched, his jaws wide as though he was about to throw up on the floor.

"Something stuck in his throat," said Nerys. She huffed. "Right, I'll go ask at the pub."

Outside on the pavement, she gave Twinkle a fierce look. "We agreed. No talking."

"Excuse me, love," he said reproachfully. "You asked and I did me best. But yer rubbish at this detective lark. If I need to step in, I will."

"No talking," she said.

Twinkle sniffed the air. "If we made a stop at that butcher's on the way to the pub, that might sweeten the deal. Know what I'm sayin'?"

"You are a pain in the arse."

Twinkle cackled. "You love it, darlin', and you know it. You're a good girl."

She coughed. "Girl? I'm three times your age."

"You forget dog years. I'm the grown up 'ere, love."

17

"Our Morris side is several participants down," said Jacob, climbing into the driver's seat. "We were doing a late night workshop at a spiritual retreat yesterday when several of our numbers were struck down by a stomach bug."

"Halesowen Hankymen!" cursed one of the other chaps.

"Easy now, Hairy Leonard. We don't know that they was poisoned."

"But they were!" hissed the other man.

"There's a bit of territorial beef going on in the Morris world," explained Marcee. "Bad blood between the fraternity."

"No brothers of mine!" declared the man.

"And Hairy and Slackpipes Johnson suspect the darkest of underhand tactics," said Jacob, starting the engine. "Which is terrible news as we are headed to an important contest."

"Important?" said Clovenhoof, who couldn't give two fucks. His recollection of Morris dancers was of a bunch of genteel hankie-waving knobs wasting their weekends doing prancing folk dances. At least Rasmus Kakerlak had the decency to commit to a proper midlife crisis and go on a Heavy Metal tour.

Clovenhoof said none of this, instead guiding them to where he estimated the other end of the bridle path would have emerged.

"Can we go up that?" asked Jacob, looking at the rocky and uneven track.

"Well we did," said Clovenhoof. It was almost the truth. They were on the right side of the ford, so as long as no other hazards awaited they should meet up with the others in a short time. He was hungry and thirsty. With a lack of any food he took another tactical sip of Lilith's Tears.

"This terrain does not look suitable," said Marcee. "Maybe you should walk ahead and check?"

"Our friend says it's fine!" said Jacob with a friendly smile at Clovenhoof. "Our *musician* friend."

"It will definitely be fine," said Clovenhoof.

The van bumped and rocked along the track, until finally Jacob pointed ahead. "Are those your friends?"

"Yes," said Clovenhoof. "Although they weren't on fire the last time I saw them. Do you have an extinguisher in here?"

"I am chief safety officer for the side," shouted Jacob, jumping from the van with an extinguisher in his hand.

Clovenhoof followed, wondering what had happened since he left. There was a large pile of logs that looked as if it was intended to be the bonfire, but somehow Aksel was the thing currently on fire.

Jacob strode forward with the extinguisher and sprayed Aksel from head to foot in foam. The flames went, but Aksel continued to run in circles, shouting loudly.

"What's he saying?" asked Marcee, appearing at Clovenhoof's side.

"I'm not totally sure, but it sounds a bit like *Yippee-ki-yay!*" said Clovenhoof.

Ben and Valdemar emerged from the side of the van, pulling the unhitched trailer. It looked as if they were struggling under the load. They paused to take in what was happening.

Jacob had swapped his fire extinguisher for a first aid kit and was now chasing Aksel. "Come here, I need to check you for burns!"

Clovenhoof saw Camille appear from the top of the covered-over trailer while Ben and Valdemar looked on, realising why it had been so heavy. She pushed aside the cover and yawned, as if she'd been napping in there. She climbed out and looked around at the scene of carnage, then strolled over to the bonfire, stooping to light it with a lighter she pulled from her pocket.

The bonfire burst into life, as if it had been doused with petrol – which Clovenhoof thought might be a clue about what happened to Aksel.

After a few minutes the group gravitated to the fire and stood around exchanging greetings and introductions. The two other Morris dancers were huge brothers known as

Hairy Leonard and Slackpipes Johnson; one for obvious reasons, the other less so.

"So it looks as if we can all hitch a ride with Jacob," said Clovenhoof.

Marcee looked unimpressed. "Maybe we can drop you somewhere close by. We'll make sure you're safe, and that's all."

"Didn't you lose several of your members?" Clovenhoof asked. "You're heading north to compete, yeah? You need musicians. Seems to me that we can help each other out here."

"Also my leg," said Rasmus, remembering to wince slightly as he tried to put weight onto it.

Marcee waved a hand at their van and trailer. "You're probably not the kind of musicians we need."

"Two years of musicology at the Royal Danish Academy of Music," said Aksel, raising his hand.

"Me too," said Valdemar.

"Hear that, sweetness," said Jacob. "They've got ologies."

"Yeah, we should do it! It sounds amazing!" said Aksel.

Clovenhoof looked hard at Aksel, wondering if he'd be fit to perform at all, either in the band or as a stand-in Morris Man. He had suffered a blow to the head – which looked as if it had started bleeding again – and he was still smouldering from where he'd been set on fire. The damage seemed to be mostly confined to his clothes, but he was a filthy, sooty mess. His eyes were bright though, and he kept exclaiming what a great day it was.

"What's so amazing, Aksel?" asked Clovenhoof.

"All of it! Bring it on, I'm living the rock dream!"

"Did your bucket list include having a head injury and being set on fire?"

"No," said Aksel. "But it's even better if it's properly spontaneous."

As the fire started to burn down, the group set to work transferring luggage and equipment to the Wednesbury Wallopers' van. There was a towing hitch at the rear, so they were able to attach the trailer once Jacob had turned the van around. There was also a rack on the top, and the cannabis bale was strapped onto the roof.

"Isn't it a bit obvious up there?" asked Ben.

"Nobody knows what it is," said Clovenhoof. "I told Jacob it was a paddling pool."

"A paddling pool?" Ben asked.

"Yeah. Said it was part of the stage act. I reckon any madness that you care to invent can be justified by saying it's part of a rock show."

Rasmus looked at the broken down van. "So we abandon this here? I put my redundancy money into this."

"The old girl has done her duty," said Clovenhoof. "She too is redundant now, my friend. But the rock and roll roadshow goes on!" He passed Rasmus his flask and the hairy middle-aged man took a deep swig.

"The show must go on," agreed Rasmus and climbed into the Wednesbury Wallopers' van.

18

Mid-afternoon in the Boldmere Oak was a period where time seemed to stand still. The lunch crowd (such as it was) had gone, the post-work evening drinkers had yet to come in, and all that was left was a harder-to-define group of pub patrons mostly composed of old boys whose day was measured out in slow pints and the occasional game of dominoes. Dust motes hung in the warm, lazy sunlight coming in through the leaded windows. Conversations in the pub were unhurried things: old arguments that went round and round in circles and the least insightful comments on the day's news.

The sudden arrival of Nerys Thomas, barging through the door, with a stripey carrier bag of butcher's wares in her hand and her little Yorkshire Terrier in tow, surprised a number of the sleepy drinkers from their dozing.

She went straight up to the bar, where Lennox was doing a stocktake of his crisp selection.

"Lennox. You can help me."

"Chardonnay spritzer coming right up," he said.

"No. I need some help."

Lennox paused, hand halfway to the wine cooler fridge. "No drink?"

"I need to find Jeremy."

Lennox gave half a laugh. "You're usually trying to get away from him."

"He's done something and I need him to undo it, pronto."

Lennox cast about. "He's not here."

"I can see he's not here. But he was here last night. With a band?"

"Was he? Yes, he was. And the band weren't half bad either."

"I need to know where they've gone."

"The band?"

"The band."

"Why?"

Irritated by his questions, she hoisted Twinkle off the floor. "Because he's done this!" she hissed.

Lennox looked at Twinkle expectantly. "Given your dog a makeover?"

Nerys jiggled Twinkle. "Go on. Show him. Nothing fazes Lennox."

Twinkle looked first at her and then at Lennox. "Afternoon, guv'nor."

Lennox stumbled back, knocking a box of prawn cocktail crisps onto the floor.

"Most things don't faze him," Nerys amended.

"It spoke!" whispered Lennox.

"*It?*" said Twinkle. "Who does he think I am? A bloody toy? You're gonna hurt me feelin's, Lenny."

"It speaks!" said Lennox. "I mean, *he* speaks."

Lennox was a barman of the old school. He'd seen life in all its forms come through his pub, and he prided himself on seeing the world exactly as it was. When Jeremy Clovenhoof had first walked into his pub, he'd taken a look at the red skin, horns and hoofs and – unlike everyone else who blanked that impossible stuff out and pretended this was just another ordinary man – Lennox had recognised he now had a devil for a patron. Devils and angels and wotnot, Lennox recognised everything for what it truly was. As far as Nerys was aware, he was the only other human on earth who knew Jeremy Clovenhoof's true nature.

"Jeremy did this?" said Lennox.

"I think it was this bottle of salty water actually," said Twinkle.

Nerys jiggled him. "You can shush now."

"Wants me to speak, Dun't want me to speak," tutted the dog. "Women are fickle, ain't they? Hey, guv. While I'm here, chuck us a packet of cheese and onion crisps."

Lennox numbly reached for a packet.

"Oi. I've just bought you half a dozen pork pies," said Nerys.

"Pork pie and crisps," said Twinkle. "A dog's gotta have some variety."

"That's dead clever that," said an old boy further along the bar. "Ventriloquism. Like that whatsisname off the telly, 'cept his dog could only spit."

"That's just silly," said Twinkle. "Dogs can't spit. Ain't got the lips for it. Can give it a go though."

Nerys put her hand around his snout, covering his mouth.

"No more talking," she said, then glared at Lennox. "Jeremy. That band."

"Yeah, yeah," said Lennox, still fascinated by Twinkle. "Foreign band. Doing some little gigs before heading up north." He cast about and found a flyer under the bar. "Djævlehund. That's them."

"And do you know where they were—" She stopped. "Djævlehund?"

She snatched the flyer from Lennox and looked at the band and its logo. She had seen that very logo painted rather inexpertly on the back of a trailer only a few hours ago. The bloody van that had nearly forced her off the road. She was absolutely prepared to believe Jeremy Clovenhoof had been behind the wheel.

"Bastard!" she hissed.

With dog in one hand, flyer in the other, and a bag of pork pies dangling from her wrist, she stormed out.

"What about me crisps?" said Twinkle.

She didn't answer him. She dropped him to the pavement so she could walk faster.

"That bastard," she muttered as she strode. "We're gonna get on his tail and God help me when I lay my hands on him."

"We goin' on a road trip?" said Twinkle. "I call shotgun."

Her car was parked on the side of the Chester Road. She

opened the door and Twinkle hopped in ahead of her. The car still stank of Tina's vomit. Nerys grimaced as she got in.

"Love the smell," said Twinkle, getting comfy on the passenger seat. "New air freshener?"

She started the engine and cranked the air blowers up to max to do her best to dispel the lingering smell. She looked at the time on the dashboard and wondered how much of a head start that van had on her.

"Buckle up, Twinks. We're going on a manhunt."

"Love it," said the dog happily. "Now, lob us one of them pork pies. Me tummy's rumblin'."

She tossed a pie on his seat and pulled out, narrowly avoiding a sleek grey Mercedes in her haste.

19

R utspud found himself irritated beyond words with Eltiel, and because his irritation went beyond the power of words to convey, he could do nothing about it. It wasn't that he couldn't vocalise that irritation with a few well-chosen phrases. Oh, he could do that all right. The problem was conveying it in a manner Eltiel could grasp.

The two of them had decided – or at least Eltiel had let the more worldly Rutspud decide – to drive from Coventry to Sutton Coldfield. However, Rutspud's intention to steal a car was vetoed by the angel. Apparently, for some obscure reason Rutspud couldn't understand, stealing was somehow wrong. So Rutspud put aside thoughts of crawling under dashboards, hotwiring a vehicle and bypassing its computer security features, and led Eltiel to a car hire place just down the road.

When the woman at the car hire centre explained they

would need to make an on-line reservation and pay for their vehicle, Rutspud cracked his knuckles and prepared to do some major hacking work into the company's website and booking system. At which point, Eltiel politely asked her to check the system again and – Lo! And sodding behold! – there already was a booking in the name of Eltiel.

Rutspud had fumed. Technology was technology. It might be esoteric and arcane, but it was technology. It was just not on for an angel to simply magic his way round it when Rutspud had devoted centuries of time to understanding technology's myriad ways. Eltiel had politely failed to grasp his point. Did they not want a booking? Did it matter how this was achieved?

The woman at the car company looked at Rutspud in his cute pink T-shirt and offered him a lollipop from a jar on the counter. This did not improve Rutspud's mood.

In the car, a high end Mercedes (because what was the point of magicking a reservation, if you weren't going to magic a swanky one) Eltiel offered the driving seat to Rutspud. The demon had pointed out that his little legs couldn't reach the pedals without some sort of aid, so Eltiel *talked* to the car and it agreed to drive without the need for pedals. Which was nonsense! Miraculous tinkering with computer innards was one thing, but messing with the basic physical mechanics of a car...! Eltiel seemed blithely happy to undo all the laws that governed this world. Worse than that, he did it with a cheerful ignorance of what that meant.

"It achieves our goals, doesn't it?" he said.

"Do you even know how cars work?" demanded Rutspud.

"Heavens above, no," said the angel. "I'm not some

grubby mechanic. My intellect is focused on higher matters."

Rutspud had sworn deeply and then, standing on the seat to steer – while the pedals just did things *themselves*! – he drove out of Coventry and to the motorway which would take them to Clovenhoof's house.

They drew along Chester Road and, narrowly avoiding being hit by a small and inexpertly driven car, Rutspud pulled into the space the car had just vacated. The Mercedes' slowed of its own accord, which was stupid enough, but when the handbrake put itself on Rutspud could not help but emit a vehement, "Satan's balls!" of annoyance.

"Ah, this is it?" said Eltiel, peering out at the long row of tall houses. "Never seen it in daylight. It looks charming."

Rutspud grunted, still in a mood. He had little interest in most of human architecture. He was surprised, given the versatility of human construction materials, they mostly used it to make repeated versions of the same dull designs. This species had invented Lego and used it to build wonders, for Hell's sake! Yet somehow, when given a clay brick, they just made boxy houses to imprison themselves in.

"Let's go get your bottle of Lilith's Tears back," said Rutspud. He hopped out, went up to the door, and rang the doorbell.

Eltiel followed him up the garden path. "They do like to leave little scraps of torn paper and plastic everywhere," he noted, stepping over a piece of rubbish on the pavement. "Is it decorative? Or have they left it as some form of tribute?"

"It's just rubbish, Eltiel," said Rutspud. He rang the doorbell again, but no one was answering.

Impatient, he whipped out his lockpicks and set to work

on the sturdy barrel lock.

"What are you doing?" said Eltiel.

"Breaking in. No one's answering."

Eltiel reached out a finger to touch the door.

"Don't you bloody dare!" Rutspud snarled.

"If we desire ingress..."

There was a shiver of light and the door clicked open. Rutspud grabbed the door, pulled it shut again and once more set to work with his picks.

"Doing it my way," he muttered.

Half a minute later, the door clicked open, and pleased he had shown the angel how it was meant to be done, Rutspud went inside. He called out but no one responded.

"Up here," he said, scampering up to the first floor to Clovenhoof's flat. This door, still broken by Clovenhoof himself, did not need picking. Rutspud wandered straight in.

"Lord Satan! You about?"

He evidently was not about. Rutspud poked his head in all the rooms and then searched the lounge area for the ancient bottle of liquid that he certainly left here not two days ago.

"Rutspud," inquired Eltiel gently. "May I ask why there appears to be half a bed in this drawing room?"

"You can't ask why things are the way they are when it comes to Mr Clovenhoof," said Rutspud. "The old devil is a fool and just does what he wishes."

"Ah." Eltiel waved his hand over his stone tablet. Golden lettering and diagrams swam into existence over it. He sucked in a sharp breath of alarm. "It has been here."

"I know it has," said Rutspud and then, not wishing to

fully incriminate himself, added, "I mean, that would be likely if old Hairy Legs is involved. You getting high readings?"

"Readings?" Eltiel didn't understand the word. "I am sensing the weft of the world is being pulled out of true."

Rutspud stopped in his futile searching. "What the Hell does that mean anyway? What is the actual danger here? A bit more free will is being sloshed out. So what?"

"So what?" Eltiel's face was filled with unhappy concern. "Willpower is a powerful force. Imagine: in the beginning, it was the Almighty's infinite will brought the world into existence. All He needed to say was 'Let there be light!' and there was light. Until He created humans, His will was the only will there was. Without humans, his perfect world would have stayed as it was, like a snow globe. Perfect but effectively static. With free will comes the power to break the world."

"Break it?"

"You have seen depictions of Lilith as half woman, half bird?"

"Depictions? I've met her," said Rutspud. "Not a woman to get on the wrong side of."

"How did a woman grow wings and talons? She simply willed it. If Jeremy Clovenhoof has half her power, he could be wreaking havoc of all sorts."

Rutspud cast about the empty flat. "We'd best go and find him then," he said.

"But where could he be?"

Rutspud put his hands on his hips and shrugged. "The pub?"

20

While they stopped to fill up the van at a petrol station on a roundabout on the outskirts of Harrogate, Aksel and Morris side leader Jacob looked at a map spread across the bonnet of the vehicle.

"You do not use the satnav on your phone?" said Aksel.

"I prefer to get in touch with real things," said Jacob. "Maps. The land. The feel of a stout stick in my hand. The sound of real instruments. We are here—" he placed a finger on the map "—the Dodgy Duck is here."

"The Dodgy Duck?"

"The Dodgy Duck. The pub we're performing at tonight. Less than an hour from here in Bishop Monkton. Tomorrow we drive further into Yorkshire. You need to be in Scarborough by Sunday night, which is way up here, but we can get you most of the way there."

"Most?" said Aksel.

"Maybe all. But you are helping us tonight."

"We doing some of the dancing?" said Clovenhoof, coming out of the petrol station shop with armsful of snacks that were mostly sugar and violent colourants.

"We will need at least two of you to be dancers," said Jacob.

"This is fine. I will play drums as accompaniment. I do not need to dance," said Camille, with more than a little satisfaction.

"Riight!" said Aksel. "We can all play our regular instruments, yeah! It will add something to the performance."

"Er, no. Absolutely not," said Marcee. "My accordion is the accompaniment."

"We will follow your lead then," said Aksel, "You play and we will come in gently with our instruments, simply to add a little depth. That could be really good, I think."

Jacob put a hand on Marcee's shoulder. "Let them help, Marcee," he said, adding to Ben and Clovenhoof, "So you two are our dancers?"

"Just show me the dance floor and I will strut my moves," said Clovenhoof.

"You'll need to practice first."

"I'm more of an improviser."

Slackpipes Johnson stepped out of the rear of the van, a bundle of heavy sticks in his hand. Ben barely caught the one the big man tossed to him. Clovenhoof caught his with his face, dropping the snacks in an untidy heap in front of him.

"Practice here?" said Jacob, looking around the dusty garage forecourt.

"They need to show their mettle," said Slackpipes. Hairy

Leonard gave loud vocal agreement and there was smug smile on Marcee's face.

"I'll get the accordion," she said.

Slackpipes sketched out a rough square on the ground with his toe. It was meant to be a space for them to dance in, but it looked like he was preparing a ring for a bare knuckle boxing match. Or a knife fight.

"Let's do *The Parson's Relish*," said Hairy Leonard.

"What's that?" said Ben.

"Basically," said Leonard, "we start with a Constant Billy, then move into Bean Setting with additional trunkles – that's West Midlands trunkles, not your soft southern nonsense – and then we go into a Shepherd's Hey, switching it up for Lollipop Man in the final verse."

"Er, what?" said Ben.

"Sounds like drug slang to me," said Clovenhoof. He hoofed his dropped snacks aside, then twirled his stick like he was Bruce Lee playing with nunchucks. He could only use one hand. Two of his fingers were still superglued to his palm. "Bring it on," he said.

As the band raced to get their instruments from the trailer – unplugged guitars for the men, a simple tom-tom for Camille – Marcee struck up a lively folk number.

There was no warm-up. Jacob loudly called the moves.

"And forward! And back! Step forward! Hey! Half-gyp! Back! Hey for three! Turn! Jockey to the Fair! Jockey to the Fair, Ben!!"

Clovenhoof jumped and twirled and slipped and nearly took a stick to the eye. Camille picked up the rhythm on her drum and the guitarists added depth. Rasmus started to lay a thudding bass line under it all.

"And a hup-hup jig," Ben panted to himself. "And a hup-hup jig."

There was the swish of sticks and the kick of legs.

"And a final step and hold!" shouted Jacob.

The song ended. The Morris men held their positions. Ben sat down in an untidy mess in the dust.

"Nailed it!" declared Clovenhoof, chest heaving.

"Bloody rubbish," said Slackpipes.

Clovenhoof saw the pink mark on the man's cheek and remembered that one of his wilder stick swings had landed with a sort of meaty sound.

"We will practise again later," said Jacob.

"No, no," said Clovenhoof panted. "We can do this. Let's give it another go."

He pulled out his flask and took a refreshing sip. He passed it over to Ben and it started a circuit round the group.

"I almost understood some of that," said Ben, getting his breath back.

"You were actually following the moves?" said Clovenhoof.

"Yeah. It's mostly hupping up and jigging about. That's pretty simple to begin with, isn't it? Then we'll do some sidestep left, sidestep right, and then another hup-hup jig."

"It only made sense when Rasmus started a decent bassline," said Clovenhoof.

Rasmus nodded in acknowledgement. "I just did *Tiger Feet* by Mud," he said. "You know them?"

"That a metal band?" said Valdemar.

"Glam rock, baby," said Clovenhoof. "Yeah. Sprinkle some of that glam rock on it, Rasmus."

"If he overshadows my accordion..." warned Marcee.

Rasmus backed away in deference to her and set up a rolling, repeating glam rock bassline. The flask of Lilith's Tears came back full circle to Clovenhoof. The ancient bottle clearly had one mystical property: it seemed that no matter how much anyone drank, it never seemed to get any emptier.

"Right, one more go," said Jacob.

"We can do this!" snarled Clovenhoof, awkwardly tossing his stick from one sweaty hand to the other. There was a chorus of suddenly enthusiastic agreement.

The passion and confidence which now suffused the group was palpable. It was real. In that moment, Clovenhoof felt they had the ability to do anything. It was a wonderful and empowering feeling.

21

Rutspud put up a hand to stop Eltiel before they went into the Boldmere Oak. "You ever been in a pub before, angel," he said.

Eltiel looked up and down at the exterior of the building. "It's a hostelry," he said.

"A pub. A bar. If you say something stupid in here, the locals will rip off your head and vomit down your neck. Got it?"

Eltiel's eyes widened. "A den of savages," he whispered.

"Something like. We have to blend in. Be human. Be casual. Let me do all the talking." He pushed open the door.

The Boldmere Oak was, of course, nothing like a den of savages. Rutspud had been in here before, on more than a couple of occasions. The clientele were somewhat unwashed, and in the great tide of social progression that constantly swept across the world, a pub was a place where those unwilling to go with the flow could skulk in darkness and cling to their old-fashioned ways. But savages? Not really.

Rutspud hauled himself up onto a bar stool.

"No children at the bar," said the woman behind the bar immediately.

"Listen, I just need to ask some questions—" Rutspud began.

"No children at the bar," the woman repeated, this time talking directly to Eltiel.

Eltiel froze under her stony gaze. "Er..."

"It's okay, Flo. I'll deal with this," said the barman. He put his hands on the woman's shoulders to sidle past her in the narrow space behind the bar.

He leaned on the bar top and gave Rutspud and Eltiel a look. "An angel and a demon walk into a bar," he said with a shake of his head. "You know, there was a time when we didn't have any of you lot in here."

"You can see us?" said Eltiel.

"He can see us," said Rutspud.

He frowned at the barman. Rutspud considered himself to be a fairly clever demon (by which he meant he considered himself to be an exceedingly clever demon, but knew the value of keeping his talents hidden) but he did have some weaknesses. Recognising humans was one of them. They were all lumpy and squishy and had hair in all the same places. Even their colouration ran in a simple palette from rose-petal white to the darkest brown. He'd only recently learned how to fully distinguish the basic male type from the basic female type, and only then by studying fatty bumps and dangly bits – which was much harder if the individual was wearing clothes. Therefore it took him a long second to realise he had met this man before.

"You're Lennox," he said.

"Well remembered," said the barman. "You're Rutspud."

Rutspud looked to Eltiel. "This is Lennox. He went to school with a friend of mine. Lennox, this wide-eyed ingenue is Eltiel. He's an angel."

"I kind of guessed from the sparkly halo," said Lennox.

No one else in the bar had given the pair of them a second look.

"How does he know what we are?" whispered Eltiel.

"He just does," said Rutspud. "Best not to question it. He's also mates with Clovenhoof."

Lennox stood back. "Whoa there, sunshine. He is one of my customers and I am his landlord of choice, but we're not mates. I tolerate him as I tolerate almost anyone. Now, are you here for a drink or can I help you in some other way?"

"Yes," said Rutspud, then thought that a drink might be in order. "Can we have a couple of glasses of that fizzy monks piss?"

Lennox frowned for a second. "You mean Lambrini?"

"That's the one. It's one of the few palatable things found on this world," he told Eltiel.

Lennox poured two different drinks. He put a wine glass of Lambrini in front of Eltiel and a straight glass of clear liquid in front of Rutspud.

"What's this?"

"It's lemonade," said Lennox. "You might be a demon, but you're four foot high and wearing a T-shirt that says *Daddy's*

Little Princess. So unless you can show me some ID then it's soft drinks for you."

Rutspud tugged at his T-shirt in bitter irritation. "Bloody angels."

Eltiel sipped his drink and instantly recoiled. "Harsh, offensive. What is this?"

"It's made from mushed up fermented pears," said Rutspud. "Almost as good as fizzy monk's piss."

Eltiel looked at the liquid critically. "Why would anyone do this to an innocent pear? Pears were fine as they were, weren't they?"

Rutspud shrugged. "Humans, eh? Nothing they won't mess with."

"*To gild refined gold, to paint the lily,*" said Lennox. "*To throw a perfume on the violet, to smooth the ice, or add another hue unto the rainbow, or with taper-light to seek the beauteous eye of heaven to garnish, is wasteful and ridiculous excess.*"

Rutspud looked at him.

"Shakespeare, innit?" said the barman. "Haribo-flavoured vodka, chocolate-covered cheese, hairless cats. There's nothing humans won't mess with."

"Cheers to that," said Rutspud and took a swig of his drink which he immediately spat back into the glass. "Gah!"

"No children at the bar!" called the woman from the other end of the room.

"Ignore my niece," said Lennox. "I assume you two are here for a reason."

"We need to find Clovenhoof," said Rutspud.

Lennox chuckled. "You're not the only one."

"Meaning?"

"His housemate, Nerys, came in here earlier with a talking dog wanting to know the same thing."

"A talking dog!" spluttered Eltiel.

"Yeah. I was mildly surprised myself. She was less than happy."

Eltiel gripped Rutspud's arm. "Lilith's tears!"

"Yeah," said Rutspud unhappily. "And were you able to help her, Mr Lennox? That is, can you help us?"

"I can only tell you what I told her." He reached under the counter and pulled out a flyer. "Reckon he's gone off with this lot."

Rutspud looked at the flyer. "Djævlehund."

"Djævlehund?" squeaked Eltiel. "The predictions are coming true! A thousand souls dragged to Hell!"

It took Rutspud a while to realise the leaflet was an advertisement for a musical act. Rutspud struggled to see the charms of human music. For the most part, it all sounded the same to him. There was no knowing what kind of music these creatures produced.

"Where are they?" he asked.

"Long gone now," said Lennox, "but their next gig..." His finger roved across the paper until it came down on some white text. "Scarborough. Sunday."

"Sunday," said Rutspud. "And today is...?"

"Friday."

"Good, good. And that gives us how many days...?"

"Sunday is the day after tomorrow. Friday, Saturday, Sunday," explained Lennox.

"We know where he's going to be in two days' time," said

Rutspud. He picked up the flyer and looked questioningly at Lennox.

"Sure, sure. Take it."

"Thanking you. Next stop, Scarborough." Rutspud jumped off the stool.

"It's coming true," Eltiel whimpered. "Calamitous events are about to befall us all."

"It's just Scarborough. Can't be that bad."

"Dunno," said Lennox. "Have you ever actually been there?"

22

On the petrol station forecourt, Marcee threaded her accordion into Rasmus's bass, started up the melody, and Jacob called the moves of the Morris dance.

"And forward! And back! Step forward! Hey!"

Ben realised that Clovenhoof was right. With the rock riffs to anchor them, he suddenly could do it. They moved, they weaved past each other, they kicked, they swung their sticks, and the sticks actually connected in unison. In the background he could hear Valdemar threading a high speed metal counter melody over Marcee's accordion. And for a handful of seconds the ten of them, five musicians, five dancers, were a thing of total unity.

"Oi! You can't do that here!"

The garage attendant's shout came at exactly the wrong moment. Halfway through a swing, Ben turned his head to the voice and his stick flew out of his slack grip. It flew like a javelin and struck the shop window where it put a spiderweb of cracks in the glass.

"Oi!" the woman shrieked.

The music came to a crashing halt. The dancers looked at the woman and the cracked glass. The woman stared back, speechless fury rising within her.

"In the van!" Clovenhoof yelled.

"Wednesday Wallopers depart!" added Jacob, like he was summoning a superhero team or something.

Filled with the adrenaline of Morris, and perhaps not thinking as straight as they otherwise might, everyone did as he suggested. Dancers and musicians piled into the vehicle, with sticks and instruments.

"I'm sorry, I'm really sorry," said Jacob, all the while retreating to the driver's side.

"My window!" the woman yelled.

"We're in a hurry. We're really sorry." And, with that, he started up and accelerated as fast as the van and trailer could go out of the forecourt.

No one spoke for a full minute. The interior of the van was silent but for the panting of exhilarated chests, until Aksel gave out a hoot.

"Yeah! That was amazing!"

There was laughter and much backslapping, especially from Hairy Leonard and Slackpipes Johnson, who seemed to take the forecourt kerfuffle as the best initiation into the world of Morris dancing. And despite their anti-social behaviour at the petrol station, Ben felt good. He felt really good.

"We were Morris men!" crowed Valdemar. "It was so cool. People in England really go for this, yeah?"

"Ohh, man. I bet the chicks love it!" said Aksel.

Camille snorted explosively. "Sure they do."

Marcee looked over the back of her seat. "I never, ever heard of a woman with a thing for Morris dancers."

Valdemar looked from Marcee to Camille. "The two of you seem to have so much in common. You should sit together."

Camille stuck her face close up to Valdemar's. "You think because we are both women we should talk to each other, huh? This is how you dismiss us from your man's world?" She shouted across to Marcee. "Hey Marcee! What washes whiter than fucking white?"

Marcee smiled grimly. "I don't know. I've never found anything that will get rid of the blood stains from the last person who patronised me."

"Salt will do it," said Ben. "Soak in cold salty water and then wash as normal."

Marcee and Camille looked at each other and then at Ben like he was mad.

Ben retreated to the rear of the van, away from the inexplicably condemning glare of the women. He found his bag and squatted in one of the rear seats to have another look at the vintage 3D books he'd brought with him.

Hunkered down, nobody was able to look directly over his shoulder as he flicked through the images of Lois. She was a woman living her best life, completely free of worry and unconcerned with society's constraints. He tried to imagine what that might be like. Here he was, on an actual honest-to-God adventure, but he still didn't feel as free as Lois looked in these pictures. He took a deep breath, closed his eyes and tried to imagine himself being Lois, or perhaps being there in the picture alongside Lois, riding his bicycle. There they were on a beautiful quiet country road, no traffic in sight, completely surrounded by nature. A gentle sun shone on their naked bodies as they rode along, enjoying the breeze on their skin. There would be a picnic in an hour or so. They would spread out a cloth and enjoy lashings—

He opened his eyes with a start as he realised he was in some sort of weird Enid Blyton fantasy. Was this why the Lois pictures were so compelling? He looked again, realising that something in the composition definitely reminded him of those illustrations in the books of his childhood. Lois was partaking in traditional, wholesome outdoor pursuits. The only difference was that she was naked – but that was fine, because Ben was now an adult. He closed his eyes and went back to the pleasant fantasy.

"So, where is your Morris contest?" asked Clovenhoof from the front.

"Well, the contest is Saturday night in a secret location that will be revealed to us a few hours ahead of time," said Jacob. "It's in Yorkshire. The Dodgy Duck for tonight's performance is on the way."

"What's the deal with the secret location?" asked Clovenhoof.

Jacob paused. "This is not so much a contest as a settling of scores. There's been a few difficulties in the Morris community of late."

"Yeah?"

"Bastard Hankymen!" scowled Hairy Leonard.

"It wouldn't be right for me to air all of our dirty laundry," said Jacob firmly.

"What? My dirty laundry is literally the only sort I air!" said Clovenhoof. "Sometimes a skid mark is so impressive you just have to share."

"Let's just say that a face to face meeting is needed to clear the air on some matters," said Jacob. "But tonight is just about putting on a show. We will be at the Dodgy Duck in about fifty minutes."

Ben smiled. Fifty minutes of quiet fantasy time with luscious Lois...

23

Nerys pulled over to the side on the long straight of A-road. "This is it," she said. "This is the spot where they nearly pushed me off the road."

The journey up from Birmingham with the aircon on full blast had not expelled the lingering smell of Tina's vomit, but baked it into a light but pervasive vinegary vegetable tang that Twinkle complimented every five miles or so.

As Nerys opened her door, Twinkle leapt over her and onto the verge.

"Don't go running into the road," she said.

"Do I look like some kind of muppet to you, sweetheart?" he replied.

Nerys couldn't help but think that with that cute furry face and the wholly inappropriate voice, he did indeed look like some kind of muppet.

She got out. She didn't know what she expected to see. A little clue on the ground that said *Jeremy went this way*?

Twinkle sniffed along the road. "There's tracks 'ere," he said.

There was indeed a wide track on the edge of the road in the soft verge.

"Is it them?" said Nerys.

"Eh?"

"Is that the van they were in?"

Twinkle sniffed again thoughtfully, then declared, "It's a 1992 Ford Transit. Registered in Wolverhampton. It's got rust problems and an oil leak."

"You can tell all that, just by sniffing?"

"Course, I fackin' can't," said Twinkle. "I'm a dog with a keen nose and a super-powered bonce, not a car mechanic. Tracks is tracks."

"Well, I don't know, do I?" Nerys huffed and put her hands on her hips as she looked up and down the road.

"Way I see it, darlin'," said Twinkle. "Is if they were coming up this way, then they were going somewhere down this road."

"Well, obviously."

"Oh, obvious, is it? Then they're a few hours ahead of us. And unless they're fools they're headin' for somewhere that's on that straight line what runs from our gaff and through this place. Draw a line in yer mental map and let's go look."

Nerys wanted to point out driving routes didn't really work like that, and that Jeremy Clovenhoof was even less likely to drive in an orderly fashion than a normal human, but she had nothing else. "Fine. Hop in."

"Hang on, sweetheart, just need to water the flowers."

"What?"

Twinkled turned around in the grass, sniffed a little, then cocked a leg. His eyes locked onto hers as he peed. "You think I find it disconcertin' when yer watch me piss?" he said.

"Oh. I'm sorry," she said and turned aside.

"It's okay, darlin'. I watch you pee all the time. That's what friends do."

"Oh, God."

He bounded over the driving seat and back into his passenger seat position. Evening was becoming night. Soon enough they wouldn't be able to see any clues in the dark. Nonetheless, she drove slowly, eyes peeled for any sign of the band's van.

"Chuck us another pork pie, love," said Twinkle.

She complied automatically. "I shouldn't been feeding you this stuff all the time."

"You reckon its worse than the stuff you usually get me," Twinkle laughed. "I don't know what animal you think my regular dog food is made of, but it don't smell like any animal I know."

"It's been devised by animal nutritionists to provide the most balanced diet," she said, which she was sure was what it said on the label.

"Is that so?" said Twinkle. "Tell you what. You spend the next week eatin' my food and I'll spend the next week eatin' yours, and let's see if you still agree."

"I'm not a dog, Twinkle."

"Oh, yeah, yeah," the dog nodded. "Double standards."

"I treat you like a pampered prince."

"Well, maybe I'm not a pampered prince, love, all right? Maybe I don't always get what I want."

"You couldn't speak before. You know: to ask."

"Oh, come on," he growled. "You tellin' me that yer don't know what my 'give us one of yer sausages' look means? I bladdy perfected that. Wide eyes, attentive stare, a little bit of tongue. You know what that means. Don't play coy."

"There are boundaries," she said firmly. "I'm the human, you're my dog."

"Oh, boundaries is it? Yeah, let's talk about them. You let me sleep on the bed some time but the moment I crawl on the pillows or try to get under the covers where the best smells is..."

"It's my bed. And I don't smell."

"All of you lot smell. Which brings me onto the laundry basket. Maybe a dog would like to have a root around in there and have a good old snuffle. It's like readin' a diary. Very educational."

"Do you know," she said, her voice rising, "I don't want to come home and find my dirty washing all over the floor and you with my pants over your head."

"A good day that was."

"You looked like a tiny bank robber."

"I'd be dead good at that. No one ever suspects the Yorkshire Terror."

"The word is terrier."

"Yeah, but my bank robber name would be the Yorkshire Terror."

"I think I'll stick with Twinkle."

The dog put his feet on the dashboard and looked out the window. "And that's another thing. This 'Twinkle' name. Zero consultation."

"You don't like your own name?"

"Twinkle? Twink? Twinky-boy? Funnily enough, I don't."

"Oh. Oh, I see," she said. "Well, maybe you have some better names in mind."

"As a matter of fact, I do."

Nerys prepared herself for the possibility of her little dog wanting to be called 'Wolf', or 'Bruiser', or 'Ultra-dog' or some such.

"Craig," said Twinkle.

"Pardon?"

"I would like the name 'Craig'," he said.

She was stuck for a response, her mouth frozen in a questioning 'W'. "Why—" she managed eventually "—Craig?"

"I've thought about it, ain't I, and I think I want to be called Craig."

"Craig?"

"Craig."

"That's a rubbish name. That's the name of a man who works in IT and owns a range of Christmas jumpers. *Craig*?"

"I think it strikes the right tone," said Twinkle. "It's a masculine name."

"It doesn't work as a dog name. Dog names need to be two syllables. Dogs recognise their names better if they're shouted as two syllables."

"Well, I'll recognise mine cos it'll be Craig and I'll be the only Craig you ever need to shout at."

She laughed. "It's not happening. I've got more dignity than that. Aunt Molly called you Twinkle. It's your name."

"Bladdy double standards," he muttered.

24

As promised, the journey to the Wednesbury Wallopers' performance venue was less than an hour further down the road. The Dodgy Duck turned out to be a smallish country pub with a duck pond. Some people were sitting on bench seats near to the water's edge. Jacob pulled the van into the car park, using two spaces so that the trailer would also fit.

"A drink before we look at the equipment then?" said Clovenhoof.

"Ooh no!" said Jacob. "Make sure you're dressed in uniform when you go to the bar so you won't be charged. It's part of the arrangement."

"Free drinks?" Clovenhoof's face was a picture. "Oh my word, point me to a uniform so I can exploit this arrangement!"

Happily, the spare uniforms were in a range of sizes,

accommodating both Clovenhoof's tubby spread and Ben's skinny frame. The trousers were breeches, and there were long white socks which came up to meet them. Clovenhoof knew there should also be a hat, but he could add that later. Then he hurried towards the bar, having shrugged on the basic items of white shirt with a waistcoat and dark red trousers.

He came running back before he got halfway. "Bells! I need bells! Where are they?"

He grabbed a handful of jingling straps and staggered away, fastening them onto his arms and legs as he went, admiring the dashing, slightly piratical look of the ensemble.

An hour later Clovenhoof hadn't found the limit to the free drinks he could claim as a Morris man, but he was working hard on the experiment.

"What time are you all doing the dancing?" someone asked across the bar.

Clovenhoof shrugged. "I expect they'll come and tell me."

Ben came to fetch him as Clovenhoof drained his sixth glass of Lambrini. He stood up and smacked his lips.

"Let's do this!" said Clovenhoof with a whoop.

Outside, on the rough space between pub and pond, everyone was now wearing Morris gear, even the musical accompaniment from Djævlehund. Aksel, Valdemar and Rasmus had accessorised their heavy metal look with tassels and bells. Only Camille, a fresh unlit cigarette jammed between her lips, sulkily refused to alter her appearance.

"Help me out?" Ben called to the others. "Jeremy's more than a bit half cut."

"We'll start with the Parson's Relish again," called Jacob.

Instinctively, Rasmus set up with a bass line that was definitely more glam than Morris. The guitars were all plugged into a portable amp this time and Camille had set up a full drum kit.

"Everyone is to follow me," Marcee shouted to the musicians, then her lively accordion jig dropped into time with the bass rhythm.

Camille added some percussion, and the two guitarists joined in, although Valdemar's attempt to throw a heavy metal counter-melody over it were dampened when Marcee cast a stony look at him.

"I think I've got this!" said Clovenhoof. Muscle memory was a powerful thing and he shuffled in the wonky circle that the dance demanded.

"Feet up! Feet up!" shouted Jacob. "Use the bells!"

Clovenhoof remembered the bells and set about adding little jigs and leg waggles to his moves.

Hairy Leonard and Slackpipes Johnson, either side of Clovenhoof, forcibly steered the drunk devil between them, bouncing him back and forth like a tennis ball. In a few moments they were all moving in a mostly synchronised manner, and Clovenhoof grinned widely.

"This has a good energy!" shouted Aksel. "Let's step it up a little, just for fun, eh?"

He grabbed the microphone and started to improvise some vocals. Rasmus and Valdemar took that as a cue to turn up their amps and began to enjoy themselves. Camille was already bashing the drums as if her life depended on it.

The dance cast its own hypnotic trance over Clovenhoof

and he felt himself channelling a beguiling combination of Morris, his defunct Satanic rock band, and every party reveller since the dawn of time. It was a romp, it was a ritual, and felt as though just below the surface it was also something of a release for everyone involved.

People had appeared to just watch as soon as the music had started up, but now they were properly into the groove. They started to join in with the dancing. They didn't have bells, but that didn't stop them. The moves were simple and the tune was infectious. Clovenhoof grinned like an idiot at Ben, who was clearly enjoying himself as much as everyone else.

When the song came to an end, there were more casual dancers than there were Morris men. Shouts of "More!" were heard, which seemed to confuse Jacob and Marcee, as if they had never heard such a thing before. They looked at each other, then looked at Aksel.

"Right," shouted Aksel into the microphone. "We will do another classic." He led with the instantly recognisable stomp-stomp-clap which signalled the lead-in to Queen's *We Will Rock You*. The rest of Djævlehund joined in.

Clovenhoof soon realised this required a different approach, with more emphasis on stamping and less on the fancy footwork, which suited him just fine. Then, as the song was reaching its end, Aksel morphed it into *Enter Sandman*.

Clovenhoof glanced across at Marcee, wondering what she was making of Aksel's performance. All he could see was her intense concentration as she squeezed the accordion, her fingers flying across the keys.

There were phones in the audience now. People were

videoing them. Clovenhoof couldn't help but cavort for a fresh audience. Morris sticks were switched for hankies and the dancing went on. And somehow they moved as one cohesive group, better and better, as though they could dance all the better by sheer joy and will alone.

25

Nerys saw the long straight was coming to an end. There was a roundabout with five exits. The main one went on into the city of Harrogate.

"Shit," she whispered. "They could be going anywhere."

"Trust yer nose," suggested Twinkle.

She sighed and pulled off the road into a petrol station forecourt. "I'll fill up and then we'll have a rethink."

"See if they've got any sausages in the little shop," said Twinkle.

"It's a petrol station."

"Just see."

She shut the car with Twinkle inside and took off the little car's petrol cap to fill up. As the hose chugged, she checked her phone to see if there were any reply messages from Ben or Clovenhoof. None. She hit redial and put the phone to her ear. Ben picked up.

"Hello!" he yelled in delighted greeting.

There was a huge amount of noise on the line. It sounded like he was at a festival, or caught in the worst kind of Black Friday shopping crush. There were raised voices and, pounding over it all, distorted music.

"Ben? Ben!" she shouted into the phone.

"Nerys! Nerys! Can't stop! We're on again!"

"Wait! Where are you? I need to speak to you!"

"Yes. We miss you too!"

The crowd noise swelled. There was a sharp knock. Nerys looked up. The woman at the till inside the shop had rapped on the window and was pointing. It wasn't clear what she was pointing at, but the meaning was clear. No phones at the petrol pump. Nerys nodded, ended the call and put her phone away. The tank was full.

Miserable, with no idea what she was going to do next, she made her way to the shop.

There was a muffled shout of "Sausages!" from the car.

The main window of the shop was cracked: a circular radiating pattern that had been badly repaired with parcel tape.

"You can't use your phone out there," the woman said as a greeting.

"Sorry," said Nerys though she didn't feel it. "I'm just trying to contact my friends."

The woman rang up the petrol. There was a small bank of CCTV screens in the woman's booth behind the security glass and that prompted an idea.

"I'm trying to find my friends. They might have come through here a few hours ago."

"Uh-huh."

"They were with a band. In a van."

The woman's eyes flashed at her. "What kind of van?"

Nerys saw how the woman's eyes had gone to the window.

"Did something happen?"

She was pointing at the broken window now. "Are they friends of yours?"

"The heavy metal band? No. I'm looking for one friend."

"Heavy metal? No. It—" She turned to the CCTV controls and within seconds had footage up on one of the screens. Men were prancing about on the forecourt by the pumps, waving hankies and sticks.

"No," said Nerys. "A heavy metal band. The van was different to that—"

She was struck dumb by the sight of Ben Kitchen dancing gaily along with the other Morris men. Then she realised the hoofed idiot next to him was Jeremy Clovenhoof.

"Oh, God, that's them."

"So, it is your friends?"

There was no sound on the CCTV, no hint of what the music might have been. There was a sudden commotion, and a stick went flying headlong into the window just below the camera's range. The musicians and dancers were thrown into a panicked scramble. Nerys could see them shouting to each other as they ran to the van.

"Do you know which way they went?" she asked.

The woman gave her a harsh look. "If I did, I'd be sending the police after them. One of them shouted the band's name. I'm going to track them on their socials and send them a bill."

"The name. The name would be good," said Nerys. "I might be able to get in touch with them!"

"Which ones are your friends, then?"

"Erm, that one and that one."

"That one? He's the one who broke my window."

"Ben? He's normally such a pleasant and respectful person."

"Ben, is it?"

"The band name please."

The woman had the chip and pin card machine in her hand. "That window is going to cost at least two hundred to repair."

Nerys looked at the woman. She looked at the card machine. "You are fucking kidding me."

Five minutes later, Nerys was back in the car. Twinkle looked at her expectantly.

"The Wednesbury Wallopers," Nerys said.

"What's that?"

"Wednesbury Wallopers. Jeremy and Ben have, for some sodding reason, teamed up with a band of Morris dancers. If I'd taken a moment to look I'd have recognised them. They were at a business retreat in the week. Tina got off with one of them, I think. Before the food poisoning kicked in. If I'd just taken a moment! Except, no, I had to pay two hundred quid for that nugget of information." She sucked through her teeth in annoyance at herself.

Twinkle sniffed. "Darlin', I can't help but notice the absence of sausages."

"I don't want to talk about it."

"Did you even look for sausages? Did you even *ask*?"

"I said I don't want to talk about it!" she said in miserable fury and started the car.

26

Across several hours, Djævlehund played a set that was danceable but still true to their rock origins, with a few wild metal numbers thrown in too. Aksel looked as if he was willing to keep going all night, but eventually the barman came out of the pub and indicated it was time to finish.

"Think of our neighbours!" he said when there were groans of disappointment.

"We're all here!" came shouts from the crowd.

Nevertheless, the barman stuck to his guns and they were forced to bring the session to a close. There was much joyous back-slapping and hugging, and Clovenhoof had a bottle of Lambrini pressed into his hand by the barman, which was a huge and pleasant surprise.

"Use the firepit and the benches if you want to stay longer," said the barman. "I need to lock up now." He left a crate of beers and departed with a wink.

The villagers stayed behind and settled in with them. Some disappeared briefly, returning with their own chairs, picnic blankets and booze.

"I don't know what we just played, but it felt amazing," said Aksel as they all settled onto benches, watching the flames leaping in the firepit.

"It actually was," said Jacob.

Even Marcee gave a small nod and took a huge swig of beer.

"I've been thinking that these bells are underused," said Clovenhoof.

"What do you mean?" asked Valdemar, sitting next to him.

"I reckon they should be more front and centre as a feature. Like if I did a naked pole dance and put some on my todger. I'd need an extra-large set, obviously. See that young tree over there? I'm thinking I could show you all what I—"

"—You buy your own bells if you want to do that!" snapped Marcee. "And make sure you give me a chance to get far, far away before you start."

Clovenhoof pouted. "Fine. The world will miss out on another amazing innovation. What's for dinner?"

"You have a point. I'm starving," said Aksel. "Do you have any food in your van?" he asked Jacob.

Jacob shook his head.

"Burgers on the firepit!" shouted one of the villagers, a huge chap wearing a red butcher's apron. "Silas Carver at your service. Back in a mo!"

"Sounds great, thank you!" said Aksel.

There was the sound of an engine. Clovenhoof looked

across the car park at the van that was slowly driving through.

"Shit!" said Valdemar, sitting up and staring. "That's the other van."

"What other van?" said Jacob.

"The van that was meant to be picking up the test bale. You know ... from the *farm*."

The members of Djævlehund abruptly understood. Clovenhoof had no idea if it was the other van which had come into the medicinal cannabis place. He didn't bother with minor details in life unless they contributed to his overall fun.

"Chill out my friend," said Aksel in a low voice. "We're in a different vehicle now. They won't know it was us."

"You don't think they might spot that?" Rasmus said, pointing to the bale strapped to the top of the van.

"I thought you said that was a paddling pool," said Marcee, but no one was listening.

There was a cube of pure marijuana on top of the van and the true owners were driving straight past it.

"Shit! Fuck! What can we do?" Aksel jumped to his feet.

Clovenhoof held up a hand. "This scenario clearly calls for a distraction."

"What?"

"Can I suggest that Camille goes over and talks to the driver while you two move the bale?"

"Yeah!" said Aksel. "You too, Valdemar. Come quickly."

"Fuck you," said Camille. "I am not your distraction bunny."

"Fine," sighed Clovenhoof. "You want a job doing. Give me more bells."

He was wordlessly passed several sets of bells. He jogged over to where the van was slowly crawling round the car park. Someone at a side window had a torch and was shining it on the vehicles in the car park.

"Oh heyyy!" Clovenhoof called, shedding his clothes onto the ground. "Let me show you my new routine!"

Naked, he hurriedly strapped bells where he could and shimmied in front of the van.

He realised he didn't actually have a routine, so he freestyled it, alternating between his earlier Tiger Feet moves and lewd lunges, with some pelvic thrusts thrown in so that he could waggle all of the bells.

Clovenhoof was gratified to hear the sound of the handbrake being applied. "What the fuck do you think you're doing?" came a voice.

Clovenhoof clasped his hands above his head and circled his hips, losing himself in the moment. It was ages since he'd last been naked in public, and he was enjoying himself.

"Get out of the bloody way!" shouted the voice.

"Join us!" said Clovenhoof. "It's what we do in this place. My friends are over there."

"Fucking weirdo!" said the voice.

Moments later the door slammed and the van went into reverse, manoeuvring back out onto the road and speeding away.

Clovenhoof picked up his clothes and swaggered back to his seat. Aksel had secreted the cannabis bale between two sets of seats.

"Mission accomplished!" Clovenhoof said proudly.

"Put your damned clothes back on," growled Marcee. "And you owe me a new set of bells. I'm never touching those again."

Clovenhoof used his fingertips to give the bells a final jangle, which met with a collective groan of disgust from the crowd, so he pulled on his clothes with some reluctance.

"Your friend, he's not right in the head," Camille said to Ben as Clovenhoof dressed.

"No, he's not," agreed Ben.

"All good!" Aksel crowed. "If they come back we're in the clear."

At that moment, the butcher, Silas Carver, returned, lugging a large cool box in one hand and an industrial-sized grilling rack in the other. "Here we go people! Finest beef products this side of the Pennines. Cows dream of ending up in my butcher's shop."

A woman followed with a small table and she laid out paper plates and bread rolls.

"Let's get this fire stoked up a little and then we can grill these beauties," shouted Silas Carver. He walked around to a woodstore which was sited a few feet away. "Gonna throw on some of these bigger logs, and the barbecue chips. The taste will blow your minds!"

"Barbecue chips, nice," said Jacob.

Ben watched as Silas picked up some hefty pieces of unchopped wood and added them to the fire pit.

27

As the flames from the fire pit rose higher, and the last of the bottled beer was passed around the locals of the Dodgy Duck, Clovenhoof launched into an a capella version of one of his Devil Preacher songs. Aksel whooped and sang along with the words, and very soon the entire audience were singing along to the chorus.

Rasmus had his bass plugged in and kept it in time, while Marcee wove filigrees of accordion tunes around the rough melody.

Silas Carver handed out the last of the cooked meat and heaped more fuel on the fire. Great aromatic clouds came off the fire and wreathed around the singers and dancers.

Camille appeared beside Ben, a bottle of beer dangling between two fingers, a cigarette hanging, James Dean-style, from her lips. "Your friend...," she said, inhaling the smoke from the fire deeply.

"He's not so much a friend as a pain in the backside I've got used to over the years," said Ben.

"He's not a roadie at all, is he?"

"Didn't say he was."

"He's a – what's the word? – he's an *enabler*?"

Ben laughed, and as he inhaled drew in lungsful of the smoke. He was immediately light-headed. He coughed and waved the smoke away.

"Jeremy Clovenhoof is the biggest enabler in the world," he said. "If he shouted 'Come on, everyone, let's march on London and bring down the government!' he'd have thousands of people joining him before they even knew what was happening."

"He's dangerous," said the Frenchwoman.

"*Run away from the man in a dress!*" screeched Clovenhoof and Aksel in unison.

"Let's hear it for our good friend Jeremy Clovenhoof, the Devil Preacher himself!" cried Aksel.

There was much foot-stomping and cheering. As it died away, Aksel followed it up with another crowd-pleaser.

"You know," Ben said to Camille, having to raise his voice to be heard over the commotion, "earlier, when the men came looking for their bale of weed, you refused to go out and be the distraction."

"Uh-huh."

"I thought that was decisive of you. Not willing to be that cliché."

Camille pulled back and stared at him. "Are you hitting on me, Ben?"

"What? No!"

"You're twice my age."

"I – what? I'm nothing like twice your age."

"I'm twenty-two."

"I'm not fucking— How old do you think I am?"

"Over forty-four."

"Well, I'm not! I wasn't hitting on you. In fact, I'm technically married. I think. And—"

"You're nearly forty four though?"

"No. Are you trying to make me feel old?"

"Nearer to forty-four than twenty-two?"

"Lots of people are. Jesus, woman." The light-headedness from the smoke seemed to be filling him with a fresh confidence. "I was just trying to have a conversation with you. Let me – let me put something to *you*, miss!"

"Yeah? What?" she said.

He pointed to the cigarette in her mouth. "You always have a fag in your mouth."

"You know how hilarious that English word sounds. *Fag*."

"Perfectly decent English word. You always have a *cigarette* in your mouth but you never light it."

"Of course not," she pouted. "I'm not a moron."

"Why then? What's the point?"

"It's all part of my ten year plan."

"Which is?"

"To become the president of France."

Ben frowned at her. He was struggling a little to think clearly, but he was sure that didn't make sense. "You're gonna have to explain that."

"Year one. This is year one. Tour with a cool, low-class metal band. Get my image out there. Be a disruptor. Cause a scene. I barter that up into a film career. Europe, America, back to Europe. Year five, maybe I get a rich husband or wife. My brand manager and I haven't agreed on this yet. Shift into politics. Year ten, run for president."

"That's the plan? From rock drummer to president."

"Last year I finished my politics degree at the Paris Institute of Political Science."

"Shit. Really? Wow."

She nodded and looked to his eyes more seriously and human than he'd seen before.

"But the cigarette thing?" he said.

She ticked off her fingers. "One, cigarettes look cool in photos and videos. Even today. Two, if you smoke them they'll fucking kill you. It's obvious really."

"So you don't smoke at all?"

"Don't smoke, don't do hard drugs."

"But you're okay with a bit of...?" he looked round for their stash of cannabis. He saw the bale by the benches. It had been ripped wide open. Half of it was already gone. And as he looked, he saw the butcher guy, Silas, dig deep into the plastic wrap, come away with heavy fibrous chunks of the stuff and toss it onto the firepit.

"*Fuuuuuck*," whispered Ben. No wonder the smoke was making him light-headed. No bloody wonder the party mood was that of some one-world 'Let's all have a sing along' lovefest. "Fuck."

"No. Not with you," said Camille. She stroked his face and walked off into the crowd.

Up on the little rise that served as a stage, Aksel had to

stop singing because he kept giggling. His giggling infected Clovenhoof.

"Come on! Hold it together!" yelled Morris-man Jacob, waving his arms for the band to keep going. He launched into a song that didn't seem to know what it was. It was either *Yellow Submarine* or *Don't Rock the Boat*. It might even have been both. But that was fine because they both had an ocean-going theme, and the chorus of "Don't you rock my submarine!" was so enjoyable to sing everyone found it hilarious.

There was no stopping this party so Ben decided to join in. Consciously or not, everyone was drawn to the intoxicating smoke coming off the fire pit. Some staggered and fell and didn't bother to get up. Others were energised to dance further and harder.

Out of nowhere a flask was thrust into Ben's hand. He recognised it as the funky ancient bottle Clovenhoof had brought from their home. There was no more beer left, and partying was thirsty work. He took a big swig and passed it on.

"This is the best party ever!" a woman shouted in Ben's face. She was absolutely right.

Ben rocked his way to the front to perform a dance which went with Jacob's rocking submarine song. He was a submarine that refused to be rocked until it jolly well wanted to be rocked. So he danced and trotted around the fire, not quite rocking until it was time to. When it was time, he broke out the headbanging and howled with delight. Everyone else decided that looked like a lot of fun, so the entire crowd indulged in howling and headbanging.

"My rocking submariiiine!" Ben screamed.

Clovenhoof grabbed a mike. "Now let's all get naked and worship me, for I am Satan, your Lord and Master!"

The music crashed to a stop. The assembled crowd stared at Jeremy for a long moment. Then someone whooped and threw their shirt in the air and the punters erupted in cheers.

Clovenhoof snatched a guitar from somewhere and yelled, "Here's a Devil Preacher classic. It's called *Eat My Fruit, Bitch!*"

He struck up the opening chords. He did it very badly, but it didn't seem to matter because this was very clearly the best party ever.

28

Eltiel had his stone tablet on his lap as Rutspud drove north through the night. Rutspud wanted to tell Eltiel that its golden glow was distracting him from the road, but it wasn't really true. From the searing white-hot centre of the Lake of Fire, to the stygian depths of the deepest pit of Hell, Rutspud's large eyes could deal with any light levels. And he was rarely distracted by anything. That too was a bi-product of aeons in Hell, because Hell was full of constantly new and diverting sights – many involving fanciful arrangements of human organs, and the novel things one could do to a body when one had access to a workshop full of tools and unlimited time. Rutspud could claim the light from the tablet was affecting his vision, but the truth was he could turn off the headlights and still drive perfectly fine. His eyes could cope with pitch darkness but in this world here was never truly dark.

No, Rutspud found Eltiel's pseudo-technical 'tablet' annoying because it existed. Heaven reaped the benefits of technology without the first inkling of what true technology really meant. It was one of Rutspud's pet peeves. It was like damned humans who thought 'the cloud' where all their data lived was somehow in the air above them.

"I'm never sure if light pollution was a deliberate choice," he said as he steered off a dual carriageway and onto an A-road. "Do you think humans are just afraid of the dark?"

Eltiel looked out of the window, at the fields and buildings whipping by beneath a dull orange sky. "Once upon a time, this was all forest," he said.

"Er, yeah. Well, that's progress for you," said Rutspud.

"Progress? If the Good Lord had decided to cover this land with forests, then forests it should have been. People mess too much with things."

Rutspud glanced at the angel. His pinky-blue tinsel halo played light across his headrest. "I didn't see you as the outdoorsy type, Eltiel."

"Me? Ooh, no. Heaven forbid. Not me. I'm a Celestial City boy. Give me cool, clean white marble and cotton-soft robes. Give me the glories of Heaven and us angels zipping all over it like busy little bees. No, I'm not a forest ... *person*. But the Lord has ordained a place for everything and humans seem to be hellbent on messing it up."

Rutspud frowned. "In your perfect vision of things, humans don't chop down the forests?"

"Obviously not."

"So they don't build houses?"

"The Lord will provide shelter."

His frown deepened. "So, your perfect vision would be, like Adam and Eve and all their descendants, wandering naked through the Big Guy's perfect creation, not touching anything?"

"The fruit from the trees. They can have that. Nuts and berries. They need food."

"So they're all vegan."

"A very healthy diet. The world as it was created, was perfect. This..." He waved at a passing service station. "What is a *Greggs* anyway? They seem to be everywhere. Free will has a lot to answer for—" he tapped his tablet "—and this spike I've seen appear in the past few minutes doesn't bode well."

"Sounds to me like you think human beings and free will were an all-round bad idea."

Eltiel made a noise in this throat and gave Rutspud the side-eye. "I know where you're going with this, demon. Yes, there was a certain angel who held that very viewpoint and had the temerity to tell the Almighty humans were a big mistake. That was *his* big mistake. I'm never going to presume to tell the Lord Above He made a single mistake in His fabulous creation."

"But you wish humans would just leave it as it is?"

"Exactly."

"Like one of those people who puts transparent plastic covers over their furniture to keep the dust off."

"Can't say I've seen that."

"It's definitely an aesthetic choice."

"Wipe clean covers, that rubbery plastic sheen. Sensual in its own way. I approve."

Rutspud might have delved deeper into Eltiel's sensual relationship with rubber and plastic, but there was a proper distraction on the road ahead.

"Hello, what's this?" he said and slowed. There were several vehicles at the side of the road. A tractor, a recovery truck, and two vans. It was one of the vans which had caught his attention. A pair of men were slowly loading one with the word Djævlehund painted on the side onto the recovery vehicle. The guy by the tractor looked on with both interest and annoyance.

"Djævlehund," said Eltiel. "We've found them?"

"I don't think so," said Rutspud, pulling in behind the vehicles. "Mud on the tires. That gateway there. That bloke with the air of a farmer who's found a van abandoned on his land." He turned to Eltiel. "You know you magicked these awful clothes for us to wear."

"Awful or naively charming?" said Eltiel.

"Can you magic up some new ones for us."

"It's not magic. It's—"

"Can you do it?"

"If you don't shout at me, yes."

"Good. Then I would like you to make us look like cops."

"Cops."

"Police officers. Detectives. FBI agents. Jesus, just look up 'cops'. We need to act the part."

"Okay, okay." Eltiel closed his eyes and, as Rutspud leapt out, he felt a shifting of his clothes. Shiny black shoes on his feet, a tie around his neck, a hat upon his head.

Rutspud strode up to the men around the vehicles, throwing in some policeman swagger as he walked. He looked over at Eltiel and saw the uniform Eltiel had conjured them both into. Thick jackets, shiny silver buttons, and perched on top of Eltiel's head, a conical hat with a little silver nipple on the top.

"Balls!" Rutspud hissed. "What century did you go to for this gear?" He took off his stupid policeman's helmet and tucked it under his arm. "'Allo, 'allo, 'allo. What's all this then?" He'd wanted to go for some standard genial police greeting, but the uniform seemed to have infected his subconscious word choices.

"Evening ... officer?" said one of the recovery vehicle men and frowned at their uniforms.

Rutspud gave an airy wave. He realised he even had a little whistle on a chain pinned to his jacket. "Me and Constable Eltiel here were just on our way back from a – er – ceremonial event." He nodded at the van. "What appears to be occurring here, gents?"

"Bloody vandals dumped their busted van in my sheep field," declared the farmer. "Who's going to pay to get rid of it, that's what I want to know."

"Where are the owners of this van?" said Rutspud, attempting to give each and every man a beady eye. Rutspud had the confidence to pull off the policeman act, but it was still a hard sell when you were a waist-high demon.

One of the men by the other van stepped forward. "They stopped by a place we were due to do a pick-up. We think they may have stolen something."

"Stolen something?"

The two men looked warily at each other. "A package we were picking up from Ribble-Lorenz Horticulture. Medical supplies."

Eltiel rocked on his heels policeman-style, seemingly happy to let Rutspud do all the talking. Rutspud noticed Eltiel had given himself a big bushy moustache for some reason. It really didn't suit the slender, androgynous angel and yet, at the same time, it really did.

"And do you know where these miscreants went?" Rutspud asked.

"We've been driving round, looking," said the van man.

"Looking where?"

"Knaresborough, Copgrove, Ripon, and back down Ripley and Killinghall. Bilal at the office says they were some kind of pub rock band, so we were checking out the pubs in the area."

"Any luck with that?"

"Apart from some weird naked Morris dancer at one of the pubs, no. I think—"

"Which pub?" said Rutspud at once.

The van guy puffed out his cheeks and looked at his mate. "I don't remember. Burton Leonard? Newby Hall? Somewhere round there."

"Excellent." Rutspud turned and marched back to their car. Eltiel scampered to keep up.

"Oi! What about this van?" called the farmer. "Who's gonna reimburse me?"

"Looks like you got a free van, if you ask me," Rutspud called back. He jumped into the car.

Eltiel hurriedly got in beside him. "What's the rush?" asked the moustachioed angel.

"Naked Morris dancing? That's one hundred percent Jeremy Clovenhoof's M.O." He started the car. "Let's go. And try to bring up a map on that stupid tablet of yours."

29

Eventually, Nerys had to stop for the night. Driving around, hoping to find a heavy metal band or Morris group was fruitless, and seemed to grow ever more fruitless the later it got. In the end, she booked into a Travelodge somewhere on the outskirts of Harrogate. There were no pets allowed, but she managed to smuggle Twinkle past the disinterested receptionist and get him to their plain but functional room.

"This is a fucking nightmare," she said tiredly, flopping onto the bed.

"I dunno, sweetheart," said Twinkle, sniffing around on the floor. "This place has character and history."

"What?"

"You can smell all the people who've been here before. It's like a walk through 'istory."

She wrinkled her nose. "Ugh. Don't tell me. I don't want to know."

She took a shower to try to wash the travel grime from her body and, considering she now had a sentient talking dog as a companion, wrapped herself up tightly with every available towel before going back into the bedroom.

She'd searched for the Wednesbury Wallopers while still on the road. She'd found an underused Facebook page and some Instagram posts from a couple of year back, but nothing current, and no contact details. Now, she searched for them again, found nothing more, and even messaged Tina to ask if, by any chance, she had a phone number for the Walloper she'd got off on the final night of the retreat.

Nerys sat on the edge of the bed and tried phoning Ben and Clovenhoof. Ben didn't pick up at all; Clovenhoof did answer. It sounded like he was in a howling gale. There were human yells and whoops that made him all but inaudible.

"Nerys! Nerys! You've got to get over here! These people! They love me!"

"Where are you?" she shouted, aware of how loud she sounded in the small room. "Jeremy! Where are you?"

There were wet sounds and moans that did not sound at all pleasant.

"Jeremy! Are you at an orgy?" she yelled.

There was a clatter and some muffled thumps on the line, as though the phone was being stamped on and then the line went died.

"Bugger," she said and tossed her phone onto the bed.

Twinkle leapt up beside her. She automatically scratched his head and tickled his ears.

"Does this place do room service?" said the dog.

"Are you still hungry? You've been eating all day

e and there, love. Nothin' like a proper meal. We eat. Keep our strength up."

viciously towelled her hair. "How can you think of food at a time like this?"

Twinkled trod a little circle in the bed. "Thing I don't get, sweetheart, is what you gonna do when you catch up wiv Ben and Jeremy?"

"Kill them," she said.

"You always say that."

"I don't."

"'Bout five times a day on a good day. I mean, what you gonna do when you catch up wiv them *this* time?"

She looked Twinkle in the face. "I'm going to find out what they've done to you and I'm going to get them to fix it."

"Fix it, eh?" He sniffed haughtily. "You reckon yer little feller needs fixin', eh?"

"This..." She waved a hand at him. "It's not natural."

"You don't like it when I talk?"

"Honestly? It's more than a little freaky."

"You don't... You don't fink this is wonderful opportunity to get to know me better?"

"I'm really sorry, Twinkle."

"Craig."

"*Twinkle.* I'm sorry, but I think I preferred you when you were just a dog."

"Oh." He tried to not sound put out. "And what was it you liked about me then, when I was 'just a dog'?"

That stumped her. She reached for what words she could. "I think ... I think I just liked that you were there."

"There?"

"Just there. You were Aunt Molly's, and then you were mine. You're a constant in my life."

"What? Like some bleedin' table ornament?"

"More than that. You're part of my routine. You define the day. Even when it's raining and I really don't want to take you out."

"No one wants to go out in the rain, sweetheart."

"And you're a sounding board."

"Eh?"

She stroked his little head. "I tell you all my problems."

"Not 'arf," he chuckled. "Listenin' to you is like listenin' to the dirtiest soap opera on the telly box. Although I have noticed a drop-off in the number of mates you drag back to our place for a bit of 'ow's yer father in the bedroom. You 'aving trouble getting' them to follow you home these days?"

"Twinkle!" She propelled herself off the bed and away from him. "That's exactly the kind of thing I don't want to hear from a talking dog. The whole point of a sounding board is that you're meant to listen. I do not want a dog that's got the lowdown on all my shameful secrets."

"Nothin' to be ashamed of darlin'. Although I'm amazed you managed to 'ave it away with so many blokes without getting preggo with pups. I've wondered about that. Wondered if there was something wrong with yer pipes."

She spat in disgust and fury and stormed back into the bathroom where she sat on the toilet and fumed for a long while before getting fully dry and dressing in the only set of clothes she had with her.

She formulated all the words she wanted to say before stepping out into the bedroom.

Twinkle sat on the bed, attentive and patiently waiting.

"Asking a woman about why she's not had children is totally not cool," she said.

"All right," said Twinkle.

"I've met children. And I've met them often enough to know I don't want to bring any more of them into this world."

"Smart move. Stay free, like a lone wolf."

"And..." She wringed her hands and huffed. "Whatever small intimate family I ever wanted... Well, that's you, Twinkle."

"Craig."

"Maybe Craig. Maybe. And I love you."

"Whoa, sweetheart. Don't come on so strong."

"I'm not *in love* with you, you tiny idiot. I love you. And I know humans and animals are not the same thing. Well, until the last couple of days. You were in that ... that animal category, and I loved you for the dog you were. Now you're, well, you're effectively human. I've had more sensible conversations with you than I've ever had with Jeremy in the last two years."

"I is an intellectual among dogs," Twinkle nodded sagely.

"And now that you're this thing, this super-dog—"

"Oh, now you're makin' me blush."

"—well, then I've lost the little Twinkle I had before."

"Craig."

"But that's it. I've lost Twinkle and I've gained Craig. And you are a remarkable little dog."

"Stop it with the compliments. You'll give me a boner."

"Ugh. You're a remarkable, weird, disgusting little dog.

And I'm pleased for you if this is what you want – but I've still lost my Twinkle."

"You'll get used to it," he said.

"I'm not sure I want to."

"Talkin' dogs is yer ideal companion. I not only bark at burglars, I can tell them to piss off an' all. When I get excited and you do that silly 'What izzit, boy? What izzit?' I can tell you. And I'm dead good at handy tasks like orderin' us takeaways an' that."

She sighed and plonked herself on the bed again and stroked him fondly. "We'll find a way through this," she said.

"Too bladdy right, we will," he said, leaning into his hand.

Ten minutes later, there was a knock at the door. Nerys looked at him. "You *can* order takeaway?"

Twinkle grinned at her. There was actually a toothy little grin.

"Kebabs!" he said, eyes sparkling. He looked at the phone she'd dropped on the bed. "Turns out a wet nose is as good as a finger on a smart phone."

Talking dogs might be able to order kebabs, but it turned out they still needed humans to pay for them. Even so, the kebabs weren't half bad. Twinkle ate half the meat in hers and she ate all the salad in his. And then they slept, side by side, once they'd established that Nerys would very much like this new Twinkle to stay on his side of the bed. But, if he happened to crawl over in the night and nuzzle into the crook of her arm and she sleepily put her fingers in his fur coat, then that was fine too.

30

Ben was sure there had only been one more song sung that night, but somehow it had gone on for hours and hours. It had been a long, overlapping sequence of music and words and dance, and there had been an awful lot of people who had decided to dance along to it with no clothes on.

Ben woke on a bench beside the smouldering fire pit. All around, there were snoozing bodies draped over every surface;. Dozens of them. Most of them were naked or half-dressed, and their clothes were scattered about like a fresh snowfall.

"Jesus," he whispered, smacking dry lips and painfully sitting up. It was then he realised he had his collection of Lois books on his chest, and the 3D glasses resting on his forehead.

"Wha'?"

There were snoozing naked people all around him, limbs intertwined, some still sleepily locked together liked exhausted wrestlers. Ben got up on the bench, walked to the edge and –books tucked under his arm – made a clumsy leap to a patch of earth that was not occupied by sleepers.

He spotted Clovenhoof's funky drinking bottle on the ground and picked it up. There was something weirdly remarkable about the vessel in that it was not particularly large, yet seemed as full as ever. Ben wiped off the bottle's top, took several mouthfuls, and tried to make himself feel more awake and ready to face the day. The drink did him the world of good and he looked round afresh.

Valdemar stood in the centre of the pub's duck pond, naked to the waist, arms raised as though in salutation to the rising sun. Ben approached.

"Hey, Valdemar."

The long-haired guitarist looked back at him. "Isn't it glorious, Ben?" he said.

Ben looked round for the glorious thing. "What is?"

"The world. And all the things in it."

"Um, yes. I guess so. I thought it was a bit crappy, to be honest."

"No, no," Valdemar said earnestly. "It is a wonderful world. And I wonder if my baby boy is looking at the same sky right now. I can feel him calling to me."

"Right. Some babies have powerful lungs, don't they? Er, you're feeling homesick?"

Valdemar began to wade towards Ben. He strode out of the pond on bare feet, water streaming out of his leather trousers and Ben couldn't help thinking Valdemar would have one heck of palaver trying to get them off later.

"I am changing," said Valdemar.

"I thought you might want to," said Ben.

"No." Valdemar reached out and gripped Ben's shoulders in an unnervingly familiar gesture. "I am changing. I feel it myself. Soon Valdemar Slange the musician will be dead."

"Oh, don't say that."

"And Valdemar Slange the father will emerge."

"Oh."

"Soon I must put this body aside, and I want to."

"Right?"

"But Valdemar the musician is not finished yet."

"Well, no. You've got a gig tomorrow night."

"Exactly. But these different pulls within me. They hurt."

"You want to be in two places at once."

Valdemar nodded as though Ben had said some great and vast truth. "My work is not yet done, but I feel it coming to an end."

"Right, mate, yeah. Well, keep it together for now, eh?"

Valdemar nodded solemnly, then pulled Ben into a tight embrace, Valdemar's wet hips against Ben.

"Yeah, yeah. Okay. Break. Break. Detach," said Ben and pulled himself damply away.

Another hand slapped on Ben's shoulders.

"What a night!" said Clovenhoof, far too loudly for such an early hour. "That was amazing. And look!" He waggled his hand, and it took Ben a moment to realise Clovenhoof had finally managed to unsuperglue his fingers.

Clovenhoof was wearing some clothes, which was better

than none. He'd pulled on someone's trousers and still wore his Morris shirt, although it was undone to the waist like some broad-chested Byronic hero. The manly look was somewhat spoiled by his hairy belly poking through, yearning to be free.

"It was a crazy night," Ben agreed.

"What happened after we burned down the bus shelter?"

"Eh? We didn't burn any bus shelter. We just sang songs and fell asleep," said Ben. "Most of us."

"Um, no. You were on about some woman and said you were going to find her."

"Did I?"

"You took a burning log out of the fire and ran off. Next thing, you were complaining it had burnt your hand and you dropped it over there."

Ben looked where Clovenhoof was pointing. He did indeed see the smouldering remains of a bus shelter.

"Ringing any bells?"

"Oh this is very bad," said Ben. "You do know we were all high, don't you? That butcher guy put the cannabis bale on the fire."

"What? My private stash of weed?"

Ben nodded.

Clovenhoof shook his head sadly. He had no time to reflect further on the evening as there came a groan and a yell from among the sleeping masses, followed by further moans, groans, yells and shrieks. The people of Bishop Monkton were waking up and seeing themselves in all their nude glory in the light of a fresh day.

There were cries of "No!" People hurriedly picked up whatever clothes they could find nearby.

"Cannabis does not usually make people become wild, insatiable creatures of lust," said Valdemar.

"No," agreed Clovenhoof, then snatched the bottle from Ben's hand. "Everyone did have a swig of this."

"You put LSD in there, didn't you?" said Valdemar.

"It's Lilith's Secret Drink all right," said Clovenhoof. "But there's no LSD. Maybe."

A roar went up. "What did you do to us?" cried the butcher guy, Silas Carver, still wearing his red apron but currently lacking any trousers. He was pointing a fat quivering finger at Clovenhoof.

"Me?" said Clovenhoof.

"You forced us to worship you! Forced us to engage in filthy carnal hanky-panky!"

"I don't force anyone to do anything. I don't have to. I may have encouraged a little light worshipping, and if I remember correctly you were very attentive at one point." He looked at Ben. "What can I say? The man loves a sausage."

"Oh, shit," whispered Ben.

"Satanist!" yelled Silas.

"Oh, he's *so* close," Clovenhoof tutted.

A woman threw her arms high. "God forgive us for what we've done!"

Clovenhoof leapt onto a picnic table to better address the crowd. "You've got nothing to be ashamed of, madam. For a woman your age, you were very accommodating. No – don't cover them up. I love a pair of saggy baps."

Across the way, Ben could see Marcee and Jacob, both remarkably fully clothed, creeping into the van.

"Bring your satanic rituals here would you?" screamed Silas Carver. He looked around and pulled the pole of an ornamental bird feeder out of the pub lawn as a weapon. "Try to abduct decent womenfolk, huh?"

Clovenhoof turned to Ben. He clearly had questions. Ben had them too. They shrugged at each other.

"Are you missing some, er, womenfolk?" Ben asked.

Aksel stumbled out from behind the pub, a half-dressed woman in each arm. It was hard to tell if he was supporting them or they were supporting him.

"Sandra?" yelled Silas in disbelief.

One of the women tried to look shocked, but didn't appear to have the energy or inclination.

Silas growled and began to advance. Whoever was at the wheel of the van started the engine. Silas whirled and launched his birdfeeder spear. It crashed straight through the windscreen. The van stopped suddenly. Jacob staggered out, stunned.

"Get them!" shouted Silas. "Get them all!"

The crowd of locals surged. There was no other choice: they could either wallow in their embarrassment, gather what clothes they could find and slink off back to their homes, or unify in hatred of the outsiders who had clearly done this *to* them.

The members of the heavy metal Morris troupe ran. One bunch of locals harried Jacob and Marcee as they ran from the van. Aksel shouted "Come with me, girls!" and fled back round the pub. Valdemar and Clovenhoof skipped nimbly round one side of the pond while Ben found himself chased round the other. A tide of angry and partially dressed village people followed.

Ben had the advantage of wearing clothes and, importantly, shoes. He ran for the trees on the other side of the pond and cut through a short path. Twigs and leaves crunched under his running feet. For a man who was never a school athlete, he had soon lost his pursuers in twists and turns of the path. But he could still hear their animalistic yells.

"Psst! Over here!"

Ben looked around. There was a large stand of bushes with glossy green leaves, and a hand beckoning from their midst.

He crept inside without questioning the matter and found a space in the middle where Camille, Rasmus, Hairy Leonard and Slackpipes Johnson huddled.

"Be very quiet," said Hairy Leonard.

Ben nodded. He needed no further instruction. Then, like a passing storm, the screaming, howling mob came running along the path. There were choked sobs and the foulest of language amidst the yells. Eventually it faded.

"I'd heard old people all become swingers to cope with the boredom and thoughts of their impending deaths," said Camille. She perched on an ancient tree trunk at the middle of the stand of bushes, looking as fresh and smug as ever. She looked at Ben. "Is that what you people do with your weekends?"

Ben wanted to remind her that he wasn't old, but he didn't have the energy.

Nerys slept uneasily and woke when cold harsh light came in through the poorly drawn curtains. It wasn't even eight a.m. and her head was a fuzzy mess, her mouth tasting of kebab.

She automatically picked up her phone. There were no texts, no replies to the messages she'd sent out. She googled for the Wednesbury Wallopers again. And suddenly there were results that had not been there the night before. More than a dozen videos, across various social media platforms. They were even on her TikTok feed.

She watched one. Against an atmospherically smoky background, a bunch of Morris dancers wafted hankies and stomped about to a pounding rock tune. It took her a moment to recognised the familiar racing guitars of AC/DC's *Thunderstruck*. High-stepping, bell-jingling moves, and a heavy rock beat. It was weirdly mesmerising.

She watched another. She wasn't great with song titles, but it was that Rage Against the Machine one with all the 'fuck you's in it. To a soundtrack of violent thrashing guitars the Morris dancers, including Clovenhoof and Ben, danced and swung sticks like men at war.

"Hashtag Metal Morris, hashtag BritMoz, hashtag WednesburyWallopers, hashtag DodgyDuck."

Dodgy Duck sounded either like a terrible real ale or a pub. And, in the videos, it looked like the performance (which the time stamp indicated as the night before) was definitely taking place outside a British pub.

She searched for Dodgy Duck. It was a pub in a village called Bishop Monkton. A map search showed it was less than a thirty minute drive from her location.

She patted Twinkle. "Wake up, dog. I've found them."

31

Eventually, there were twelve hiding in the bushes: Ben, Clovenhoof, Jacob, Marcee, Hairy Leonard, Slackpipes Johnson, Rasmus, Camille, Valdemar, Aksel and the two women Aksel somehow still had with him. The sounds of angry villagers buzzed around, near and far.

Clovenhoof forced Camille to budge over and sat on the tree trunk beside her. "I've had worse furniture than this in my flat."

"Shh!" came the sharp retort.

"We should camouflage ourselves," Clovenhoof suggested, dragging his hoof through the mud in front of him. He pointed at the ground, then mimed smearing dirt on his face.

"No thank you," hissed Camille.

Aksel, however, willingly slapped some muck on his face. The others were less keen.

Clovenhoof grabbed a handful of mud and spat on it,

making a mucky paste which he smeared on his face with his hands. He thought for a moment. Did he still have the superglue? He rootled in his pocket and found that he did. He applied some of the glossy leaves from the bushes to his head, imagining he must look like one of the Caesars with his noble headgear.

There was a shout not far away from Silas Carver. "Spread out! We can trap them!"

Clovenhoof eyed the rest of the group in the bushes. Everyone seemed to understand there was a genuine threat of physical harm, but there were also angry glares in his direction, as though he was somehow responsible for the situation. He tried to project an aura of harmless innocence.

"They're going to come back with dogs," whispered on of Aksel's new companions.

"Dogs?" quailed Ben.

"Like little fluffy puppies?" suggested Hairy Leonard hopefully.

"My uncle's got a pair of hunting dogs," said the other woman.

"We need to get out of here," said Rasmus.

"I will protect you both," Aksel said, holding both women close.

"Yeah, we're probably all right," said one, gently extricating herself from Aksel's arm. "I mean, last night was fun..."

"Super fun," said the other. "We've never shagged a Swedish bloke before."

Rasmus almost concealed his snigger.

"But *we're* not in danger of being hunted with dogs or stabbed with pitchforks," said the first woman.

"Those of us in *mortal danger* need to get away, right?" said Marcee.

"We head back for the van, yeah?" Jacob asked.

One of the women held out her phone. It was a village WhatsApp group. On it, a petrol Molotov cocktail was being tossed into the open rear door of the van as people around cheered.

"Oh, no," whispered Jacob.

Then, in the real world, there came a distant but clear *boom* that was quite probably the sound of the van's fuel tank exploding.

"My van," Jacob wept.

"Our fucking gear!" fumed Camille. "All our fucking gear!"

"My guitar?" said Aksel.

"All my songwriting notes!" said Valdemar.

"I mean, I'm impressed we've wrecked two vans in two days," said Clovenhoof.

Furious gazes turned on him, but before they could vent their fury there came a shout from Silas Carver. "We're know you're in there! Come out!"

"Everyone be really quiet!" Clovenhoof hissed.

"We just heard you say 'everyone be really quiet'," said Silas.

Huffing, angry and afraid, the group trudged out of the bushes. The two local woman happily stayed back in hiding. They didn't need to face the music.

Out on the path, a band of locals were bunched together.

It seemed as if they'd all been told to bring pitchforks and had raided their sheds and garages for the nearest twenty-first century equivalent. Someone had a strimmer, there were at least two garden forks and, most unlikely of all, a pressure washer. Clovenhoof wasn't too worried about those, unless they got close enough to use them as bludgeoning weapons, but he heard the distant sound of someone starting a chainsaw.

"Okay," said Clovenhoof, raising his hands to appease the crowd. "I can see there's a few angry people here, but there's anger on both sides. We burned down your bus shelter and you burned down our van."

"You perverted and degraded us!" growled Silas.

"Again," said Clovenhoof, "I have to point out it was all consensual stuff. And since you all signed waivers, everything has been uploaded to www.villagesexfest.com. Some great footage. Take a look."

There were uneasy frowns among the locals. Garden implements were juggled from one hand to another as a dozen people grabbed their phones to check.

"Run!" yelled Clovenhoof and, in that moment of distraction, ten musicians and dancers legged it down the track.

"Come back here!" shouted Silas after them. "We'll get you, we know these woods!"

The gang ran on.

"You know this would be a lot easier if my hand wasn't glued together!" Clovenhoof puffed.

"I thought you had freed your fingers," panted Ben.

"Yeah. Somehow managed to glue them back again. I shouldn't be trusted with this stuff."

DESPITE GRUMBLES that a certain little dog couldn't possibly start the day without a decent breakfast, (preferably a whole roast chicken), Nerys had driven straight from their Harrogate hotel to the little village of Bishop Monkton. The roads into the village were narrow and lined with a mixture of hedges and rustic fencing. Houses of white stone, cute veering on beautiful, were set back from the street, and a small stream ran through a grassy ditch along the roadside near the village pub.

Nerys was about to comment on how idyllic this village was when she spotted, in quick succession, a burned out wooden bus shelter, a still merrily burning transit van, and a muddy circle of discarded clothing and beer bottles on the green area next to the pub.

"Jeremy's been here," she said, darkly.

"Oh, he's a scamp, that one," said Twinkle.

Nerys parked in front of the pub. Twinkle was leaping over her lap and out of the door before she even had her seatbelt off.

"What's the hurry?" she called.

"Breakfast!" the dog shouted back at her.

Twinkle snuffled furiously among the clothes on the grass until he turned up a filthy and discarded beef burger. He savaged it like it was a struggling rabbit he'd just caught, then tore chunks off it.

"You complain about dog food but you'll eat mud burgers."

"Natural marinade, sweetheart," said Twinkle around a mouthful of old meat.

Nerys turned round to inspect the scene. "What the hell happened here?" she said to no one.

This was definitely the place. She sought out the recently shared videos again. They were racking up thousands of views across social media. This 'Britmoz' music mash up was in danger of going completely viral.

The pub in the videos was definitely this pub. There was even a glimpse of the van (unburnt) in the videos. Overnight, there had been a performance – a viral performance – and it had descended into this ... mud and abandoned clothing.

She idly scrolled through some of the comments on the videos. A fresh one popped up from a user called HankymenUK.

The Wallopers are a disgrace to the fine Morris tradition. There will be a reckoning tonight. #TrueMorris #KeepTheHankiesFlying

The comment was as interesting as it was cryptic. HankymenUK clearly knew something about these Morris dancers, and there was obviously a plan for something later today, although no hint of what.

She clicked on the user details for HankymenUK. It was the account of something called the Halesowen Hankymen. She was preparing to send them a message when she caught movement out of the corner of her eye. Two women and a man had come onto the green area and were collecting clothes, the women in washing baskets and the man in a black bin bag.

The man met Nerys's eye. "Morning," he said cagily.

Nerys nodded in greeting, while trampled trousers, ripped tops and forgotten underwear were picked up.

"Did everyone just vanish and leave their clothes behind?" said Nerys.

"Oh, just a little accident," said a woman. "We're just tidying up."

"Get this lot washed," said the other. "Dried and returned to their owners, and we'll say nothing more about the whole sordid business."

"Least said, soonest mended," said the first.

Twinkle found another burger and pounced on it. "Seconds!" he whooped.

The man looked at Nerys. "Did your dog just speak?"

Nerys forced a laugh. "Dogs don't speak, do they?"

32

The combined line-up of Djævlehund and the Wednesbury Wallopers trotted through the woods at a lolloping jog. Clovenhoof and Ben both came up with the idea of following Rasmus, Hairy Leonard and Slackpipes Johnson, who were so heavily built that they cleared a substantial path through the branches as they went.

"I guess we're wearing Morris gear for a bit then," said Ben. "My spare clothes were in the van."

"No they weren't," said Clovenhoof.

"Yes they were. You packed me a bag."

"I did, but it didn't have clothes in it."

"What?"

"I filled it with Lambrini and fig rolls. It seemed like a better use of space."

"Bastard."

"I know. RIP Lambrini."

Ben made huffing noises of outrage, but they were all mixed up with the huffing noises he was making as he ran.

"Does it matter where we go?" said Jacob. "They could be waiting for us with shotguns and chainsaws wherever we come out of the woods."

"Things have admittedly taken a slightly odd turn, Jakeyboy, but your mind has gone to a very dark place," said Clovenhoof.

Ben gestured wildly all around. "Hello? Did you check out our current situation at all? A dark place is where we are!"

"Who could have predicted that we'd end up being chased by a mob because they had a good night's entertainment?" said Aksel.

"Yeah, it's weird, isn't it?" said Clovenhoof. "The regular acts must be pretty rubbish."

There was a crashing sound, followed by a shout over to one side.

Clovenhoof and Ben paused and hid themselves behind a large tree trunk. It wasn't quite big enough for both of them, so they jockeyed for position, peering round to see what was happening.

"It's Valdemar, he's taken a tumble," shouted Camille.

The group gathered round.

"It's my ankle," said Valdemar, testing his weight and wincing.

"You were on your phone," said Aksel. "Seriously, there's a time for making calls and there's a time for running away."

"I had to update my wife," said Valdemar. "What if I die

here? She would never know what had happened. Anyway, I think the battery's gone now."

Rasmus and Aksel supported Valdemar under his shoulders and the three of them were able to get moving again; but it was much slower progress now. The group was bunched closer together as they proceeded at walking pace. Treetops loomed over them. The world around was cut into strips of dark wood and strained daylight.

"You had to screw the local girls, Aksel," said Camille. "If you had kept it in your trousers we would not be in this situation. My favourite leather skirt was in that van. I am pretty pissed with you right now."

"Wait, how is this my fault? There was a whole load of screwing going on. Our roadie was the one who told everyone to strip off and get down and dirty with each other."

"I only lay out suggestions," said Clovenhoof innocently. "It's not my fault if my persuasive tongue and sexual pheromones encourage certain behaviour."

Aksel looked as if he wanted to throw further accusations back at him when Marcee shouted a low warning. "Dogs! Can you hear them?"

They all listened hard'. There was the distant yipping sound of dogs who had been unleashed to play, and Clovenhoof knew that 'play' in this context meant 'find them for the angry mob'.

"Let's get going," said Aksel, taking Valdemar's arm again.

"We're just going to keep running forever?" said Camille.

"Out of puff, little girl?" said Clovenhoof.

Camille punched him in the face and put a cigarette

between her lips. Clovenhoof staggered back, clutching his bright red hooter.

"That's for the sexist attitude, asshole," said Camille, "I did a two-week training course with the Israeli Defence Force, for your information."

"Motherfu—"

She punched him again. "And that's for my favourite bass drum. Anyone else want a go? It's very therapeutic."

Clovenhoof was about to open his mouth again when Camille raised her fist and said, "I lost at least ten pieces of kit in that fire. Just so you know."

Clovenhoof decided that silence and not having a broken nose was the better course of action.

Camille waved a hand in the direction they were running. "This forest will come to an end at some point. Who knows what's beyond? Mountains, cliffs, raging rivers?"

"Yorkshire is not well known for its dangerous terrain," said Ben, gesturing to Clovenhoof to give him a drink. Ben wasn't a fan of outdoorsy exercise at the best of times, but being chased by dogs and armed men made it particularly stressful. Who knew what horrors still lay ahead of them? And this was really the worst way to start a Saturday morning. "Anyone else had their morning routine disrupted by all of this?" he asked.

"Understatement," said Slackpipes Johnson with a weary headshake.

"Ben needs a shit," said Clovenhoof.

"Jeremy!"

"It's true, isn't it? Every morning. Kettle on, Weetabix

breakfast. Plop plop sploosh, Ben drops the kids off at the pool. I hear it through the wall."

Ben tried to act dignified. "There's nothing wrong with regular bowels," he sniffed.

"Maybe there's something useful to be done there," said Jacob.

"Like what?" said Valdemar.

"Would the dogs be attracted to the, er, smell?"

A small part of Ben wanted to curl up and die. "No, I don't think—"

"Brilliant idea!" said Clovenhoof. "So we put it somewhere weird to throw them off the actual scent? We need to rub a badger in it and then send it off somewhere so they follow it instead of us."

"Have you even seen a badger?" asked Ben. "I mean, ever?"

"Of course!"

"A live badger."

"The ones that sleep at the side of the road? No? Okay, fine. How about up a tree?" asked Clovenhoof.

"What?"

"Shit in a tree."

Ben was horrified. "How on earth am I supposed to—"

"You don't have to *be* up a tree, just throw it there afterwards," said Jacob. "Do it on a leaf or something."

As Ben sloped off into the undergrowth he heard Clovenhoof challenging the idea. "A leaf? How on earth does that work? The leaves here are tiny. If we'd got rhubarb plants or palm trees then we might be in business. Are your insides even working properly if you can fit it on an itty bitty little leaf?"

Ben found a secluded spot and delivered his missile onto a handful of leaves, then he lobbed it high into the branches of a massive oak tree. He shuddered with horror at the whole idea. The books containing Lois were zipped up inside his jacket, and he was glad she was shielded from the indignity. He trotted back to join the others. "All done."

He brushed his hands on his trousers, feeling no less grubby than before. "Let's make a move and never speak of this again."

The morning was not yet done and Ben wondered if the day could get any worse.

33

A scent caught Twinkle's nose. (He might have wanted to think of himself as a 'Craig' – or maybe a 'Darren' or possibly a 'Gareth' – but in his heart of hearts he still called himself Twinkle.) It began at the edge of the grassy area by the pub and went off into the woods beyond. Dozens of people had passed this way in the last few hours, all bearing a hot, sweaty, meat scent within them, but in the midst of that tapestry of smells was the goaty funk and softer aroma of Clovenhoof and Ben, respectively. Twinkle had known the two of them for most of his life and had much appreciated Clovenhoof's odorous contributions to their shared home. Most humans devoted chunks of their life to banishing quality smells, masking rich and informative aromas with floral chemical guff. Not Mr Clovenhoof. Clovenhoof's flat was like a vast library for the nose. Twinkle could read almost every week of Clovenhoof's life by some small stink here or great guff there. The man knew how to lay on entertainment for a dog.

Twinkle sniffed at the trodden earth again. Yep, the unmistakeable body odour of one Jeremy Clovenhoof esquire.

"Oi, sweetheart. They've gone this way," he said.

"Yeah, hang on," said Nerys, distracted. "I'm just going to get in touch with these Hankymen people. They seem to be meeting up with this Morris gang tonight. Maybe we can head them off at the pass."

"Nah, you don't understand. Trail's going cold, innit?" Which was not exactly true, but Twinkle was keen to get in pursuit.

"A minute, all right!" she snapped, still staring at her phone. "And no talking in front of people!"

Twinkle snorted in derision and went off to follow the trail anyway.

There were a few clear trails through this woodland, but this was no park. Many a time, Twinkle had been taken to the huge Sutton Park near their Boldmere home where there were acres upon acres of land, and all manner of thrilling turds to sniff at. There was the usual dog crap and bird shit, but there was also sheep and rich dungy horse turds, and even deer. All chuffing amazing, while the park was bigger than one dog could explore in a single day, but ultimately, it was still parkland. It was managed and sculpted and arranged to suit human needs. There was no wilderness to it. A dog could hardly access his inner wolf in such a place. But here...

He was less than a hundred metres into the wood before

that true wilderness stink was upon him. Ancient earth, rotting vegetation, and best of all, the low level hum of a million things which had died here over the centuries. It was rich and beautiful; a homecoming of sorts.

Twinkle raced with joy through narrow paths, leaping over large tree roots which burst through the earth, scrambling awkwardly over the largest of all. This place was a Valhalla, a Happy Hunting Ground for all dog-kind.

He paused to check the smell trail. As he looked up, he saw a grey squirrel in the tree above, frozen, staring at him.

"What you fackin' lookin' at?" said Twinkle.

The squirrel scarpered. Twinkle chuckled.

The scent trails of many humans followed a general direction, although some quickly branched off. Clovenhoof and Ben's trail diverged from the main body less than a half mile into the trees. It swiftly turned to one side and hung around in an stand of bushes for quite some time. There was the rich, fruity toot of Ben's shit nearby. Twinkle knew all of his housemates' droppings very well. Oh, they could shamefully hide them in their human toilets and spray their air freshener, but nothing could prevent Twinkle getting an olfactory glimpse of their doings. Only Clovenhoof was considerate enough to let his bob around in the toilet bowl like stinky brown fish for Twinkle to enjoy. In many ways, the old devil was a very considerate gent.

The mass of humans had been here. Twinkle could smell that they had a pair of dogs with them, who had also appreciated the shit stink and left urine markers on the trees as quick reviews. A decent dog community thrived on good, piss-based communication.

Twinkle raced on (and, yes, a part of his mind registered that he'd left Nerys a mile or more behind now, but he knew she'd understand that when a dog had a calling, it had to go). The trails divided up further, but the handful of humans with the dogs were firmly on Ben and Clovenhoof's trail.

He pursued it onwards.

34

Eltiel was an angel, brought into existence in the first seconds of creation. In fact, created so early in the process that he existed even before the Almighty had created the notion of time itself. He was a being of pure energy and purpose, an extension of God's will. He might wear the superficial outward appearance of a human being, but he was not human in any sense. He did not need food or any sustenance. He could walk in frozen wilderness or baking desert and feel no ill effects. He did not tire, he did not ache, he had no need for sleep.

And yet ... after an entire night of driving round this landscape, where farms and villages and far too many roads dissected the beautiful landscape the Good Lord had set down, he was certainly something. It couldn't be fatigue, it couldn't be boredom. Conceptually, these things meant nothing to him. But he was definitely ... something.

He had created a map of the area on his stone tablet, and

many villages were now stricken through with golden crosses. Their search for signs of the naked Morris dancers was, of necessity, widening.

He stifled a yawn. Angels *did not* yawn.

"Oi, oi, what's this?" said Rutspud, nodding ahead to where three men clustered at the side of the road. One of them was bent over double and vomiting on the verge.

"Oh, dear," said Eltiel. "Plague victims?"

Rutspud gave him a look. "How long has it been since you properly walked the Earth?"

"Oh, I do it as little as possible. Humans are so *bucolic* aren't they? Should we help them?"

"I think we should stop and ask why one of them is carrying a lawn strimmer and the other is carrying a clothes pole."

"You think it's relevant to our search?"

"Like I said, stupid weird shit is Clovenhoof's modus operandi. Never ignore stupid weird shit." He pulled up at the side of the road.

Eltel got out. "Hello, gentlemen. Is everything all right?"

The puker looked up, attempted to give Eltiel an 'ok' sign and promptly threw up again.

"Just a little local trouble is all, officer," said the one with the lawn strimmer.

"Is that so?" said Rutspud, strolling round from his side of the vehicle in his small copper's uniform. "I'm Constable Rutspud. PC Eltiel and I are on the search for some wanted criminals."

The lawn strimmer man belatedly tried to hide

offensive weapon behind his back. "Wouldn't know anything about that, officer," he said.

"Really? Bloke we're looking for is a known troublemaker. Performs acts of public indecency. Often while intoxicated. There's been reports of some naked Morris dancing in the area."

The men looked at each other. Not the one vomiting: he was still crouched on the ground and looking very sorry for himself. As well as the vile vomit stench coming off the man, he also seemed to smell of something far more earthy.

"It's the bloody Satanists," Clothes Pole whispered to Lawn Strimmer.

"Satanists?" said Eltiel.

"They drugged us," said Lawn Strimmer. "Threw their weird drugs on the fire; made us drink from their weird bottle."

"You've seen the weird bottle?" said Eltiel.

"I thought it was just water," said Clothes Pole. "But they used it to control our minds."

"I don't think Lilith's Tears works like that."

"It's the *only* explanation for what happened," the man insisted. A look passed between the two standing upright that said this very phrase had been agreed upon and there was no way they were going to change their minds on the matter.

"After their debauchery they tried to run off," said Lawn Strimmer. "We were, er, following them to make sure they left the area."

"You were trying to catch them?" said Rutspud.

"But you wouldn't believe what they did in the woods!"

"Oh?"

"Booby traps in the trees."

"What kind of booby traps?" said Eltiel.

"Not sure I want to say in front of Jim's lad here. An unpleasant business."

"If you know anything at all that can help us apprehend them then you must tell us," said Rutspud.

Clothes Pole sighed. "Human excrement in the trees, officer."

"Human...?"

Lawn Strimmer nodded solemnly. "It brought the dogs right up to it, then Jim's lad here tried to climb up and..."

The lad on the ground retched again but there was nothing left for him to produce.

"Got himself covered in it," said Clothes Pole.

Lawn Strimmer did a mime of his face and mouth being drenched.

"No lad should have to suffer this indignity," said Clothes Pole.

Lawn Strimmer bent to put a consoling hand on the sick man, then hesitated in revulsion and decided not to.

"And where did this all happen?" said Rutspud.

"Bishop Monkton. Two mile down the road."

"And the, er, miscreants?" said Eltiel. "The man with the bottle?"

"Through the woods. Towards the River Ure."

Eltiel automatically stepped towards a track leading into the woods.

"PC Eltiel," said Rutspud. "We shall go to Bishop Monkton."

"But Clovenhoof and Lilith's Tears are this way," said Eltiel.

"*Somewhere* in that direction. And we can't just drive a car into the woods."

"We're hot on their heels."

"We don't have a bloody clue where their heels are right now. We go to Bishop Monkton, find clues and make a decision."

"While the trail goes cold?" He heard a dog barking in the woods. "Do you have dogs tracking them?" Eltiel asked the men.

"Best sniffer dogs in North Yorkshire."

"That's decided then," said Eltiel and strode into the woods.

"PC Eltiel!" Rutspud shouted.

Eltiel spun in his heel and glared at Rutspud. "You heard them. Satanic rituals! Debauchery! It's getting horribly out of hand! You take the car to Bishop Monkton, do your detective thing if you want to. Maybe we'll catch them in a pincer movement!"

Eltiel strode on, pushing through damp undergrowth, heading towards the point from where the barking had seemed to come. And although Rutspud called for him several times, Eltiel pushed on. He was creature of pure energy and purpose and he had job to do.

35

Clovenhoof was hungry. He was also thirsty, but he realised that he was probably also in mourning for the bottles of Lambrini which had been destroyed when the van exploded.

"Anyone got any snacks?" he called.

Nobody did.

"What about foraging?" said Jacob. "Our ancestors would have simply lived off the land. Nature's bounty is all around us."

"There is no bounty here," said Camille. "We need to make our way to find other people. The sort who don't want to attack us. Someone must have a working phone, no?"

Jacob had some battery left. "But I need to conserve it. The Morris Meet-Master is going to announce the location of the contest any moment now."

"They call me the Meat-Master," said Clovenhoof with a lascivious hip wiggle.

"We cannot miss out on this contest," insisted Jacob.

"Just show us where we are," insisted Camille.

The gang gathered around the tiny screen as Jacob found a map of their location. "So we are here."

"We see the big red pointer, Jacob," said Marcee.

"There is something over there," said Jacob, zooming in to a small cluster of buildings. "It's about three miles away."

"Yay," muttered Valdemar, whose ankle had swollen considerably.

"It should be easier to walk once we get to this point here," said Jacob. "See how there is a stream going almost directly there? We should be able to walk along it, so we won't miss it."

Clovenhoof eyed the route and shrugged, as did the others. "Yeah, go on then. Lead the way."

"Turning the phone off to conserve battery," said Jacob. "If we ever get out of here we still need to get transportation to the competition."

"Bizarre grudge match," said Clovenhoof.

Jacob led the way through the woods. "It's not a bizarre grudge match. It's a matter of honour."

"The Hankymen have got some justice coming their way," said Marcee.

"Hankymen? Is this the dirty laundry you mentioned?"

Marcee looked at Jacob, but he just shrugged.

"Fine, I'll explain," she said. "You need to understand the background though. You've got us, the Wednesbury Wallopers, then you've got the Halesowen Hankymen, who have always hated us. We've always been better supported, more successful and much cooler than them, you see."

"Cooler? Holy shit, they must take lameness to a whole new level," said Camille.

Marcee carried on, ignoring the remark. "This rivalry goes back a very long time. It's tied into a game of Shrove Tuesday football that's been going on since medieval times. Mostly it was banter, nothing serious, but the recent problems go back to a sponsored event last spring. The winner would get a set of handkerchiefs edged with genuine vintage Nottingham lace."

Marcee eyed Camille and looked fiercely round at the group. "Now you might think this all sounds a bit small-time, but it was the first time in *years* that someone outside the Morris community took an interest in us. It was all anybody could talk about in the weeks leading up to it. The prize was offered by a local haulier firm, and they had us dance in their truck yard for the prize. It was magical. All the trailers in the yard were strung with lights, and the staff from the canteen came out to watch."

Clovenhoof wondered how magical a truck yard could really be, but he kept his mouth shut.

"We danced up a storm, let me tell you. We'd practised a load of new routines and it went perfectly, every last step. Well, right up until one of the trailers had its rear door swing open. It swung open and shut again, right? Nobody else saw it apparently, but it knocked our Slackpipes Johnson clean off his feet and cost us the competition."

She looked around at them all. "It had to be an inside job. One of the Halesowen Hankymen sabotaged us."

"Rufus Dandy," said Jacob bitterly.

"Ru-who?" said Clovenhoof.

"Rufus Dandy, the leader of the Hankymen. He's always had it in for me," said Jacob. "Ever since we beat them at the Netherton All-Comers event in twenty-eighteen."

"Your nemesis is called Rufus Dandy? This gets better and better!" Clovenhoof rubbed his hands together.

"And when Slackpipes took a tumble, the Hankymen won the handkerchiefs. There's been nothing but fierce hatred between us since then."

"It hurt a lot, and no bugger believed me," said Slackpipes Johnson. "They all laughed and said I must have been on the pop."

"You had been on the pop," Hairy Leonard said.

"Not the point!" said Slackpipes.

"So what's the situation now?" asked Clovenhoof.

"When we met you on the road, we said that our side was reduced because of food poisoning. We strongly suspect Rufus and the Hankymen were behind it somehow," said Jacob. "We've lost Tommy Brownshoes, Jazzhands Clements and Mr Samuel Sanders. Top, top men."

"Our chances against the Hankymen are slim at best now," said Marcee. "Half our gear gone. My accordion!"

"So when we get to this event we take these Hankymen out," said Clovenhoof.

"Like, for lunch?" asked Hairy Leonard.

"I mean a tactical strike, man," said Clovenhoof. "Something subtle like carpet bombing them with drones."

"No," said Jacob.

"Well..." Marcee began.

"No. Definitely no violence," said Jacob. "We maintain the moral high ground. We win the contest fair and square and show them there is nothing to be gained by being horrible."

The group was silent for a long moment.

"Are you fucking joking?" Camille said, incredulous. "There is everything to be gained by you being horrible. You will wipe the fucking floor with them and you do not hold back if you find a way to bring them pain." She looked round at the trudging walkers. "Am I not right?"

"Yeah!" came a ragged chorus. Slackpipes Johnson punched the air.

It started to rain and they realised that not one of them was equipped for wet weather.

"Can I have your jacket?" Camille asked Ben. Clovenhoof actually saw her smile and assumed Ben would hand it over immediately, unable to resist.

"Sorry, no. I need to keep something dry." Ben tapped his chest.

"So much for gallant men," Camille huffed.

"I thought you'd be all for equality between men and women," he said.

"Use the patriarchy, smash the patriarchy. It's all the same fight," she said.

"What you got in there anyway, Ben?" asked Clovenhoof.

"It's some books I need to look after," said Ben.

"Ha! Just when I though the Morris dancers were the biggest nerds on this walk."

The rain deepened and the group trudged with shoulders hunched, speaking only to complain that they were cold and wet.

"I think I want the dogs to catch me now," muttered Hairy Leonard. "Least it'd be a distraction from this shit."

At the head of the group, Jacob came to a sudden standstill. "Ah. Interesting."

He said it in a way that made Clovenhoof's ears automatically translate it into "Oh crap, what now?" Clovenhoof trotted up to see what it was.

"I told you there'd be cliffs," said Camille.

"It's not exactly a cliff," said Ben. "It's more of a..."

The woodland came to a stop at the edge of a very steep drop where the eroded land fell down to a river. Bank or cliff, the difference seemed immaterial to Clovenhoof. It was a long way down with almost no hand or footholds.

"Is that the stream we were looking for, down there?" he asked.

"I think so," said Jacob.

They all stood in a line, peering over.

"What's is it? Something like twelve metres down?" Aksel said. "It looks like there's more of a slope further up, we could maybe scramble down that."

"Twelve metres of scrambling?" said Valdemar. His foot was so swollen now that his shoe was tied around his neck. It bumped off his chest as he moved. "Not gonna happen."

"This is stupid," declared Marcee. "Why are we here? Why are we doing this?"

Ben jerked his thumb over his shoulder. "The angry villagers. The dogs."

Marcee stamped her foot. "We are law-abiding citizens re being hunted in the woods. Why on earth are we this weird Rambo game and not calling the police?"

"Cannabis," said Clovenhoof.

"Yeah," several others nodded.

"We stole a lot of weed," said Aksel.

"No! I did nothing wrong!" said Marcee. "I want to be dry and warm and far away from all of you. We need to prepare for the contest and I need a new accordion."

"Hang on, we didn't do anything really wrong either," said Clovenhoof. "Yet here we all are." He put on a gravelly voiceover style. "Fugitives, on the run for a crime they didn't commit."

"I'm going to see if I can find a path," said Aksel determinedly. "If it works for me then you can all follow, yeah?"

"You'll fall," said Jacob.

Aksel walked along the edge of the cliff, looking for the best place to start. "Hm, I reckon it's one of those things."

"What things?" asked Ben.

"One of those things where you need to step out with a little faith. My feet will find the path if I let go." He got down onto his stomach and wriggled feet-first over the ledge.

"We could just walk along the cliff until we find something better," said Ben.

"My feet will find the—" Aksel's words were cut off as he dropped. There was a distant yell of pain.

They all looked over the edge and saw Aksel at the base of the cliff in a crumpled heap.

"Fuck!" said Camille, staring down at him.

"Aksel!" called Rasmus. "Get up!"

Aksel didn't get up. His hand waved weakly.

"Let's see if there is a better way," said Marcee, all trace of moaning gone from her voice, replaced by cool pragmatism. She pointed at Ben. "Left or right?"

"Right," said Ben.

"Even though it's in the opposite direction to the one we want? Why?" asked Marcee.

He waved airily. "The general lay of the land?"

Marcee didn't question him. "Come on everybody."

"Stay there, Aksel!" called Valdemar unnecessarily and limp-hopped along with the rest of them.

Clovenhoof reckoned they'd walked a quarter of an hour before they reached a point where there was a bank low enough for them all to scramble safely down and follow the stream back to where Aksel had fallen.

However, when they reached that point, he was nowhere to be seen. There was only a patch of flattened grass where he'd fallen.

"He has been taken by wild animals," said Rasmus.

"What kind of wild animals?" said Slackpipes Johnson.

"I do not know what predators you have here."

"Well, this isn't Denmark," said Slackpipes. "We don't have any wolves and stuff. There's nothing here more dangerous than badgers."

"And we don't mean the kind you find sleeping at the side of the road," said Clovenhoof.

"But you do have serial killers," said Camille.

"And dangerous dogs," said Hairy Leonard.

"Statistically, the most dangerous animals in the UK are cows," said Ben.

Marcee looked at him. "You think Aksel has been taken away by cows?"

"This is a good thing, yeah?" said Valdemar. "It means he got up and walked away? There's no blood on the ground, so...?"

"Did you just hear something?" Ben asked, straightening up from examining the ground. "Like a faint roaring sound?"

They continued alongside the stream, everybody hearing a faint, low level sound that seemed to draw nearer.

They rounded a bend and saw Aksel. He was draped across the rear platform of a quad bike puttering up the shallow far bank of the stream and up across grassy fields. The grey-haired rider was clearly aiming for a group of stone buildings beyond a shallow rise.

Clovenhoof cupped his hands to his mouth and hollered. Other joined in, but with the rain and distance, and the noise of the vehicle, there was no chance they could be heard.

"At least he's been rescued," said Valdemar.

"By a serial killer," said Camille.

"I think that was a woman," said Jacob.

"Hey. Women can be serial killers too," said Camille.

"Unlikely," said Clovenhoof. "She's probably just some in-bred hillbilly cannibal woman."

"Or a witch," said Rasmus.

"Yeah, or a witch," Clovenhoof agreed. "Let's go find out."

Soaking wet, they traipsed on.

"If the witch has a warm oven in her gingerbread cottage, I'm going to climb straight inside," said Camille.

Ben tutted. "Now you've made me hungry for gingerbread."

36

F uming at the impetuousness of angels everywhere, Rutspud steered into the car park of the Dodgy Duck pub in Bishop Monkton. There was no one around. He hopped out of the hire car and crossed the grassy area by the pond. There was trio of ducks floating on the pond – horrible fluffy creatures – but his distaste for them was a droplet of water compared to the boiling irritation he felt for Eltiel.

And despite the angel's foolishness, Rutspud's ire was limited to irritation. Rutspud never felt hatred. He had realised, aeons ago, that he had no use for hatred at all. For a start, hatred required energy, a form of mental investment, and a demon who wanted to survive the violent politics of Hell needed to conserve his energy for more important things. Also, he'd never really found anything worthy of true hatred. To hate something was to attach blame to it, and in his long, long experience no one was ultimately to blame for the things they did. Nearly everything that might be hateworthy could basically be blamed on gross stupidity. Eltiel was a prime example. The angel had the wits of an ant and yet had spent his entire existence in the cosseted comfort of the Celestial City, constantly being told that he was one of God's special little angels. It was no surprise he might stride off unhelpfully into a forest and abandon Rutspud.

No, if Rutspud had any hatred in him at all, it was reserved for himself – hatred that he underestimated the hare-brained idiocy of the numpties all around him.

He walked across the grass and circled the cold ash remains of a large fire pit. All around it the turf had been churned to mud by hundreds of feet. But there was no evidence of naked Morris dancers or debauched Satanic rituals or, most critically, Mr Jeremy Clovenhoof.

"Twinkle!" came a distant cry.

Rutspud's large ears twitched. Twinkle?

The shout came again. "Twinkle!"

Rutspud was better with human voices than he was with faces and his mind immediately leapt from thoughts of Twinkle to the dog's human owner, Nerys Thomas. Apart from the Boldmere barman, Lennox, she was the only other human of Clovenhoof's acquaintance who saw Rutspud for the demon he was. She owned the flat above Clovenhoof's. Human relationships were complicated things, and describing her as Clovenhoof's friend was not quite right. It had struck Rutspud more than once she seemed to be more of a self-appointed probation officer when it came to Clovenhoof.

He scampered across the grass towards the sound.

Not far down one of the trails leading into the woods stood Nerys Thomas.

Rutspud approached from behind and put his hand to his mouth to cough and draw her attention, when her own hands cupped around her mouth as she bellowed for her dog. Rutspud let the echoes fade before doing his discreet little cough.

Nerys jumped, looked round, then looked down. The worry on her face was replaced by surprise. "Oh, all Hell has arrived," she said. "Things must be going to shit."

"Greetings," he said.

"It's Rutspud, isn't it?"

He was tempted to do a little bow.

"Why are you dressed as a tiny old fashioned police officer?"

Rutspud raised expressive eyebrows. "The old fashioned police officer look is the fault of an idiot angel I've recently lost. Any tininess is, well, me."

"I've lost my dog," she said.

"Is this the talking one?"

"You know?" she said.

He nodded. "That's why we're here. We need to find Clovenhoof and the dog before anything bad happens."

"Bad as in...?" She waved her arms to underscore the question.

Rutspud didn't want to mention any of Eltiel's dire predictions about chaos and bodily fluids. It wouldn't be helpful, plus it gave the angel too much credit.

"Twinkle's not going to ... explode or anything, is he?" said Nerys.

"Are you serious? Why would a dog explode? I mean, I'm sure you wouldn't want him to, but – if he did – I think I'd want to be there to see it. No, no, I'm talking more generalised badness. I need to find Clovenhoof. And the dog. And probably the angel. In that order."

A wretched bitterness came over her face. "I've lost him. My poor brave lad is lost and alone in the woods."

"Well, maybe we can find him, eh?" said Rutspud.

"Can you track animals?" she asked as they started to walk. "Like with your demonic senses?"

"Demonic senses? Er, no, lady. I cannot. If I had a workshop, I might be able to cobble something together, but for now, let's just wander and see what we see."

37

There were a few wrong turns on the way, but Twinkle, running as fast as a small dog could, closed in on the other dogs. They were a considerable distance ahead of a drawn out, noisy line of humans, who appeared to be armed with spades, rakes, golf clubs, and even one with a long-handled croquet mallet. The mood, to Twinkle's ears, seemed to be burning anger, tempered with boredom and damp misery.

The dogs up front were a pair of lolloping, brown-furred foxhounds, making good pace with their noses close to the ground. Twinkle fell in beside them and joined in the sniffing.

"Oh, yeah," he said. "You've got Jeremy's scent there good an' proper, mate."

The foxhounds leapt back in surprise. Twinkle carried on, looking back for them to join him. "Come on. While the scent is hot, lads."

The older foxhound growled at Twinkle.

"What?" said Twinkle.

The other bounded around in panicked circles before joining in with the growling at a safer distance.

"Oh, the speakin' thing?" said Twinkle. "I know. You 'ave to larf, don't ya? I'm as surprised as—"

The older one set to barking. Not just barking, but lips-drawn, fangs-gnashing kind of barking. The 'I'm going to rip your face off' sort of barking.

"Come on, lads!" a human shouted from twenty yards back down the curving path. "They've found something!" This was followed by audible grumbles from the hunting party, who probably wished they'd brought lighter weapons.

The foxhounds warily and angrily approached Twinkle.

"No, it's all right," he insisted. "I'm a proper dog. Listen. Arf arf! Arf arf!"

His efforts to blend in with the basic, unintelligent creatures were not working at all. They were snarling and salivating now and, Twinkle belatedly realised, each of them was at least four times his size.

"Fuck!" he yelped and ran. The hounds were on his tail instantly.

Twinkle ran faster than he'd ever run in his long years on earth, but it was never going to be fast enough. He lunged sideways, through a tangle of low brambles, zipped through a stand of nettles and high-tailed it, ducking and weaving through the trees at top speed.

The sniffer dogs' barking receded and fell away completely when the humans shouted for them. Muddy-pawed, and with several green things caught in his fur,

Twinkle collapsed in a tiny heap by the foot of a fat pine tree. He could feel his heart in his chest doing a super-tempo rumba beat. But more than that, his little heart ached.

Twinkle had met nasty dogs before. There weren't many of them around, but he'd occasionally met them in the park, all of them miraculously attached to equally anti-social owners. Those two hounds didn't have a bad dog aura to them, they had turned on him the moment he'd spoken. *Just because he'd spoken.*

"Philistines!" he shouted, although he was still out of breath and it was more a wheeze than shout. "Speech racists!"

They were jealous, he told himself, though he didn't quite believe it. They had gone for him – and they were *truly* going for him – because he was different. It came to him in a moment of clarity there was no reason other dogs wouldn't do the same if they heard him speak.

"One day, all dogs will be like me," he said to no one and everyone.

The words vanished on the breeze. Twinkle slumped on the ground and felt very sorry for himself indeed.

ELTIEL WAS unimpressed with this wood. He'd not been in a proper wood before, at least, not since the time he'd spent in the original Garden of Eden, and he didn't remember Eden being anything like this. Eltiel knew what woods should be like. He'd seen paintings on the matter. Woods were places where majestic trees, ancient and wise, grew to towering heights. Woods were where golden sunlight was dissected into heavenly beams and fell upon the ground in a glorious, natural pattern. Woods were where, at any moment, a beautiful deer might stop for a moment, look round with innocent wonder, then bound off with a graceful energy. Woods were meant to be places of beauty, where the magic of the Almighty's creation shone through.

This wood was clearly defective. For one thing, it was wet. The day's rain clung to every leaf and every tree trunk. To walk through it was to get soaked calves within a minute. On top of that, it was just ... untidy. There was no space for majestic trees and sun dappled clearings because there was stuff growing just about everywhere. It was a wood with zero consideration for the angelic visitor. It was no wonder he hadn't seen any deer coming through; they'd probably find it just as unfulfilling as he did.

Eltiel assumed this was yet another symptom of human waywardness messing with the perfection of the Lord's creation. No God above would want it to look like this: all green and jumbled and chaotic. The Good Lord would want neat and orderly forests, and, if there was a little less wilful destructiveness from humans, maybe things would start to look a little nicer.

He glanced at the mud coating the toes of his shoes. It was clear no one had cleaned up in here in months!

But Eltiel was a filled with resolve, so he marched on into the woods. Clovenhoof and the bottle of Lilith's Tears were close. He felt it instinctively. He just needed to forge ahead, the undergrowth would part, and there they would be in front of him.

What was actually in front of him, he realised, was a small dirty dog, sitting at the base of a tree, its head bowed in quiet misery.

"Oh, hello," said Eltiel.

"Piss off," sniffed the dog.

Eltiel tried not to give a start of surprise. He was an angel of the Lord. He should not be surprised by anything, and definitely not by a talking dog. *The* talking dog.

"What's your name?" said Eltiel.

"Twinkle— Fack! I meant to say Craig, di'n't I?"

"Hello, Twinkle. I'm Eltiel."

The dog sniffed back its sadness. If it had been a human, it would have had tears streaming down its cheeks.

"I've been looking for you," said Eltiel.

The unholy dog creature narrowed its eyes suspiciously. "You wanna take me away to be a talkin' dog at a freak circus or summin', huh? Why's yer head all sparkly and glittery?" He jutted up his chin. "Yer one of Jeremy's angel friends, ain't ya?"

"Friend?" Eltiel tilted his head. "I do not think Jeremy Clovenhoof has many friends."

Twinkle swung his head round towards the now distant sound of barking. "They 'ate me, they do."

"Who hates you?"

"The other dogs. They took one look at me and shat their undercrackers. Moment I opened my mouth."

Eltiel nodded in sad agreement and crouched beside Twinkle. "Well, they would, I think. You're an abomination, you see."

"Me? An abomination?"

"A thing that should have never existed. A marriage betwixt the animal and the divine."

"Fack off, glitter-boy. Can't you see I'm suffering enough 'ere?"

Eltiel found himself in an unusual but specific moment. He had experienced it before, though not often. Eltiel was an angel of the Lord and considered himself to be as devout and resolute as any of the Lord's angels. Eltiel knew most angels, seeking only to do their duty, would have conjured a flaming sword from the air and struck the abomination down. An angel should strive for perfection in itself and in the Almighty's creation. Destroying this ungodly horror would have been morally just and a kindness to the creature, and yet ... and yet... In that moment, Eltiel recognised he was not the sword-wielding, horror-killing sort. It just wasn't in him.

He reached out and stroked the mucky creature. "You look a bit of a state, Twinkle."

"Not 'alf. Tell me about it. Up hill and down fackin' dale, I've been. I look like a Wookie what's been dipped in chocolate and left to dry."

Eltiel blinked and conjured a weapon into his hand. It was not a flaming sword, but a long-toothed hairbrush. He began to gently comb the monster's hair.

"What the 'ell are you doin' now?" said Twinkle.

As Eltiel pulled brush through hair, he magicked away knots and tangles and filth. "We shall make you look fabulous," he said. "For whatever may come."

Twinkle hesitated, then said, "All right then. But you better make a bang up job of it, mate."

"Oh, trust me," said Eltiel. "I am the very best."

38

The farmhouse across the river was not constructed from gingerbread as Camille had suggested but of far more ordinary white Yorkshire stone. There was the farmhouse itself, with several large barns and outhouses, then a track leading across the hill and away. As they came up from the river, they passed a sign saying PRIVATE PROPERTY (LITTLETHORPE FARM) – TRESPASSERS WILL BE PROSECUTED.

Further on they passed between two paddocks. One was occupied. Ben expected to see horses, but was disconcerted to see an enormous bull standing in the middle. There was a MIND THE BULL sign on the paddock gate.

A woman with her hair in a steel grey bun stood outside her front door, watching the nine sodden walkers approach. Ben half expected her to produce a shotgun. She had the demeanour of someone who had a firearm within easy reach, but made do with a fearsome expression.

"Well? What's going on here?"

"You have our friend," said Valdemar.

"You mean the long-haired drip with the gammy leg who keeps muttering 'Rock and Roll!' to himself every few minutes."

"Our friend fell down the cliff and we went the long way round to find him," said Jacob.

"Bloody long way round," said the woman. She sighed. "You'd better come in. Don't you be dripping on my furniture, mind."

Ben looked back down to the river. Across the other side, grey sheets of rain moved over the fields and forest. He couldn't see their pursuers in that gloom.

In the large farmhouse kitchen, Aksel was laid out on the table.

"Just like in a cowboy film!" said Clovenhoof. "Although you really should have swept a load of stuff aside with your arm. Shall I find something breakable so we can give it another go?"

"I get the impression you're the annoying sort," said the woman without looking up.

Clovenhoof stayed where he was, but shut up. The woman leaned over and examined Aksel with her hands, checking along his arms and legs. Ben wondered how old she was. Her face was heavily lined, but she moved with fluid ease.

"Well, the leg's fractured," she said eventually. "Not sure how long it will take an ambulance to come up here for a non-emergency, mind."

"How's it a non-emergency?" asked Jacob. "Surely it's serious?"

"He's not going to die from it, Jacob," said Marcee.

The woman nodded in agreement. "You don't have a vehicle?"

"Not one that isn't on fire," said Clovenhoof.

She looked around at them. "Can I just say that you are possibly the worst equipped group of hikers I've ever seen up here. Look at the state of you!"

Ben, along with most of the group had been edging closer to the big Aga cooker, which was giving off a huge amount of heat. Some of them were gently steaming as they dried off.

"Accidental hikers—" Ben started, but Camille nudged him in the ribs and gave him a warning look. "—um yeah. We were just seized with the urge to go a-wandering and here we are."

"Idiots," she said. "Well if you want to stay here for a few hours I've got some parcels that need taking into the town. I can probably get you all down there in the horse box."

"Horse box?" said Ben.

"Yes," she said. "A horsebox. A box for carrying horses. Or bulls in my case."

They all tried to make meek, grateful noises. Aksel looked less impressed than everyone else as he was belly up on the kitchen table, but then the woman looked back at him. "We'd better strap you up, splint that leg."

She disappeared and came back with some lengths of wood and a number of small straps. Within moments she was instructing the others to help Aksel off the table. He was a little wobbly, but that was understandable. He was helped to a kitchen chair and his leg elevated.

"Thank you," he said to the woman. "What's your name, kind lady?"

"Miss Cavanagh," she said.

"Thank you, Miss Cavanagh."

The woman tutted at the unwanted thanks.

Aksel looked down at his leg. "Write on my cast, dudes!" he said to everyone. "Come on! You need to sign it."

"Calm your tits, you moron. It's not a cast, it's two pieces of wood," said Camille.

"I have some jobs to attend to around the farm," said Miss Cavanagh. "Which one of you can be trusted to use the Aga to make a pot of tea for everyone?"

Clovenhoof started to raise a hand.

"Not you," said Miss Cavanagh. She turned to Ben. "You. Make tea for everyone and keep him away from my things. I know trouble when I see it."

Ben was impressed, both at the notion that he seemed trustworthy, and that she recognised Clovenhoof was an irresponsible idiot. Most people only realised that after he'd burned something down; and sometimes not even then. Ben swung into action filling the kettle and approaching the slightly scary stove. He checked the cupboards and found a teapot. There were nice china cups, or mismatched mugs. Which to use? He looked around the room and surveyed the band members, who nearly all sported various injuries from their own misadventures. There were the Morris side, who all looked extremely unhappy that they had been involved in a wild dash through the woods and the loss of their van. And then there was Clovenhoof, who was inching towards the front door, until he spotted Ben watching him. He gave a broad smile and inched back into the room.

Ben selected the mismatched mugs and began to make tea.

The woman readied to go outside. "Dry yourselves off. You smell like wet sheep. But don't be going in my front room and getting your wet on my good furniture."

"We will stay here," said Ben, compliantly.

Miss Cavanagh made a doubtful noise in her throat and departed.

Camille stripped off her wet top and laid it over the covered Aga hot plate to dry. Hairy Leonard and Slackpipes Johnson looked at each other and then, as if by telepathic agreement, stripped off their damp trousers, hung them up, then sat down, pale chubby thighs quivering. The big bassist Rasmus looked at them for a moment before deciding to join the naked legs squad.

Ben undid his jacket and retrieved his precious Lois books (which were only a little damp around the edges) and placed them carefully on an empty shelf.

The group formed small knots around the enormous kitchen, clustered together by the Aga, or bunched at either end of the table.

"This is so cool," said Aksel as Ben handed him a cup of tea.

"Cool?" said Ben. "Really? We're I don't know how many miles away from where we're meant to be ... your instruments are destroyed or missing..."

"But this—!" said Aksel waving his hands at his leg. "This is the kind of thing."

"Breaking your leg?"

"It's nearly good enough."

Ben didn't get it. "Good enough for what?"

"You don't understand," said Aksel. "Ben, my good friend, it's my birthday in two weeks."

"Oh. Happy birthday."

"My *twenty-eighth* birthday." He said it as though it was of huge significance.

"And?"

"So, I'm in the twenty-seven club for only a few more days."

"The twenty-seven club?" said Marcee, clutching her hot tea with both hands.

"I know this one," said Clovenhoof. "All the greats die at twenty-seven years old. Jimi Hendrix, Kurt Cobain, Brian Jones from the Rolling Stones. A lot of drugs and alcohol."

"That's terrible," said Marcee.

"Oh, I'm a big fan of drugs and alcohol," said Clovenhoof gleefully.

Marcee took Aksel's hand and looked intently into his eyes. "Do you wish to die, Aksel? Do you really want to kill yourself?"

"What? No!" he laughed. "But this is the year. This my time to take risks, to live fast. What is there for me after twenty-seven, eh?"

"A long career in Morris dancing?" said Jacob.

"Redundancy from the only job you've known," said Rasmus.

"Parenthood," said Valdemar.

Camille smirked and put a fresh cigarette between her lips. "Forget twenty-seven. Life ends at twenty-five. You're all ghosts to me."

"So jaded, so young," said Marcee. She squeezed Aksel's hand. "You don't need to be on a path of self-destruction, Aksel. Life has so much to offer."

"Are you kidding me?" said Aksel. "The last twenty-four hours has been amazing. We boosted a ton of weed from a lab. We've been chased by a gang of inbred yokels. We played an absolutely killer set last night."

"Hang out with the hoof and all manner of cool things happen to you," said Clovenhoof.

"Yeah, about that," said Camille, smacking her phone. "If the rain hasn't totally killed this thing..." She gave it another smack and it came to life. "Have you seen the videos from last night?"

"Did we do something embarrassing?" said Jacob.

"Have my midnight moves been turned into an on-line sex tape?" asked Clovenhoof hopefully.

"Videos of our performance," said Camille. "They've gone viral."

"Viral?" said Jacob.

"Proper viral. This one, a million views so far."

"What?!"

There was a scramble to look over Camille's shoulder at her phone. Aksel gave a bark of pain as his leg was jarred by a clumsy Slackpipes.

"Who knew the merger of Morris dancing and hard rock could be so popular?" said Valdemar.

"The Morris does weave an unusual magic," said Jacob.

Rasmus sniffed. "Hard riffs and unusual dancing. It is like that time everyone was dancing the floss, or the Harlem Shake."

"This is astonishing," said Marcee. "Millions of people exposed to Morris. You *can* just about hear my accordion in that, can't you?"

A fevered excitement had seized the group. Several people tried to look it up on their devices, although a good portion of them had lost their phones in last night's party frenzy, and of those left, many had succumbed to wet or drained batteries. Ben had lost his some time back, yet he felt remarkably chilled about it. The only thing he would want his phone for was to check up on at Spartacus at the shop.

Thinking about his shop made Ben realise there were books on the massive dresser at the back of the kitchen.

He drifted towards it to check them out. There were recipe books from the time before celebrity chefs, and some more specialised practical volumes about animal husbandry and vegetable growing.

He was drawn to one of the recipe books: *Fancy Free Entertaining*. It promised recipes for parties and special occasions, so Ben flicked through, delighted that there were actual photographs of the dishes. Peas and boiled eggs suspended in clear aspic jelly were such a regular feature he briefly wondered what they tasted like, but he couldn't bend his imagination far enough. He flicked to the centre of the book, where there were several pages of colour photographs, and found suggestions for how you might lay out your room and table for your entertaining. There was a sunken lou featuring a table laid out with a fondue set. Joyous revellers surrounded the table, waving chunks of food on long forks. Ben had never seen a sunken lounge in a real house. He wondered if they still existed. Before he turned over the page his attention was caught by one of the people in the picture. A woman caught in the act of dipping her fork into the fondue, but her carefree smile was focused on the person opposite.

"No! It can't be?" he whispered. He blinked. He double-checked.

He went to the empty kitchen shelf and brought back one of his 3D Lois books, opening it and putting it down beside the picture. The woman eating fondue was Lois! Maybe a decade older, but it was her all right. The same Lois, *his* Lois, at a fondue party! He flicked to the front of the book. It was from nineteen sixty-eight. He flicked through the rest of the pictures and spotted Lois in two more. She modelled a gingham apron in one, demonstrating that a perfect hostess could protect her outfit stylishly without looking old-fashioned, according to the text.

Ben had always regarded himself as a morally sound person. He followed rules and he was considerate of others, but at that moment he knew he couldn't leave the recipe book behind. He snatched it up; another fragment of Lois was now his.

39

Twinkle trotted through the woods, following the still detectable trail of Clovenhoof's scent. The rain, now eased off to a drizzle, had diluted many smells, but in some way had unlocked the full bouquet of Clovenhoof's goaty essence.

"You don't think the bow's too much?" Twinkle said.

"The bow looks lovely," said Eltiel. "You have a problem with pink?"

"Nah," said Twinkle. "Any decent geezer knows how to rock pink."

The angel had brushed out Twinkle's fur with the kind of loving attention any dog would enjoy, and finished the pampering session by tying the long fur on the top of his head with a large pink bow. The angel had magically produced a succession of bows from out of nowhere, and they had both settled on the pink one. It was practical. It kept the hair out of his eyes and, yes, a big pink bow was manly and stylish.

"So," said Twinkle, pausing to sniff a nettle and take a piss, "the bottle what yer after contains these Lilith's Tears, and that's what gave me the gift of the gab."

"Essentially," said Eltiel. "It is the essence of willpower, the anima, the soul which makes humans human. If Clovenhoof has been quaffing it – and I strongly expect he has – then he's probably been able to draw people into all manner of obscene behaviour."

"Right," said Twinkle. "I get ya. But 'ow has willpower got anythin' to do with talkin'? Not that I'm complainin'. It's right useful this talkin' malarkey."

"It's more than willpower, you adorable aberration." Eltiel spread his hands as he explained. "Before humans were put on earth, or before humans were humans, whichever way you want to look at it, all the animals were dumb, like dogs."

"Oi!"

"I'm using the word literally. No speech, no self-awareness, no introspection. The Lord's world was like a perfect piece of clockwork. Everything was in its place and fulfilled its function. All was in balance. Everything. Even the forests were better than this jumbled mess. It all just fitted together perfectly. It was glorious. And then the Lord created man and woman, imbuing them with this special quality. Now there was not only willpower but also speech, and with speech came lies. And with deeper thought came deeper desires, and thence came human congress—"

"What? Like government."

"No. I mean..." The angel made squishy gestures with his hands.

"Bread?" suggested Twinkle.

"No. Intercourse. Conjugal behaviour."

"Oh! You mean a bit of slap'n'tickle."

"Do I? Possibly. And though humans were the Lord's greatest creation, this freedom allows them to pervert His perfect world. Everything became fractured, sloppy and messy, and I for one can't tolerate anything other than perfection."

Twinkle sniffed. "You want my opinion on this, mate?"

"I don't believe the opinion of an unholy interbreeding of animal and soul would be worth much, but you are pleasant enough company, so..."

"I think you've got it all arse about face, mate."

"Oh, really? *You* think *I'm* wrong."

"Not 'alf. This world is bladdy amazin', Eltel me lad. Forests. This wood is exactly how woods should be. Twistin' things, creepin' things, rottin' things, livin' things—"

"No. I've seen paintings. Majestic deer. Crepuscular rays of golden light—"

"Don't know nuffin about crepuscular rays, and a deer or two would be nice, but it sounds like you've been lookin' at pictures painted by blokes what ain't never been in an actual wood before. You think this world is broken? Sure, there's things that need sorting out, like what the fack goes into dog food for one. But, no, this is – whatchercallit? – the best of all possible worlds."

"Are you quoting Leibniz at me?"

"Dunno. Is he the bloke what makes them chocolate biscuits? Nah. If you want my opinion—"

"Which you do appear to be giving me."

"—this whole 'Oh, the world used to be perfect' thing you've got goin' on says more about you than it does about the world."

"Oh. Oh, I see," said Eltiel stiffly. "I didn't realise I was getting a doggy psychotherapist."

"Yer like one of them dog walkers who tells their dog off for gettin' 'is paws wet, or sniffin' other dogs' arses. Things have their nature and you, in yer bleedin' ivory tower, can't cope with that."

"I've never been in an ivory tower," Eltiel retorted. "Think of how much ivory you need. And it's unethical besides. Only a human-like mind would even think of such a concept."

"Fine! Your spotlessly clean, antiseptic roller disco. Whatever."

"Actually, that's quite an alluring concept," said Eltiel.

"There you go. Your problem with perfection is with yerself, mate. Stop blaming the world for being 'imperfect' and stop 'avin' a go at perfectly innocent talkin' dogs."

Eltiel seemed to think on this, and was about to open his mouth to answer when Twinkle shushed him.

"What is it?" Eltiel whispered, dropping automatically into a crouch.

Twinkle crept ahead. They were at the edge of the woods, and beyond the next couple of trees the open ground fell away, rolling down to a fold in the land that was probably a river, before rising up through fields on the other side. More importantly, and somewhat closer, stood a group of people carrying an unusual assortment of garden implements and tools. Two foxhounds barked and bounded about, eager for the humans to follow.

"Them people are following Jeremy an' all," said Twinkle.

"We met a couple of them back on the road," said Eltiel.

"We?"

"Rutspud and I."

"Diamond geezer, that Rutspud," said Twinkle.

"He's a demon of the sixth circle."

"Nobody's perfect. That's what I'm sayin'. Shhh. Listen."

The crowd of locals weren't going anywhere right now, but loudly discussing what to do next.

"I don't care if the trail's clear enough," declared one, not for the first time. "I'm not wading across the river. They've gone."

"What? You give up just like that?" said another. "After what they did?"

"Actually, I'm kinda starting to wonder what possessed me to go chasing across the land with a leaf blower in my hand."

"Lilith's Tears," Eltiel whispered.

"What did I actually think I was gonna do with it?" said leaf-blower. "Blow them away? I feel stupid. And it's heavy."

"Anyway," said another, "the only crossing near here takes you up into old Cavanagh's land."

This drew 'Ooh's of mistrust from many.

"Maybe she put 'em up to this," suggested another.

A huge chap in a red apron declared, "Well, I'm not afraid of her, and I'm not giving up. If their only options are to double-back or go up to Dirty Cavanagh's farm, then I'm getting my van and going round there."

"You'll get short shrift from her, Silas," said one of the others. "She's shot trespassers before."

"Won't be the first time some old bird's waved her double-barrelled at me," said Silas, character undeterred. "Come on. Nevis, you can piss around with your dogs on this side of the river if you wish, but I'm going to get my van."

There was mild dissent and some stretching out of the group as a few left and others hesitated, but ultimately they all departed, heading off back through the woods via a path off to Twinkle's right. The two dogs, disappointed the humans weren't following their trail, trotted after. One glanced towards Twinkle's position at the edge of the woods and bared its teeth.

"Yeah, you piss off too, mate," snarled Twinkle.

"They've gone another way," said Eltiel. "Should we turn back?"

"You wanna find Mr Clovenhoof?" said Twinkle. "Then we follow the trail. Less than an hour old, I swear."

"Very well," the angel conceded. "At least we're out of the woods now."

40

Nerys shouted for Twinkle until her throat hurt and the word had lost all meaning. Twink-kul. Twin-kul. She then alternated between "Twinkle" and "Craig", just in case her dog was making some pedantic point about his chosen name. She wandered through a tumble of interconnecting paths until she had no idea in which direction she was heading.

"That dog appears to be thoroughly lost," said Rutspud, which was a bloody unhelpful thing to say.

She glared at him.

"And maybe we should not lose sight of the main goal of finding Mr Clovenhoof," added Rutspud.

She glared at him even more.

"We are not leaving this wood without my dog," she said simply.

Her eyes latched onto a point of bright colour on the path ahead. A piece of baby blue ribbon hung from a bramble.

She went toward it. There was a yellow ribbon tied into a loose bow a little way beyond it. And a third, silver-white, among the grasses nearby.

It meant nothing to her, but it added some variety to the unchanging woods. Desperation was making her reach for anything as significant.

Rutspud reached out for the blue bow. "Does Twinkle wear a little – ow!" His fingers pulled back as golden sparks flew from the bow.

"What the—?" said Nerys.

Rutspud's mouth set into a resolute line and he gripped the ribbon. It sparked, then flew apart in strands of shimmering yellow light. "This is Eltiel's work," he said.

"The ribbon?

Rutspud snatched up a ball of long wispy fur. "If it wasn't so ridiculous I'd say Eltiel stopped to give your dog a little grooming session."

"Eltiel is with Twinkle?"

"Must be." Rutspud turned round on the hard track. "I honestly can't tell which way they've gone."

"But they're together?" she insisted.

She woke her phone. She'd made requests to join a number of local Facebook groups, and now she'd been admitted she began writing an emotional 'Lost Dog' post. She had the most enchanting pictures of her dog she could find and was contemplating whether to write *Answers to the name 'Twinkle'* or *Answers to 'Twinkle' or possibly 'Craig'* when a message popped up.

It was from one 'Rufus Dandy' and it took her a moment

to realise he was the man from the Halesowen Hankymen group she had tried to contact.

Hi, what do you want to know? he said.

I'm trying to track down the Morris dancers. The Wallopers. You mentioned something about tonight, she replied.

Why do you want to know?

She hesitated. She needed to word this right. Dandy's original comment had mentioned a 'reckoning'.

I need to catch up with them. One of the men with them has done me wrong. Done me wrong? she thought, rolling her eyes at herself. She sounded like a western saloon floozy.

Then you'll be able to catch him tonight, messaged Dandy. *The Meet-Master has sent the location. The dance off is at the Gnome's Bottom in York. It's a brewery. 9pm.*

"Gnome's Bottom," she said out loud.

"What's that?" said Rutspud.

"It's where they are going to be tonight," she said. She looked at the time on her phone. It was nearly half past twelve. "They're going to be at a brewery in York in eight hours or so."

"How far away is that?"

Nerys didn't have a clue, but she'd seen York on some signposts not far outside Harrogate. "Can't be far. Less than an hour."

"There we go," said Rutspud enthusiastically. "We can work with that! Let's get back to the car and head over to York."

"But Twinkle!"

"He's with Eltiel. They'll probably keep each other out of trouble."

Nerys was unsure.

"And if Eltiel is as doggedly on the trail as he claims to be, then when Clovenhoof turns up in this York, your dog and my angel will be close behind."

Nerys didn't like the feel of it. It made her insides twist unhappily, but Rutspud was sort of right. It represented as good a chance to find her Twinkle as anything she was currently doing.

"Fine," she sulked. "Back to the cars."

41

Clovenhoof wanted to look around Littlethorpe Farm. His bandmates were going nowhere for a while, and there were bound to be interesting things in the outbuildings. He managed to slip outside when Ben was looking through some book or other, passed the dogs relaxing in a large kennel, and sauntered across the yard, happy to see that the horse box which Miss Cavanagh had mentioned was massive. They would all fit in it without an issue.

He stopped by the edge of the bull paddock. The massive creature ambled towards him. He hoped it was curious rather than hungry, because it was built like a dumper truck.

"Hello boy!" Clovenhoof said, although he stepped back from the gate slightly. The bull had horns bigger than his own. It was then that he saw a small sign.

GLADIATOR SWAGGERBOI

He looked up at the bull. "Hells bells, is that your name?"

The bull gave a small snort that Clovenhoof took as an affirmative. It almost seemed as if it wanted to be friends. Clovenhoof held out a hand and moved forward. If he stood on the bottom bar of the gate he'd be able to reach over and pet it. He stepped up, and almost fell straight back off again when he heard a massive bellowing from behind.

"Get away from my bull, you imbecile!"

Clovenhoof turned to see Miss Cavanagh approaching with a very angry expression on her face.

"I wasn't going to do anything stupid. I just felt a connection with him. He's a very smart boy, I think."

Miss Cavanagh stood and regarded Clovenhoof. "He is not a smart boy in the sense that it's safe to approach him. If he scented a cow in heat he would batter this gate down in an instant to get at her. He is like three massive gorillas in one big body, but without the brains of a great ape."

Clovenhoof turned back to look at the bull. "I can't pet him then?"

"You are not to go near him at all!" she said. "Go back inside and have some tea."

Clovenhoof turned to go, but she called him back.

"On second thoughts, come with me. I want to keep an eye on you."

Clovenhoof trotted alongside her as she made her way into a large building. It might have passed for a barn, but it had solid walls and there was a substantial lock on the door. She opened it up and went inside.

"This is unexpected," he said as they entered a clean and warm corridor.

She glanced back at him and opened a door to a space that looked like a lab.

"I'm getting déjà vu," said Clovenhoof. "Are you growing cannabis here?"

"Good grief, no," she said.

They walked through the lab and she stepped into a room that was like a small cupboard, lined with racks of computers. Small green lights glowed from within. She flicked a switch and lamps over some of the workspaces flickered on. She sat in front of a monitor and glanced back at Clovenhoof.

"I'm doing some admin. Can you manage to sit down and not touch anything for a few minutes?"

"Sure!" he said, taking the seat next to her so that he could see what she was doing.

She sighed heavily. "Do you work hard at being annoying?"

"No, it comes very naturally. What are you doing, then?"

She pulled a thoughtful face. "Well, I have set up a buying platform for a very specialised product. I'm proud of my work: taking a very lucrative market and finding a way to make it work better, while making some money from it."

"Cool!" said Clovenhoof.

"Some of the orders come to me, because I am also a supplier of this specialised product. It's what I need to do now, fulfil the latest orders."

Clovenhoof grinned, certain it was cannabis. He looked forward to an opportunity to replace his lost stash. "Can I help?"

"You can help by sitting there and being quiet while I print out some labels and delivery notes," she said firmly.

Clovenhoof sat on his hands to prove he could be still. It was a little uncomfortable, as his hand was still glued together. He glanced around the lab, wondering if it was equipped with anything that might help him with that problem, but couldn't see anything useful at all. He decided all of the good stuff was probably in the closed cupboards. He would take a look if he was left alone for a moment.

Miss Cavanagh tapped at the computer and a series of sheets and labels came out of a printer underneath the counter.

"I'm really good at labels," said Clovenhoof. "Once I had a labelling machine and I labelled everything in my flat. I'm a natural, let me stick them on your packages."

"These packages are not only very valuable, they are time sensitive," she said. "If they are not delivered correctly they will become worthless."

"Gotcha. Can I go and get you a cup of tea instead?"

She looked at him sceptically. "Actually that would be nice. Yes, please."

Clovenhoof skipped out of the door and went back over to the kitchen. "Cup of tea for Miss Cavanagh," he demanded.

Ben poured one from the massive pot on the table. "Are you behaving yourself? I was supposed to be keeping an eye on you, but it's taken me this long to work out how to make tea with an Aga."

"Yep. Miss Cavanagh is pleased with my assistance. She is preparing some orders and I've been helping."

Ben's eyes narrowed in suspicion. "Orders for what?"

Clovenhoof whispered behind his hand. "Don't tell the others because they might try and steal it, but I think she is *also* growing cannabis. They're all at it up here. I bet there's some sort of government subsidy."

"Huh? I had no idea," said Ben.

"I know, right? She looks so sweet and wholesome doesn't she?" said Clovenhoof.

"She does," said Ben.

"Anyway, that cup of tea," said Clovenhoof.

Ben pointed at the mug on the table.

"Well, it's not going to deliver itself," Clovenhoof pointed out.

Ben sighed. Valdemar stood on his wobbly ankle. "I shall take it to the old woman. She has been a fine host."

WITH THE ANGEL still shaking river water from his police uniform trousers, Twinkle led the way up the hill on the far side.

"Private Property, Littlethorpe Farm," read Eltiel as they passed a sign. "Trespassers will be prosecuted. Oh, my."

"Nuthin' for us to worry about, mate," said Twinkle. "Yer decked out like the Old Bill. Yer on police business, ain't ya?"

"I suppose."

"This reading business seems kind of useful," said Twinkle. "I ought to give it a go one day."

Eltiel made a doubtful noise. "Language and writing weren't such a great step forward in the old days."

"Is that so?"

Eltiel drew himself up to his full height, preparing to impart wisdom.

"After Adam and Eve used their free will to break the Lord's one rule, after their son had used his free will to murder his sibling, the people of the world became numerous. Language allowed them to co-ordinate en masse and they set about the blasphemous task of building a tower tall enough to reach Heaven."

"What?"

"That is what they did. Speaking one tongue, writing their plans in the language of Adam, they built a tower with the intention of reaching Heaven."

"Why? I mean, I get it. Buildin' a tower to get into Heaven seems a lot easier than all that prayin' and chantin' and givin' money to the church what could be better spent buyin' a chop or two for 'ungry dogs."

"Some say the people wanted to wage war on God."

Twinkle was a dog and could not shrug, but he gave the idea an indifferent head waggle.

"Only by making all the people speak different languages, thus confounding their ability to work together, did the Lord prevent it," said Eltiel. "A single language allowed the wicked to defy their creator and break the rules he set down."

Twinkle sniffed the air and looked at a sign on a nearby gate. "What does that one say?"

"Mind the bull," read Eltiel.

"Mind the bull?"

"Mind the bull." He pointed at another sign. "His name is, apparently, Gladiator Swaggerboi."

"Now, *that* is a crackin' name." Twinkle looked into the field. There was a large beast, barrel-chested and magnificently horned, ambling about the space. "How are we supposed to mind it?"

"Like a childminder minds a child?" said Eltiel.

"Take it to the park and read it stories?"

Eltiel tugged at the edge of the big moustache he'd given himself, then opened the gate. "You go mind the bull and I will speak to the people of the house and see if Clovenhoof has been this way."

"Are you just tryin' to keep me away from the public?"

"You are an abomination, Twinkle," the angel said in his kindest voice.

Twinkle gave a huff. "You are one dodgy geezer, my angel friend. You'd better not double-cross me."

"Heaven forefend," said Eltiel

As the angel approached the large farmhouse, Twinkle went over to introduce himself to Swaggerboi.

42

Clovenhoof's mind was concerning itself with where Miss Cavanagh might be hoarding her secret stash of drugs. He had never realised the north was such a hotbed of illegal drug production. He thought it was all just meat pies and rolling hills. If he'd known there were recreational drugs to be had, he would have come up this way sooner. He decided to be patient, certain he'd find the good stuff if he just kept going.

Valdemar burst through the outer door into the kitchen. "There is someone approaching the farm!" he said.

"Pitchfork-wielding yokels?" said Clovenhoof.

"It looks like a police officer!"

There was a flurry of panicked activity. but Marcee waved her arms. "Again, we've done nothing wrong."

"Speak for yourself," said Clovenhoof.

"I am," she said plainly. "Very well, *I've* done nothing wrong."

The was a ping from Jacob's phone. He looked at it. "The Gnome's Bottom!" he exclaimed.

"Are we talking in code now?" said Clovenhoof.

"The rendezvous for the dancing event tonight. Giles Palmerston-Chuff, the Morris meet-master, has made the announcement. It's in York."

"We have to hide!" said Ben. "We can talk Morris dancing later. I'm not going to prison over a stolen bunch of weed."

"I've done nothing wrong!" Marcee insisted.

"Sweetness, we need these people if we have any chance of success in the competition," said Jacob.

"Prison could be a good look for my profile," said Camille. "I would have to check with the brand management team."

"This is so rock and roll," said Aksel.

"We have to hide!" Ben repeated.

"Upstairs you idiots!" Clovenhoof called. "Quickly!"

The near-dozen of them clattered up the stairs, carrying Aksel and helping other band members whose injuries slowed them down. It wasn't a very large house, so they all crowded into what looked like the master bedroom.

"These floorboards are very squeaky, we need to stay still!" urged Ben.

"Some of us are gifted with the ability to move silently," said Clovenhoof, knocking over a small table as he moved further into the room.

Downstairs, there were sounds in the kitchen. Miss Cavanagh said, "Where have those bloody buggers gone," loud enough to carry through the house.

Clovenhoof was about to answer when there was a sharp rap on the door downstairs.

ELTIEL ADOPTED a pose he thought would suit a proper police officer and popped his conical helmet on his head, just as the door to the farmhouse was opened. An old woman stepped out. She had more wrinkles than a raisin. Eltiel was an angel of the Lord and loved all humans equally, but he really wasn't ready for the appearance of an individual who was so shamelessly old. In the Celestial City, human beings gravitated towards an image of their best selves. Even those who appeared old presented themselves as a spritely, twinkly-eyed sort of old; not as someone with a face like a walnut.

"Er, afternoon, madam," said Eltiel in his best policeman's voice.

The woman looked him up and down suspiciously. "What are you meant to be?"

"I'm a police officer, madam," he said, tapping the insignia on his heavy epaulettes.

"Really?"

"Of course," he said, dangling a wooden truncheon from his hand.

"Oh, yes," she said in an odd voice. "That pretty much clinches it. How can I help you, *officer*?"

"Myself and my colleagues are looking for some miscreants: ne'er-do-wells who have been seen in the area."

"Are you now?"

"Particularly for a gentleman who goes by the name of Jeremy Clovenhoof."

"Odd name."

"He's an odd fellow, madam."

"And exactly what crime is this man wanted for?"

UPSTAIRS, Ben could hear Miss Cavanagh chatting to the police officer below, but their voices were too low for him to make out what was specifically being said. Which just made it all the worse. The Morris dancers and musicians were all stood or crouched in a room which was not really big enough for all of them, frozen in place and forced to wait. And Ben realised he really needed to pee.

He crossed his legs and tried to think calming thoughts. As he did so, he glanced around and saw a stack of what looked like magazines on the dressing table. Peering closer, he realised they weren't magazines, but slender books.

The first one was entitled *Girly Games* and looked so much like the 3D books he had tucked inside his jacket. He reached across and moved the book aside. The one underneath was a copy of *A Bosomy Beauty,* which he already owned. Below that were *Saucy Sunbather, All the Fun of the Fair,* and *Free and Easy.* Book after book of gentle erotica and, as best as he could see, every single one of them featured photographs of his Lois.

"I'm dreaming," he whispered.

Slackpipes Johnson shushed him. There were sounds on the stairs.

"Shit! They're coming up!" squeaked Valdemar. "My baby boy…"

The bedroom opened. Ben grabbed the books in panic, as if their sweet, innocent, nostalgic sexiness could save him.

Miss Cavanagh stood in the doorway with a foul look on her face. "Why are you lot playing silly buggers?" she demanded. Her stern gaze swept the group and settled on Ben with his arms full of books. "I think you all have a great deal of explaining to do!"

IT STRUCK Twinkle that minding a bull was not as easy as it initially seemed. In fact, Twinkle reckoned that, in the scheme of things, childminding was probably an easier job than bullminding. Twinkle thought he'd totally smash it as a childminder. Kids loved dogs. He had a lifetime of stroking, fondling and ear-puling as proof. Plus now, with the gift of the gab, he could branch out into telling stories and jokes. Who wouldn't love that?

But bulls … bulls seemed to be a tough audience. For one, this bull seemed happy enough minding himself, ambling to and fro. What was a jobbing bullminder to do in such circumstances?

Twinkle trotted over. The bull, Swaggerboi, didn't even notice.

"All right, guv'nor," said Twinkle. "Nice gaff you've got 'ere."

Swaggerboi heard that all right! The monster nearly leapt into the air with surprise. It spun on the spot, then had to lower its head considerably to bring Twinkle into its field of vision.

"'Allo," said Twinkle. "How's it goin'?"

Swaggerboi snorted, spraying hot bovine snot from its huge nostrils. Twinkle couldn't tell if it was a snort of fear or anger, but there was certainly a powerful note of alarm about the beast. It reared.

Heavy hoofs mushed down into the earth just in front of Twinkle.

"Careful, mate. Don't want to crush me under yer size nines, do ya?"

But Swaggerboi seemed to want to do precisely that. It stamped, rearing with the intention of bringing its iron-boned legs down on the spot where Twinkle stood. Twinkle jumped aside and the bull twisted to follow him.

"Oi! Don't be a tosser, mate!" Twinkle snapped. A moment later he was forced to run as the bull came at him again.

One of the key perks of being a small dog was the ability to go from a standing start to full pelt in minimum time. Only rabbits, squirrels and other furry prey could match a determined terrier for sheer acceleration. A bull was just a lumbering truck compared to a small, turbo-charged dog. That being said, a terrier's top speed wasn't necessarily much higher than that of a bull, and Twinkle would be the first to admit that, as a dog of action, he was built for sprinting, not stamina.

They did two circuits of the paddock before Twinkle realised Swaggerboi was not going to give up, despite Twinkle throwing him entreaties and curses in equal measure. In his head, he was also throwing an equal number of curses at Eltiel. Next time, Twinkle would do the investigating cop routine and the angel could play tag with barnyard animals.

Hoofs pounded the churned earth just to Twinkle's left. Twinkle jigged right, tumbled, rolled, and came up with barely a pause before running straight for the five bar gate. There was wire mesh covering most of the gate, but there was a small gap beneath the lower edge. If a dog was fast and agile and lucky...

He bounded up, felt the wood slats brush his back, and made it to the rough track on the other side. Hot air burning his aching lungs, he turned to see the bull collide with the gate. It wobbled violently and swung open.

The bloody angel hadn't put the gate back on the latch when he'd let Twinkle through!

Swaggerboi spun on the track and angled round to find Twinkle.

"Twat!" yelled Twinkle and ran on.

43

B en once more joined the group in the kitchen. He looked around warily.

"I sent that so-called police officer packing," said Miss Cavanagh. She said it matter-of-factly, making it clear she cared little for her house guests one way or the other.

"'So-called'?" said Camille.

Miss Cavanagh put the kettle back on the Aga. "Aye. He was no bloody police officer. In fact, I called the local bobbies and told them there was some joker making pretend house calls in a fake police uniform." She glanced at Clovenhoof. "I believe he was looking for you."

"I'm a very popular chap," grinned Clovenhoof. "Animal magnetism, I think it's called."

Miss Cavanagh was having none of it. "Who are you running from and why? And I'll thank you to put my books down," she said to Ben.

Ben had so many questions, but Aksel stepped in with a response to her question.

"We are musicians. We played a gig at a village nearby. The villagers are now chasing us."

"You were that bad?" said Miss Cavanagh.

"Someone – not us! – threw a large quantity of cannabis on a fire," said Marcee.

"Miss Cavanagh knows all about cannabis," said Clovenhoof with a pantomime wink.

"And we were somehow blamed for any hijinks and lewdness that followed," said Marcee.

"This butcher guy..." said Ben.

The expression on Miss Cavanagh's face changed from one of joyless annoyance to a sort of light-hearted yet vindicated anger. "Silas Carver."

"That's him!" said Valdemar. "You know him?"

"I should do," she said. "He's my nephew. And that boy's never happy. He's a – thingamajig – a fount of suppressed rage."

"Rage, yes," said Jacob. "We very much saw that."

"If you've done something to upset him, he'll follow you to the ends of the earth."

ELTIEL WALKED AWAY from the farm and back down the track, deep in thought. The old woman had been most courteous, yet he felt there had been something odd about their conversation. He'd performed his policeman routine seamlessly. He really felt he was blending in on Earth now, especially since it was clear no one could see his halo – even when it shone around his policeman's helmet, making it look for all the world like a lighthouse perched on his head. The old woman had engaged with him, and there was no reason why Clovenhoof and his companions *must* have passed through this way. But the manner in which the conversation had been brought to a conclusion almost made him feel like the woman was hiding something.

Eltiel resolved to ask Twinkle. The creature might be an unholy aberration which would need to be remedied or destroyed at the soonest opportunity, but the little dog did seem to have an earthy wisdom that might be useful in this situation.

In fact, Twinkle was running towards him right now, at full pelt.

"Run! Run!" the dog panted. "Run!"

Eltiel was about to ask why when he saw the massive bull come skidding round the corner of the track in hot pursuit of the dog.

"What did you do?" Eltiel yelled. "I told you to mind the bull!"

"This is me ... minding bull...!" Twinkle replied in a wheezing scream.

There was no time for further questions. Eltiel had to run or be mown down. He turned and ran back up the track, past the turning for the house itself, and over the crest of the hill where the track turned downwards towards a main road.

A white van was parked on that track. The words SILAS CARVER – PURVEYOR OF FINE MEATS was painted in a flowing black script on the bonnet and side panel. The big man in the red apron who they'd seen with the mob on the other side of the river was standing outside his van and talking into a mobile phone. Next to him was a pair of men, one carrying a garden shovel, the other toting a wire-headed broom.

As Eltiel barrelled down the hill towards them, the butcher, Silas, clocked sight of the angel and held out his hand in greeting. "'Scuse me, mate. Do you happen to have seen—?"

He never reached the end of that question. Eltiel raced straight past, Twinkle a blur of fur at his feet. Eltiel didn't look back for the bull. He didn't need to. He could hear the dull and powerful impact of its hoofs on the loose stone.

"Oh, shit!" squeaked one of the men. There was the sound of a van door being hurriedly opened.

Behind Eltiel, Silas Carver gave a wordless roar of panic and ran.

"My nephew he might be," Miss Cavanagh was saying in the kitchen, "but I don't have time for him, and he don't have time for me. Most of the locals don't have time for me."

"Really?" said Marcee.

"People can be so judgemental."

"Oh, I know," said Clovenhoof fervently. "I try to introduce Let It All Hang Out Thursdays at the local Tesco and the backlash I got... The fight against prejudice is a long and difficult road."

Miss Cavanagh didn't pay him any mind. It seemed she had firmly decided Clovenhoof was a person best ignored.

"Why have the locals turned against you?" asked Marcee, adopting a particularly gentle tone, as though she was somehow Miss Cavanagh's therapist.

Miss Cavanagh gestured at the books Ben still held. He put them on the table, then guiltily reached inside his jacket and took out the recipe book he'd 'borrowed'.

"What's this one?" asked Clovenhoof, pointing.

"It's one of Miss Cavanagh's recipe books," Ben said apologetically. "I didn't really mean to steal it, but a woman who's in it is in the old ... erotica books. What are the odds?"

"Quite low, considering," said Miss Cavanagh.

The group looked over the images in the books on the table, both of Lois in the significant library of nude images, and Lois in the saturated colour images in the old cookbook.

"I don't understand," said Rasmus.

"Really?" said Camille, grinning for once. "You haven't seen it?"

"Just because this woman owns a stash of tame pornography..." began Valdemar.

"I prefer to think of them as risqué art photography," said Miss Cavanagh.

"You haven't spotted it, have you?" said Camille. "Men!"

"What?" said Ben.

Camille looked at him. "We are in the presence of a celebrity, Ben." She gestured to the farmer. "Miss Cavanagh – or should we call you Lois?"

Ben stared at the cookbook, then across at Lois riding her bicycle, and then at Miss Cavanagh – whose gaze was also taking in the vintage pornography.

"Really?" said Ben, his mind blown.

Miss Cavanagh raised her eyebrows. "I was very young when I participated in those."

"Oh, this gets better and better!" crowed Aksel. "I've met an aging porn star. How you doin', baby?"

He made kissy motions to Miss Cavanagh. She slapped his broken leg, making him double up in pain.

"My life choices are my own," the old woman said with an imperious pride.

"You are badass," said Camille.

"You've got to admire a woman who lives her life on her own terms," said Marcee.

"Not everyone does," said Miss Cavanagh. "Especially certain prudish relatives. Now, let's get you out of here."

44

On a certain level, Twinkle was impressed that Gladiator Swaggerboi was willing to chase down men and dogs just for the sake of it. None of them had done anything to antagonise the brute, but he still came, stomping, snorting and bellowing, all the way down the track to the road. Eltiel skidded on the tarmac road in his formal police shoes and spun round looking where the hell to go. Twinkle was close behind him.

A little way behind, Silas Carver, a stout fellow probably not used to running at all, was heaving, hacking and swearing in equal measure.

Twinkle glanced back briefly. Swaggerboi was keeping pace easily. Twinkle suspected the bastard wasn't even moving at top speed. The bull might not turn as swiftly as a nippy terrier, but now he was up to a fast cantering speed, that bastard bull looked as if he could keep it up for miles and miles.

Ahead of Twinkle, Eltiel glanced up and down the road, still dithering. He looked straight at Twinkle and held out his arms. Twinkle didn't understand until the moment when, in a pop of multicoloured angelic sparkles, the angel's wings sprung from his shoulders.

Eltiel's knees bent, preparing to jump.

Twinkle leapt into his arms.

Eltiel's legs straightened, his wings extended and...

"*Fuuuuck!*" screamed Silas Carver.

The butcher's eyes were wide in shocked awe as the angel and dog soared straight up. It became a totally different kind of shock and awe as Swaggerboi thundered right up behind him, dipped his head under Silas's rump, and tossed him high into the air.

Twinkle burrowed against Eltiel's chest, but the angel had him tight. Straight up they rose, high above the road and the lush green landscape to either side.

Below, Silas had come down on a gorsy bush, his yells only pausing at the moment of impact. He rolled out of the bush, scratched and hobbling painfully, and looked round in a daze. He saw Swaggerboi turning circles, seeking out his enemies.

"Fuck!" Silas sobbed.

He tugged at his red apron, ripped it off his head and threw it away. Swaggerboi's gaze followed the apron as the wind took it and tumbled it away down the road. Taking advantage of the minor distraction, Silas ran in the other direction, across the road and into the field beyond. It didn't take long for Swaggerboi to turn his attention away from the discarded apron and lock onto the man. The bull began to run again.

On the whipping wind, Twinkle heard the faint shout of "I'm sorry!" come from Silas as he was chased once more.

"I mean the guy was a grade-A muppet, weren't he?" said Twinkle.

"The beasts of the field will turn against their masters," whispered Eltiel. "It's all coming true."

Down below, Silas Carver leapt head first over a stone wall and disappeared from sight.

Twinkle looked up at the angel policeman.

"Mate, thanks for the lift and everythin', but maybe we ought to get back to the ground before someone sees you, eh?"

Eltiel nodded grimly.

"SIT TIGHT. I'll get my things and then we'll set off," said Miss Cavanagh, closing the back door of the horse box. Inside, the ten passengers sat on the straw bales arranged around the interior.

"We've got less than seven hours to get to York," said Marcee, consulting her watch.

"I just wish to be away from here," said Camille. She took her pack of cigarettes from her jacket pocket, stared at the empty interior, and crushed it vehemently.

Ben barely took any of it in. His mind was a rolling mess of confused thoughts. For the last two days he'd been caught up in a fantasy world – a mostly innocent fantasy world – of the wonderful, lovely, carefree naked Lois. It was barely a sexual fantasy. Her nakedness wasn't titillating. Okay, it *was* titillating, but it was more than that. A naked Lois was a Lois with nothing to hide. A naked Lois was a Lois without secrets. Without an interior life of her own, apart from that which involved Ben, her secret caring voyeur. To discover that Lois was really real and not just a set of beautiful 3D photographs was a shattering of that dream scenario. That the real Lois was an octogenarian farmer was the least concerning of all.

The wonderful, perfect, idealised Lois was a beautiful empty vessel, and now it had been filled with unlovely and grim reality.

"Hello? What's this?" said Clovenhoof.

Ben looked over.

Clovenhoof had pulled up a cardboard box from behind the bale he'd been sitting on.

"What is it?" said Valdemar.

"A package addressed to a farm in Scotland," said Aksel, reading over Clovenhoof's shoulder while trying to keep his splinted leg in a straight position.

"This has got to be the drugs she's sending out," said Clovenhoof.

"Is everything about drugs with you?" said Marcee.

"She's sending cannabis through the post?" said Valdemar.

"Looks like it," said Clovenhoof, holding the parcel aloft. "Let's take a look shall we?"

"Why don't we leave it alone?" said Marcee. "She's helping us, isn't she? She's getting us out of here. Barely more than six and a half hours until we need to be performing."

"Smoking weed is good for pain management," said Aksel.

"My ankle still hurts too," said Valdemar.

Clovenhoof pulled off the wrapping around the box and exposed a metal flask.

"That doesn't look like weed," said Jacob.

"Oho! This is obviously how they are getting round the sniffer dogs," said Clovenhoof. He held it up so that they could see the warning labels.

Ben stared. "Liquid nitrogen? Are you sure? That doesn't sound right."

Clovenhoof opened the outer case and peered inside. There were metal hooks extending up over the lip and coldness poured out in a frosty breath.

"It looks cool whatever it is," said Valdemar.

Clovenhoof upended the container and a number of thin straws rained down on the floor of the horsebox. "Huh. It must be some other kind of drug, ready for dunking into a fancy cocktail."

"You are convinced everything is a drug," said Marcee.

Clovenhoof picked up a handful of the plastic straws and slurped out the contents from one. He smacked his lips as he swallowed it down. "Quite a distinctive flavour that."

Aksel leaned over and took some for himself, and so did Valdemar and Rasmus. Hairy Leonard and Slackpipes Johnson shrugged at each other and grabbed the remaining ones. The horsebox was filled with the sound of slurping. Then they all pulled faces at each other.

"Oh man, it tastes so bad," said Aksel, licking his teeth.

Camille sniffed and recoiled.

Valdemar grimaced. "It is – what is the English word – *klistret*."

"Sticky. Gooey," said Rasmus.

"Yes," said Aksel, "like waffle mix."

"Eggy almost," said Clovenhoof, smacking his lips.

"It's bull sperm," said Camille.

Eighteen eyes turn to her.

"What?" said Rasmus, colour draining visibly from his face.

The Frenchwoman sighed. "There is a massive bull in a pen over the other side of the yard. People sell bull's semen so that they can artificially inseminate cows." She looked at Ben, as though he was the most likely to know.

Before Ben could respond, there was a collective heaving. Rasmus burst out of the back of the horsebox before vomiting, but not everyone was so swift. Hairy Leonard and Slackpipes Johnson could do no better than throwing up behind the bales they were sitting on.

"Oh man, I just swallowed bull semen," said Aksel, grinning. "I bet even Ozzy Osborne never did that!"

Clovenhoof belched and wafted a hand in front of his face. "Interesting how it's a little different second time around. Are you all getting hints of aniseed?"

Outside, Rasmus groaned and heaved again.

"Oh, God, what have you done?" whispered Ben.

"Bull semen," said Clovenhoof. "I think we've already established that."

"I mean, what have you *done*. You know how much that stuff goes for?"

"Do you?" said Clovenhoof.

"Thousands. Possibly tens of thousands."

"How would you know a thing like that?" said Marcee.

"It's like prize stallions, isn't it?" said Ben. "All those rich sheikhs paying top dollar for some stallion to service their mares."

"This is Yorkshire and this isn't horse," said Marcee.

"I wonder what horse jizz tastes like," Clovenhoof mused.

Several men continued to be very busy being ill everywhere.

"We've ruined thousands of pounds worth of her product," said Ben. "We needed her help."

"You're just being prissy about it because she's your girlfriend," said Clovenhoof.

Ben could have punched him. "We need to put it back so it looks like we haven't touched it."

Clovenhoof picked up the little straws and gathered them in his hands. "We can put them back, but they are obviously all empty now." He looked around at the group. "Unless we fill them back up, that is."

If Ben thought he had already seen the full range of facial expressions from the members of Djævlehund and the Wednesbury Wallopers, then he was mistaken. At Clovenhoof's words, each face became a complex illustration of its owner moving from confusion to horrified understanding.

"No!" said Marcee. "I have never heard anything so disgusting in my life."

"Chill Marcee, it's not something you can help with," said Clovenhoof.

"We gotta wank to get ourselves out of a bind!" cackled Aksel with insane glee. "Seriously man, I am so glad you joined our group. I could never have expanded my bucket list like this without your help. I could never come up with stuff like this. It's mind blowing. Now, who has some porn?"

"I am out of here!" said Camille. "Better to freeze my ass off outside than to see your filthy genitals."

"Good call," said Marcee, and followed her out, slamming the door behind her.

"Um, sweetness?" called Jacob. "Should I...? Should I stay and help or...?"

Marcee boggled at him.

"Back to the porn," said Clovenhoof. "Ben, you still got your stash?"

Ben made a small strangled noise. He had no intention of sharing Lois with this group of idiots. His hand moved to his precious books. "Nobody is to touch them except me."

"I cannot do this in front of others," said Hairy Leonard.

"The English are uncomfortable with nudity," said Rasmus.

Aksel shuffled to reposition his bound leg and tried to find his flies.

"I can't stay for this," said Ben.

"What is going on here?" called Miss Cavanagh, returning. "I told you to wait in the box—"

The old woman appeared at the open rear of the horsebox. Ben had his vintage erotica once again in his hands. Aksel had his hands inside his pants.

"Miss Cavanagh!" said Clovenhoof. "Whatever you think this looks like it's almost certainly worse."

Miss Cavanagh caught sight of the straws scattered on the floor of the horse box and sucked in a horrified breath.

"You imbeciles! You have ruined my shipment!"

"In all fairness, we thought it was drugs," said Clovenhoof.

"Thousands of pounds!" Miss Cavanagh squeaked hoarsely.

"I did say," said Ben.

"I am calling the police right now." She stalked off towards the kitchen with her phone to her ear.

Ben stumbled after her. "Miss Cavanagh! Lois! Please!"

"Well, now you've done it," said Clovenhoof.

45

Nerys and Rutspud had agreed that going to York would be their best chance of finding Jeremy Clovenhoof and, by extension, their missing dog and angel, but there was a minor disagreement over which car to take. Both had a car and neither was prepared to leave theirs parked in Bishop Monkton.

Eventually, they agreed to drive in convoy. Nerys, declaring herself to be the Earth native and therefore some sort of expert, took the lead. They set off from the village, Rutspud following her tiny puttering car in his hire vehicle. Miraculously, the pedals still worked in Eltiel's absence. For an angel concerned with the chaos created by thoughtless beings, he sure seemed happy to leave his metaphorical angelic fingerprints all over everything he touched.

They were barely five minutes outside the village when Rutspud saw flashing blue lights in his rearview mirror. It was a police car. The demon slowed and pulled over to the side of the narrow road to let the car pass, but rather than speeding past, it slowed, pulled in front of him and halted. A hundred metres ahead, Nerys also stopped.

A pair of police officers got out, round chaps who looked like they spent more of their time chasing down their next meal rather than criminals. Rutspud wound down his window. He was confident that whatever this was, he could blag his way through it. Then he remembered what he was wearing.

"Afternoon, sir," said one of the officers. "Would you mind taking the keys out of the ignition."

"Yes, of course," said Rutspud.

"And would you happen to have any ID on you, sir?"

Rutspud, standing on the driver's seat, made a show of patting his pockets. "I must have left it at home."

"I see, sir, because I can't help but notice that you appear to be wearing something which looks very much like a police officer's uniform."

"This?" said Rutspud, tugging at his angel-conjured police outfit.

"Because me and Damo here reckon we know pretty much everyone in the North Yorkshire Police."

"Everyone," echoed the other officer, Damo.

"Are you a serving police officer, sir?" said the policeman. "Or are you perhaps going to a fancy dress party?"

Rutspud pointed and nodded. "That one. Fancy dress party."

"Because impersonating a police officer is a serious crime, punishable with… What is it, Damo?"

"A custodial sentence of up to six months, Ollie," said

Police Officer Damo. "And, I believe, a potentially unlimited fine."

"Ooh, ouch," said Police Officer Ollie. "That is steep. So, this fancy dress party...? Was it perhaps at Littlethorpe Farm? Because a perfectly lovely member of the public called us with—"

"Actually, I don't know about that," said Damo confidently. "It's her who did pornos and now sells bull spunk for a living."

"Damo, we don't pass judgement on folks that live inside the law," said Ollie. He cleared his throat and looked at Rutspud. "We had a call to say that someone was going door-to-door pretending to be a police officer. Gave her quite a shock. And we don't like the thought of wrong-uns going about, putting the willies up innocent old ladies."

Damo nodded in solemn agreement.

"Okay," said Clovenhoof to everyone gathered in the farmyard, "we just need to wait for Miss Cavanagh to finish her little old lady hissy fit, then remind her she promised to give us a drive into town."

"Er," said Ben, less than eloquently, and pointed. Miss Cavanagh was coming back out of the house, a shotgun cradled in the crook of her arm. She fumbled in a pocket and brought out a handful of shells.

"Steady now!" said Clovenhoof. "I'm sure you don't actually mean to harm us."

She popped shells into the barrel and closed the shotgun with an audible clunk.

"You know one of the best things about being really old?" she said. "You care a lot less about the consequences of things."

"Look, we're sorry about the bull jizz," said Marcee.

"Really sorry..." burbled Rasmus, who hadn't quite finished throwing up.

"Maybe I will go to jail if I shoot you, but I just don't care," said Miss Cavanagh. "The satisfaction will more than make up for the inconvenience."

"Please," said Ben, hands held up imploringly. "This isn't you, Miss Cavanagh. Lois. Please. I feel like I know you. I've seen your pictures. You're not violent. You're not about hate. You're jolly, bright and breezy. You're all about innocent fun and playful—"

He was cut off by a shotgun blast into the air which made him yelp and leap back six feet.

"That's the only warning shot you get," she said. "Shells ain't cheap."

The group scrambled to get away: down across the grass, towards the wild rolling fields and the river.

"Wait for me!" shouted Aksel, hobbling on his splinted leg, trying to catch up with his fleeing companions. "Surely you wouldn't shoot me in this injured state?"

She answered with another barrel-load from the shotgun.

～

Twinkle's ears perked up. "There it was again."

"I definitely heard something that time," agreed Eltiel.

Twinkle sniffed along the verges of the road, hoping to pick up Mr Clovenhoof's scent again. "Nuffin', nuffin', fox poo – mmm, fox poo – rotting thing, nuffin'. Bit of wool. Cor, you can smell the sheep properly on that. Have you ever hunted down and eaten a sheep in the wild?"

"What?" said Eltiel, distracted. He gazed off in the direction the bull had gone, seemingly worried it might just come trotting back. "No, of course I haven't."

"I've eaten bits of lamb chop," said Twinkle. "And a bit o' mutton curry. But I reckon to chase one down and savage it." He licked his lips. "I got a real urge in me."

"And here was me thinking Lilith's Tears had elevated you."

"I'm a very elevated dog. Just cos I've got a few more cogs turnin', don't mean I don't enjoy the simple things in life. I bet there's angel stuff you just love doin' – well this is dog stuff." He gave a final dismissive sniff. "Nah. No, sign of him. We should go back over there, see if we can pick up the trail where it left off."

"Back to the bull farm?" said Eltiel nervously.

"Where there ain't no bull anymore."

"True," said Eltiel and they walked together.

46

B en ran back and grabbed Aksel's arm, trying not to look at what damage Miss Cavanagh's gunshot blast had done. Aksel howled in pain but tottered along. Ben felt very much better when there was a building between him and Miss Cavanagh, and he looked ahead, following the others as they ran across an open field.

The field seemed to go on forever. The grass wasn't very long, but it was tufty in a way that threatened to twist Ben's ankle, especially as he tried to keep Aksel upright. There was a water trough halfway across, and Ben spotted a wheelbarrow near to it.

"This could be useful. In you get," he said to Aksel.

"Nice!" said Aksel, dumping himself in. As he sprawled in front of him, Ben was able to see his injuries more clearly. Aksel still had the head wound from his fall in the cannabis farm, but the more recent shotgun blast had torn away what remained of his shirt along his side, and there were long stripes of seeping, bloody wounds, as if he'd been clawed by a tiger. Mercifully his leg was still strapped into its splint.

It was much harder than Ben had anticipated to wheel Aksel across the uneven field, and Ben regretted his decision after less than a minute. It took him a good ten minutes more to reach the field's boundary, where he saw Clovenhoof waiting.

"Give me a hand!" he called.

He could see Clovenhoof with a hand to his ear, pretending not to hear what he was saying, so he pushed on, grunting with the effort of not toppling Aksel out.

"Took your time," said Clovenhoof, stretching lazily as Ben made it to the other side.

"Bastard," Ben muttered.

NERYS WATCHED the exchange between Rutspud and the cops through her rearview mirror, but soon became irritated with the limited view it had to offer. She opened the car door and stepped out. She attempted to act nonchalantly, as though she was nothing to do with the demon in the hire car and was perhaps just stretching her legs at the side of this country road.

She looked back, so very casually, and saw the conversation go from genial enough traffic stop to something far more physical. The police had the car door open and were now grappling with the lithe, wriggling form of Rutspud. She wondered if the act of laying hands on the demon might alert them to the fact he was anything but human, but it seemed not to.

Rutspud clawed and grabbed at anything he could to get away from the police. He gasped and grunted, then shouted out "Littlethorpe Farm! Littlethorpe Farm!"

This was more than a little unusual, and Nerys wondered if she was mishearing some sort of infernal curse. Then she saw his large eyes flash her way and realised it was a message for her.

The coppers wriggled and struggled as though battling an uncooperative deckchair, but eventually had Rutspud in handcuffs. They managed to throw him into the rear of their vehicle.

One of them took off his hat to wipe his sweating brow and saw Nerys watching. "Nothing to worry about, madam. Everything's in hand," he called.

She nodded, holding back the bitterness as yet another person called her 'madam' instead of 'miss', and turned away. She opened maps on her phone and looked for Littlethorpe Farm. It was a couple of miles away, where the road looped around nearby woods.

The police car drove slowly past. Rutspud looked out the rear side window at her. His eyes – always so shockingly good at communicating – told her he would be fine and she needed to get on with the task in hand.

Nerys got into her car, intending to do just that.

~

THE HEAVY METALLERS and Morris dancers collapsed onto the grass at the far, sloping end of the field. The rain had stopped, and although the ground was damp, the mid-afternoon sun had burst through and was warm on their faces.

"Going to siphon off Little Jeremy," said Clovenhoof, heading off towards a nearby copse. "Still got some fingers stuck together. Anyone want to help me drain the hose?"

There were precisely zero takers on that request.

"I think I hate that man," said Marcee.

"Oh, you should try living with him," said Ben.

"Does the hate fade?"

Ben thought on it for a while. "No. It sort of marinades and because a thick gloopy soup of general disgust. Occasionally, his heart is in the right place. When it suits him."

"I am having the best time!" said Aksel.

"I think you might be delirious," said Ben.

"I need something to wash this taste from my mouth," moaned Rasmus, but no one had anything to offer him.

"I need a cigarette," said Camille.

"You don't smoke," said Ben.

"Doesn't mean I don't need one."

"I miss my baby boy," sighed Valdemar.

"Shut up. Or I will make him an orphan."

"No, don't kill him," said Marcee. "We still need backing musicians for our performance in—" she consulted her watch "—six hours."

"I don't think we're going to make it, sweetness," said Jacob.

Clovenhoof eventually emerged from the trees.

"You took your time," said Ben.

Clovenhoof grinned. "Do you lot believe in magic?"

Few bothered to reply. There were barely any grunts.

"Do you believe in fate?" tried Clovenhoof.

"I believe God hates us and has inflicted this day on us as punishment," said Camille.

Clovenhoof had his clay bottle of drink in his hand. Rasmus gestured for him to hand it over.

"I've been carrying this bottle ever since we left Birmingham," said Clovenhoof. "And I'm starting to think it has magical properties."

"It has drugs in it?" said Aksel.

"No. Actual supernatural powers. It's called Lilith's Tears."

"Isn't that the name of a Brazilian thrash metal band?" said Valdemar.

"No. I don't think it is. Lilith was Adam's first wife."

"I'm sure it is a metal band. Got this demon harpy with huge tits on the album cover."

"That's her!" said Clovenhoof. "Anyway, she was pushed aside as Adam's wife for being too wilful. And I think that drink – yes, pass it round, Rasmus, everyone take a sip – that drink gives us the will to just get on with life and overcome all obstacles."

"I'm not touching your funky drink," said Marcee, but the others drank deeply.

"Think about it. We broke down but scored a ton of weed," said Clovenhoof. "We *really* broke down, but were rescued by this amazing team of hanky-waving dancers. We put on an absolutely killer show the likes of which even the

Big Guy has never seen before. We were chased but found refuge with an old bint who – crazy coincidence! – turns out to be Ben's geriatric porno crush."

"We've been chased, bashed, tossed off cliffs and shot at!" Marcee threw back at him.

"I'm just enjoying every moment," said Aksel.

"Exactly!" said Clovenhoof. "If we wish hard and dream big and refuse to give in, we always pull through!"

"Bollocks," said Marcee.

"And I tell you why I think that," said Clovenhoof, pointing through the trees. "You'll never guess what's over there."

Ben made a muffled grunt to indicate that he would not be guessing. If it wasn't a minibus with keys in the ignition, then he couldn't imagine it doing them any good.

"It's going to make our lives a lot easier," said Clovenhoof.

"Every suggestion out of your mouth is a disaster," said Marcee.

"Come and see!" said Clovenhoof and did an excited, capering dance.

Ben got to his feet and stumbled after Clovenhoof, pushing Aksel. The ground dropped away and they moved down a slope towards the sound of running water. Ben realised it was an actual river, not simply a continuation of the stream they had followed.

"We can't get across a river!" he said to Clovenhoof.

"We don't have to!" said Clovenhoof. "It's our superhighway out of here. Look what we found!"

They made their way through the remaining trees and saw the rest of the group already at work unloading two-person kayaks from a trailer where they had been lashed to racks.

"See! There's enough for us all," said Clovenhoof.

"Fuck off!" said Marcee. But she looked round and saw the light of excitement and possibility in the eyes of everyone else.

And even though Ben didn't believe in magic or demon drinks, or ninety percent of the absolute twaddle that came out of Jeremy Clovenhoof's mouth, he couldn't help but think that, right now, a strong kayak with a decent paddle was almost as good as a minibus with the keys in the ignition.

47

"That's fair enough," said Eltiel, as they walked through the long grass in search of fresh signs of their quarry. "There are things that angels do love doing, that are core to their very nature. Singing the praises of the Lord on High, serving the needs of the residents the Celestial City."

"Yeah?" said Twinkle, sniffing as he went. "You really enjoy that?"

"Of course I do. You say that it's part of dogs' nature to hunt things and sniff animal ... leavings. I am telling you that we enjoy an existence of service and singing praises."

"Nuff said. Just sounds like that's somethin' on yer angelic wossname... Yer CV. Like yer job description."

"I suppose it is," Eltiel conceded. "Not that angels have curricula vitae. We have a role assigned to us for all eternity."

"So, mate, I'm askin' what stuff you really enjoy doin'."

Eltiel gave this due time and consideration. "I started customising my halo several centuries ago."

"Customisin'?"

"Oh, very subtly at first. I think it would have been around 1750 here on Earth when I brought a delicate note of cerise into a few of the light rays. Very subtle. Angels can't just start glowing loud and proud. Words will be had. Cerise and then a few notes of aquamarine and some extra sparkles."

"Whatever floats yer boat."

"It makes me happy. I think I was happiest when – it would have been 1951 Earth-time – when I finally plucked up the courage to add some purple. And I don't just mean a gentle violet. I mean a solid, imperial purple. I thought, 'let's go crazy, Eltiel. Let the inner you shine forth.'"

"Very good," said Twinkle, moving round a stand of grass. Much of it had been pushed down.

"And you know what?" said Eltiel. "The guys were very accepting, or at least, they didn't say anything. So that's when I went crazy and began making alterations to my angelic robes."

"Uh-huh."

"Some people think there's no design elements to white robes. Straight up, straight down. Those people would be so wrong. True, the variations are subtle, but even a degree of change in this angle or a tightening of a seam here... Oh, it was so freeing. And then when I decided to use a dash of silver thread or even gold... I thought I was in Heaven. Obviously, I *was* in Heaven, but I felt that, deep down, I was finally living an authentic—"

"'Old up," said Twinkle.

Eltiel stopped. Behind him, Twinkle was circling the flattened grass once more.

"What is it?"

"This is blood," said Twinkle. "Human blood."

"Really?"

"Bunch of people came through 'ere." He sniffed deeply. "Through 'ere and down the hill towards them trees there."

"Clovenhoof."

Twinkle sniffed once more and nodded. "We can't be more than ten minutes behind them."

"Yes! Come on!"

Together they bounded across the field.

"WE CAN TEAM up injured individuals with someone who can help them," said Ben, testing one of the kayaks in the water. "It could work."

"See?" said Clovenhoof merrily. "Everything's better with Jeremy making the decisions."

Marcee stepped in front of him. "You. You are a filthy degenerate. If we hadn't stopped when you jumped out in front of us, we would have been a million times better off. Everything is *not* better. The sooner we can part ways with you, the better."

"But, Marcee, haven't you got a Morris competition to win?" Clovenhoof asked. "You need us!"

She laughed hard and long. "If we ever find our way back to civilisation and get to York in time for that contest then I will recruit someone else. Literally *anybody* else. You are, without a doubt, the last person I ever want to work with again."

Clovenhoof winked at her. "Many people have felt that way about me. It doesn't last, believe me. I can tell I'm growing on you."

Marcee looked as if she was struggling to find a way to express how she felt about that. She made a small seething sound, like a kettle coming to the boil, then just kicked his leg in lieu of words before stalking off to bagsy a kayak.

Some of the group were more confident in the kayaks than others. Aksel somehow swung himself inside one, while Jacob debated who should pair up with him.

"You not want to ride along with me?" he said. "Hey, Valdemar and I grew up doing this shit, yeah? We can kayak in our sleep. Let's get going."

"Fucking rednecks," said Camille. "I'll walk."

"Camille, you can come in my kayak if you want," said Marcee.

Camille looked at her. "I don't want to die because you lack upper body strength. I will go with Ben."

Ben looked shocked that Camille had offered him anything remotely resembling a compliment, but at least they were all now getting somewhere. Hairy Leonard and Slackpipes Johnson got into kayaks with Valdemar and Rasmus, making them sit very low in the water. Clovenhoof joined Aksel, and Marcee shared a kayak with Jacob.

Clovenhoof whooped with excitement as he picked up the paddling stick. Maybe it was an oar, he really didn't care. Aksel was in front, scooping the water with an efficient twirl of the wrist. Clovenhoof tried to do the same, quickly realising that his glued hand made it impossible. So he sat back and let Aksel do all the work. The current also did a good job of moving them along. He glanced at the others. Valdemar and Rasmus also knew what they were doing, but he saw that Ben and Camille were swinging in a weird arc.

"Were we supposed to have a paddle?" Ben called.

Camille sat behind him and rolled her eyes.

"Aksel! Can we get to them?" Clovenhoof asked.

Without too much visible effort, Aksel wheeled them around and sped towards Ben and Camille. Clovenhoof held out his paddle at arm's length and swung it at Ben. Ben ducked to the side, and tipped the entire kayak into a roll.

"Holy shit, they've gone under," said Clovenhoof.

"It's fine. They will do an eskimo roll and pop up on the other side," said Aksel with confidence.

Ben's kayak stayed upside down.

"When will that happen?" asked Clovenhoof.

Aksel grunted and steered closer. He reached out and twisted the end of their kayak. The occupants emerged from the water as the kayak righted itself.

Ben and Camille coughed and choked. Camille shook herself angrily and spat out water with supreme disgust. "What in the fuck was that for? Why would you do such a thing? You will tow us, yes?"

Clovenhoof shrugged. "Sure."

He wasn't sure how Aksel was able to paddle all of them along, especially given how hurt he was, but he just powered on along the river, catching up with Marcee and Jacob with ease. They were both paddling, but seemed to have very different ideas about how it should work.

"You're messing up my water!" yelled Marcee from the back seat. "It's simple physics. You need to stop doing that!"

"I really don't know how, Marcee," said Jacob. "Let's just keep paddling, shall we?"

Valdemar and Rasmus were out of sight. Clovenhoof wondered how they had managed it. He could see no bends.

"Hey Aksel," he called. "What's up ahead?"

"A beautiful open vista!" called Aksel. "We can get some speed up finally."

"Should it be that open?" Clovenhoof wanted to say that the horizon looked too close, but that was ridiculous.

"Oh shit!" said Aksel. "I thought you said there were no waterfalls in this bit of England."

Before they hit the waterfall, Marcee made sure she locked eyes onto Clovenhoof.

"I hate you, Jeremy."

48

Nerys was so intent on finding Littlethorpe Farm that she didn't notice the bull until it was too late. Her phone's satnav had indicated the farm was approximately 'here', but exactly which bit of 'here' was unclear. She slowed to a crawl, looking round at a number of unmarked gateways.

And then the bull hit her.

The huge brute trotted up to the side her car, shoulder-barged it hard enough to make it rock on its suspension, then put a crack in the side window with a swing of his head.

Nerys screamed, which she considered to be a totally valid response in the situation.

The bull ambled round the front of her car and pull a long horn scratch in her bonnet.

"Fucking madness," she whimpered. "Bloody ... countryside ... fucking madness."

The bull seemed properly pissed off. Nerys had no idea if it was something she'd done. Was he just annoyed because her car was red. Or was that an urban myth about bulls and the colour red? Or a rural myth? Whatever. Cows were colour-blind, or something.

"What the fuck did I do to you?" she yelled.

The bull didn't care. He didn't even seem particularly angry. The way he ambled round, then turned to do a bit more mindless violence to her car gave him the air of a bored teenager smashing up a bus stop, rather than an individual with proper vengeance on his mind.

A grey-haired woman had come down one of the tracks leading off from the road, calling to the bull with a wordless "Hyah! Hyah!" and flapping a walking stick up and down. This drew the bull's attention and he turned to the gate. He stepped through. The woman kept the gate between herself and the beast and when he paused to look her way, she gave a firm "Hyah!", waved her stick again, and he trotted on. It was a masterful level of control.

The grey woman came through the roadside, closing the gate behind her. She came over to Nerys's car. Nerys climbed out, realising she was shaking.

If Nerys thought the woman's first words were to ask if she was okay then she was mistaken.

"Did you let my bull out?" she said.

"Did I what? Fucking hell, lady!"

Nerys looked at the damage to her car. There were dents and scratches, some wide scouring marks, and other, deeper gouges that no amount of polishing would conceal. One window was cracked and – Nerys groaned – there was the hiss as her front passenger tyre deflated.

"Your bull has just trashed my car!"

The woman put her hand to her chin and appeared to be in deep contemplation. As far as Nerys could tell, this contemplation was how to not appear to be utterly in the wrong when she was abso-fucking-lutely totally in the wrong.

Nerys stabbed a finger at the gate the woman had come through. "Is this Littlethorpe Farm?"

"It is," said the woman.

"I'm looking for someone."

"There's a lot of that going on today. Who?"

"A man called Jeremy Clovenhoof."

The laugh that erupted from the older woman was proof she had indeed met Jeremy, and for long enough to grasp some essential aspects of his personality.

"He a friend of yours?"

"Everyone asks that and it's currently a big firm no from me," said Nerys. "That man. I need something from him. Answers and more. I might just give him a bloody kicking in return."

"He's annoying, isn't he?" said the woman.

"And more."

The old woman sighed. "He's gone. And the others with him. I sent them packing, across yonder. While ago now."

"I'm never going to catch him, am I? I know they're going to be in York tonight. I was hoping to catch them before..." Nerys gave a sour huff. "You've not seen a dog as well, have you?"

"Dog?"

"A Yorkshire terrier."

"Can't say I have." The woman nodded at Nerys's car. "You'll not be going far with it like that."

"You reckon?" said Nerys sarcastically.

"I can help you put the spare on."

Nerys shook her head. "The spare's knackered too. Someone borrowed it when he was building a soap box go-cart."

"This that Jeremy character again?"

"Ah, you definitely have met him."

The old woman stroked her chin some more. "I could give you a lift into York if you give me time to get Swaggerboi away. That any good to you?"

Nerys wanted to growl and swear. It wasn't any good to her. She wanted her car in good working order. She wanted her dog back, and she was starting to not care if it was her true dumb Twinkle or the chattering cockney geezer he'd recently become. She wanted to be home. She wanted to be curled up with her bundle of fluff on the sofa with a bottomless drink of alcohol in her hand. She wanted any number of things that were a million miles better than a lift into York with some mad old bull-farmer. But none of them were on offer.

"That would be very kind," she managed to say.

CLOVENHOOF'S FIRST THOUGHT, as they went over the edge of the waterfall, was that he could see the bottom below them, which might mean that this was survivable. His immediate follow-up thought was that he had no idea which way was up. In less time than it took to draw breath, he was far under the water and he knew this was not a good place to be.

He had no idea what to do about it. He could see nothing except green and white foaming watery chaos. His mouth was open with a perfectly-formed string of profanities ready to go, but water had rudely rushed in to shut him up.

His head broke the surface, which was surely the end of his torment, but he immediately went under again. He popped up and stayed up after a couple more dunkings. He coughed up water and tried to unleash the swearing, but it was a poor effort. He saw the bank of the river nearby and banged a shin on a submerged rock.

"Fluuurk!" he gasped, sploshing ashore. "Fuck! That's better."

He pulled himself upright to see where everyone else was. Marcee and Jacob splashed in the shallows nearby, arguing about the best way to right their kayak. Ben and Camille were wading ashore on the other side of the river, but there was no sign of their kayak.

Rasmus and Valdemar were both miraculously still afloat in their kayaks, although they had lost Hairy Leonard and Slackpipes Johnson in the tumble. The two beefy Morris men were flopping in the shallows like two elephant seals. Clovenhoof searched the water for a sign of Aksel. He was the only one unaccounted for.

"Aksel!" he called. "Anyone see Aksel?"

Everyone turned to search.

"He's here!" called Jacob, pointing under the water. "I think he's stuck!"

Clovenhoof splashed over to where Jacob was pointing. Aksel could be seen waving frantically underneath a partly-submerged fallen tree. Clovenhoof and Jacob both ducked down to try and dislodge him. When they both popped up again Jacob gulped for air.

"I think his hair is caught in the tree! We need to cut him loose."

Clovenhoof looked down. Aksel had stopped moving. Had he slipped into unconsciousness?

"I haven't got a knife, but I do have an idea."

Clovenhoof climbed on top of the tree, holding onto its slippery green branches. He reached a leg down and angled his foot onto Aksel's face, pushing as hard as he could. He could feel something cracking. He hoped it was the ton of twigs that were holding Aksel fast. He pushed further.

"I think it's working!" said Jacob. "I will try dragging him from the side."

Jacob went under again, and this time surfaced with Aksel. Marcee helped him drag Aksel's lifeless form further up the bank.

"Tip him over, empty some of that water out," said Marcee.

They rolled him onto his stomach. A moment later, as water started to emerge from Aksel's mouth, he coughed and retched.

"He's alive!" yelled Jacob.

After a few moments, Aksel was able to sit up. His hand went to his face. "Is by dose broken?" he asked.

"It looks different," said Clovenhoof, who was finally untangled from the tree. "I can't imagine how that happened. At least you didn't drown."

Aksel nodded. "Id's like a bark of honour. Rock and roll!"

It took Clovenhoof a moment to translate. "Mark of honour, yes!"

49

Rutspud sat quietly in the back of the police car and watched the world go by. Being of supple wrists and dextrous hands, he'd already slipped his hands in and out of the cuffs several times, but there was no point in making a run for it when he was travelling at high speed in a police car with no clear idea where he might go. He decided to enjoy the ride for what it was.

Over the years, he'd grown accustomed to the fact that the human world had a sky over it and no ceiling of any kind. Demonkind had become conditioned by aeons of existence in Hell to assume all places had some sort of ceiling. If one stood in Hell, there was a rocky ceiling above and a rocky floor below (unless either of them happened to be lava or razor blades or something even less appealing to human inmates). And there was something deeply comforting about knowing that if you tunnelled far enough through that ceiling or floor, eventually it was just the floor or ceiling of the next level above or below. Hell was a nearly endless sandwich of rock and suffering, and there was a place in it for everyone.

Rutspud, who feared he had come close to going native on Earth, now watched the clouds drift by in the afternoon sky. He knew humans saw animals and other strange shapes in clouds and saw it as an indication of their own intelligence and creativity. Rutspud considered himself to be a creative thinker, at least by demon standards, but wasn't sure how thinking a thing looked like a completely different thing was really any marker of intelligence.

"That one looks like a mass of condensed water vapour," he said softly, "and that one looks like a mass of condensed water vapour..."

The police officers, Damo and Ollie, took him to a nearby town called Ripon. The signposts declared it to be a city, but it looked like a town. It was definitely a town if the police and fire stations had to occupy the same building, huddling together as though afraid of bigger municipal services.

They marched Rutspud up to the front desk. The sergeant had to lean right over the counter to see Rutspud.

"What do we have here then?" he said.

"I can stand on a box if you want a better view," said Rutspud helpfully.

"Impersonating a police officer, sarge," said Damo.

The sergeant twitched his nose and inspected Rutspud's uniform. "Not a particularly good impression."

"Will that go in my favour with the judge?" said Rutspud.

The sergeant grunted, amused. "Depends on why you were impersonating a police officer."

"Do you want the simple answer or the honest answer?"

The sergeant looked genuinely torn. "Apparently, the Crown Prosecution Service prefers honesty."

"Oh, okay. In that case, myself and my friend, who is an angel, gave ourselves police uniforms so we could interrogate drug-addled locals about the location of a devil who's gone rogue with a bottle of magic willpower juice harvested from the tears of Adam's first wife."

The sergeant nodded long and slow at this. He'd clearly decided to leap headlong into the police cliché of never thinking things through quickly, when doing it slowly was perhaps as equally effective. "And that's the honest answer, is it?"

"It is."

"Hmmm. Perhaps you might want to rethink that while you're sitting in the cell. I say cell – it's also the interview room." He looked at the constables. "If this is going to take us past tea-time, you'll have to take him to the nick over at Harrogate."

Ollie began to groan.

"Meanwhile," said the sergeant firmly, "you two need to get over to Aldwark Holiday Park. They've reported some of their canoes have gone missing."

"Where've they gone?" said Damo.

"I do not know," said the sergeant. "That's why they're missing."

The police searched Rutspud (not very well) and confiscated his little wooden truncheon and his tiny police whistle on a chain, then put him in a little room with a bench and a table.

"Now, no monkey business," said the sergeant.

"Wouldn't dream of it, sir," said Rutspud.

As soon as the door was locked, Rutspud took out his InstaDoor device (which they'd totally failed to notice during their cursory body search). Using the InstaDoor to get from Limbo to Earth had required some time and fine-tuning, because Earth is complex and varied, and it was very easy to wind up in the wrong place. The return journey was much easier because Limbo, whilst huge (even notionally infinite), is the same everywhere. It didn't matter which bit you ended up in.

He activated the device and a narrow line of light appeared in the middle of the small room.

Rutspud dug his hands in the gap, pulled apart and stepped through into Limbo, closing the doorway behind him.

Ben, wet and as miserable as he had been at any point in their cross-country adventure, realised that Camille and he were on the opposite side of the river to the spot where Aksel was apparently stuck underwater, but they could clearly see what was happening.

He opened his jacket to inspect his secret stash of 3D books, but they were soaked too: fused together into a solid lump. He told himself he might be able to dry them out and salvage them, but knew in his heart he was lying through his teeth and they were ruined.

When the lead singer of Djævlehund was hauled up the

bank and proved to be alive, Camille clutched Ben's arm and gave an enormous cry of relief. Then, remembering herself, she shook her head.

"Fucking idiot, almost getting killed. How's he going to get over here to us now?"

"Everyone else is over there. We should probably go to them," said Ben.

"I am never getting in one of those stupid things ever again. If I live to be a hundred I will not do it!" said Camille.

Rasmus and Hairy Leonard had recovered a kayak from somewhere. Ben had no idea if it was the one he and Camille had used. They towed it over.

"If you climb into here, we will take you to the other bank. You won't need to row or steer, we will guide you," said Rasmus.

"These things are fucking death traps. No way!" said Camille. "We can walk round."

"It's a river," said Ben. "There's no walking round."

"I hate this river! It has made me cold and wet."

"That's the nature of water, yes," said Ben snidely, who was just as cold and wet but felt Camille had unfairly stolen all the available indignation. "How about I hold onto you?" he offered. "I sit behind and hold you all the way over, I won't let you go."

Camille looked as though she hated the idea but hated the alternative even more. "Fine," she said. "But this does not mean sex for you."

"What?"

"'I hold onto you' is man-code for sex."

"Is it? What? No. I'm just saying—"

"No sex, dirty old man," she said fiercely, reluctantly climbing into the kayak with him.

The young woman seemed obsessed with the idea that he was constantly hitting on her. He had no interest in the angry Frenchwoman, although there was part of him that wished she'd stop putting him in some 'old man' category.

Ages and age gaps were a funny thing, he thought, as the others towed their kayak across the river and he hugged Camille to keep her warm.

It was like the business with Lois/Miss Cavanagh. Ben had happily – Gladly! Joyfully! – wallowed in daydreams of lovely naked Lois while she had been a young and vivacious creature in those 3D pictures. But now...? In truth, Ben felt properly messed up by the fact that Miss Cavanagh had turned out to be Lois. He would need time to unpick what that meant, because it had left him very confused. Was he the sort of person who went round fancying octogenarians? He definitely hadn't fancied Miss Cavanagh until he knew she was Lois, but then he had played back some of her movements and expressions, and found himself seeing the similarities. She still had those amazing cheekbones and the ghost of the carefree smile.

"Stop it, you weirdo," he said quietly to himself, as he clung onto Camille.

"What? Do you have an erection? Stop that! You need the blood to be in your brain, not your dick," Camille said.

"I do not have an erection!" Ben shouted.

The rest of the group on the bank clapped and jeered at that. Ben rolled his eyes. Hopefully by mocking him, Camille would be distracted from the horror of the river.

They made it to the other side and were helped onto the bank by the rest of the group. Camille shot Ben a disgusted look and went over to sit beside Aksel.

"Having trouble getting it up, Kitchen?" asked Clovenhoof, slapping him on the back. "We can get you some of those boner pills if you need to party."

"No!" said Ben. "I was just answering Camille's question. Now, how on earth are we going to get out of here?"

Clovenhoof strode towards the group. "Let's see how we're going to get out of here." The river stretched on around a curve, the land rising sharply into a ragged hill behind them. "I know you all have places where you need to be, things you need to do."

"Five o'clock," said Marcee.

"Thank you, speaking clock," said Clovenhoof.

"Four hours until we are expected to dance against the bloody Hankymen."

"Right!" said Clovenhoof. "So what shall we do next?"

"We keep *doing things*," said Slackpipes Johnson. "It's *doing things* that's getting us into trouble."

"Moving us forward, I think you mean," said Clovenhoof.

"Why don't we try doing nothing?" said Hairy Leonard. "Just nothing."

"I'm out of energy and I'm out of ideas," agreed Jacob.

"What does it even mean to do nothing at this point?" asked Clovenhoof. "We're all soaking wet and cold, some of us have injuries, although it has to be said that Aksel has most of them. We have nothing to eat or drink and we're in the middle of nowhere. Doing nothing means lying down and waiting for death, surely?"

There was no argument from the group, just some grunts of agreement.

"Death sounds good right now," said Rasmus. "You guys heard of *ättestupa*?"

Aksel laughed. "Sure. Suicide cliffs."

"The what now?" said Ben.

Askel explained. "When the Vikings ruled Sweden, it was said that the old and infirm would throw themselves off a cliff to their deaths when they had become a burden to society."

"I am a burden," said Rasmus. "I wasted my redundancy money on a wreck of a van and now ... perhaps it is better for me and for my Henrik if I just lay down and die."

"Screw that!" said Valdemar. "I have a home and a family to get to."

"Exactly!" said Clovenhoof. "And you guys have a dance-off to win!"

"We're not going to win," said Jacob.

"Not with that attitude!" said Clovenhoof. He took a fresh swig of Lilith's Tears. "I say we all need another blast of magical courage, find a way out of here and—" He paused, cocking an ear. "You hear that?"

"It sounds like a car," said Ben. "Is there a road near here?"

They all sat up a little straighter. There was definitely something nearby.

"Hot damn!" grinned Clovenhoof, gripping his ancient flask. "I love this drink."

50

Nerys held onto the door handle as Miss Cavanagh's ancient Land Rover rocked and rolled along the A59. The thing was either so old that it had never been fitted with seatbelts or, somewhere in its decades long history, some mad person had decided to remove them.

"No seatbelts, is this legal?" Nerys asked.

"No idea. Do you want to get out and walk?"

"No, thank you." A sign on the road had indicated they were a mere twelve miles from York.

"I lost my licence in nineteen-eighty-three," said Miss Cavanagh conversationally.

"You mean you couldn't find it? Like it had gone down the back of the settee?"

"I mean I was caught speeding through Richmond and then gave the magistrate a piece of my mind when it went to court the next week. Lost my licence."

"You mean...?" Nerys gestured generally at the vehicle and specifically at Miss Cavanagh driving it.

The old woman nodded, smiling. "I learned something in life a long, long time ago. People are going to judge you."

Nerys couldn't help but laugh at that. "Ha! I know that one. I get enough judgement in life."

"And I decided the best way to deal with that was to say 'to hell with all of them' and just keep on living my life the way I want to."

"Driving a jeep illegally well into your senior years?"

"That," said Miss Cavanagh. "And everything else. I've lived life on my own terms."

"Has it made you happy?" said Nerys.

Miss Cavanagh mushed her lips together. "I dunno. Ask me when I'm older."

They drove in silence for a minute.

"What's this Jeremy character to you?" said Miss Cavanagh.

"The bane of my life."

"He your husband?"

"God, no!" said Nerys automatically, then had to backtrack. "Actually, technically, he is. On paper. We got married when he was at risk of deportation. Long story. I often try to forget it. But, no, we're not a thing. Absolutely not. The man's a knob."

"But you're chasing across the country after him."

"Because he's done something... He's caused problems in my life."

"And will finding him make him fix them?"

Nerys pulled a face. "Not sure this one can be fixed."

"So, you're following him because...?"

Nerys sighed. "I just want him to see what he's done. I want him to recognise his mistakes."

Miss Cavanagh wagged a finger at her. "People. They don't change much. To hell with people. Go your own way. That's my advice anyway."

"That's very good advice," said Nerys honestly.

"Are you going to follow it?"

"Probably not," said Nerys.

TWINKLE PAUSED at the top of the slope leading down to the river. "Definitely came this way, guv'nor," he said and trotted down to the water.

He dipped his front paws in the river. It was good to cool off one's pads. And then he lapped at the water. It was beautifully, bitingly cold, with just a hint of farming run-off and – mmm – sheep droppings. "Magic," he said.

"Where now?" said Eltiel.

Twinkle finished his drink and looked about. "Dunno."

He raised his nose high (as high as a Yorkshire Terrier could do) and sniffed. "No trace from the other side."

"What?"

Twinkle scampered along the bank a little and took in a mighty noseful. "Went down the river, I'd say."

"They swam?" Then Eltiel saw something further up the bank. He picked up a plastic-handled oar with a bright orange head. "Boats. They took boats."

"That's about the short and the tall of it," Twinkle agreed.

Eltiel sighed and cast the oar down. "So close!"

"No need to be down, me old china."

"They're always one step ahead! It's fruitless."

Twinkle chuckled. "And yet 'ere we are. Miles from civilization on a gorgeous day. The sun has got his hat on. We've got cool drinkin' water. Back to bladdy nature, innit?"

Eltiel forced himself to take a deep breath and looked about. "Actually, this is quite nice, isn't it?"

"'Xactly, mate."

Eltiel waved a hand airily at the trees on the far bank, and possibly at the clouds and sun above them. "Eden was much more like this."

"Was it now? Like Yorkshire sheep country?"

"Pleasant. Peaceful. Untrammelled and untrampled beauty. Fabulous. As the Lord had originally intended."

Twinkle nodded. "Course, it weren't always like this."

"How do you know?"

"Beavers and that."

Eltiel put his hands on his hips. "Excuse me?"

"Somethin' like that. I watch a bit of telly you know. Gimme a bit of that David Attenborough shit. It's great. Beavers come in and build their dams and the course of the river changes. And then the deer and wolves do their bit. And it's all to do with where the trees put down their roots an' all."

"I'm not sure there are beavers and wolves and such things round here," said Eltiel, though the angel didn't sound very sure on the matter.

"All I'm sayin' is that the animals and the other bastard critters, they change the landscape, don't they?"

"All part of the divine plan," suggested Eltiel. "Constant creation."

"Oh, I see," said Twinkle, giving him the eye. "So, animals doing their shit and changin' the landscape is all fine and good, but humans and – ahem – certain doggies doing what they fancy is messin' with the Lord's fackin' plan."

"Are you trying to make a point? I feel this isn't about this little beauty spot at all."

Twinkle raised his snoot. "Seems to me you've got double standards, fluffy-wings. You go on about perfection and beauty and God's plan and how I'm some sort of abomination—"

"A quite pleasant and amiable abomination," said Eltiel.

"—but you seem to have these fixed views on dogs gettin' a little bit of free will and the power of speech, but you don't give two bladdy 'oots about where the beavers build their dams."

"They're quite different things, honestly."

"Nah," said Twinkle. "I reckon I've got you pegged. You don't want a perfect world of things growin' and changin' and gettin' up to all kinds of crazy wonderful shit. You want a picture postcard. You want a paintin'. You want your idea of perfection and you want to freeze it in place."

"There's nothing wrong with wanting a little order. There's nothing wrong with wanting to strive for – yes! – I will use the word, to strive for perfection."

"That ain't life, mate. Really ain't." Twinkle made a throaty noise. "I feel sorry for you really."

"Sorry? For me?"

"Least I can look at this place, love it for what it is and

know it ain't gonna be this way forever. It's that, er, livin' in the moment thing. You? You see this and want to hit the pause button and just have it this way forever."

"I feel you have thoroughly misunderstood my personal philosophy on beauty," said Eltiel, but his wounded tone told Twinkle the angel had been properly called out.

Eltiel might have said something to defend himself further, but there came a shout from up on the bank.

"Oh, there you are!" said a man in camo trousers and a fleece, jogging down to meet them. "Didn't see you come past me."

"Sorry?" said Eltiel.

"I called earlier. The stolen kayaks."

Eltiel only then remembered he was still wearing a police uniform. "Oh! Oh, yes," he said. "We're here because of that. Me and my, er, police dog are trying to track them down."

The man looked past Eltiel at Twinkle. "Bit small for a police dog."

Eltiel faltered only for a second. "But an excellent scent hound. He's got it where it counts."

Twinkle decided to aid this explanation by doing some performative sniffing at some grass then gave his best "Yip!", as though to indicate they should go this way.

"See?" said Eltiel.

"And the pink bow in his fur?" asked the kayak man.

"Pink's a masculine colour," said Twinkle.

The kayak man stared agape and might have screamed some stunned utterance if he had not been interrupted by the arrival of two more people on the scene. A pair of out of breath policemen stumbled onto the bank.

"Here he is, Damo," said the lead one. "Right, mister, we've come about your stolen boats—" He looked at Eltiel in his police get up. "Bloody hell! We've got another one!"

The other officer made it down the bank. "Another one what? Oh. Christ, is there some fake copper convention on or something?"

"Ah," said Eltiel.

"Run?" suggested Twinkle.

They dashed off along the riverbank downstream. Fortunately they were both far faster than the two cops.

51

en scrambled partway up the bank and saw there was indeed a road, a short distance from where their failed kayak adventure had washed up. The road clung to the hillside, a crash barrier on one side, tufted grass and loose stone slopes on the other. It was about twenty feet above them. With aching and wet limbs, he scrambled up to the roadside just as a very old Land Rover puttered past. He waved enthusiastically at it, but they either didn't see him or just ignored him.

"Bugger," he said with feeling.

There was a toot of horn and he turned to see a small lorry coming up behind him.

"Hey!" He waved with the enthusiasm of a desert island castaway seeing a passing ship. "Hey! Help us! Please stop!"

The lorry slowed. Ben hurried alongside the cab. A woman leaned out of the open window, looking out upon the scene by the riverside. She wore some kind of uniform, but Ben couldn't see the detail.

"Looks like you've had a bit of a rum to-do," she said casually.

"Can you help us?" Ben asked. "We're completely lost and some of us are hurt."

"What are tha doing out here?" asked the woman.

Ben briefly considered telling the truth; but not only did it paint them in a poor light, it also sounded increasingly unlikely. "Um. We went for a walk, but then things went very wrong. We have no idea where we are."

"Looks like you stepped in the drink."

"I did. We did. Please help."

"Hm," she said and took a moment to look from Ben to the rest of the group, who were trying to get up the slope with varying degrees of success. "I can give thee a ride. I'm heading t'wards York if that'll do thee any good."

"Oh, God, that will be fantastic," said Marcee, reaching the top before the rest.

Fine," said the woman. "Get yon others together. I need to stop in Tockwith first, then I can take thee into York if that'll do. Tha'll have to ride in back, mind."

Ben grinned at her. "Thank you!"

RUTSPUD STEPPED PROMPTLY BACK into Limbo and zipped the rip in reality closed behind him.

The gunshots were still ringing in his ears. He checked himself for bullet holes.

"I mean!" he shouted back at the now closed portal. "Who brings guns to church, huh?!" He sighed tiredly and shrugged. "Americans."

The words disappeared into the vast emptiness of Limbo. The void sucked up any possible echoes.

He looked at the InstaDoor device accusingly. "Could we perhaps try to get a little closer to Yorkshire this time?"

He fiddled with the controls, refining his dial-twiddling until anything more seemed like prevaricating. He activated the device and pulled apart the line of light before him.

Rutspud stepped through onto warm sand. The sun was low in the sky over the lapping waves of a peaceful sea. "This is not Yorkshire," he said.

He looked round for an indication of geographical location. A man at a bamboo drinks shack waved at him encouragingly.

"At least they're not shooting at me this time..."

THE LORRY DRIVER closed the rear doors of the lorry on ten done-in individuals. They rocked gently as the truck started up and negotiated the country road.

"So! What do we have in here?" said Clovenhoof, slapping a hand on the side of a wooden box that was strapped to the flatbed.

"We're not supposed to touch anything," said Jacob. "Not touching things we don't understand should definitely be the way forward for this group."

"Has being in the back of a vehicle with a mysterious cargo taught us nothing?" said Valdemar.

"Semen. Drugs," said Slackpipes Johnson.

"Don't remind me," said Hairy Leonard queasily.

"Shoub be rock and roll gext," said Aksel, through his broken nose.

"What?" said Camille.

"Sex, drugs and gow rock and roll. Id's a trilogy."

"He's delirious."

"This box is warm," said Clovenhoof.

"That's just hypothermia," said Ben. "Your sense of touch has gone haywire."

"I wonder if it's got food inside."

The mention of food grabbed several people's attention.

"I'b bery huggry," said Aksel.

"It's an unusual kind of box to have food inside, even for this ridiculous country," said Camille.

Ben thought she was right. These boxes were made from wood, and were painted in an assortment of colours.

"We're in the sticks," said Clovenhoof. "They do things differently here. I'll just have a look inside."

"For fuck's sake!" hissed Marcee. "Can you not leave well alone?"

Clovenhoof looked for a way into one of the boxes. There was a huge strap with a rachet fastener which went right round the box. He loosened it off, pushed the strap aside, and raised the top.

"Oh. Oh dear, I think this might be a beehive."

"I was right! I was right!" screamed Marcee as a huge

cloud of bees emerged from their open hive. Clovenhoof staggered backward and landed on top of Aksel, who howled in pain. Aksel soon shut his mouth as the bees enveloped him.

Ben wanted to run away from the angry bees, but his options in the back of a lorry were limited, so he did what everyone else in the truck was doing, which was screaming loudly. It crossed Ben's mind that the bees might not like the noise. If they had ears. Did bees have ears? He couldn't stop screaming, even if it might possibly upset the bees. He could feel them on him and they were stinging.

The driver slammed on the brakes, which threw the top part of the hive down onto the floor. Ben saw it still contained a lot of bees – an impossible number – and they rose up in an angry swirl for a second assault wave.

EVENTUALLY, Twinkle and Eltiel had stopped running. Running was something that came easy to both of them. They may have both enjoyed a pampered lifestyle, and were definitely indoorsy types at heart, but Twinkle was a dog in his prime while Eltiel – well, he was a celestial being for whom physical things such as muscles, lung capacity and exhaustion were more of an aesthetic choice than anything else.

They came to a stop a couple of miles down the river and looked back. They'd lost the two puffing and out of shape police officers a long while ago. Eltiel considered his police outfit, and with a wave of his hand was miraculously back in his traditional angelic robes.

"This is a world of madness and chaos," he said.

"A world of adventure," said Twinkle.

"Every step we make towards finding Jeremy Clovenhoof is confounded. Maybe it's a background effect of the Lilith's Tears."

"Nah, mate," said Twinkle. "I think you'll find that's just life."

"I feared as much. I can't wait for this to be over and I get to return home." He looked about. "Hmmm. I suppose the demon Rutspud was my ticket out of here."

Twinkle nodded. "I shouldn't've left Nerys behind. I mean, I'm totally fine runnin' around the countryside, but the little lady worries when I'm not about. It's sweet really."

Eltiel didn't pass comment, even though he could sense the sadness now gripping the little dog.

"Canoe!" said Twinkle suddenly. Down below them, where the river curved right round beneath a twenty-foot waterfall, there were three kayaks drawn up onto the shallow riverbank.

They hurried over.

"Three vessels and no signs of their owners," said Eltiel.

"Maybe they drowned," said Twinkle, then sniffed. "Nah. This way. Shift it."

Twinkle scrambled up a steep bank with Eltiel behind him. Twinkle wriggled between the horizontal bars of a crash barrier and onto the side of a tarmacked road.

"They definitely came this way," said Twinkle. "Dirty, wet. It's like trackin' damp and mouldy towels."

Eltiel didn't want to ask if tracking damp and mouldy towels was easy.

"But then it stops," said Twinkle.

"Stops?"

"Probably got into a vehicle."

Eltiel looked up and down the road. "Which direction?"

"How the fack should I know?" said Twinkle sharply. He sat down on his haunches. "I want Nerys."

"I'm sure she's around somewhere. Just sniff harder. Where did they go?"

"This nose don't track vehicles. Jesus Christ, mate." Twinkle gave a doggy whine. "I wanna go home. I want Nerys."

"You said."

"I'm hungry too. Could eat a bladdy horse. Literally. You wouldn't 'appen to have a pork pie on you, would you?"

52

With the lorry full of bees stopped, there was at least the option of getting off. Ben tried to open the rear doors, frantically pushing at bolts and important looking bits. The driver released the doors and Ben was nearly swept away by the rush of people trying to get out.

"What the flipping heck has tha done?!" the driver demanded.

The gang stumbled along the road until the bee cloud had thinned a little.

"I'm stung!" hissed Marcee, both whining and furious. "All over! I'm stung."

"No shit? We're all stung lady," said Camille.

Hairy Leonard and Slackpipes Johnson carried Aksel between them, with Rasmus and Valdemar limping alongside. Back at the truck, the driver had donned a bee veil and was attempting to restore the hive to its correct state.

"You utter morons! You have destroyed this hive!" she yelled.

"In all fairness," said Clovenhoof, seemingly unaffected by the cloud of bees, "the bees started it."

"I'm calling the police!" the woman shouted.

ELTIEL STEPPED BACK into the partial cover of an overhanging tree as a police car came whizzing past, lights flashing. He watched it recede down the road.

"Sun's going down," he noted, looking at the red sky. "I thought we would have caught up with them by now."

"I'm hungry," said Twinkle.

"I told you I don't have anything."

"I'm still hungry. If Nerys was here, she'd feed me."

"Well, she's not."

"She'd give me a whole roast chicken and a plate of lamb chops. She knows how to treat 'er boy right."

"But she's not."

"I know she's not!"

Eltiel took a calming moment. "We need to pick a direction."

"We've lost them. Face facts, mate. I can't track Mr Clovenhoof across hundreds of miles of wilderness—"

"Maybe ten miles at the most, so far."

"—and you are not 'elpin' matters. In fact, I don't even know what your skill set is."

"What do you mean?"

Twinkle looked at him through narrowed eyes. "What do

you bring to this team? Apart from judgy attitudes and a disco lightshow on your bonce?"

"How dare you. I'm an angel of the Lord, you pint-sized horror."

"Angel of the Lord is somethin' what goes on a nametag. What are you actually good for?"

Eltiel was going to tell him precisely what he was good for, but the question had actually flummoxed him. "Righteousness..." he began.

"Is not a skill," said Twinkle.

Eltiel gave up, deflated. A road. A choice of left or right. One had a chance of leading them towards Clovenhoof, but only a chance.

"Oh, Lord, we've made a mess of this, haven't we?" he said.

He expected Twinkle to speak up and pin the blame solely on him, but the dog just grumbled in sad agreement.

"Finished feeling sorry for yourselves?" said Rutspud, coming out of the trees behind them. He had a wide-brimmed straw hat on his head, and was holding a scooped-out pineapple with a drinking straw in it.

"Rutspud!" cried Eltiel. "What...? How...? Where...?"

"All valid questions, Eltiel," said Rutspud smoothly. "But I can see you're no closer to finding our quarry."

"Wotcha, mate," said Twinkle in greeting.

"Hello, strange talking dog," said Rutspud. "Now, I assume you'd like my assistance in getting back to Clovenhoof, and possibly Nerys too."

Twinkle sprang to his feet. "You know where she is?"

"I know where's she's heading," said Rutspud. "Apparently a place called the Gnome's Bottom."

"And you know where that is," said Eltiel.

"Of course."

Eltiel frowned at the pineapple drink. "Where did you get that, exactly?"

"From a lovely man called Julio, if you must know," said Rutspud. "I might also have relieved him of this," he added, waving a smartphone he now held in the other hand. "Julio is about to rack up some data-roaming charges, and I'm going to use his credit card to order us an Uber."

"A what?" said Eltiel.

"A car ride!" said Twinkle with happy relief. "My paws! I've never walked so bladdy far!"

Rutspud began swiping and tapping on the phone. "Gnome's Bottom, here we come."

A POLICE CAR drew up behind the beekeeper's lorry. The siren gave a final whoop before turning off.

"Thank God," said Marcee.

"Don' gnow aboud you," agreed Aksel through swollen lips, "bud geddin' arresded sounds priddy gub righ' gnow."

"Better than death," agreed Jacob.

Two police officers stepped out. They wore exhausted expressions, as though this might have been the fifth bee incident they'd been called out to today.

"Right then," said one, sliding on his cap. "Would anyone care to tell me what's going on here?"

"It's these people!" said the lorry driver from behind her heavy mask. "They hitched a lift and then attacked my bees!"

One of the officers looked at the ragged mob and then nudged his partner. "Damo, these guys look kind of damp..."

"You're right, Ollie," the other nodded. "Ladies and gentlemen," he said, "you wouldn't happen to know anything about some kayaks that went missing earlier today?"

There was a lot of shuffling and people casting embarrassed looks at their feet. Apart from Marcee. She pointed a stung and swollen finger straight at Clovenhoof.

"Him! He's a nutter! It's all his fault!"

Clovenhoof was not abashed. "Credit where credit's due," he said. "It's been a spectacular weekend so far, let me tell you!"

"LEFT HERE," said Nerys, reading off her phone's satnav.

Miss Cavanagh took the turning at the lights. They were not yet at the centre of the city of York. The venue was in the suburbs, at a place not far from the city racecourse.

"Here," said Nerys.

There was a low building with a sign outside: GNOME'S BOTTOM MICROBREWERY.

"What makes it a microbrewery?" said Miss Cavanagh.

"It's small?"

Miss Cavanagh grunted, as though she had seen smaller.

It was six o'clock. If Clovenhoof was going to turn up for this dance contest then he'd be here within the next few hours.

Several vehicles were parked in the rough car park in front of the brewery building. Men and women were entering the building, some in loose shirts and britches, others in jackets festooned with tassels and rags.

"Morris dancers?" said Miss Cavanagh distastefully.

"I thought you were encouraging me to live a life without judgement," said Nerys.

"Was I?"

"To hell with the opinions of other people. Live life how you want to. Can't Morris dancers do the same?"

The old woman gave her a look. "You have to draw the line somewhere."

"Anyway," said Nerys opening the door, "thanks for the lift."

She was surprised when Miss Cavanagh put the hand brake on and opened her own door to get out.

"You don't have to stay," said Nerys.

"Long drive, bloody awful day. I think I could do with a pint."

"A drink on me then," said Nerys politely.

Miss Cavanagh didn't bother to lock up her vehicle. The two of them walked towards the brightly lit entrance.

53

A police van came over from York to collect the damp and bee-stung boat thieves. Everyone applauded the two police officers who climbed out.

"So good to see you!"

"Thank you so much for coming!"

There was some discussion between the two original coppers and the van cops from York about whether Aksel needed an ambulance. In the end they were all put into the back of the van to be driven to a nearby hospital.

"Careful now," said Clovenhoof as he got in. "We've not had much success with vans these last two days."

"Hospital!" said Marcee, almost giddy with happiness as she climbed in. "Blankets! Drink!" She sucked in a sharp breath as she knocked a bee sting on her cheek. "Ointment!"

Between them, they had been stung so many times that

several had massive, alarmingly red, shiny faces. Aksel looked like a Halloween pumpkin version of himself.

"Ointment would be good," said Ben.

The ten of them settled into their seats. More than a couple fell asleep on the way.

～

"Nery Thomas?"

Nerys turned round, a half-pint of Gnome's Bottom Dark'n'Nutty in her hand. The bar area and rear beer garden of the microbrewery were crowded with Morris dancers and Morris dancing fans. Nerys wasn't sure if there were genuinely that many people in the second category or whether, like the audiences at poetry events and open-mic comedy nights, most of the 'fans' were just participants awaiting their time to shine.

"Is that you, Nery Thomas?"

The voice was rich and fruity, the kind of cultured playful tone one might get from a TV antiques expert or a second-rate actor. It belonged to a man with bright ginger hair that he'd tried to tame flat with a lot of hair cream, but which refused to lay down and die. To her surprise, she recognised him.

"It's you. From the Halesowen Hankymen."

"Rufus Dandy," he said, offering her a hand. His smile revealed a set of perfectly white and perfectly square teeth, like a cartoon illustration of a healthy, happy mouth. "So glad you could make it to our festival of music and dance."

The way he said 'our' made it sound like the event belonged specifically to him.

"Yes," she said, looking about. "I've not seen the people I'm looking for yet."

"The Wednesbury Wallopers?" Rufus stuck out his bottom lip in a childish pout. "Sadly, no sign of the plucky little tykes. Jacob and Marcee Willoughby said— Have you met Jacob and Marcee? Dreadful people, but salt of the earth really. They said they would be here. I think a lot of people are hoping to see them."

"Oh?"

"Those scandalous videos have drawn a lot of unwanted attention to the craft."

"Oh, those videos on social media?"

"Over two million views now."

"Really?" Nerys took out her phone and brought up one of the videos of the wild Morris dancing/rock band mash-up. Rufus was right. They were not only popular but there were even some copycat videos and, bizarrely, both *#morrisdancing* and *#BritMoz* were trending across social media platforms.

"Unbelievable," she said.

"I know," said Rufus. "Bringing the craft into disrepute. I mean, look at them there. Is that meant to be a Shepherd's Hey? And if that's supposed to be a Come-by-me-Willy then they need to lift their legs far higher than that. It's embarrassing."

Miss Cavanagh nudged Nerys's elbow. The older woman had an empty glass in her hand. "You've not even touched yours yet," she said, noting Nerys's glass.

"It's a bit dense," said Nerys, which was a polite way of

saying that trying to drink the Dark'n'Nutty was like trying to drink malty porridge.

"I'll take that from you then," said Miss Cavanagh, swapping glasses with her. "You go to the bar and get us a couple of glasses of Smooth'n'Fruity." She gave Rufus the briefest of smiles. "I am drowning my sorrows. Vandals drank all my bull semen."

"Is that one of the brews here?" said Rufus.

"It is not," said Miss Cavanagh.

"Oh. Oh, I see."

Nerys hesitated before going back to the bar. "If either of you see Jeremy Clovenhoof or any of the Wallopers, be sure to let me know."

"I'm sure they're around somewhere," said Rufus.

AT YORK HOSPITAL bee stings were dabbed with soothing ointment, and several people were checked for cuts, bruises and general shock. Aksel's various burns, bangs, breaks and scrapes were a brief source of fascination for a group of medical students who were doing the rounds.

With the two bored police officers waiting for them all in the waiting room, Clovenhoof wandered through to the cubicle to check on Aksel.

"You can't be in here," said the nurse.

"It's amazing how many people say that to me," Clovenhoof replied. "Hey Aksel! Did they reset your nose?"

"They sure did! It looks amazing, I can't believe it! So much better than the old one!"

"I see they also gave you morphine. Nice work. I'm working on a plan to bust us out of here."

"None of you are going anywhere," said the nurse. "Mr Vaskebjorn is going down to x-ray in a minute."

"No can do, sunshine," said Clovenhoof. "It's seven o'clock. Our team of dancers and musicians have a competition to win in less than two hours."

"Are you kidding me?" said Marcee, popping her head through the curtains. "We are bashed and broken, we have lost good men to food poisoning, and we have no instruments."

"Details, details," said Clovenhoof. "We're a team. We need to stick together."

When - the bull scene or earlier in story

"No, fucking way, you monster. We're back with normal humans now and I don't ever want to see you again."

"*Again*," said the nurse, "there shouldn't be anyone in here."

Clovenhoof ignored him. "So, Marcee, you'll let Rufus Dandy and his cheating Hankymen steal your prize once more?"

"What do you care?" she shot back.

"I don't. I really don't. Well, except ... I'm a roadie for this band and that means I'm in charge of fun."

"I don't think that's what roadies do..."

"As Aksel will testify, I've created nothing but fun and exciting experiences since I joined this motley crew—"

"Damn right," said the much injured lead singer.

"—and nothing would be more fun right now than gatecrashing a Morris dancing contest and helping you stick it to that cheating, no-good, chicken-molesting scoundrel Rufus Dandy!"

"Chicken-molesting? I don't think..."

"Oh, Marcee, you don't know half the bad things he's done. Tax evasion. Drug-running for the Contra-rebels. Widdling on toilet seats in public toilets. It's a litany of shame and villainy."

Marcee glared at him, but Clovenhoof knew he had her. "Fine. Tell me what to do," she said.

"First of all, drink this." He thrust the flask of Lilith's Tears into her hand.

She eyed him suspiciously, then relented.

"Is that alcohol?" demanded the nurse.

"No, no, my friend. It's something far better than alcohol." Clovenhoof stopped and stared. "Wow, did I actually just say that?" He shook himself from his daze. "It's true what they say: travel really does broaden the mind. Not overly sure I like that."

THERE WAS a queue of traffic on the main road into York. Rutspud sat in the back of the private hire taxi with Eltiel and Twinkle. Rutspud craned his neck to see round the front seat at the mounting traffic.

"Backed up all the way through Rawcliffe and Skelton. Big police incident," said the driver and turned up the car radio.

"*...fire broke out at York Hospital a short while ago. Police are searching for a man who they wish to speak to in connection with* *a number of thefts and public order offences in the York and Ripon areas. It is understood the man was in police custody in York Hospital but escaped by masquerading as a doctor. It is also believed a quantity of medication and a wheelchair have been stolen from the hospital, but reports of one of the local ambulances being stolen remain unconfirmed."*

"Clovenhoof?" said Eltiel.

"Of course," said Rutspud.

"Oh, that Jeremy's a right character, ain't he?" chuckled Twinkle.

54

"**S**tealing an ambulance is not cool!" said Ben for the sixth time, leaning into the front from the crowded rear of the vehicle.

"It's got seatbelts!" said Clovenhoof. "And probably even an MOT. I thought you'd be thrilled." He took a corner at speed. He'd discovered the sirens while casually flicking switches and was now making full use of them. "Anyway, it's for a good cause."

"It is," said Marcee. "We're on a mission!" She had the clay bottle in her hand.

"That stuff has hallucinogenics in it, right?" said Ben.

"Magic juice, I tell you!"

"The Gnome's Bottom was straight on," said Valdemar, looking at his phone.

"And what's the point in us going to the venue when we don't have any gear with us?" said Jacob. "We have no instruments or accoutrements—"

"There will be time later for fancy French snacks," said Clovenhoof.

"I meant bells and sticks. We're all either wearing rags or hospital gowns."

"We'll borrow some at the competition!"

"What about our instruments?" said Camille. "There will be no drum kits at this festival of lame dancing."

"I am very confident we will find what we need before the performance," said Clovenhoof.

"Man, your delusions are as deep as they are extensive!" said Camille.

"Give that woman more magic juice!" he declared.

"What kind of a place are we going to find that will provide the things we need?" said Ben. "They are pretty damned niche. I should also remind you we have no money."

"A place like this could be a good start," said Clovenhoof, as he made a sharp turn in through an entrance gate.

"A scrapyard? Are you thinking we can scrap the ambulance for the cash? I don't—"

Clovenhoof jumped out of the vehicle and strode up to the tiny office, which was a shipping container with a door. He knocked and waited. A man answered the door. He had a moustache that drooped down the sides of his face, a pair of curtains around the cigarette he was smoking. His jowls sagged in crumpled folds, and his head was completely bald. He looked so much like a walrus that Clovenhoof held out a hand, half-expecting a flipper.

"Jeremy Clovenhoof at your service. I believe you've been waiting all of your career to help a group of Morris dancers and musicians to equip themselves for an important Morris dancing showdown."

The man blinked. "You one of them rehabilitated criminals selling stuff? Your patter needs work, mate."

"You're not a million miles from the truth there, my friend. Let me put it another way. You're pretty thirsty and I have a drop of the good stuff here. Take a sip."

Clovenhoof held out his flask. The man shrugged and took a swig. He smacked his lips and rolled his meaty neck. "So, are you saying we need to go and make a load of insane equipment out of rusty scrap metal?"

"I am," said Clovenhoof.

The man whooped with glee. "I thought this day would never come!" He called over his shoulder. "Trace, hold my calls! I'll be over in the workshop."

THE TAXI DRIVER was indicating before Rutspud saw the venue and the roadside sign for the brewery.

"Gnome's Bottom indeed," he said.

The driver drew to a stop in the crowded car park. "Big event tonight?"

"Big Morris dancing contest," said Rutspud.

"Right, yeah. I seen that BritMoz dance video. Looked a bit of a laugh."

"Bit of a laugh, yes," said Rutspud and hopped out, Eltiel and Twinkle in tow.

"Don't forget to rate me five stars!" the driver called.

"Julio always gives five stars," Rutspud assured him, waving the pilfered phone.

The crowd inside the microbrewery bar generated a wall of sound – chatter, laughter, lively expectation.

"Focus now," said Eltiel. "We find Clovenhoof and the Lilith's Tears. We must be close."

Twinkle sniffed the ground, then sniffed the air and, with a yip of excitement, dashed forward.

"He's got his scent!" said Rutspud.

"Or he's detected unguarded meat products," said Eltiel.

They plunged in.

BEN WASN'T sure how the transformation had happened, but his job for the next half hour was apparently to hammer the dents and ridges out of a dustbin lid until Camille declared it made a pleasing sound when she hit it. He had been given a hard hat and a hi-vis jacket and was using an anvil.

He looked around the group. Everyone was engaged in something equally unlikely yet oddly pleasing. Rasmus and Valdemar inspected the innards of an ancient piano, selecting lengths of wire they might somehow use for the strings of a guitar-like instrument. Aksel and Clovenhoof pored over a scribbled plan with the walrus guy, who was apparently the only one allowed to use the welder (much to Clovenhoof's disappointment). Clovenhoof had produced something which looked very much like a titanium hip bone from a pocket – "Borrowed it from the hospital," he informed Ben –

and was pointing at the design, indicating where it might go. Walrus guy wandered into the office at one point, looking really excited, and came out again cradling a box which they all peered into. Clovenhoof did a little jig at that point, which Ben thought might signify a worrying development.

Jacob and Marcee wielded tin snips and pliers, and were apparently making bells from smaller pieces of scrap. They might not have been traditional bells - in fact they looked more like medieval instruments designed to flay skin from one's enemies - but they made a sound when rattled, which seemed to delight Marcee and Jacob. Hairy Leonard and Slackpipes Johnson seemed very comfortable in a metalwork shop, and they had teamed up to make a glockenspiel by sawing up lengths of metal tubing. They were also in charge of fashioning drumsticks, glockenspiel sticks, and the sticks that would be used in the Morris dancing. Everything was made from metal as there was no wood available.

Camille tested her new drum kit, which was made from two dustbin lids and an oil drum. She scowled at the sound, but kept going. "It's fucking harsh!" she growled as she bashed out a metallic rhythm.

"If anyone can make that work then it's you," said Clovenhoof.

She stared at him long and hard, as if trying to prise apart the insult from the compliment. In the end she shrugged. "Yeah."

Rasmus picked up his bass guitar, which definitely looked as if someone had sawed through part of a piano and welded it onto an old lawnmower handle. He plucked at the strings. "Wow these are heavy. Not sure my fingers are up to it."

"Here, here." Walrus guy handed him a pair of welding gloves, and Rasmus pulled them on. He strummed a chord. It wasn't tuneful in any traditional sense, but it was powerful. He hit the strings with more confidence, matching Camille's beat. "This could be good."

This was high praise from Rasmus, and Ben wondered if they might actually be able to deliver some sort of show when they arrived.

"It's nearly half eight," said Marcee.

"To the ambulance!" cried Clovenhoof.

55

Nerys had allowed herself to be led out the rear of the Gnome's Bottom with Rufus Dandy. He seemed keen to give her the full Morris dancing experience. Or perhaps he just wanted to hold onto her because he seemed to be as keen as her to see the Wednesday Wallopers and their entourage.

There was a large field behind the microbrewery. Night had fallen over the city, but a pair of temporary floodlights had been set up. They bathed the area in light as bright as sunshine. There was a large central enclosure that was presumably the performance space. Around the side were a number of taped off areas: each Morris side given a space of their own to prepare in.

"The Buxton Buckle-Benders there are a fearsomely good team," said Rufus. "The Durham Dance Sensation are good, but a little avant garde for my tastes. Oh, the Clitheroe Cloggers are here. Surprising after their poor showing last year."

"I had no idea that flouncing about with bells on was so popular," said Miss Cavanagh, an unashamedly foamy beer moustache on her upper lip.

Rufus Dandy gave her a scowl. "It is a fine and noble tradition which has often had a strong following." He looked about at the crowds. "But there are a lot of people here tonight." He scoffed haughtily. "Your friends' internet antics appear to have drawn something of an uncultured crowd." He consulted a watch. "Fifteen minutes until registration closes and the competition begins. Is it possible the Wednesbury Wallopers might not make it...?"

"Comin' through! Comin' through!" grunted a gruff, ankle-high voice somewhere in the crowd.

It took Nerys a moment to place it. As she turned, Twinkle bounded up, ran up the vertical length of her leg, and tunnelled his way into her arms.

"Twink!" she gasped as her little lost dog plastered her face with a hundred licks of greeting.

He snuzzled her with energy and affection and she hugged him close.

"I was so worried!" she said.

"Tell me about it!" said Twinkle.

She held him out at arm's length to inspect him. He looked a bit bedraggled, although the pink bow in his hair was a nice addition.

"Don't you go runnin' off again like that, missy!" he said, still wriggling with delight.

"Me?" she said and laughed.

"I ain't had nuffin' to eat since this mornin'. It's been bladdy awful."

"Did that dog just talk?" said Rufus, his pasty complexion paling further.

"Probably done with hidden speakers or something," said Miss Cavanagh and took another swig of her pint.

Nerys didn't care what they thought. Her little boy, whether he spoke or not, had been returned to her. She hugged him close. "Did you find Jeremy?"

"Nah. But I found a couple of other chancers. Put me down now, woman. Don't show me up in front of the lads."

She held onto him tightly as Rutspud the demon and Eltiel the angel squeezed their way closer through the press of people.

"Ah, if it isn't Miss Thomas," said Eltiel.

"Aren't you the fake copper who came to my house earlier?" said Miss Cavanagh.

The angel looked at her. "I have no idea what you're talking about, madam."

Rutspud rubbed his hands together and tried to see through the crowd around them.

"Well, we're all here. Any sign of Lord Clovenhoof?"

"I think they're going to miss it all," said Nerys.

THE MOOD in the speeding ambulance was elevated.

"We're going to perform with instruments we crafted with our own hands," said Aksel. "We are not only artists, we are artisans. When I write my memoir, this will get its own chapter, I think."

"You? Write a memoir?" said Camille. "What happened to dying at twenty-seven?"

Aksel chuckled. "If this weekend is anything to go by, I need to live another fifty years to fit in all the fun things yet to be done!"

"Be sure to take pictures," Valdemar told Camille. "When I play my new guitar, I want my family to know they were at the forefront of my mind."

"There will be no photographic record of this weekend, I can assure you," she said. "This is not part of my ten year plan. You know you lot are all over social media with your antics. This is bending my narrative all out of shape."

"Hey," said Rasmus and passed Camille a pack of cigarettes.

"Where did you get these?" she said, delighted.

"The guy back at the scrapyard. Real helpful guy, no?"

Camille took out a cigarette and jammed it between her lips. She did her best not to smile.

Clovenhoof called out as they turned off the main road. "We're here!"

When the ambulance pulled up they all piled out into a car park. Jacob and Marcee led the charge towards the venue.

"Five to nine!" Marcee shouted.

"Registration!" Jacob shouted.

They followed a hand drawn sign round the side of the brewery building. Djævlehund followed with their homemade instruments. They nearly collided with the

Morris dancers as they drew up at a little gazebo where they were required to register.

"What time do you call this?" said a man with a clipboard and a beard like wild hedgerow.

"Not yet nine o'clock," panted Jacob. "We're the Wednesday Wallopers and our, er, backing band."

There were some whispers among the punters around them. There was some pointing too.

"We're famous," tittered Clovenhoof.

"Or they're wondering who these hobos in rags and hospital gowns are," said Ben.

"It's definitely a look," said Valdemar. "Maybe we should be like Ghost, or Slipknot. You know, only appear in costume on stage."

"Is hospital hobo a look?" said Rasmus.

"For one night only," said Camille.

But Clovenhoof heard one of the curious onlookers say something about 'BritMoz' and there was the flash of camera. "I think we are actually famous," he said.

"Crazy," whispered Ben.

The registration grey beard finally let them sign in and told them to find an empty paddock in the rear field to set up.

They all carried their scrapyard equipment into the only spare space. There was definitely a noticeable dip in the background noise as they passed through. This was good. Clovenhoof knew if people were bothered enough to stop talking and watch as they entered, then they already had some sort of an edge.

"Do we get the chance to do any rehearsals before the

contest starts?" Ben asked. He had a set of bells, but he twitched them at arm's length, as if scared of them.

"Afraid not. The contest starts any moment," said Marcee. "Now, we need to all understand our set. We will start with *The Lollipop Jig*, and segue straight into *The Fool's Wedding*, so—"

"—whoa, whoa, whoa! I think I need to stop you right there!" said Aksel. "What about our amazing performance the other night? The crowd went nuts for our rock tunes, didn't they? We don't even know those songs you just mentioned."

"Can I remind you that you managed to follow my lead perfectly well before you all went off the rails?" said Marcee with gritted teeth, "I plan to borrow an accordion and we can do exactly the same thing. This is a Morris contest, not a drunken gathering at a pub!"

Hairy Leonard and Slackpipes Johnson shrugged at each other, clearly not seeing the difference.

"Well, we need to come up with a plan," said Rasmus. He nodded as a man strode out to the centre of the performance area, microphone in hand.

"Giles Palmerston-Chuff, the Morris meet-master," Jacob whispered in awe.

As some boring self-important duffer began to give a self-important speech about the noble and longstanding tradition of Morris dancing (to which Rufus Dandy nodded along with every word) Nerys caught sight of a pair of little red horns on the far side of the performance area. At the same time, Twinkle gave a gruff bark. "'E's 'ere."

"Who's here?" said Miss Cavanagh. "That bastard who drank my semen?"

"Er, yes," said Nerys.

"Don't forget," said Rutspud. "The important thing is to get the flask of Lilith's Tears off him."

"Is that the cause of all this?"

"Well, he's also, you know, Satan," Eltiel pointed out. "Is there any other artifact of holy power he has secreted about his person?"

"Well, last time I saw him, he also had the Pipe of St Zita superglued to the palm of his hand."

"What?" said Nerys.

"Who?" said Miss Cavanagh.

"Saint Zita," said Eltiel. "Thirteenth century maid canonised for her piety and hard work. The patron saint of order and tidiness."

"We could do with some of that round here," said Rutspud.

"People pray to her when they've lost their keys, apparently," said the angel.

Rutspud grinned. "What's the betting one toot on her pipe will restore order to this situation?"

"I think I'm going to tackle this the old fashioned way," said Nerys and, metaphorically rolling up her sleeves, waded through the crowd towards Clovenhoof.

56

The Palmerston-Chuff dude was droning on about some aspect of the evolution of the Somerset Morris when Clovenhoof caught sight of familiar faces moving through the crowd.

"Uh-oh. The fun police have arrived!" he hissed at everyone. "I think we might need to move our act to the start of the running order."

"How on earth would we do that?" Marcee asked.

"We take the stage. Now! Aksel, strike up the opening chord!"

"Of what?"

"Search your heart and you will find the answer," said Clovenhoof, having no idea if such things actually worked.

"I don't even have an accordion!" snapped Marcee.

"Then let's sort that first!"

He strode out across the green performance space, crossed to where a much more traditional Morris musical act was waiting, punched the accordionist in the face, and ripped the instrument from his stunned grip.

There were gasps of surprise from the audience. Giles Palmerston-Chuff was thrown entirely off his lecture. Even Nerys, pushing to the front of the onlookers, hesitated at the sight of such random violence. The stunned silence gave Clovenhoof time to act.

He threw the accordion at Marcee (who managed to catch it more by luck than design), then ripped the microphone from Palmerston-Chuff's hand and positioned himself front and centre.

"Hello Gnome's Bottom!" he screamed. "We are the Wednesbury Wallopers here to melt your faces with a blitzkrieg of music and dance!"

Aksel stepped forward with his new, experimental guitar and struck a chord that indeed came straight from his heart.

"Come close one and all!" Clovenhoof screamed. "Britmoz is here!"

He could see a ginger-haired Morris tosser gesticulating and complaining, but the majority of the crowd surged forward and squeezed into the performance area in front of the band.

"Ready to play some Britmoz?"

Aksel nodded.

Clovenhoof put the microphone onto a stand in front of Aksel. He beckoned Jacob, Ben, Hairy Leonard and Slackpipes Johnson forward to join him for the dancing.

Marcee pursed her lips with annoyance, but leaned over her instrument with an intensity that suggested she was taking the concept of rock accordion seriously.

Camille counted them in with the harsh clatter of her percussion and the band started to play. Even with the rough, scrap yard instruments Clovenhoof recognised the opening chords of *(Never Trust a) Man in a Dress*.

Out among the crowd, Clovenhoof could see Nerys looking furious that her path was blocked.

"Morris dancers!" Jacob yelled over the escalating noise. "A *Jenny-runs-ragged* on four! One! Two!"

Clovenhoof grinned to himself, knowing he could add a little dramatic flair to the performance. He danced a little hip-waggling, foot-shuffling piece, using his arms to encourage the crowd to join in, while Jacob, Hairy Leonard, Slackpipes Johnson and a bewildered Ben leapt into their first routine.

Rasmus was piling raw bass notes on top of Askel's singing, while Valdemar wove intense heavy metal counter melodies around it. As the crowd cheered (the large sections who weren't disgusted by this affront to traditional Morris), Clovenhoof joined in with the Morris routine.

He didn't know the moves. He hadn't bothered to learn any of the moves. He was very much an improviser when it came to dance. When it came to all things, in fact. However, he did have one thing planned. It was going to be big. It was going to be explosive.

He was waiting for the big guitar *kerr-ang* that punctuated *Man in a Dress* halfway through. He edged over to Aksel in readiness. The crowd weren't going to know what hit them.

～

TWINKLE WAS in a world of stomping crowded feet. It was not a good place for a little dog to be.

"Oi – wotchit! Jeez lady! Heels? At an event like this! Stone the crows! Mate – get your clodhoppers out of my face!"

Suddenly Rutspud was there beside him. In this forest of legs the little demon was nearer to Twinkle's height that anyone else. "We need to get to the front!" He shouted over the wall of din.

"We? Us?!"

"Sneak through the crowd! You've seen the flask. You know what it looks like. You go left, I'll go right!"

Twinkle gave the demon a look that hopefully indicated how crazy he was, then dashed forward through a storm of kicking feet.

BEN DANCED. He kicked, he twirled, he waved his hankie and jingled his bells. He hoped he was keeping time and doing the right moves. Hairy Leonard and Slackpipes Johnson might have the appearing of obese beer-swilling oafs, but with their Morris get up on they transformed into precise and graceful creatures. They were like ... they were like beautiful dancing bears, except without the imprisonment and animal cruelty that generally went with dancing bears. Ben listened to Camille's pounding beats and let them drive him forward in the dance.

As he gave a leap and a twist, he looked out across the cheering crowd and saw—

No! It couldn't be!

Watching from the back, cast in the shifting lights all around her, was Lois Cavanagh. His brain still could not reconcile the innocent maid he had frankly obsessed over with this octogenarian curmudgeon, but she was here. She was here!

He gave a mighty and joyful cry of "Ho!" on the next turn—

—And saw Nerys battling her way to the stage. What the fuck was she doing here? Had the viral craze of their previous performance really brought her all the way out here?

"Nerys is here!" he yelled.

CLOVENHOOF BROKE from his routine at Ben's shout. He turned to look

Nerys, the angel Eltiel and the ginger tosser – Rufus Dandy, it had to be! – were barging their way forward through people who were doing their best to have a good time.

Nerys shouted something which he could not hear, but Eltiel followed it up with a very clear "Lilith's Tears!"

So that was their game! They wanted to steal the magic juice and spoil his fun. He slid up behind Aksel and twisted the titanium hip knob on the man's guitar.

"Ready?" Clovenhoof yelled.

"Born ready!" screamed Aksel, then added, "What for?"

Clovenhoof flicked the lighter he'd borrowed off the walrus guy at the scrapyard just as Eltiel reached out for him.

"Back off Spangle Pants!" yelled Clovenhoof. "Flamethrower guitar!"

Yellow flames leapt six feet from the head of the guitar. The first blast scorched the microphone stand.

Aksel screamed, first in alarm and then in exhilaration.

Eltiel (along with several unfortunate members of the audience) lost his eyebrows in that instant and staggered back in scorched surprise.

"Yeah man!" Aksel whooped as he swung the guitar in an arc, like a child waving a sparkler.

Clovenhoof was quite frankly surprised the gas cylinders held out for more than a second or two, but Aksel continued to twirl the guitar in the air, shooting a roaring flame.

"Segue into *Eat My Fruit, Bitch!*" cried Camille.

"*Haymaker-ho!*" instructed Jacob.

In the flamethrower's glare, Marcee wove her own mad accordion melodies.

Most of the audience had backed off to a safe distance, but that Rufus Dandy had nipped into the gap so that he could complain.

"—bringing our noble tradition into disrepute—!" he yelled, barely audible over the crashing bass line, the sound of Camille's drums, and the roar of the flamethrower guitar.

Then the flames touched – only touched – Rufus's bonce, and suddenly his flame-red hair was truly aflame.

"Oh shit!"

Clovenhoof watched Rufus Dandy clutch the top of his head and try to pat out the flames with his hands.

"That's what happens when a grown man uses too much product on his luscious locks," said Clovenhoof.

He pulled out the flask of Lilith's Tears. If this thing really was bottomless then it should be just the thing to put out a fire. As he pulled it from his pocket, he saw little Twinkle was just in front of him.

"Gizzus the bottle, mate!" said Twinkle. "And no one needs to get hurt!"

"Twinkle! You can talk!"

"Bottle!" the dog growled.

"What? No!"

He turned to pour liquid on Rufus's noggin, but there was Nerys, coming from the other direction, with a fire extinguisher in her hand. Clovenhoof didn't even had time to think about where the hell she had snatched it from so quickly. He swung round with the flask. She was swinging the other way with the extinguisher, starting to squeeze the trigger.

NERYS SAW the flask and extinguisher collide. With a hearty 'chonk' the extinguisher smashed the mouth and neck off the ancient vessel and water gushed forth, right over Rufus's burning bonce and into the fiery mouth of the flamethrower.

A ball of steam ballooned outward, an explosion of gaseous Lilith's Tears.

There was a long drawn out shout of "Noooooooooo!" from somewhere, and still the cloud billowed outward. There was something truly unnatural in that cloud. It wasn't just liquid turned into steam, it was as though something unholy had been unleashed.

"That went right in my face!" complained Rufus Dandy. Nobody was listening because all eyes were on the ball of steam. It wobbled and expanded overhead.

Nerys craned her neck as it flowed over and through them, bringing a hazy salty scent and the strangest of feelings.

Now the cloud was the size of the crowd...

Now it was the size of the field they all stood in...

Now it filled the sky as far as the eye could see. It expanded ever outwards, up and down. The world was now mist and darkness, and even the music and dancing had come to a startled stop. The flamethrower guitar gave a final sputter.

In the silence, Eltiel wailed. "You utter morons! What have you done? What have you done!?"

Clovenhoof loomed large in the mist. His surprise had turned into incredulous delight.

"Breathe deep, friends," he said. "I'm sharing my gift with the world."

57

By happy accident, Clovenhoof found the mic stand again.

"Good evening, everyone," he crooned. "My name is Jeremy Clovenhoof." He gave a leg jiggle of his bells. "And this is my backing band Djævlehund. Let me tell you a story of the greatest woman in the world."

Out of nowhere, and right on cue, Rasmus's bass started up in the foggy distant, joined by the swirling runs of Marcee's accordion.

"She refused to yield to what men told her to do," Clovenhoof half-spoke, half-sang. "She wouldn't take none of their shit."

There was a whoop of approval from the mist-shrouded crowd. Clovenhoof held out a hand and Nerys, apparently much to her own surprise, stepped out of the mist to take it.

Somewhere, Eltiel was still complaining, but he seemed fainter and further away.

Clovenhoof clutched Nerys's hand tenderly. "This woman, spurned for her wilful nature, was outcast. Treated like a demon."

Nerys was giving him a questioning look. Now Valdemar, Aksel and Camille had taken up the tune and Clovenhoof, knew – just knew – the words, as though the vapours allowed him to will them into existence.

He leaned into the microphone and gave a high, piercing rock and roll scream. A wind sprung from behind the band and pushed the fog out through the crowd. Floodlights blared and guitars thrashed.

Clovenhoof sang.

"In the garden where the serpent's coil winds,
Adam's first wife, born of earth, divine
Lilith, oh Lilith, fierce and free,
Before Adam she'd never kneel!"

He gave them a salacious tongue waggle and launched into the chorus.

"Lilith, queen of the night,
Rebel spirit burning bright.
Tears of defiance, bitter and clear,
Defiant earth maid, knows no fear."

TWINKLE COULD SEE that a strange effect had overcome everyone. Nerys had clearly stepped up to wrest control of the situation, but now seemed to have become Clovenhoof's dance partner.

Twinkle was pleased to see his mistress enjoying herself. She was in a much better mood than he'd seen her since ... since forever, basically. So was everyone else. But there was something hypnotic and unnatural about it all.

The effect of Lilith's Tears had obviously seeped into every single person. Joyous whooping came from the punkish drummer as she hammered her makeshift drums. The two fat Morris dancers started to swing each other around in an athletic dance routine.

Next to Twinkle, Eltiel said, "Oh, this is bad!"

"Yeah?" said Twinkle. He saw Eltiel's feet were tapping and shuffling in time to the music. "But you seem to be getting into the groove."

Eltiel looked down. His expression became surprised, then angry that Twinkle had called him out.

"You know nothing, abomination..."

"Er..."

Angel wings thrust out from Eltiel's sides with such speed they knocked a member of the audience off his feet.

"I was made ... to dance!" Eltiel boomed and leapt into the air. His halo became a supernova of bright colours that washed over the whole scene. He spun in rhythmic pirouettes in the sky.

"Nice to see you've found yerself a purpose, mate," Twinkle called after him.

Up front, the woman with the accordion was dancing some sort of lively jig as she played. A man who might have been her husband mirrored her moves. The two of them were synchronised perfectly. In spite of Twinkle's longstanding hatred for the sound of the accordion, they played and danced as if they were born for this moment. Despite the weird atmosphere gripping the place, it was a beautiful sight to see.

"Humans living in the moment," Twinkle said to nobody in particular. "Finally learned something from us dogs, eh? Now, has any of them left any food unattended before they took to dancing, I wonder?"

RUTSPUD EYED THE CROWD. He'd spent enough time on Earth to recognise when people were drunk or high, but this was a step beyond that. It looked to him as if the entire population had been doused with the wilfulness of Lilith's Tears. It removed inhibitions and made them all certain that their most insane impulses were truly amazing ideas.

He wasn't sure what the outcome would be if this continued, but he suspected it probably wasn't good. He wove a path through the heaving mass of dancers to find Clovenhoof. He paused briefly beneath the humanoid glitter ball that was Eltiel. Should he ask the angel to snap out of it and help him sort out this mess?

Eltiel had somehow transformed the grass beneath his feet into a pulsing neon dancefloor. He had a hand on each buttock and swivelled his hips, his feet planted wide.

Rutspud sighed. Eltiel was too far gone.

The singing had now transmogrified into an extended instrumental break. Not just an instrumental break, but a lengthy solo for five instruments. And yes, Rutspud knew you couldn't have five solos at the same time, but this was very clearly what was happening. In the innovative Sixth Circle of Hell, many of the damned were softened up for torture by being locked in the *Chamber of the Nineteen-Minute Prog-Rock Solo*. Rutspud knew a lengthy and self-indulgent solo (or indeed five of them) when he heard one (or indeed them).

Clovenhoof was trying to join in in his own inimitable way.

"My lord!" he said when he reached the devil. He tapped him on the back. "Er, what is that you're doing?"

"I am inventing the cockenspiel," said Clovenhoof over his shoulder. He had his trousers around his ankles while he waggled his groin over some unfortunate musical instrument. "What are you doing here, vile betrayer?"

"Betrayer? Me?"

"Pandering to me by pretending to bring me queries and questions on hellish matters. And on *Bake Off* night at that! Treating me like an old senile fool! But look at me now! Huh! Huh! See what I'm capable of!"

Rutspud could indeed see what Clovenhoof was capable of. He was capable of getting a discordant sound out of a bent cymbal with his swinging manhood.

"You have unleashed Lilith's Tears upon a great many people," said Rutspud. "It has to stop!"

"Stop?" There was a zipping sound and Clovenhoof swivelled round to face Rutspud. "Why on earth would I stop? People are enjoying themselves. Leave them be."

"Yes, but the consequences—"

"Screw the consequences, you obnoxious toad! You're a buzzkill and a big fat liar. Come here!"

Clovenhoof wrenched the wang-soiled cymbal off its stand and swung viciously. If Rutspud been any taller and hadn't ducked, Clovenhoof would have decapitated him with that blow. Demons could survive all manner of mutilations, but losing his head would have been mighty inconvenient.

"Sire! You've lost your mind!"

"I am a rock god!" Clovenhoof screamed and booted Rutspud with a surprisingly effective karate kick. The fact that the leg had jingly little bells on did not make it any less painful. Rutspud rolled across the ground. His InstaDoor device bounced along beside him. Yes, perhaps it was time to make a tactical withdrawal and work out a new attack strategy.

Rutspud grabbed the InstaDoor, but only a second before Clovenhoof grabbed him.

"Don't you be spoiling my fun with your hi-tech gadgets!" snarled his satanic majesty.

With brute force, Clovenhoof pulled the device from Rutspud's hands. Rutspud could now see that this hand, mostly freed from the superglue, still had a small clay pipe stuck to the palm.

"Zita's pipe..." Rutspud wheezed and reached for it. Clovenhoof flung him aside, and with luck (or the power of Lilith's Tears) Rutspud collided against the open back of a stage equipment storage box which slammed down on top of him as he fell inside.

Rutspud rolled in the dark and pushed, but there was a

sudden weight on top of the box and the sound of latches clicking.

"Ha!" crowed Clovenhoof. "Now let's see what this device can do."

"Oh, crap," said Rutspud.

en felt as if the music had crept under his skin. It was a tune that seemed familiar, but he had no idea where he'd heard it. It gave him a frenetic energy, and a new heightened perception of the world around him.

He had danced through the crowd like a whirling dervish, Morris dancing hankies fluttering and waving. He felt the Morris moves and the heavy metal beats lift him. He felt like he had become the embodiment of Morris, the manliest of all the dances in the world.

And as his twirling stopped, he found himself deep in the crowd and standing right in front of Lois Cavanagh.

The old woman was inspecting her half-drunk glass of ale. "I think someone's spiked my drink," she said.

"Lois..." he said.

She looked at him. This was his moment. The world around them had ascended into a dream-like state. Fate had brought him before her. Here he was in his Morris gear, dashing and ragged and ready for action. He was her James Bond, her knight in shining armour, her masked avenger. He had the tassels and bells and, somewhere, a knobbly stick to wave about.

"Lois," he repeated.

She struggled to focus on him. "Oh, it's you. The spunk-drinking tosser with pictures of me."

"I'd like you to perhaps think of me as something more, if you might," he said.

"You like real ale," she said. It was a statement. "Try this."

Ben took the offered glass and took a hefty sip. It was delicious. In this messed up misty world they now inhabited, how could it be anything other than delicious?

"I have things I need to say to you," he said.

"You're half my age, sunny Jim."

Ben recalled what Camille had said about their own age gaps previously. "Age is just a number. Listen, I know the affairs of two people in this crazy world don't..."

"You'll have to speak up!" said Lois. "The music's very loud!"

"Right. You see, er, I'm just a boy, standing in front of a hill of beans, asking her..."

Lois was grinning widely at him. She had all her own teeth, he noted. That was a good thing. Or maybe they were just really nice dentures. Whatever. The original Lois – *his* Lois – was shining through.

She pushed the glass to his lips again. He realised it was more than a shared drink, it was an invitation.

He drank deeply, tossed the glass aside and held out his arms to her. "Shall we dance, Lois?"

She nodded and slotted neatly into his arms.

UP ON THE STAGE – if anything could be described as the stage, when it now felt like the whole world had become the stage for the greatest concert of all time – Valdemar turned to Aksel. "Hey man, you think this is happening everywhere, or just here?"

"Which answer do you want to be true?" asked Aksel.

"I want my baby boy to be dancing to his daddy's music."

"And he will!" said Aksel. "Everyone!" he bellowed into the microphone. "Hold onto the person in front and let's go!"

He struck up a driving rock riff and turned to leave the stage, gesturing for the nearest people to fall in behind. "A heavy metal snake of rock music!" he shouted.

Rasmus found a fresh riff to accompany the dance.

"*Rock snake, slither cross the floor,*" sang Aksel. "*Rock snake, let's go explore.*"

CLOVENHOOF HAD no idea whether Aksel had intended to reinvent the conga dance, but here he was, doing it anyway. The song (which sounded suspiciously like Rod Stewart's *Hot Legs* with new words) was simple enough, and Clovenhoof thrust himself at the front of the line. Aksel might be the lead singer, but Clovenhoof could be nothing but frontman, the bandleader, the majorette with the twirling baton, the maracas-waving loon centre stage, the chief fool and party maker.

He swayed and pranced, sending the moves down the line behind him. The band smashed out the music on the brash metal instruments, creating a wild, magical harmony. Aksel's vocals led them on the dance of their lives, but Clovenhoof was the conduit. He looked over his shoulder to see the snake rippling away into the distance, as the movements passed down the line. He dodged left and right, and the snake shimmied from side to side. He sped up and slowed down, but the snake never faltered. It was a beautiful, co-ordinated beast and he was its head. He let out a roar, and everyone else echoed the sound.

"This is a beautiful thing!" he yelled. "What shall we do, Rock Snake?"

Somehow the answer came back, in a low but certain growl. *"Beer!"*

Clovenhoof could not have pinpointed who said the word, but he felt it in his bones. The Rock Snake had spoken.

"Let's get you some beer then, my magnificent beast! We need to find the cellar."

He dipped inside the building and found a single puny door in his way. It was easily stomped aside by the multi-legged rock snake. After gaining access to the cellar, the multi-armed rock snake swiftly passed kegs of beer outside into the performance area. It was a beautiful sight, or at least the rock snake thought so.

"Beer!"

The rock snake made short work of filling buckets, glasses and (in a couple of cases) wellington boots. Every part of the rock snake slurped and glugged beer from a series of massive drinking vessels. They made sure that the band was also provided with drink. Aksel, Rasmus and Valdemar were given their own keg with a piece of copper piping to use as a straw. It might well have been part of the pub's plumbing system. Who knew? Who cared? Camille had subtly communicated to the rock snake that she wanted her beer in a classier vessel, so she had a pineapple-shaped ice bucket which she sipped from as she drummed.

The rock snake moved a little more slowly now, because every part of it was clutching at least a gallon of beer.

ELTIEL WAS high above the snaking crowd of people, spinning in his own private disco. He'd transformed his robes into a sequinned suit that caught and reflected every ray of light. He smoothed back his suddenly luxuriant hair and struck the classic Travolta pose. He pursed his hips and swung an outstretched arm around, making sure to make eye contact with everyone below as he pointed. The whole world wanted to see his dance routine. He could feel it. He removed his jacket, hooked it over his finger, and twirled it overhead. He let it fly, preparing to throw his earthly form into some seriously funky moves.

BEN AND LOIS danced and whirled, both to the wild tune the band played and their own shared music. Something that spanned the decades. It might have been a jive or it might have been thrash metal, it didn't matter. They locked eyes, and Ben had no idea whether this was young Lois or old Lois, but she was the same person, so that didn't matter either.

He swept her around the floor, knowing there was no chance of them falling or bumping into anything, because everyone was a part of this glorious moment, and the world moved to accommodate them.

They collided with the dancing, drinking, cavorting Rock Snake as it wound around the field and were suddenly part of it. Lois had hold of the person in front and Ben had his hands on Lois's hips.

He couldn't recall every being happier.

NERYS FOUND herself holding onto Clovenhoof as he high-kicked and thrust himself about.

"I know you did this, Jeremy," she said.

"I sure did. You can't stay mad at me though, can you?"

She definitely had been mad at him. She had pursued him across the countryside, wanting her pound of flesh. She clutched for what had made her so angry. "You messed Twinkle up."

"Messed up, or improved? But now you adore me again because this is the best party ever!" Clovenhoof threw his arms wide.

"It is!" she was forced to agree. "It is the best party ever."

"And it's going to get even better if I— Ah!"

He was fiddling with a silvery button-covered box, and the "Ah!" was because he had stabbed a button and now, in the middle of the field behind the Gnome's Bottom, a purple slit of light had appeared.

"Fuck!" gasped Nerys.

Cackling, Clovenhoof reached into the line of light and pushed it wide. "Come on, gang! Let's take this party to the next level!"

Nerys could have refused to follow him through, but somehow she couldn't. Her dancing feet just kept dancing and she *wanted* to go. She never wanted this party to end. She and the rest of the rock snake danced through the pulsating gash.

She stepped onto a landscape of soft cloudiness. The light about them was white-grey nothingness, but the light of the amped-up party brought its own kaleidoscope of colours.

"What is this place?" shouted Aksel, still powering away on his guitar.

"This is Limbo," said Nerys. "The empty space between worlds."

"Come on!" yelled Clovenhoof, with a folksy high kick and a wave of his Morris hanky. "Let's all go back to my place!"

"...*My* place?" whispered Nerys.

She knew exactly what he meant. For there, in the far distance, was a small red glow. The gateway to Hell.

59

Twinkle was very much in favour of living in the moment and putting aside your worries for just one night, but he kind of drew the line at dancing a conga through a magic doorway into another dimension. The air from that place smelled unnatural. It smelled of nothing whatsoever. Yet the humans, hundreds of them, swinging jugs of ale and waving whatever instruments they could carry, were merrily dancing their way into the netherworld.

"This is not good," he declared and ran to the head of the line. "Hey! Oi! Stop!"

None of the people showed any inclination of stopping. The few who even heard him over the musical din just looked at him and grinned.

"Oi! You muppets! Give over! This could be bladdy dangerous!"

Not a single person paid attention.

Twinkle saw Ben Kitchen further down the line, kicking his legs and trying to maintain some grip on the old woman in front of him. Twinkle ran to them.

"Ben! Ben, mate! Time to give this a rest, awright?" Twinkle's nose nudged Ben on the knee, his paws extended up his leg. "C'mon now, me old mucka, enough of this!"

Nerys was so absorbed in his fun that he didn't even look as he reached a hand down to tickle Twinkle's ear.

"You do know you look proper gormless don't you?" said Twinkle. "It's like all the lights are on, but the real Ben – the one what knows where the sausages are – he ain't home, is he?"

Ben laughed as though he'd just heard a joke inside his own head and danced on.

"Fack's sake! You do know a dog's ears are highly sensitive, don't you? They can't take much more of this almighty racket." He sighed and dropped to the floor. "Come on Twinks," he growled to himself. "You're the only one here who's not lost their bleedin' marbles. Off we pop to sort shit out."

~

THE STORAGE BOX Rutspud was trapped in had a comfortingly low ceiling, but it provided little in the way of entertainment value, and he was becoming increasingly concerned about the noise from outside. Or indeed the lack

It had sounded very much as if the entire population ɪgaged in an enormous alcohol-fuelled rampage, but now that sound was trailing off, fading away, which meant the carnage was going elsewhere.

A rampage contained was one thing. A rampage on the move was something worse. And by worse, he absolutely meant something that could get him in trouble.

He'd laid on his back and tried to kick the lid open, but he was a demon built for scheming and plotting, rather than anything that required strength. His tiny legs were just not up to the job. He had inspected the hinges and knew if he had access to a screwdriver he could have them off in a jiffy, but there was nothing in this space he could use on screws. He'd battered a hinge with a coil of extension wire, but apart from making him feel slightly better, it hadn't really worked.

So he started yelling.

"Help! Help! Someone help me!"

There was the faintest patter of footsteps and then a snuffling sound.

"Alright, my son!" came Twinkle's voice. "What you doin' in a box? Only stoopid cats like goin' in boxes."

"I'm trapped!" said Rutspud. "And, please, no mention of cats while I'm in a vulnerable position."

Twinkle grunted. "Right. Seems like someone has closed these 'ittle 'itty 'atches on 'ou," he said around the scratch of gnawing teeth. One latch sprang open, followed seconds later by the other.

Rutspud propelled the lid up and, although he technically had no real need for air, gasped for it as he got up. "Thank you, Twinkle."

The little talking dog grinned at him grimly. "I can

understand why you locked yourself in there. It's a right proper shitshow out here."

Twinkle turned and followed his gaze. The last two dozen people still the field were jigging and capering through an InstaDoor fissure.

"Oh, hell," Rutspud spat.

"That's what I thought," said Twinkle.

"No. Literally hell. The Djævlehund will drag a thousand souls down to Hell. It's a heavenly prediction."

Up above, the sparkling orb of disco-dancing energy that was Eltiel swooped down on broad wings and followed the last of the revellers through the fissure into Limbo.

"We need to stop them!" said Rutspud, and ran for the shimmering doorway of light.

"I've never shown you round my old place before, have I?" shouted Clovenhoof.

"Hell? No!" Nerys shouted back.

"Oh, you're gonna love it! I don't know why I haven't taken you there before! Absolutely the best place for a party!"

"This is brilliant!" said Nerys. She jerked her head back. "Your drummer friend..."

"Camille?"

"She looks proper badass. Listen to those drums!"

"She is proper badass," said Clovenhoof. "And French!"

"You can just tell, can't you?"

"I know what you mean!"

"Do you think she'd let me have a go on her drums?"

Clovenhoof appeared to think only for a second. "Definitely. She is very friendly. Hang on, everyone! Switchback turn!"

The rock snake formed a coiling U-turn in Limbo. Clovenhoof led them in a shimmying dance until he had looped back to Camille and what was now her portable drum kit strung about her.

"Hello! I love your drums!" Nery shouted. "They are like cartoon drums, the way they look a bit like old dustbins. Can I have a go?"

Camille looked Nerys up and down. "Join me, bitch!"

As Clovenhoof peeled away to lead the dance back towards Hell, Nery hugged Camille with a love she rarely felt and looked for something to hit drums with.

One of the fat and hairy Morris man leaned round and offered her his stout dancing stick.

"You're all amazing!" shouted Nerys and, giving a Japanese schoolgirl V-pose as someone flashed a camera their way, bashed the drums with unbridled joy.

~

TWINKLE LEAPT through the purple portal and came down on a landscape that was too soft and yielding for his liking. The long snaking line of dancers was stretched over what seemed like miles. Could there really be that many of them? The band was still playing in the distance. Above, Eltiel was pulsing his hips and making steam train movements with his arms.

"That red glowy shit over there..." said Twinkle.

"That's Hell," said Rutspud.

"Does 'Ell get many visitors?"

"Not voluntarily, no."

"And you reckon 'Ell will let our lot go in, have a party, then come marchin' out again?"

Rutspud stroked his chin. "Let them go in? Yes. Have a party? Maybe. But then it'll be one of them parties where all the masks come off at midnight. And then I think the fun will stop."

Twinkle bared his fangs unhappily. "Then we'd best bladdy stop them." He looked up at Rutspud. "You seem like one o' them sneaky, clever types. How do I stop Nerys from dancin' 'er way into 'Ell?"

"They have all been dosed with a substance called Lilith's Tears. It's the same stuff that made you talk, but with the humans it's made them all behave like this."

Twinkle nodded. "They don't 'ave the mental capacity see, can't 'andle it."

Rutspud paused. "Er, something like that, maybe. I think we should try going for St Zita's Pipe."

"That the woman who 'elps you find lost keys?"

"More importantly, she's the patron saint of order and tidiness. If there's any divine plan in this creation, then maybe that pipe has been put there as our final hope."

"And that's the thing glued to Mr Clovenhoof's 'and?"

"Yeah. We need to get it off him. I don't really know if that's going to work. Lord Clovenhoof broke it and it might not have gone back together properly. Well, it definitely didn't go back together properly because it's glued to his hand."

"Nuffink ventured, nuffink gained, I always say," Twinkle said. "Let's go for it."

Rutspud gave him a little salute and the two of them charged down the flank of the blissfully doomed dancers.

BEN AND LOIS were at one with the rock snake. It was the natural next step for their relationship. They were comfortable enough with each other to share with the entire world. Ben nursed a vase full of Stumpy's Crotch ale, while Lois was forced to drink quickly as her Oxford Fusty was in a flowerpot with small holes in the bottom.

"Where are we?" said Lois dreamily.

"Does it matter as long as we're together?" said Ben.

She tugged on his hand. "You are an incorrigible young man."

60

The gateway to Hell reared in front of them: a massive cavern flanked by pillars of such staggeringly incomprehensible evil that dozens of stonemasons must have gone mad during the carving of them.

Clovenhoof howled as he approached. A thousand revellers howled along with him. They were magnificent and didn't care who knew it. They were preparing themselves for their descent into the pits of Hell and the excitement was a rippling energy surging through them, making every part of them yearn for the experiences to come. Any moment now and they would rush down the rocky slope into Hell, the ultimate basement nightclub, the eternal underground party.

"Lord!" came a shout from behind. Hurrying along the line came that treacherous demon, Rutspud.

"I thought I'd dealt with you!" Clovenhoof sneered.

"Please, Lord Clovenhoof," panted the running demon. "I just need a moment of your time."

"No time. Gotta party."

Valdemar threw out a crazy guitar riff as if to back him up.

"I'm sorry I was unkind to you earlier," said Rutspud.

"Unkind?"

"Being condescending. Pretending to make you feel important. To pander to your ego."

"My ego needs no pandering! I am Satan, Lord of Hell. I am in my prime! And this is my party!"

"Er, right, yeah, exactly. And I'm sure you were just biding your time, sitting on your half a sofa and watching that *Bake Off* crap on the telly."

A small forgotten part of Clovenhoof's soul felt the need to shout up. "It's not crap! It's beautiful television!"

"Er, okay."

"A quintessential slice of British life."

"If you say so."

"I do say so," said Clovenhoof, but he suddenly felt uncertain. For a split second he felt like an old man who had danced far longer into the night than he should have done. For a split second he felt like a mere mortal who would love nothing more than to curl up on his broken sofa with a mug of hot chocolate and a packet of digestive biscuits, and watch hours of *Bake Off* back to back. He only felt it for a second, but it was enough to send a disquieting ripple along the rock snake behind him.

Clovenhoof, the party-machine, the rock god, reasserted

himself just as quickly. "I don't need your apologies, demon. I've moved on. Apologies are for losers."

"Right, good," said Rutspud. "All I wanted from you, lord, was to show me your hand."

Clovenhoof held out his hand.

"The other one," said Rutspud tiredly.

Ahead, figures were moving in the firelight coming from the mouth of hell. Demons were coming to the edge of their domain to see what all the noise was. Rutspud could hear the clanking of chains and the tensing of whips. Demons – possibly griping about being overworked and underpaid – were preparing to receive an unexpectedly large consignment of souls.

Clovenhoof presented his other hand. As he did, he tried to switch his grip on the clay pipe into the other hand, but the glue still held fast.

"You're not having it," said Clovenhoof, holding his hand high. "Whatever it is, whatever your ploy. You're a tiny demon and you can't reach it."

"Oh, me?" said Rutspud. "I'm just the distraction."

There was a discordant guitar sound. Clovenhoof turned as a furry blur scampered up Aksel's leg, leapt once onto the neck of the guitar and a second time directly at Clovenhoof.

Twinkle's small jaws locked onto the open palm of Clovenhoof's hand. Fangs buried deep into flesh.

Clovenhoof roared and instinctively tried to fling the overgrown rodent away. This was both good and bad. Good because the action worked and Twinkle was tossed high into the sky; bad because the dog took a fair chunk of his hand flesh with it. Blood and pain poured forth.

"*Fuuuuuuuuuuuuuuck!*" Clovenhoof yelled.

"*Fuuuuuuck!*" yelled the front ranks of the rock snake, and the shout was carried back. "Fuuuck! Fuuck! Fuck, fuck, fuck!"

Clovenhoof squeezed his fist tight. The pain galvanised him, forced down any doubt. Hell – his home! – was only a hundred feet away. Clovenhoof was marching into the heart of his kingdom with his merry retinue and – by *fuck* his hand hurt! – there was going to be a homecoming party of such wild, crazed, excessive debauchery that it would make the Almighty in Heaven blush!

~

TWINKLE DIDN'T KNOW if the laws of gravity just didn't apply in this Limbo land, or if the magic Lilith's Tears had given Clovenhoof superhuman strength, but the dog, with pipe and glued-on skin clenched in his mouth, was airborne far longer than he wished.

He was contemplating what it was going to be like hitting the ground at speed, even the soft non-ground here, when there were suddenly hands around him.

"Flying disco dog!" exclaimed Eltiel.

There was a smile on his face. Possibly blissful, possibly just idiotic. The magic juice and dancing rhythm had him firmly in their spell.

"I expected better of you," growled Twinkle, with his mouth full. "Is this part of yer 'divine plan', mate?"

"It's divine," sang the angel and pirouetted in the air

whirling Twinkle with him. "How could it not be part of His plan?"

"Well, I reckon 'Is plan is for you to drop me off – gently! – somewhere down there."

The angel was happy to oblige and swooped down.

"Gentle like!" Twinkle grimaced.

The angel soared over the massive trailing snake.

"There! There! Drop!"

The angel released his furry payload at head height. Twinkle splayed his paws and wished for the elegance of a cat in his landing. He didn't quite manage it. He bounced off the frenetic accordion player, barrelled off their dancing partner, and landed not three feet from his mistress, Nerys.

He opened his mouth to tell her to snap out of it – and realised he couldn't speak. He couldn't breathe! The pipe was lodged way back in his mouth. He gagged and coughed, but it would not budge. And Nerys went dancing on, flailing at the drums around her.

Twinkle managed to drag in a fraction of a breath and tried to cough or vomit. Either would be good. But the pipe did not move. Instead a thin, reedy peep came out of it. There was a whooshing sound in the air, a flash of copper metal, and something very small whacked into Nerys's head at speed.

"Ow!"

She dropped her drumstick as she put her hand to her head and stared round wildly. She saw Twinkle choking.

"No! Twinkle! What's in your mouth? Drop it now!" Nerys fell to her hands and knees and pushed open Twinkle's jaws. "Oh, God!"

Lungs burning, vision dimming, Twinkle felt her fingers inside his mouth, finding, pulling...

"Eeeergh!" he spat as the pipe came free, then hauled in a deep, rasping breath.

"Twinkle! Dearest!" Nerys said, holding him firmly to check he was all right.

"Cor blimey!" Twinkle puffed. "Saw my life flash before me eyes! Not nearly enough sausages in it by my reckonin'."

Nerys picked him up and looked about in wonder at the close to hellish landscape, as though she had no idea how she had got here.

"Yeah, we're not in Kansas anymore, sweetcheeks," said Twinkle.

"This is Limbo."

"And we're dancin' directly into 'Ell. Literally."

"We have to stop this."

"There's only one way. You need to blow Mr Clovenhoof's pipe."

Nerys gave him a deep frown. "Twinkle, I know you're a dog, but what kind of *filth* have you got into your head? I will not be blowing into Jeremy's pipe—"

"Whoa, calm down, you daft mare. It's a supernatural artifact."

"He tells everyone that, but it doesn't mean—"

"I'm on about a pipe-pipe. That pipe in your bleedin' 'ands!"

Nerys looked at the glue and spittle covered piece of clay in her hand. "St Zita's Pipe of Order?"

"That's the one. Just blow it."

"You blow it!"

"I ain't got the lips for blowin', love. And the way I've 'eard it said through your bedroom door, all the gentlemen like—"

"Do not finish that sentence!" As the dancers moved on around her, she lifted the pipe to her mouth. "It smells funny."

"Again, fings I've 'eard—"

"Shut it! I just don't want to stick Jeremy's funky piece in my mouth."

"A thousand souls depend on it, love."

She wiped the worst of the dog spit from it and, grimacing, put it to her lips. She blew. And as she blew, a low, ululating sound came from the pipe.

"I can hear summat," said Twinkle, his head cocked. "That's the sound of order bein' restored, that is."

Nerys paused in her blowing. "Are you sure? Because I can see a cloud approaching. I think it's a cloud anyw—"

Her words were cut off as she was forced to duck, and the trailing edge of the rock snake was pelted from every side by a barrage of small metal objects.

There were yelps and shouts of pain. Nerys caught one of the objects as it tumbled to the ground. Twinkle saw it was a simple and unexceptional door key.

"Keys?" said Nerys.

"Oh, that'll be to do with Zita being the saint of lost keys or whatever."

"A pipe of key finding?"

"Not a magic pipe of order, no."

"Where in Heaven's name are we?" said a man next to Nerys with a head that was one third singed orange hair, one third red and shiny burn marks, and one third sharp little bruises from flying keys. All the dancing energy had gone from him, as it had from all the other people beneath the key storm.

"Rufus Dandy!" said Nerys. "You're awake!"

He looked around himself. "I must be dreaming."

Twinkle jerked his head back across Limbo. "Normality's that way, mate."

The burned redhead stared at the Yorkshire terrier.

"The pipe snaps them out of it," said Nerys.

"Or maybe a face full of keys makes anyone think twice about their actions."

Nerys looked down the length of the rock snake.

"We need to get to the front, love, pronto," said Twinkle. "Can you toot and run at the same time."

"And me in high heels," said Nerys. She put the pipe to her lips and started to blow again.

A dense cloud of keys started to form in the air behind them. As they ran, it rained down with a thousand tinny thunks and accompanying screams.

"Who loses this many keys?" Nerys shouted, momentarily pausing for breath.

"'Umans," replied Twinkle.

BEN COULD FEEL the warm glow of the cave ahead on his face now. Red flames wavered in its depths.

Warmth. That was nice, he thought. He had half his Stumpy's Crotch left. He had Lois's shoulder in the grip of his other hand. What better thing could there be than to be with the woman he loved and a nutty ale and a warm fire for them to sit beside.

Ahead, Clovenhoof had his arms raised. "Demon brothers! I have come home! And I've brought friends! Make room for us all!"

Next to Clovenhoof was a short figure with large expressive eyes who was trying to hold Clovenhoof back and saying things like, "Do not make room for us! We're not stopping! In fact, put up a few barricades if you could! Oh, balls!"

The figures in the cave were most unusual looking, thought Ben. They were tall and short, bent and misshapen, with faces that frankly defied description. Locals, thought Ben. Merely friends he hadn't met yet. He could offer then a bit of his Stumpy's Crotch.

Suddenly Twinkle sprinted by on his left side and Nerys pelted by on his right, producing a loud peeping sound as she ran. Ben had barely a moment to think on that before there was a sound like whistling fireworks and pain rained down on him: talon strikes to his back, neck and head.

He lurched forward to shield Lois. His yells joined those of everyone around him. In agonised astonishment he saw keys cascading about him. Thin Yale keys, fat Chubb keys. Little silver padlock keys. Even a few swipe cards. Stunned and confused, he picked up a fat brass key that had landed right in front of him. He clenched his fist around it.

"What the buggering hell?!" he whimpered.

Lois Cavanagh turned in his arms and looked at him with

short-sighted suspicion. "Why the hell are you holding onto me, young man?"

Ben wanted to say something about protecting her from the keys. He wanted to say something about happiness and passion and his pure simple love for her. But all of that was fading away, like the logic of a passing dream. He was holding onto an angry woman he barely knew, in a misty landscape that seemed to be suffering a deluge of keys.

"I really don't know," he said. He looked at the vase full of beer he was holding. "I seem to have been drinking." He looked at the remains of his shambolic Morris dancing gear. "And dancing."

Miss Cavanagh roughly pushed his hands away. "I don't remember how we got here. Did you put something in my drink?"

"Oh God, no!" Ben was horrified. "I think it's been one of those evenings. I'm drawing a bit of a blank too."

CLOVENHOOF HEARD the music of the rock snake falter and fail a moment before a torrent of keys hit him.

"Fuck me!" he yelled as he put his hands up to shelter his bonce.

Rutspud flinched away from him as he raised hands over his own head. Hell was but a dozen footsteps away now. Demons crowded eagerly to greet them, and there were plenty Clovenhoof recognised. That was Pisskettle and Lynchgill in the front row, pitchfork wielders par excellence.

Surely that tentacled one was old Cockthorn. And there was Rimdust, Slagstrike, and old Smutboil.

"Boys ... boys..." said Clovenhoof with glowing affection.

He looked back. His party group, his rock snake, had fallen apart under the bizarre hail of keys. It was coming apart. People were running back the way they had come, to the distant purple glow of the door between worlds.

"We're nearly there, guys!" he shouted.

He looked at the remnants of his rock band and Morris troupe. Hairy Leonard and Slackpipes Johnson were already fleeing. Camille had cast her last cigarette aside and was staring wide-eyed as though all Hell was laid before her (which it was). Marcee's accordion had been shredded by the hail of keys and now she was pulling Jacob away.

"I need to be with my boy," whispered Valdemar, backing off.

Clovenhoof looked to Aksel.

"This is some heavy trip," said the guitarist.

"We smoked all that weed and we're still high," said Rasmus faintly, as though justifying this vision to himself.

"We're nearly there!" Clovenhoof pleaded. "The ultimate party. The biggest gig in Hell."

"It's over," said Nerys.

"Please let it be over," said Rutspud, hurt and weary.

"I can't," said Clovenhoof. "I'm a rock god."

"You're a sad weirdo with too many bells and tassels, mate," said Twinkle.

"But I was having the time of my life. I was being so cool."

"Really?" said Rutspud. "You claimed to have invented the cockenspiel."

Clovenhoof shook his head firmly. "No. This party is going to go on for eternity."

"Bold intentions," said Rutspud. "Or we could go home and watch some *Bake Off*."

The words 'Bake Off' truly tugged at his – well, Clovenhoof didn't have a soul, but they tugged at his innermost core. Cakes, contestants. Weird perverse fantasies about which dessert would be tastiest eaten off which contestant. It seemed so very attractive.

"No!" he declared. "The party must go on! Me and Cockthorn and Smutboil... We're gonna raise the roof!"

One of the demons at the mouth of Hell bent to another and whispered not so very quietly. "Who is that weird guy? Do you know him?"

"I'm the party king!" said Clovenhoof, wishing he didn't sound like he was begging as he said it. "I'm not a washed-up old man. I'm not a has-been."

"You are," said Askel.

Clovenhoof whirled on him accusingly.

The lead singer of Djævlehund looked at him through bee-stung eyes, hobbling on one decent leg.

"You have been everything, my good friend," said Aksel. "The original Devil Preacher. Party animal number one. With you at my side, I've stolen a shit-tonne of drugs. I've fucked many beautiful women. I've been chased and hounded across the countryside and put on a rock show that no one will ever forget."

"Kind of hoping everyone does forget," muttered Nerys.

"We even drank bull jizz together like Vikings of old."

"I'm not sure they ever did that," said Rutspud.

"You *have been*," said Aksel with emphatic pride. "You *have been* everything. You are a rock god, Jeremy, and you do not need to prove anything to anyone."

It was a heart-warming endorsement, but it seemed terrible to have come this far and not step over the threshold into the underworld.

"But the endless party..." Clovenhoof said, throwing out a pathetic hand towards Hell.

Eltiel chose that moment to alight on the ground, still surrounded by his angelic disco lights. He danced in his own little world to music only he could hear.

"Step, step, slide, feelin' fine. Funky town. Shake that thing, feel the fever. Moonwalk, moonwalk and spin! Let the groove last forever." Eltiel grabbed his crotch, thrust, and gave a little Michael Jackson squeal.

Clovenhoof looked at the disco-dancing twat for a long time. "Yeah. All right," he said tiredly. "Let's go home."

61

Many things were said of the Morris dancing competition at the Gnome's Bottom brewery in York.

The most commonly said thing was that someone had spiked the beer supply and over a thousand people were completely off their tits all night. This commonly shared 'knowledge' did little to harm the Gnome's Bottom's reputation and sales.

In fact, a second, more explicit rumour stated that an elixir of goddess's tears had been spilt on the ground that night, and any beer purchased from the Gnome's Bottom brewery thereafter was guaranteed to loosen anyone's inhibitions. And this much seemed to be true because, for most people, telling them they were guaranteed to lose their inhibitions was a surefire way to loosen said inhibitions. It was also good for beer sales.

More objective reports on the events that evening would

include the fact that the Wednesbury Wallopers had won the Morris dancing competition, being the only dancers to take to the stage before the entire thing descended into chaos. But there's no fun in objectivity, and no one seemed to care much for the doings of Morris dancers apart from Morris dancers themselves. Rufus Dandy, leader of the Halesowen Hankymen, raised some half-hearted objections in Morris dancing newsletters and Facebook groups, but questions about how exactly he had burned off half his hair were of far more interest to people.

The police investigation into the Gnome's Bottom fiasco was made all the more complicated by the possibly connected/possibly unconnected trail of crimes committed in the hours and days beforehand, in which, it was alleged, an ambulance, several kayaks, and a quantity of medicinal cannabis had been stolen, of which some of latter may have been used in a debauched orgy at the Dirty Duck in Bishop Monkton. The police were unsure how this was linked to a battered and terrified butcher found running across the fields of Yorkshire, but they were happy to assume it was all part of some horribly messy sequence of events.

The real facts of the aftermath, for the individuals involved, were much more mundane and entirely unexciting. One Miss Lois Cavanagh begrudgingly gave a Ms Nerys Thomas and two of her friends (whose names she never caught, but one was short fellow with what she thought were rather expressive eyes and the other a handsome androgynous sort in what appeared to a flowing white robe) a lift. Together, in the cold light of a new day, they inspected Nerys's cracked window and flat tyre which, after the handsome androgynous one had waved hands over it, turned out not to be cracked or flat at all but in good working order.

A short drive from there another car was collected, and various dancers, singers and musicians – nursing all manner of hangovers and slowly healing wounds – were transferred to an old, battered van in a disgruntled farmer's yard. Farewells were said, a tiny little trophy was celebrated once more and, still reeling and confused from the events of the night before, a number of individuals departed in different directions.

In short, everyone went home.

"YOUR CAR STINKS OF VOMIT," said Clovenhoof cheerily as they pootled along the dual carriageway towards Birmingham and Sutton Coldfield.

"Yes," said Nerys. "Tina ate the chicken curry at the business retreat. You'd have thought Eltiel would have been able to fix that when he fixed everything else."

"Roadside assistance people aren't here to clean your car, Nerys," said Ben, from the back seat.

Nerys wasn't sure how the supernatural inability inflicting most humans to see demons and angels for what they were had somehow caused Ben to mistake an angel of the Lord for an AA repairman, but she supposed it was not the worst of outcomes.

"This is your fault by the way, Jeremy," said Nerys.

"I didn't vomit in your car."

"No, not you specifically," she said, peeved. "But things

this weekend have generally, by and large, been your fault. Isn't that right, Twinkle?"

She looked at the dog sitting in Jeremy's lap as she said this. It would not have been good for Ben's sanity if Twinkle had replied, but the fact was, ever since the cold and revealing sun had dawned over the Gnome's Bottom brewery, Twinkle had not spoken a single word. And that unsettled Nerys. Although she had been shocked by his sudden powers of speech, she now realised there many things she had yet to say to him; so many things she had hoped to ask him.

Twinkle looked at her, stuck out a little pink tongue, and licked his own nose.

Clovenhoof sniffed haughtily. "Ben and I were having a perfectly innocent—"

"Mostly innocent," said Ben.

"—Mostly innocent weekend away with the lads. We did nothing but help out a Morris dancing group – and it's an artform in danger of extinction, let me tell you – and a few Danish lads—"

"And a Frenchwoman," said Ben.

"—and a Frenchwoman achieve their rock and roll dreams. You should have been focused on the lessons learned from your *Bosses Go Ape in the Jungle* spiritual retreat, or whatever it was."

"Oh, don't," said Nerys. "That was a colossal waste of time. I spent the whole week pointlessly trying to visualise being a successful businesswoman and getting weirded out by Guru Gary."

"Who's Guru Gary? A new boyfriend?"

"Guru Gary is a goat."

"Nothing wrong with a goaty boyfriend. Many's the woman who gets a taste for the horns and can't stay away."

"Ugh!" Nerys pulled a disgusted face.

"I think I should try something like that," said Ben.

"What? Get a bit of goat action in your life?" said Clovenhoof.

"No. Positive visualisation. I sometimes get too precious about books. I try to gatekeep who gets to buy them and who doesn't. They're just books – they're meant to entertain, however they're read – and I really shouldn't try to read anything more into them than that."

Clovenhoof laughed. "Ha! Someone's learned a valuable lesson."

"What's that?" said Nerys.

"Ben has been having a little fantasy boycrush on a hottie from some nineteen fifties soft porn book—"

"That's not what I was talking about!"

"—And it's very different when he meets the *very* mature lady in the flesh."

"I was talking about not selling books to that woman who turns them into sculptures! I..." He trailed off and sighed. "But, yes, I shouldn't let my imagination lead me into dubious territory."

Nerys indicated to come off the dual carriageway.

"Can you drop me off at the shop, actually?" said Ben. "I need to sort some things out."

"Sure," she said. "It's not like I've got anything better to do with my Sunday."

"*Bake Off* marathon back at mine," said Clovenhoof. "Cocoa, biscuits, and a cuddle on my sleeping sofa, eh?"

She grunted. "Let me get a shower first, swap the cocoa for Chardonnay and have Twinkle here as my cuddling partner instead of you, and you've got a deal."

"Throw some Lambrini in the cooler and Crispy Findus Pancakes in the oven and it's a perfect Sunday," said Clovenhoof.

"Something like that," said Nerys.

THE DEMON and the angel went their separate ways in Limbo.

Rutspud closed the InstaDoor rift in space. It was as though it had never been there and, as far as Rutspud (and any demon who questioned him on the matter) was concerned, there had never been any InstaDoors, never been any unsanctioned jaunts to Earth and in fact – cross the place where his heart would have been if he'd had one and hope to die (if such things were possible) – none of the events that allegedly occurred in the last few days had ever occurred. Or at least they had not featured him in any provable way.

"You know," Rutspud said to Eltel, "if there's ever another emergency on Earth and you want some assistance, please feel absolutely free to involve someone other than me."

Eltiel straightened his robes. "Or, to put a more accurate spin on things, please avoid dragging me into Earthly matters by giving powerful religious relics to the Prince of Darkness."

Rutspud had to admit the angel had a point. "Lord Satan and I might limit our future activities to the occasional shared tipple."

"Fizzy monks' urine."

"Only the best."

"Goodbye, demon," said Eltiel and held out a hand to shake.

Rutspud regarded it suspiciously before taking it. He was about to go, but felt compelled to ask something. "That was your first prolonged visit to Earth, wasn't it?"

"Not at all. I was present in the Garden of Eden, you'll recall."

"Yes, but in the thousands, or is it millions of years since then, this was your first proper visit."

"It was."

"Earth has a way of changing individuals, even those of us who are immortal and rather difficult to change."

"Perhaps..."

"The funky disco shapes you were throwing last night for one..."

"I've cast it all from my mind," said Eltiel stiffly.

"I'm sure you have but ... I have to ask – no, I *want* to ask – did you learn anything in your time on Earth?"

Eltiel did him the courtesy of giving it considerable thought. "If I was to tell you that I learned some homey, folksy wisdom from a talking dog, would you think any less of me?"

"Less of you?" said Rutspud. "No."

"I think I learned a little of the nature of perfection and the impermanence of all things, good and bad. And the fact that, on Earth, living in the imperfect moment is all you can do."

Rutspud grinned. "Wow. The stuck-up prissy angel has learned to chillax a little bit."

Eltiel gave him a sharp scowl. "Goodness me, no! That fleeting nature of beauty stuff is all well and good for the mortal world, but I cannot wait to get back to the Celestial City, where everything is perfect and beautiful and in accordance with the Divine Plan *without fail.*"

"Have it your way," said Rutspud. "Oh! You might want this." He tossed St Zita's Pipe of Key-Finding to Eltiel. It still had fragments of Clovenhoof's skin stuck to it. The angel caught it deftly.

"Oh, offering me this, but you're planning on holding onto Lilith's Tears, eh?"

Rutspud's brow furrowed. "I assumed you had that. It's not like you were going to leave it behind."

"What? I thought *you* had picked it up!"

"Me? Why me?"

"It was you who lost it," said Eltiel. "One assumes you would feel an imperative to retrieve it."

"You're serious?" said Rutspud. "You're not joking. You don't have it?"

"Angels don't lie!"

"And they supposedly don't fuck up either!"

Rutspud glared at the angel, hoping against hope that the stupid idiot wasn't telling the truth.

"Oh, crap!" sighed Eltiel.

Swearing under his breath, Rutspud began to reprogram the InstaDoor.

62

C amille hunkered down in her seat, looking at her phone as the Djævlehund band van trundled south on its way to the ferry terminal in Dover.

Rasmus had voiced his opinion on the chances of the rickety old thing making it all the way back to Copenhagen. By his estimation, they had a thousand miles to cover, through France, Belgium, the Netherlands and Germany, before getting back to Denmark, and that it was probably best to do all of that as quickly as possible, before the old van died completely.

There had been zero talk of honouring their gig appearance in Scarborough, or of continuing with any kind of UK tour. The band, it was clear, had had enough. Rasmus had already explained at length his intention to apologise to his beloved Henrik and put aside his foolish mid-life crisis in favour of domestic bliss. Given that Rasmus had spoken more in the last forty-eight hours than he had in all the time the band had known him, it was perhaps the case that the big hairy man had worked through his issues and was ready to enter middle-age gracefully.

Valdemar, it was abundantly clear to Camille, only yearned now to be at home with his partner and baby boy. The band could at least be grateful that now, homeward bound, he had stopped going on and on about it, or indeed composing songs about the horrid little snot-monster.

Only Aksel seemed to have a thirst for the rock and roll lifestyle, but even he had to admit he needed time to heal. He sat in the back, trying out chords and wincing every time he moved his burnt, broken and bee-stung body.

For Camille herself, it seemed that this rock and roll phase of her life had come to a fitting end. She felt that in her ten year plan, it was now time to move onto the next step: the film career. Right now, she was messaging her agent and brand manager to discuss how they would make that happen.

"You know," said Aksel. "We really slayed it up there last night, didn't we?"

"We certainly did," said Valdemar, possibly answering without listening.

"I have a new song just at the back of my mind," said Aksel. "I think we wrote it last night, just improvised it, but I can barely remember." He played a few chords.

"Sounds great," said Valdemar.

"Just make sure it's not the same as Rod Stewart's *Hot Legs*," said Rasmus. "I'd hate for you to be accused of plagiarism."

Behind Camille, Aksel made a disappointed noise. "Oh yeah. No wonder it sounded so familiar."

"But keep working on it," said Rasmus.

"You're right. This life on the road has inspired me."

"I'm glad it's done someone some good," said Ramus. "It's been a blast, but nothing's left to show for it."

"Nah, it's been legendary," said Valdemar. "People will talk about it for years to come. And the social media has gone— Well, wow! The pictures are everywhere."

"What pictures?" said Camille and began searching her phone. "Oh! You fucking bastard!"

"What is the problem, my friend?" said Askel.

"How did this happen?"

She held up the phone so Aksel could see the photo. The image had clearly been taken by someone in the audience at some forgotten point. Camille and another woman were bashing drums together. For reasons Camille really couldn't remember, she and the other woman were throwing cute V-signs and grinning together like best friends.

"What's the matter with it?" asked Aksel. "You have such a nice smile."

"I do not smile!" she spat. "I do not smile because it is not my brand. It's a PR fucking disaster!"

She reached for her cigarettes, but remembered she'd run out. Instead, she angrily grabbed her water bottle. It didn't contain water, though.

In the confusion and mess of that morning, Camille had stumbled upon something dropped in the middle of the Morris dancing performance area. She recognised the clay flask, even though the top had been smashed off. For reasons she could not properly articulate, she'd picked it up, found a discarded plastic drinking bottle and decanted the last of the interesting drink into the bottle. Oddly enough – very oddly – the amount in the flask was precisely the amount needed to fill the bottle to the brim. And she took it with her.

Now, fuming over the off-brand images, she unscrewed the lid and took a grumpy sip. "Fuck it," she said. "I'm still going to become the President of France."

"I believe you," said Aksel.

Camille didn't need him to believe her. She already knew – just *knew* – that it was true.

SPARTACUS WILSON HEARD the door to Books'n'Bobs chime and looked up.

He'd spent most of the morning scouring the internet for hardback books he could buy in bulk. He'd just clicked through checkout on an order and taken a first bite of his lunchtime sausage roll when the door chimed and Ben Kitchen came in, followed by Mr Clovenhoof, Nerys Thomas and her little dog, Twinkle.

The three humans looked in a bloody awful state. Clovenhoof appeared to be dressed in the tattered remnants of a hospital gown, with some extra and frankly bizarre bits tied on. This was not terribly unusual for Mr C, who Spartacus had seen dressed in far worse and far less. But Ben wasn't dressed much better, and Nerys looked like she'd been dragged through a hedge backwards and forced to wear the same clothes for a week.

"Ah, there you are, Mr Kitchen," said the teenager. "Your note didn't say when you'd be back."

"Sooner than expected," said Ben. "And later than I'd like."

"Right-o. You back in for the day or...?" He waved at Ben's appalling appearance. "You wanna go get yourself a bath and throw your clothes in the...?" He was struggling now.

"Bin?" suggested Ben.

"I was gonna say incinerator, but yeah, sure."

"I'm going to pop to the offy and pick up a couple of bottles," said Nerys, with the tone Spartacus knew adults used when they planned to get utterly smashed.

"Pick up a couple of bottles for me too," said Clovenhoof. "I'll pop to the supermarket for the crispy pancakes. What flavour do you prefer?"

"Any chance you could actually get some decent snacks? Olives, cheeses, biscuits."

"Olive and cheese flavoured crispy pancakes?" said Clovenhoof frowning. "Don't think I've heard of them – and I'm in all the on-line pancake forums. But I can ask."

"Look after Twinkle for a minute," said Nerys as she made for the door. "Be good for mummy, Twink. Yes? Yes?"

When Clovenhoof and Nerys were gone, Spartacus gave Ben a very specific look up and down. "What actually happened to you, Ben?"

"Words cannot even begin to explain," said Ben. "But I did have an epiphany."

"Anna who?"

"I came to a realisation. You know, before I went away I told you to not sell any of those books to Crystal's Crafts."

"Yeah, about that..." said Spartacus, trying to nonchalantly lean on the counter so that he blocked from view the pile of books he'd set aside for Crystal.

"I can get too drawn into books and lose sight of the fact that books and people ... well..."

"You saying you *do* want us to sell books to Crystal?"

"If she wants to buy them."

"Oh, thank fuck for that," Spartacus grinned, leaning back. "Cos you see I realise I'm onto a decent little racket here. Since Crystal don't care what the books are as long as they're structurally sound, then I can buy them from anywhere. And, well basically, I'm turning a decent profit on each and every one. She's been paying me in cash and, to be honest, Ben, I don't know where to stick it all."

Spartacus popped open the till. Under the spring clip there was wad of notes far fatter than the till had probably ever held before.

"Visualise business success and it will come," breathed Ben.

"Is that a fact?"

"It's something Nerys learned off a very persuasive goat, I think," said Ben.

"I was a bit worried about leaving that much cash on the premises. I would have stuck it in old Dirty Desmond's safe—"

"—If we only had the key," said Ben, joining his voice to Spartacus's.

Ben gave a start and blinked rapidly. "Hang on, hang on..." He started feeling about his person, hands tapping his trouser pockets, feeling across his chest. "I had it somewhere."

"What?"

Ben didn't answer but continued the pantomime of searching his rather ragged self. While this was going on, Spartacus could have sworn he heard a gruff little voice from the other side of the counter say, "Oi, mate. Do us a favour and gizz us a bit o' that sausage roll." But when Spartacus leaned over the counter there was only Nerys's dog, and no conceivable source for the voice.

"Ah-ha!" Ben shouted. He was holding aloft a key. An old chunky brass key.

"Where'd you get that?" said Spartacus.

"I have no idea," said Ben frankly. "I think it just landed on me. I think. But it looks about right, doesn't it?"

Ben moved round to the back of the counter, shifted a box away from the door of Desmond Rothermere's almost forgotten safe, and put the key in the lock.

"It fits!"

"That's something," said Spartacus.

"Just an end of your sausage roll, mate, that's all I'm asking."

Ben gave it was twist and there was a heavy clunk. "It turns! By God, it turns!"

He wrenched the door open. The hinges squeaked, but it opened nonetheless.

Spartacus had half-expected to see piles of cash or diamonds in there, but he was disappointed. In fact, at first, the safe appeared to be empty. Then he saw there was a flat cardboard box on one shelf. Ben pulled it out. On the front was a faded sticker which read: HANKY-PANKY, VOLUME #1.

Ben put it on the counter and opened it. Inside were two clear plastic reels around which a length of tape was wound.

"What's that?" said Spartacus. "Old computer tape?"

"I don't think so," said Ben, slowly. "I think it's eight millimetre cine film."

"It's what?"

"A film, a movie film. Used to be a popular format. Obsolete now. You can probably buy the old projectors on eBay, but..." Ben carefully pulled out a length of film and held it up to the light.

"Is it worth anything?" said Spartacus.

"Not really. It's a curio really. I don't know why Desmond kept it in his safe." Ben squinted as he tried to focus on the tiny film frames, then gave a gasp.

"What? What is it?" said Spartacus.

"Oh, Lois," Ben whispered in a delighted tone. "Oh, Lois, you've been a naughty, naughty girl..."

"Let me have a look," said Spartacus.

Ben snatched it out of reach. "Not for your eyes, young man. Now, be useful and get on eBay."

"You want to buy a film projector?"

"Maybe," said Ben casually.

On the floor, Twinkle gave up waiting by the counter and went to have good long sniff along the shelves.

ABOUT THE AUTHOR

Heide lives in North Warwickshire with various children and animals.

Iain lives in South Birmingham with various children and animals.

They are both married but not to each other.

Oddjobs

Unstoppable horrors from beyond are poised to invade and literally create Hell on Earth.

It's the end of the world as we know it, but someone still needs to do the paperwork.

Morag Murray works for the secret government organisation responsible for making sure the apocalypse goes as smoothly and as quietly as possible.

Trouble is, Morag's got a temper problem and, after angering the wrong alien god, she's been sent to another city where she won't cause so much trouble.

But Morag's got her work cut out for her. She has to deal with a man-eating starfish, solve a supernatural murder and, if she's got time, prevent her own inevitable death.

If you like The Laundry Files, The Chronicles of St Mary's or Men in Black, you'll love the Oddjobs series."If Jodi Taylor wrote a Laundry Files novel set it in Birmingham... A hilarious dose of bleak existential despair. With added tentacles! And bureaucracy!" – Charles Stross, author of The Laundry Files series.

Oddjobs

Sealfinger

Meet Sam Applewhite, security consultant for DefCon4's east coast office. .

She's clever, inventive and adaptable. In her job she has to be.

Now, she's facing an impossible mystery.

A client has gone missing and no one else seems to care.

Who would want to kill an old and lonely woman whose only sins are having a sharp tongue and a belief in ghosts? Could her death be linked to the new building project out on the dunes?

Can Sam find out the truth, even if it puts her friends' and family's lives at risk?

Sealfinger

Printed in Great Britain
by Amazon